WORTH POCKET COMPANIONS

ROMANCE

Short Stories by Great Writers

WORTH POCKET COMPANIONS

Other titles in the series

CRIME

MYSTERY & SUSPENSE

TRAVEL & ADVENTURE

Romance

Short Stories by Great Writers

Selected by
ROSEMARY GRAY

WORTH POCKET COMPANIONS

This edition published in 2012 by
Worth Press Limited, Cambridge, UK
www.worthpress.co.uk

A catalogue record for this book is available
from the British Library

ISBN 978 1 84931 070 3

Cover design Bradbury & Williams
Typeset in Great Britain by Antony Gray
Printed and bound in China by Imago

Contents

F. SCOTT FITZGERALD

F. Scott Fitzgerald was born in St Paul, Minnesota, in 1896. He went to Princeton University but left before graduating to join the army in 1917 when America entered World War I. He was assigned to a camp in Alabama where, at a social event, he met Zelda Sayre. *This Side of Paradise* was published in March 1920 to great critical acclaim and the couple were married a week later. Together they embarked on an extravagant celebrity life-style that epitomised the 'Jazz Age'. *The Beautiful and Damned*, the second novel, was published in 1922 and *The Great Gatsby* in 1925. Fitzgerald earned only modestly from his novels, living on short stories and screenwriting. His fourth novel, *Tender is the Night*, appeared in 1934, and he was midway through his last when he died in 1940.

Love in the Night

1

The words thrilled Val. They had come into his mind sometime during the fresh gold April afternoon and he kept repeating them to himself over and over: 'Love in the night; love in the night.' He tried them in three languages – Russian, French and English – and decided that they were best in English. In each language they meant a different sort of love and a different sort of night – the English night seemed the warmest and softest with the thinnest and most crystalline sprinkling of stars. The English love seemed the most fragile and romantic – a white dress and a dim face above it and eyes that were pools of light. And when I add that it was a French night he was thinking about, after all, I see I must go back and begin over.

Val was half Russian and half American. His mother was the daughter of that Morris Hasylton who helped finance the Chicago World's Fair in 1892, and his father was – see the *Almanach de Gotha*, issue of 1910 – Prince Paul Serge Boris Rostoff, son of Prince Vladimir Rostoff, grandson of a grand duke – 'Jimber-Jawed Serge' – and third-cousin-once-removed to the Tsar. It was all very impressive, you see, on that side – house in St Petersburg, shooting lodge near Riga, and swollen villa, more like a palace, overlooking the Mediterranean. It was at this villa in Cannes that the Rostoffs passed the winter – and it wasn't at all the thing to remind Princess Rostoff that this Riviera villa, from the marble fountain – after Bernini – to the gold cordial glasses – after dinner – was paid for with American gold.

The Russians, of course, were gay people on the Continent in the gala days before the war. Of the three races that used Southern France for a pleasure ground they were easily the most adept at the grand manner. The English were too practical, and the Americans, though they spent freely, had no tradition of romantic conduct. But the Russians – there was a people as gallant as the Latins, and rich besides! When the Rostoffs arrived at Cannes late in January the restaurateurs telegraphed north for the prince's favourite labels to paste on their champagne, and the jewellers put incredibly gorgeous articles aside to show to him – but not to the princess – and the Russian Church was swept and garnished for the season that the prince might beg Orthodox forgiveness for his sins. Even the Mediterranean turned obligingly to a deep wine colour in the spring evenings, and fishing boats with robin-breasted sails loitered exquisitely offshore.

In a vague way young Val realised that this was all for the benefit of him and his family. It was a privileged paradise, this white little city on the water, in which he was free to do what he liked because he was rich and young and the blood of Peter the

Great ran indigo in his veins. He was only seventeen in 1914, when this history begins, but he had already fought a duel with a young man four years his senior, and he had a small hairless scar to show for it on top of his handsome head.

But the question of love in the night was the thing nearest his heart. It was a vague pleasant dream he had, something that was going to happen to him someday that would be unique and incomparable. He could have told no more about it than that there was a lovely unknown girl concerned in it, and that it ought to take place beneath the Riviera moon.

The odd thing about all this was not that he had this excited and yet almost spiritual hope of romance, for all boys of any imagination have just such hopes, but that it actually came true. And when it happened, it happened so unexpectedly; it was such a jumble of impressions and emotions, of curious phrases that sprang to his lips, of sights and sounds and moments that were here, were lost, were past, that he scarcely understood it at all. Perhaps its very vagueness preserved it in his heart and made him for ever unable to forget.

There was an atmosphere of love all about him that spring – his father's loves, for instance, which were many and indiscreet, and which Val became aware of gradually from overhearing the gossip of servants, and definitely from coming on his American mother unexpectedly one afternoon, to find her storming hysterically at his father's picture on the salon wall. In the picture his father wore a white uniform with a furred dolman and looked back impassively at his wife as if to say, 'Were you under the impression, my dear, that you were marrying into a family of clergymen?'

Val tiptoed away, surprised, confused – and excited. It didn't shock him as it would have shocked an American boy of his age. He had known for years what life was among the Continental rich, and he condemned his father only for making his mother cry.

Love went on around him – reproachless love and illicit love alike. As he strolled along the seaside promenade at nine o'clock, when the stars were bright enough to compete with the bright lamps, he was aware of love on every side. From the open-air cafés, vivid with dresses just down from Paris, came a sweet pungent odour of flowers and chartreuse and fresh black coffee and cigarettes – and mingled with them all he caught another scent, the mysterious thrilling scent of love. Hands touched jewel-sparkling hands upon the white tables. Gay dresses and white shirt-fronts swayed together, and matches were held, trembling a little, for slow-lighting cigarettes. On the other side of the boulevard lovers less fashionable, young Frenchmen who worked in the stores of Cannes, sauntered with their fiancées under the dim trees, but Val's young eyes seldom turned that way. The luxury of music and bright colours and low voices – they were all part of his dream. They were the essential trappings of love in the night.

But assume as he might the rather fierce expression that was expected from a young Russian gentleman who walked the streets alone, Val was beginning to be unhappy. April twilight had succeeded March twilight, the season was almost over, and he had found no use to make of the warm spring evenings. The girls of sixteen and seventeen whom he knew, were chaperoned with care between dusk and bedtime – this, remember, was before the war – and the others who might gladly have walked beside him were an affront to his romantic desire. So April passed by – one week, two weeks, three weeks –

He had played tennis until seven and loitered at the courts for another hour, so it was half-past eight when a tired cab horse accomplished the hill on which gleamed the façade of the Rostoff villa. The lights of his mother's limousine were yellow in the drive, and the princess, buttoning her gloves, was just coming out of the glowing door. Val tossed two francs to the cabman and went to kiss her on the cheek.

'Don't touch me,' she said quickly. 'You've been handling money.'

'But not in my mouth, mother,' he protested humorously.

The princess looked at him impatiently.

'I'm angry,' she said. 'Why must you be so late tonight? We're dining on a yacht and you were to have come along too.'

'What yacht?'

'Americans.' There was always a faint irony in her voice when she mentioned the land of her nativity. Her America was the Chicago of the nineties which she still thought of as the vast upstairs of a butcher's shop. Even the irregularities of Prince Paul were not too high a price to have paid for her escape.

'Two yachts,' she continued; 'in fact we don't know which one. The note was very indefinite. Very careless indeed.'

Americans. Val's mother had taught him to look down on Americans, but she hadn't succeeded in making him dislike them. American men noticed you, even if you were seventeen. He liked Americans. Although he was thoroughly Russian he wasn't immaculately so – the exact proportion, like that of a celebrated soap, was about ninety-nine and three-quarters per cent.

'I want to come,' he said. 'I'll hurry up, mother. I'll – '

'We're late now.' The princess turned as her husband appeared in the door. 'Now Val says he wants to come.'

'He can't,' said Prince Paul shortly. 'He's too outrageously late.'

Val nodded. Russian aristocrats, however indulgent about themselves, were always admirably Spartan with their children. There were no arguments.

'I'm sorry,' he said.

Prince Paul grunted. The footman, in red and silver livery, opened the limousine door. But the grunt decided the matter for Val, because Princess Rostoff at that day and hour had certain grievances against her husband which gave her command of the domestic situation.

'On second thoughts you'd better come, Val,' she announced coolly. 'It's too late now, but come after dinner. The yacht is either the *Minnehaha* or the *Privateer*.' She got into the limousine. 'The one to come to will be the gayer one, I suppose – the Jacksons' yacht –'

'Find got sense,' muttered the Prince cryptically, conveying that Val would find it if he had any sense. 'Have my man take a look at you 'fore you start. Wear tie of mine 'stead of that outrageous string you affected in Vienna. Grow up. High time.'

As the limousine crawled crackling down the pebbled drive Val's face was burning.

2

It was dark in Cannes harbour, rather it seemed dark after the brightness of the promenade that Val had just left behind. Three frail dock lights glittered dimly upon innumerable fishing boats heaped like shells along the beach. Farther out in the water there were other lights where a fleet of slender yachts rode the tide with slow dignity, and farther still a full ripe moon made the water bosom into a polished dancing floor. Occasionally there was a swish! creak! drip! as a rowboat moved about in the shallows, and its blurred shape threaded the labyrinth of hobbled fishing skiffs and launches. Val, descending the velvet slope of sand, stumbled over a sleeping boatman and caught the rank savour of garlic and plain wine. Taking the man by the shoulders he shook open his startled eyes.

'Do you know where the *Minnehaha* is anchored, and the *Privateer*?'

As they slid out into the bay he lay back in the stern and stared with vague discontent at the Riviera moon. That was the right moon, all right. Frequently, five nights out of seven, there was the right moon. And here was the soft air, aching with enchantment, and here was the music, many strains of music from many orchestras, drifting out from the shore. Eastward lay the dark Cape of Antibes, and then Nice, and beyond that Monte Carlo, where the night rang chinking full of gold. Someday he would enjoy all that, too, know its every pleasure and success – when he was too old and wise to care.

But tonight – tonight, that stream of silver that waved like a wide strand of curly hair towards the moon; those soft romantic lights of Cannes behind him, the irresistible ineffable love in this air – that was to be wasted for ever.

'Which one?' asked the boatman suddenly.

'Which what?' demanded Val, sitting up.

'Which boat?'

He pointed. Val turned; above hovered the grey, sword-like prow of a yacht. During the sustained longing of his wish they had covered half a mile.

He read the brass letters over his head. It was the *Privateer*, but there were only dim lights on board, and no music and no voices, only a murmurous k-plash at intervals as the small waves leaped at the sides.

'The other one,' said Val; 'the *Minnehaha*.'

'Don't go yet.'

Val started. The voice, low and soft, had dropped down from the darkness overhead.

'What's the hurry?' said the soft voice. 'Thought maybe somebody was coming to see me, and have suffered terrible disappointment.'

The boatman lifted his oars and looked hesitatingly at Val. But Val was silent, so the man let the blades fall into the water and swept the boat out into the moonlight.

'Wait a minute!' cried Val sharply.

'Goodbye,' said the voice. 'Come again when you can stay longer.'

'But I am going to stay now,' he answered breathlessly.

He gave the necessary order and the rowboat swung back to the foot of the small companionway. Someone young, someone in a misty white dress, someone with a lovely low voice, had actually called to him out of the velvet dark. 'If she has eyes!' Val murmured to himself. He liked the romantic sound of it and repeated it under his breath – 'If she has eyes.'

'What are you?' She was directly above him now; she was looking down and he was looking up as he climbed the ladder, and as their eyes met they both began to laugh.

She was very young, slim, almost frail, with a dress that accentuated her youth by its blanched simplicity. Two wan dark spots on her cheeks marked where the colour was by day.

'What are you?' she repeated, moving back and laughing again as his head appeared on the level of the deck. 'I'm frightened now and I want to know.'

'I am a gentleman,' said Val, bowing.

'What sort of a gentleman? There are all sorts of gentlemen. There was a – there was a coloured gentleman at the table next to ours in Paris, and so –' She broke off. 'You're not American, are you?'

'I'm Russian,' he said, as he might have announced himself to be an archangel. He thought quickly and then added, 'And I am the most fortunate of Russians. All this day, all this spring I have dreamed of falling in love on such a night, and now I see that heaven has sent me to you.'

'Just one moment!' she said, with a little gasp. 'I'm sure now that this visit is a mistake. I don't go in for anything like that. Please!'

'I beg your pardon.' He looked at her in bewilderment, unaware that he had taken too much for granted. Then he drew himself up formally.

'I have made an error. If you will excuse me I will say good-night.'

He turned away. His hand was on the rail.

'Don't go,' she said, pushing a strand of indefinite hair out of her eyes. 'On second thoughts you can talk any nonsense you like if you'll only not go. I'm miserable and I don't want to be left alone.'

Val hesitated; there was some element in this that he failed to understand. He had taken it for granted that a girl who called to a strange man at night, even from the deck of a yacht, was certainly in a mood for romance. And he wanted intensely to stay. Then he remembered that this was one of the two yachts he had been seeking.

'I imagine that the dinner's on the other boat,' he said.

'The dinner? Oh, yes, it's on the *Minnehaha*. Were you going there?'

'I was going there – a long time ago.'

'What's your name?'

He was on the point of telling her when something made him ask a question instead.

'And you? Why are you not at the party?'

'Because I preferred to stay here. Mrs Jackson said there would be some Russians there – I suppose that's you.' She looked at him with interest. 'You're a very young man, aren't you?'

'I am much older than I look,' said Val stiffly. 'People always comment on it. It's considered rather a remarkable thing.'

'How old are you?'

'Twenty-one,' he lied.

She laughed.

'What nonsense! You're not more than nineteen.'

His annoyance was so perceptible that she hastened to reassure him. 'Cheer up! I'm only seventeen myself. I might have gone to the party if I'd thought there'd be anyone under fifty there.'

He welcomed the change of subject.

'You preferred to sit and dream here beneath the moon.'

'I've been thinking of mistakes.' They sat down side by side in two canvas deckchairs. 'It's a most engrossing subject – the subject of mistakes. Women very seldom brood about mistakes –

they're much more willing to forget than men are. But when they do brood – '

'You have made a mistake?' enquired Val.

She nodded.

'Is it something that cannot be repaired?'

'I think so,' she answered. 'I can't be sure. That's what I was considering when you came along.'

'Perhaps I can help in some way,' said Val. 'Perhaps your mistake is not irreparable, after all.'

'You can't,' she said unhappily. 'So let's not think about it. I'm very tired of my mistake and I'd much rather you'd tell me about all the gay, cheerful things that are going on in Cannes tonight.'

They glanced shoreward at the line of mysterious and alluring lights, the big toy banks with candles inside that were really the great fashionable hotels, the lighted clock in the old town, the blurred glow of the Café de Paris, the pricked-out points of villa windows rising on slow hills towards the dark sky.

'What is everyone doing there?' she whispered. 'It looks as though something gorgeous was going on, but what it is I can't quite tell.'

'Everyone there is making love,' said Val quietly.

'Is that it?' She looked for a long time, with a strange expression in her eyes. 'Then I want to go home to America,' she said. 'There is too much love here. I want to go home tomorrow.'

'You are afraid of being in love then?'

She shook her head.

'It isn't that. It's just because – there is no love here for me.'

'Or for me either,' added Val quietly. 'It is sad that we two should be at such a lovely place on such a lovely night and have – nothing.'

He was leaning towards her intently, with a sort of inspired and chaste romance in his eyes – and she drew back.

'Tell me more about yourself,' she enquired quickly. 'If you are Russian where did you learn to speak such excellent English?'

'My mother is American,' he admitted. 'My grandfather was American also, so she had no choice in the matter.'

'Then you're American too!'

'I am Russian,' said Val with dignity.

She looked at him closely, smiled and decided not to argue. 'Well then,' she said diplomatically, 'I suppose you must have a Russian name.'

But he had no intention now of telling her his name. A name, even the Rostoff name, would be a desecration of the night. They were their own low voices, their two white faces – and that was enough. He was sure, without any reason for being sure but with a sort of instinct that sang triumphantly through his mind, that in a little while, a minute or an hour, he was going to undergo an initiation into the life of romance. His name had no reality beside what was stirring in his heart.

'You are beautiful,' he said suddenly.

'How do you know?'

'Because for women moonlight is the hardest light of all.'

'Am I nice in the moonlight?'

'You are the loveliest thing that I have ever known.'

'Oh.' She thought this over. 'Of course I had no business to let you come on board. I might have known what we'd talk about – in this moon. But I can't sit here and look at the shore – for ever. I'm too young for that. Don't you think I'm too young for that?'

'Much too young,' he agreed solemnly.

Suddenly they both became aware of new music that was close at hand, music that seemed to come out of the water not a hundred yards away.

'Listen!' she cried. 'It's from the *Minnehaha*. They've finished dinner.'

For a moment they listened in silence.

'Thank you,' said Val suddenly.

'For what?'

He hardly knew he had spoken. He was thanking the deep low horns for singing in the breeze, the sea for its warm murmurous complaint against the bow, the milk of the stars for washing over them until he felt buoyed up in a substance more taut than air.

'So lovely,' she whispered.

'What are we going to do about it?'

'Do we have to do something about it? I thought we could just sit and enjoy – '

'You didn't think that,' he interrupted quietly. 'You know that we must do something about it. I am going to make love to you – and you are going to be glad.'

'I can't,' she said very low. She wanted to laugh now, to make some light cool remark that would bring the situation back into the safe waters of a casual flirtation. But it was too late now. Val knew that the music had completed what the moon had begun.

'I will tell you the truth,' he said. 'You are my first love. I am seventeen – the same age as you, no more.'

There was something utterly disarming about the fact that they were the same age. It made her helpless before the fate that had thrown them together. The deckchairs creaked and he was conscious of a faint illusive perfume as they swayed suddenly and childishly together.

3

Whether he kissed her once or several times he could not afterwards remember, though it must have been an hour that they sat there close together and he held her hand. What surprised him most about making love was that it seemed to have no element of wild passion – regret, desire, despair – but a delirious promise of such happiness in the world, in living, as he had never known. First love – this was only first love! What must love itself in its fullness, its perfection be. He did not know that what he was experiencing then, that unreal, undesirous medley of ecstasy and peace, would be unrecapturable for ever.

The music had ceased for some time when presently the murmurous silence was broken by the sound of a rowboat disturbing the quiet waves. She sprang suddenly to her feet and her eyes strained out over the bay.

'Listen!' she said quickly. 'I want you to tell me your name.'

'No.'

'Please,' she begged him. 'I'm going away tomorrow.'

He didn't answer.

'I don't want you to forget me,' she said. 'My name is – '

'I won't forget you. I will promise to remember you always. Whoever I may love I will always compare her to you, my first love. So long as I live you will always have that much freshness in my heart.'

'I want you to remember,' she murmured brokenly. 'Oh, this has meant more to me than it has to you – much more.'

She was standing so close to him that he felt her warm young breath on his face. Once again they swayed together. He pressed her hands and wrists between his as it seemed right to do, and kissed her lips. It was the right kiss, he thought, the romantic kiss – not too little or too much. Yet there was a sort of promise in it of other kisses he might have had, and it was with a slight sinking of his heart that he heard the rowboat close to the yacht and realised that her family had returned. The evening was over.

'And this is only the beginning,' he told himself. 'All my life will be like this night.'

She was saying something in a low quick voice and he was listening tensely.

'You must know one thing – I am married. Three months ago. That was the mistake that I was thinking about when the moon brought you out here. In a moment you will understand.'

She broke off as the boat swung against the companionway and a man's voice floated up out of the darkness.

'Is that you, my dear?'

'Yes.'

'What is this other rowboat waiting?'

'One of Mrs Jackson's guests came here by mistake and I made him stay and amuse me for an hour.'

A moment later the thin white hair and weary face of a man of sixty appeared above the level of the deck. And then Val saw and realised too late how much he cared.

4

When the Riviera season ended in May the Rostoffs and all the other Russians closed their villas and went north for the summer. The Russian Orthodox Church was locked up and so were the bins of rarer wine, and the fashionable spring moonlight was put away, so to speak, to wait for their return.

'We'll be back next season,' they said as a matter of course.

But this was premature, for they were never coming back any more. Those few who straggled south again after five tragic years were glad to get work as chambermaids or *valets de chambre* in the great hotels where they had once dined. Many of them, of course, were killed in the war or in the revolution; many of them faded out as spongers and small cheats in the big capitals, and not a few ended their lives in a sort of stupefied despair.

When the Kerensky government collapsed in 1917, Val was a lieutenant on the eastern front, trying desperately to enforce authority in his company long after any vestige of it remained. He was still trying when Prince Paul Rostoff and his wife gave up their lives one rainy morning to atone for the blunders of the Romanoffs – and the enviable career of Morris Hasylton's daughter ended in a city that bore even more resemblance to a butcher shop's than had Chicago in 1892.

After that Val fought with Denikin's army for a while until he realised that he was participating in a hollow farce and the glory of Imperial Russia was over. Then he went to France and was suddenly confronted with the astounding problem of keeping his body and soul together.

It was, of course, natural that he should think of going to America. Two vague aunts with whom his mother had quarrelled many years ago still lived there in comparative affluence. But the idea was repugnant to the prejudices his mother had implanted in him, and besides he hadn't sufficient money left to pay for his passage over. Until a possible counter-revolution should restore to him the Rostoff properties in Russia he must somehow keep alive in France.

So he went to the little city he knew best of all. He went to Cannes. His last two hundred francs bought him a third-class ticket and when he arrived he gave his dress suit to an obliging party who dealt in such things and received in return money for food and bed. He was sorry afterwards that he had sold the dress suit, because it might have helped him to a position as a waiter. But he obtained work as a taxi driver instead and was quite as happy, or rather quite as miserable, at that.

Sometimes he carried Americans to look at villas for rent, and when the front glass of the automobile was up, curious fragments of conversation drifted out to him from within.

'– heard this fellow was a Russian prince.' . . . 'Sh!' . . . 'No, this one right here.' . . . 'Be quiet, Esther!' – followed by subdued laughter.

When the car stopped, his passengers would edge around to have a look at him. At first he was desperately unhappy when girls did this; after a while he didn't mind any more. Once a cheerfully intoxicated American asked him if it were true and invited him to lunch, and another time an elderly woman seized his hand as she got out of the taxi, shook it violently and then pressed a hundred-franc note into his palm.

'Well, Florence, now I can tell 'em back home I shook hands with a Russian prince.'

The inebriated American who had invited him to lunch

thought at first that Val was a son of the czar, and it had to be explained to him that a prince in Russia was simply the equivalent of a British courtesy lord. But he was puzzled that a man of Val's personality didn't go out and make some real money.

'This is Europe,' said Val gravely. 'Here money is not made. It is inherited or else it is slowly saved over a period of many years and maybe in three generations a family moves up into a higher class.'

'Think of something people want – like we do.'

'That is because there is more money to want with in America. Everything that people want here has been thought of long ago.'

But after a year and with the help of a young Englishman he had played tennis with before the war, Val managed to get into the Cannes branch of an English bank. He forwarded mail and bought railroad tickets and arranged tours for impatient sightseers. Sometimes a familiar face came to his window; if Val was recognised he shook hands; if not he kept silence. After two years he was no longer pointed out as a former prince, for the Russians were an old story now – the splendour of the Rostoffs and their friends was forgotten.

He mixed with people very little. In the evenings he walked for a while on the promenade, took a slow glass of beer in a café, and went early to bed. He was seldom invited anywhere because people thought that his sad, intent face was depressing – and he never accepted anyhow. He wore cheap French clothes now instead of the rich tweeds and flannels that had been ordered with his father's from England. As for women, he knew none at all. Of the many things he had been certain about at seventeen, he had been most certain about this – that his life would be full of romance. Now after eight years he knew that it was not to be. Somehow he had never had time for love – the war, the revolution, and now his poverty had conspired against his expectant heart. The springs of his emotion which had first poured forth one April night had dried up immediately and only a faint trickle remained.

His happy youth had ended almost before it began. He saw himself growing older and more shabby, and living always more and more in the memories of his gorgeous boyhood. Eventually he would become absurd, pulling out an old heirloom of a watch and showing it to amused young fellow clerks who would listen with winks to his tales of the Rostoff name.

He was thinking these gloomy thoughts one April evening in 1922 as he walked beside the sea and watched the never-changing magic of the awakening lights. It was no longer for his benefit, that magic, but it went on, and he was somehow glad. Tomorrow he was going away on his vacation, to a cheap hotel farther down the shore where he could bathe and rest and read; then he would come back and work some more. Every year for three years he had taken his vacation during the last two weeks in April, perhaps because it was then that he felt the most need for remembering. It was in April that what was destined to be the best part of his life had come to a culmination under a romantic moonlight. It was sacred to him – for what he had thought of as an initiation and a beginning had turned out to be the end.

He paused now in front of the Café des Étrangers and after a moment crossed the street on impulse and sauntered down to the shore. A dozen yachts, already turned to a beautiful silver colour, rode at anchor in the bay. He had seen them that afternoon, and read the names painted on their bows – but only from habit. He had done it for three years now, and it was almost a natural function of his eye.

'Un beau soir,' remarked a French voice at his elbow. It was a boatman who had often seen Val here before. 'Monsieur finds the sea beautiful?'

'Very beautiful.'

'I too. But a bad living except in the season. Next week,

though, I earn something special. I am paid well for simply waiting here and doing nothing more from eight o'clock until midnight.'

'That's very nice,' said Val politely.

'A widowed lady, very beautiful, from America, whose yacht always anchors in the harbour for the last two weeks in April. If the *Privateer* comes tomorrow it will make three years.'

5

All night Val didn't sleep – not because there was any question in his mind as to what he should do, but because his long stupefied emotions were suddenly awake and alive. Of course he must not see her – not he, a poor failure with a name that was now only a shadow – but it would make him a little happier always to know that she remembered. It gave his own memory another dimension, raised it like those stereopticon glasses that bring out a picture from the flat paper. It made him sure that he had not deceived himself – he had been charming once upon a time to a lovely woman, and she did not forget.

An hour before train time next day he was at the railway station with his grip, so as to avoid any chance encounter in the street. He found himself a place in a third-class carriage of the waiting train.

Somehow as he sat there he felt differently about life – a sort of hope, faint and illusory, that he hadn't felt twenty-four hours before. Perhaps there was some way in those next few years in which he could make it possible to meet her once again – if he worked hard, threw himself passionately into whatever was at hand. He knew of at least two Russians in Cannes who had started over again with nothing except good manners and ingenuity and were now doing surprisingly well. The blood of Morris Hasylton began to throb a little in Val's temples and made him remember something he had never before cared to remember – that Morris Hasylton, who had built his daughter a palace in St Petersburg, had also started from nothing at all.

Simultaneously another emotion possessed him, less strange, less dynamic but equally American – the emotion of curiosity. In case he did – well, in case life should ever make it possible for him to seek her out, he should at least know her name.

He jumped to his feet, fumbled excitedly at the carriage handle and jumped from the train. Tossing his valise into the check room he started at a run for the American consulate.

'A yacht came in this morning,' he said hurriedly to a clerk, 'an American yacht – the *Privateer*. I want to know who owns it.'

'Just a minute,' said the clerk, looking at him oddly. 'I'll try to find out.'

After what seemed to Val an interminable time he returned.

'Why, just a minute,' he repeated hesitantly. 'We're – it seems we're finding out.'

'Did the yacht come?'

'Oh, yes – it's here all right. At least I think so. If you'll just wait in that chair.'

After another ten minutes Val looked impatiently at his watch. If they didn't hurry he'd probably miss his train. He made a nervous movement as if to get up from his chair.

'Please sit still,' said the clerk, glancing at him quickly from his desk. 'I ask you. Just sit down in that chair.'

Val stared at him. How could it possibly matter to the clerk whether or not he waited?

'I'll miss my train,' he said impatiently. 'I'm sorry to have given you all this bother – '

'Please sit still! We're glad to get it off our hands. You see, we've been waiting for your enquiry for – ah – three years.'

Val jumped to his feet and jammed his hat on his head.

'Why didn't you tell me that?' he demanded angrily.

'Because we had to get word to our – our client. Please don't go! It's – ah, it's too late.'

Val turned. Someone slim and radiant with dark frightened eyes was standing behind him, framed against the sunshine of the doorway.

'Why – '

Val's lips parted, but no words came through. She took a step towards him.

'I – ' She looked at him helplessly, her eyes filling with tears. 'I just wanted to say hello,' she murmured. 'I've come back for three years just because I wanted to say hello.'

Still Val was silent.

'You might answer,' she said impatiently. 'You might answer when I'd – when I'd just about begun to think you'd been killed in the war.' She turned to the clerk. 'Please introduce us!' she cried. 'You see, I can't say hello to him when we don't even know each other's names.'

It's the thing to distrust these international marriages, of course. It's an American tradition that they always turn out badly, and we are accustomed to such headlines as: ' "Would Trade Coronet for True American Love," says Duchess', and 'Claims Count Mendicant Tortured Toledo Wife'. The other sort of headlines are never printed, for who would want to read: ' "Castle is Love Nest," Asserts Former Georgia Belle', or 'Duke and Packer's Daughter Celebrate Golden Honeymoon'.

So far there have been no headlines at all about the young Rostoffs. Prince Val is much too absorbed in that string of moonlight-blue taxicabs, which he manipulates with such unusual efficiency, to give out interviews. He and his wife only leave New York once a year – but there is still a boatman who rejoices when the *Privateer* steams into Cannes harbour on a mid-April night.

W. S. GILBERT

W. S. Gilbert was born in London on 18 November 1836. He studied at King's College and became a clerk in the Privy-Council Office from 1857 to 1862. He was called to the Bar in 1864 but he failed to attract lucrative briefs and made his living writing humorous contributions to magazines like *Punch*. Under his boyhood nickname 'Bab', he wrote and illustrated a series of highly popular comic verses, primarily for the magazine *Fun*, known as the 'Bab Ballads'. But it is as the librettist of Sir Arthur Sullivan's Savoy Operas that he is best remembered. He died in Harrow Weald, Middlesex, on 29 May 1911.

An Inverted Love Story

I am a poor paralysed fellow who, for many years past, has been confined to a bed or a sofa. For the last six years I have occupied a small room, giving on to one of the side canals of Venice, and having no one about me but a deaf old woman, who makes my bed and attends to my food; and there I eke out a poor income of about thirty pounds a year by making watercolour drawings of flowers and fruit (they are the cheapest models in Venice), and these I send to a friend in London, who sells them to a dealer for small sums. But, on the whole, I am happy and content.

It is necessary that I should describe the position of my room rather minutely. Its only window is about five feet above the water of the canal, and above it the house projects some six feet, and overhangs the water, the projecting portion being supported by stout piles driven into the bed of the canal. This arrangement has the disadvantage (among others) of so limiting my upward view that I am unable to see more than about ten feet of the height of the house immediately opposite to me, although, by reaching as far out of the window as my infirmity will permit, I can see for a considerable distance up and down the canal, which does not exceed fifteen feet in width. But, although I can see but little of the material house opposite, I can see its reflection upside down in the canal, and I take a good deal of inverted interest in such of its inhabitants as show themselves from time to time (always upside down) on its balconies and at its windows.

When I first occupied my room, about six years ago, my attention was directed to the reflection of a little girl of thirteen or so (as nearly as I could judge), who passed every day on a balcony just above the upward range of my limited field of view. She had a glass of flowers and a crucifix on a little table by her side; and as she sat there, in fine weather, from early morning until dark, working assiduously all the time, I concluded that she earned her living by needlework. She was certainly an industrious little girl, and, as far as I could judge from her upside-down reflection, neat in her dress and pretty. She had an old mother, an invalid, who, on warm days, would sit on the balcony with her, and it interested me to see the little maid wrap the old lady in shawls, and bring pillows for her chair, and a stool for her feet, and every now and again lay down her work and kiss and fondle the old lady for half a minute, and then take up her work again.

Time went by, and as the little maid grew up, her reflection grew down, and at last she was quite a little woman of, I suppose, sixteen or seventeen. I can only work for a couple of hours or so in the brightest part of the day, so I had plenty of time on my hands in which to watch her movements, and sufficient imagination to weave a little romance about her, and to endow her with a beauty which, to a great extent, I had to take for granted. I saw – or fancied that I could see – that she began to take an interest in *my* reflection (which, of course, she could see as I could see hers); and one day, when it appeared to me that she was looking right at it – that is to say when her reflection appeared to be looking right at me – I tried the desperate experiment of nodding to her, and to my intense delight her reflection nodded in reply. And so our two reflections became known to one another.

It did not take me very long to fall in love with her, but a long time passed before I could make up my mind to do more than nod to her every morning, when the old woman moved me from my bed to the sofa at the window, and again in the evening, when the little maid left the balcony for that day. One day, however, when I saw her reflection looking at mine, I nodded to her, and threw a flower into the canal. She nodded several times in return, and I saw her direct her mother's attention to the incident. Then every morning I threw a flower into the water for 'good-morning', and another in the evening for 'good-night', and I soon discovered that I had not altogether thrown them in vain, for one day she threw a flower to join mine, and she laughed and clapped her hands when she saw the two flowers join forces and float away together. And then every morning and every evening she threw her flower when I threw mine, and when the two flowers met she clapped her hands, and so did I; but when they were separated, as they sometimes were, owing to one of them having met an obstruction which did not catch the other, she threw up her hands in a pretty affectation of despair, which I tried to imitate but in an English and unsuccessful fashion. And when they were rudely run down by a passing gondola (which happened not unfrequently) she pretended to cry, and I did the same. Then, in pretty pantomime, she would point downwards to the sky to tell me that it was destiny that had caused the shipwreck of our flowers, and I, in pantomime, not nearly so pretty, would try to convey to her that destiny would be kinder next time, and that perhaps tomorrow our flowers would be more fortunate – and so the innocent courtship went on. One day she showed me her crucifix and kissed it, and thereupon I took a little silver crucifix that always stood by me, and kissed that, and so she knew that we were one in religion.

One day the little maid did not appear on her balcony, and for several days I saw nothing of her; and although I threw my flowers as usual, no flower came to keep it company. However, after a time, she reappeared, dressed in black, and crying often, and then I knew that the poor child's mother was dead, and, as far as I knew, she was alone in the world. The flowers came no more for many days, nor did she show any sign of recognition, but kept her eyes on her work, except when she placed her handkerchief to them. And opposite to her was the old lady's chair, and I could see that, from time to time, she would lay down her work and gaze at it, and then a flood of tears would come to her relief. But at last one day she roused herself to nod to me, and then her flower came, day by day, and my flower went forth to join it, and with varying fortunes the two flowers sailed away as of yore.

But the darkest day of all to me was when a good-looking young gondolier, standing right end uppermost in his gondola (for I could see *him* in the flesh), worked his craft alongside the house, and stood talking to her as she sat on the balcony. They seemed to speak as old friends – indeed, as well as I could make out, he held her by the hand during the whole of their interview which lasted quite half an hour. Eventually he pushed off, and left my heart heavy within me. But I soon took heart of grace, for as soon as he was out of sight, the little maid threw two flowers growing on the same stem – an allegory of which I could make nothing, until it broke upon me that she meant to convey to me that he and she were brother and sister, and that I had no cause to be sad. And thereupon I nodded to her cheerily, and she nodded to me, and laughed aloud, and I laughed in return, and all went on again as before.

Then came a dark and dreary time, for it became necessary that I should undergo treatment that confined me absolutely to my bed for many days, and I worried and fretted to think that the little maid and I should see each other no longer, and worse still, that she would think that I had gone away without even hinting to her that I was going. And I lay awake at night wondering how I could let her know the truth, and fifty plans flitted through my brain, all appearing to be feasible enough at night, but absolutely wild and impracticable in the morning. One day – and it was a bright day indeed for me – the old woman who tended me told me that a gondolier had enquired whether the English signor had gone away or had died; and so I learnt that the little maid had been anxious about me, and that she had sent her brother to enquire, and the brother had no doubt taken to her the reason of my protracted absence from the window.

From that day, and ever after during my three weeks of bed-keeping, a flower was found every morning on the ledge of my window, which was within easy reach of anyone in a boat; and when at last a day came when I could be moved, I took my accustomed place on my sofa at the window, and the little maid saw me, and stood on her head (so to speak) and clapped her hands upside down with a delight that was as eloquent as my right-end-up delight could be. And so the first time the gondolier passed my window I beckoned to him, and he pushed alongside, and told me, with many bright smiles, that he was glad indeed to see me well again. Then I thanked him and his sister for their many kind thoughts about me during my retreat, and I then learnt from him that her name was Angela, and that she was the best and purest maiden in all Venice, and that anyone might think himself happy indeed who could call her sister, but that he was happier even than her brother, for he was to be married to her, and indeed they were to be married the next day.

Thereupon my heart seemed to swell to bursting, and the blood rushed through my veins so that I could hear it and nothing else for a while. I managed at last to stammer forth some words of awkward congratulation, and he left me, singing merrily, after asking permission to bring his bride to see me on the morrow as they returned from church.

'For,' said he, 'my Angela has known you very long – ever since she was a child, and she has often spoken to me of the poor Englishman who was a good Catholic, and who lay all day long for years and years on a sofa at a window, and she had said over and over again how dearly she wished she could speak to him and comfort him; and one day, when you threw a flower into the canal, she asked me whether she might throw another, and I told her yes, for he would understand that it meant sympathy for one sorely afflicted.'

And so I learned that it was pity, and not love, except indeed such love as is akin to pity, that prompted her to interest herself in my welfare, and there was an end of it all.

For the two flowers that I thought were on one stem were two flowers tied together (but I could not tell that), and they were meant to indicate that she and the gondolier were affianced lovers, and my expressed pleasure at this symbol delighted her, for she took it to mean that I rejoiced in her happiness.

And the next day the gondolier came with a train of other gondoliers, all decked in their holiday garb, and on his gondola sat Angela, happy, and blushing at her happiness. Then he and she entered the house in which I dwelt, and came into my room (and it was strange indeed, after so many years of inversion, to see her with her head above her feet!), and then she wished me happiness and a speedy restoration to good health (which could never be); and I, in broken words and with tears in my eyes, gave her the little silver crucifix that had stood by my bed or my table for so many years. And Angela took it reverently, and crossed herself, and kissed it, and so departed with her delighted husband.

And as I heard the song of the gondoliers as they went their way – the song dying away in the distance as the shadows of the sundown closed around me – I felt that they were singing the requiem of the only love that had ever entered my heart.

EDITH WHARTON

Edith Wharton was born in 1862 into a wealthy New York family. In 1885 she married a Boston socialite; the couple travelled widely and settled in France in 1907, but the marriage was unhappy and they divorced in 1913. Her first major novel was *The House of Mirth* (1905); many short stories, travel books, memoirs and novels followed, including *Ethan Frome* (1911), *The Reef* (1912) and *The Age of Innocence* (1920). Wharton was decorated for her humanitarian work during the First World War. She died in France in 1937.

The Long Run

1

It was last winter, after a twelve years' absence from New York, that I saw again, at one of the Phil Cumnors' dinners, my old friend Halston Merrick.

The Cumnors' house is one of the few where, even after such a lapse of time, one can be sure of finding familiar faces and picking up old threads; where for a moment one can abandon oneself to the illusion that New York humanity is less unstable than its bricks and mortar. And that evening in particular I remember feeling that there could be no pleasanter way of re-entering the confused and careless world to which I was returning than through the quiet, softly-lit dining-room in which Mrs Cumnor, with a characteristic sense of my needing to be broken in gradually, had contrived to assemble so many friendly faces.

I was glad to see them all, including the three or four I did not know, or failed to recognise, but had no difficulty in classing as in the tradition and of the group; but I was most of all glad – as I rather wonderingly found – to set eyes again on Halston Merrick.

He and I had been at Harvard together, for one thing, and had shared there curiosities and ardours a little outside the current tendencies: had, on the whole, been freer and less amenable to the accepted. Then, for the next few years, Merrick had been a vivid and promising figure in young American life. Handsome, free and fine, he had wandered and tasted and compared. After leaving Harvard he had spent two years at Oxford. He then accepted a private secretaryship to our ambassador in England, and came back from this adventure with a fresh curiosity about public affairs at home, and the conviction that men of his kind didn't play a large enough part in them. This led, first, to his running for a state senatorship which he failed to get, and ultimately to a few months of intelligent activity in a municipal office. Soon after a change of party had deprived him of this post he published a small volume of rather hauntingly delicate sonnets, and, a year later, an odd uneven brilliant book on municipal government. After that one hardly knew where to look for his next appearance; but chance rather disappointingly solved the problem by killing off his father and placing Halston at the head of the Merrick Iron Foundry at Yonkers.

His friends had gathered that, whenever this regrettable contingency should occur, he meant to dispose of the business and continue his life of free experiment. As often happens in such cases, however, it was not the moment for a sale, and Merrick had to take over the management of the foundry. Some two years later he had a chance to free himself, but when it came he did not choose to take it. This tame sequel to an inspiriting start was slightly disappointing to some of us, and I was among those disposed to regret Merrick's drop to the level of the merely prosperous. Then I went away to my big engineering job in China, and from there to Africa, and spent the next twelve years out of sight and sound of New York doings.

During that long interval I learned of no new phase in Merrick's evolution, but this did not surprise me, as I had never expected from him actions resonant enough to be heard across the globe. All I knew – and this surprised me – was that he had never married, and that he was still in the iron business. All through those years, however, I never ceased to wish, in certain situations and at certain turns of thought, that Merrick were in reach, that I could tell this or that to Merrick. I had never, in the interval, found anyone with just his quickness of perception and just his sureness of touch.

After dinner, therefore, we irresistibly drew together. In Mrs Cumnor's big easy drawing-room cigars were allowed, and there was no break in the communion of the sexes; and, this being the case, I should have sought a seat beside one of the ladies who so indulgently suffered our presence. But, as generally happened when Merrick was in sight, I found myself steering straight for him past all the minor ports of call.

There had been no time, before our passage to the dining-room, for more than the barest expression of delight at meeting, and our seats had been at opposite ends of the longish table, so that we got our first real look at each other in the screened secluded sofa-corner to which Mrs Cumnor's vigilance now tactfully directed us.

Merrick was still handsome in his long swarthy way: handsomer perhaps, with thinnish hair and graver lines, than in the young excess of his good looks. He was very glad to see me and expressed his gladness in terms of the same charming smile; but as soon as we began to talk I felt a change. It was not merely the change that years and experience and altered values bring. There was something more fundamental the matter with Merrick: something dreadful, unforeseen, unaccountable. Merrick had grown conventional and dull.

In the face of his frank pleasure in seeing me I was ashamed, at first, to analyse the nature of the change; but presently our talk began to flag – fancy a talk with Merrick flagging! – and self-deception became impossible as I watched myself handing out platitudes with the unconvinced gesture of a salesman offering something "equally good". The worst of it was that Merrick – Merrick, who had once felt everything! – didn't seem to feel any lack of spontaneity in my remarks, but clung to me in speech and look with a harrowing faith in the resuscitating power of our past. It was as if he treasured the empty vessel of our friendship without perceiving that the last drop of its essence had gone dry.

I am putting all this in exaggerated terms. Through my surprise and disappointment there glowed a certain sense of well-being in the mere physical presence of my old friend. I liked looking at the way his thin dark hair broke away from the forehead, at the tautness of his smooth brown cheek, the contemplative backward tilt of his head, the way his brown eyes mused upon the scene through indolently lowered lids. All the past was in his way of looking and sitting, and I wanted to stay near him, and knew that he wanted me to stay, but the devil of it was that neither of us knew what to talk about.

It was this difficulty which caused me, after a while, since I could not follow Merrick's talk, to follow his eyes in their slow circuit of the room.

At the moment when our glances joined, his happened to have paused on a lady seated at some distance from our corner. Immersed, at first, in the satisfaction of finding myself again with Merrick, I had been only negatively aware of this lady, as of one of the few persons present whom I did not know, or failed to remember. There was nothing in her appearance or attitude to challenge my indifference or to excite my curiosity: I don't suppose I should have looked at her at all if I had not noticed that my friend was doing so.

She was a woman of about forty-seven, with fair faded hair and a young figure. Her smoke-grey dress was handsome but ineffective, and her pale and rather serious face wore a small unvarying smile which might have been pinned on with her ornaments. She was one of the women in whom the years show rather what they have taken than what they have bestowed, and only on looking closely did one see that what they had taken must have been exceptionally good of its kind.

Phil Cumnor and another man were talking to her, and the very intensity of the attention she bestowed on them betrayed the straining of rebellious thoughts. She never let her eyes stray or her smile drop; and at the proper moments I saw she was ready with the proper sentiment.

The party, like most of those that Mrs Cumnor gathered about her, was not composed of exceptional beings. The people of the old New York set were not exceptional: they were in fact mostly cut on the same neat, convenient and unobtrusive pattern; but they were often exceedingly 'nice'. And this obsolete quality marked every look and gesture of the lady I was scrutinising.

While these reflections were passing through my mind I was aware that Merrick's eyes were still turned in the same direction. I took a cross-section of his look and found in it neither surprise nor absorption, but only a certain sober pleasure just about at the emotional level of the rest of the room. If he were looking at the lady in question it was only, his expression seemed to say, because, all things considered, there were fewer reasons for looking at anybody else.

This made me wonder what were the reasons for looking at her: and as a first step towards enlightenment I said: 'I'm sure I've seen the lady over there in grey – '

Merrick, with a slight effort, detached his eyes and turned them on me in a wondering look.

'Seen her? You know her.' He paused for my response. 'Don't you know her? It's Mrs Reardon.'

I wondered that he should wonder, for I could not remember, in the Cumnor group or elsewhere, having known anyone of the name he mentioned.

'But perhaps,' he continued, 'you hadn't heard of her marriage? You knew her as Mrs Trant.'

I gave him back his stare. 'Not Mrs Philip Trant?'

'Yes; Mrs Philip Trant.'

'Not Paulina?' I insisted.

'Yes – Paulina,' he said, with a just perceptible delay before the name.

In my stupefaction I continued to stare at him, instead of turning my gaze towards the lady whose identity was in dispute.

He averted his eyes from mine after a moment, and I saw that they had strayed back to her. 'You find her so changed?' he asked.

An odd note in his voice acted as a warning signal, and I tried to reduce my astonishment to less unbecoming proportions. 'I don't find that she looks much older.'

'No. Only different?' he suggested, as if there were nothing new to him in my perplexity.

'Yes – awfully different,' I confessed.

'I suppose we're all awfully different. To you, I mean – coming from so far?'

'I recognised all the rest of you,' I said, hesitating. 'And she used to be the one who stood out most.'

There was a flash, a wave, a stir of something deep down in his eyes. 'Yes,' he said. 'That's the difference.'

'I see it is. She – she looks worn down. Soft but blurred, like the figures in the tapestry behind her.'

He glanced at her again, as if to test the exactness of my analogy.

'Life wears everybody down, I suppose,' he said.

'Yes – except those it makes more distinct. They're the rare ones, of course; but she was rare.'

He stood up suddenly, looking old and tired. 'I believe I'll be off. I wish you'd come down to my place for Sunday . . . No, don't shake hands – I want to slide away while they're not looking.

We were standing near the door of the inner drawing-room, and I placed myself before him to say a last word and screen his retreat.

'You will come down, won't you?' he repeated. 'I want to see you. There'll be no one else.' He had backed away to the threshold and was turning the noiseless door-knob. Even Mrs Cumnor's door-knobs had tact and didn't tell!

'Of course I'll come,' I promised warmly. In the last ten minutes he had begun to interest me again.

'All right. Goodbye.' Half through the door he paused to stammer: ' – She remembers you. You ought to speak to her.'

'I'm going to. But tell me a little more.' I thought I saw a shade of constraint on his face, and did not add, as I had meant to: 'Tell me – because she interests me – what wore her down?' Instead, I asked: 'How soon after Trant's death did she remarry?'

He seemed to require an effort of memory to recall the date. 'It was seven years ago, I think.'

'And is Reardon here tonight?'

'Yes; over there, talking to Mrs Cumnor.'

I looked across the broken lamplit groupings and saw a large glossy man with straw-coloured hair and a red face, whose shirt and shoes and complexion seemed all to have received a coat of the same expensive varnish.

As I looked there was a drop in the talk about us, and I heard Mr Reardon pronounce in a big booming voice: 'What I say is: what's the good of disturbing things? Thank the Lord, I'm content with what I've got!'

'Is that her husband? What's he like?'

'Oh, the best fellow in the world,' said Merrick, going.

2

Merrick had a little place at Riverdale, where he went occasionally to be near the Iron Works, and where he hid at weekends when the world was too much with him.

Here he awaited me on the following Saturday afternoon, and at tea-time I found myself with him in a pleasant careless setting of books and prints and faded parental furniture.

We dined late, and smoked and talked afterwards in his low-ceilinged book-walled study till the terrier on the hearth-rug stood up and yawned for bed. When we took the hint and picked up our candles in the hall I felt not that I had found the old Merrick again, but that I was on his track, had come across traces of his passage here and there in the thick jungle that had grown up between us. But I had an odd poignant feeling that when I finally came on the man himself he might be dead . . .

As we started up the shallow country stairs he turned with one of his abrupt shy movements, and walked back into the study.

'Wait a bit!' he called to me.

I waited, and he came out in a moment carrying a limp folio.

'It's typewritten. Will you take a look at it? I've been trying to get to work again,' he lamely explained, thrusting the manuscript into my hand.

'What? Poetry, I hope?' I exclaimed.

He shook his head with a gleam of derision. 'No – just general considerations. The fruit of fifty years of inexperience.'

He showed me to my room and said good-night.

The following afternoon – it was a mild winter day with soft wet gusts, I remember – we took a long walk inland, across the hills, and I said to Merrick what I could of his book. Unluckily there wasn't much to say. The essays were judicious, polished and cultivated, but they lacked the freshness and audacity of his youthful work. I tried to conceal my opinion behind the usual ambiguities, but he broke through these feints with a quick thrust to the heart of my meaning.

'It's worn down – blurred? Like the figures in the Cumnors' tapestry?'

I hesitated. 'It's a little too damned resigned,' I said.

'Ah,' he exclaimed, 'so am I. Resigned.' He switched the bare brambles by the roadside. 'A man can't serve two masters.'

'You mean business and literature?'

'No; I mean theory and instinct. The grey tree and the green. You've got to choose which fruit you'll try; and you don't know till afterwards which of the two has the dead core.'

'How can anybody be sure that only one of them has?'

'I'm sure,' said Merrick sharply.

We turned back to the subject of his essays, and I was astonished at the detachment with which he criticised and demolished them. Little by little, as we talked, his old perspective, his old standards came back to him, but with the difference that they no longer seemed like functions of his mind but merely like attitudes assumed or dropped at will. He could still, with an effort, put himself at the angle from which he had formerly seen things; but it was with the effort of a man climbing mountains after a sedentary life in the plain.

I tried to cut the talk short, but he kept coming back to it with nervous insistence, forcing me into the last retrenchments of hypocrisy, and anticipating the verdict I held back. I perceived that a great deal – immensely more than I could see a reason for – had hung for him on my opinion of his book.

Then, as suddenly, his insistence broke and, as if ashamed of having forced himself so long on my attention, he began to talk rapidly and uninterestingly of other things.

We were alone again that evening, and after dinner, wishing to efface the impression of the afternoon, and above all to show that I wanted him to talk about himself, I reverted to the subject of his work. 'You must need an outlet of that sort. When a man's once had it in him, as you have – and when other things begin to dwindle – '

He laughed. 'Your theory is that a man ought to be able to return to the Muse as he comes back to his wife after he's ceased to interest other women?'

'No; as he comes back to his wife after the day's work is done.' A new thought came to me as I looked at him. 'You ought to have had one,' I added.

He laughed again. 'A wife, you mean? So that there'd have been someone waiting for me even if the Muse decamped?' He went on after a pause: 'I've a notion that the kind of woman worth coming back to wouldn't be much more patient than the Muse. But as it happens I never tried – because, for fear they'd chuck me, I put them both out of doors together.'

He turned his head abruptly and looked past me with a queer expression at the low grey-panelled door at my back. 'Out of that very door they went – the two of 'em, on a rainy night like this: and one stopped and looked back, to see if I wasn't going to call her – and I didn't – and so they both went . . . '

3

'The Muse?' said Merrick, refilling my glass and stooping to pat the terrier as he went back to his chair – 'well, you've met the Muse in the little volume of sonnets you used to like; and you've met the woman too, and you used to like her; though you didn't know her when you saw her the other evening . . .

'No, I won't ask you how she struck you: I know. She struck you like that stuff I gave you to read last night. She's conformed – I've conformed – the mills have caught us and ground us: ground us, oh, exceedingly small!

'But you remember what she was: I saw at once that you remembered. And that's the reason why I'm telling you this now . . .

'You may recall that after my father's death I tried unsuccessfully to sell the Works. I was impatient to free myself from anything that would keep me tied to New York. I don't dislike my trade, and I've made, in the end, a fairly good thing of it; but industrialism was not, at that time, in the line of my tastes, and I know now that it wasn't what I was meant for. Above all, I wanted to get away, to see new places and rub up against different ideas. I had reached a time of life – the top of the first hill, so to speak – where the distance draws one, and everything in the foreground seems tame and stale. I was sick to death of the particular set of conformities I had grown up among; sick of being a pleasant popular young man with a long line of dinners on my engagement list, and the dead certainty of meeting the same people, or their prototypes, at all of them.

'Well – I failed to sell the Works, and that increased my discontent. I went through moods of cold unsociability, alternating with sudden flushes of curiosity, when I gloated over stray scraps of talk overheard in railway stations and omnibuses, when strange faces that I passed in the street tantalised me with fugitive promises. I wanted to get away, among things that were unexpected and unknown; and it seemed to me that nobody about me understood in the least what I felt, but that somewhere just out of reach there was someone who did, and whom I must find or despair . . .

'It was just then that, one evening, I saw Mrs Trant for the first time.

'Yes: I know – you wonder what I mean. I'd known her, of course, as a girl; I'd met her several times after her marriage to Trant; and I'd lately been thrown with her, quite intimately and continuously, during a succession of country-house visits. But I had never, as it happened, really seen her till then . . .

'It was at a dinner at the Cumnors', I remember; and there she was, in front of the very tapestry we saw her against the other evening, with people about her, and her face turned from me, and nothing noticeable or different in her dress or manner; and suddenly she stood out for me against the pinkish-smoky background, and for the first time I saw a meaning in the stale phrase of a picture's walking out of its frame. For you've noticed, haven't you, that most people are just that to us: pictures, furniture, the inanimate accessories of our little island-area of sensation? And then sometimes one of these graven images moves and throws out live filaments towards us, and the line they make draws us across the world as the moon-track seems to draw a boat across black water . . .

'Well, there she stood; and as this queer sensation came over me I felt that she was looking steadily at me, that her eyes were voluntarily, consciously resting on me with the weight of a deep interrogation.

'I went over and joined her, and she turned silently and walked with me into the music-room. Earlier in the evening someone had been singing, and there were low lights there, and a few couples still sitting in those confidential corners of which Mrs Cumnor has the art; but we were under no illusion as to the nature of these presences. We knew that they were just painted in, and that the whole of sentient life was in us two, and flowing back and forward between us in swift innumerable streams. We talked, of course; we had the attitudes, even the words, of the others: I remember her telling me her plans for the spring and asking me politely about mine! As if there were the least sense in plans, now that this thing had happened to us!

'When we went back into the drawing-room I had said nothing to her that I might not have said to any other woman of the party; but when we said goodbye I knew we should see each other the next day – and the next . . .

'That's the way, I take it, that nature has arranged the beginning of the great enduring loves; and likewise of the little epidermal flurries. And how's a man to know where he is going?

'From the first, I own, my feeling for Paulina Trant seemed

to me a grave business; but then I knew that the enemy is given to producing that illusion. Many a man – I'm talking of the kind with imagination – has thought he was seeking a soul when all he wanted was a closer view of its tenement. And I tried – honestly tried – to make myself think I was in this case. Because, in the first place, I didn't just then want a big disturbing influence in my life; and because I didn't want to be a dupe; and because Paulina Trant was not, according to hearsay, the kind of woman for whom it was worth while to bring up the big batteries . . .

'But my resistance was only half-hearted. What I really felt – all I really felt – was the flood of joy that comes of heightened emotion. She had given me that, and I wanted her to give it to me again. That's as near as I've ever come to analysing my state in the beginning.

'I knew her story, as no doubt you know it: the current version, I mean. She had been poor and fond of enjoyment, and she had married that pompous monolith Philip Trant because she needed a home, and perhaps also because she wanted a little luxury. Queer how we sneer at women for wanting the thing that gives them half their grace!

'People shook their heads over the marriage, and divided, prematurely, into Philip's partisans and hers: for no one thought it would work. And they were almost disappointed when, after all, it did. She and her wooden consort seemed to get on well enough. There was a ripple at one time over her close friendship with young Jim Dalham, who was always with her during a summer at Newport and an autumn in Italy; then the talk died out, and she and Trant were seen together, as before, on terms of apparent good-fellowship.

'This was the more surprising because, from the first, Paulina had never made the least attempt to change her tone or subdue her colours. In the grey Trant atmosphere she flashed with prismatic fires. She smoked, she talked subversively, she did as she liked and went where she pleased, and danced over the

Trant prejudices and the Trant principles as if they'd been a ballroom floor; and all without apparent offence to her solemn husband and his cloud of cousins. I believe her frankness and directness struck them dumb. She moved like a kind of primitive Una through the virtuous rout, and never got a fingermark on her freshness.

'One of the finest things about her was the fact that she never, for an instant, used her plight as a means of enhancing her attraction. With a husband like Trant it would have been so easy! He was a man who always saw the small sides of big things. He thought most of life compressible into a set of by-laws and the rest unmentionable; and with his stiff frock-coated and tall-hatted mind, instinctively distrustful of intelligences in another dress, with his arbitrary classification of whatever he didn't understand into 'the kind of thing I don't approve of', 'the kind of thing that isn't done' and – deepest depth of all – 'the kind of thing I'd rather not discuss', he lived in the service of a shadowy moral etiquette, of which the complex rites and awful penalties had cast an abiding gloom upon his manner.

'A woman like his wife couldn't have asked a better foil; yet I'm sure she never consciously used his dullness to relieve her brilliancy. She may have felt that the case spoke for itself. But I believe her reserve was rather due to a lively sense of justice, and to the rare habit (you said she was rare) of looking at facts as they are, without any throwing of sentimental lime-lights. She knew Trant could no more help being Trant than she could help being herself – and there was an end of it. I've never known a woman who 'made up' so little mentally . . .

'Perhaps her very reserve, the fierceness of her implicit rejection of sympathy, exposed her the more to – well, to what happened when we met. She said afterwards that it was like having been shut up for months in the hold of a ship, and coming suddenly on deck on a day that was all flying blue and silver . . .

'I won't try to tell you what she was. It's easier to tell you what her friendship made of me; and I can do that best by adopting her metaphor of the ship. Haven't you, sometimes, at the moment of starting on a journey, some glorious plunge into the unknown, been tripped up by the thought: 'If only one hadn't to come back'? Well, with her one had the sense that one would never have to come back; that the magic ship would always carry one farther. And what an air one breathed on it! And, oh, the wind, and the islands, and the sunsets!

'I said just now "her friendship"; and I used the word advisedly. Love is deeper than friendship, but friendship is a good deal wider. The beauty of our relation was that it included both dimensions. Our thoughts met as naturally as our eyes: it was almost as if we loved each other because we liked each other. I'm inclined to think that the quality of a love may be tested by the amount of friendship it contains, and in our case there was no dividing line between loving and liking, no disproportion between them, no barrier against which desire beat in vain or from which thought fell back unsatisfied. Ours was a robust passion that could give an open-eyed account of itself, and not a beautiful madness shrinking away from the proof . . .

'For the first months friendship sufficed us, or rather gave us so much by the way that we were in no haste to reach what we knew it led to. But we were moving there nevertheless, and one day we found ourselves on the borders. It came about through a sudden decision of Trant's to start on a long tour with his wife. We had never foreseen such a possibility: he seemed rooted in his New York habits and convinced that the city's whole social and financial machinery would cease to function if he did not keep an eye on it through the columns of his morning paper and pronounce judgement on it in the afternoon at his club. But something new had happened to him. He caught a cold, which was followed by a touch of pleurisy, and instantly he perceived the intense interest and importance which ill-health may add to life. He took the fullest advantage of it. A complaisant doctor recommended travel, insisted on a winter in a warm climate; and suddenly, the morning paper, the afternoon club, Fifth Avenue, Wall Street, all the complex phenomena of the metropolis, faded into insignificance, and the rest of the terrestrial globe, from being a mere geographical hypothesis, useful in enabling one to determine the latitude of New York, acquired reality and magnitude as a factor in the convalescence of Mr Philip Trant.

'His wife was absorbed in preparations for the journey. It took an army to mobilise him, and weeks before the date set for their departure it was almost as if she were already gone.

'This foretaste of separation showed us what we were to each other. Yet I was letting her go – and there was no help for it, no way of preventing it. Resistance was as useless as the vain struggles in a nightmare. She was Trant's and not mine: a part of his luggage when he travelled as she was part of his household furniture when he stayed at home . . .

'The day she told me that their passages were taken – it was on a November afternoon, in her drawing-room in town – I turned away from the tea-table and, going to the window, stood looking out at the torrent of traffic interminably pouring down Fifth Avenue. I watched the senseless machinery of life revolving in the rain and mud, and tried to picture myself performing my small function in it after she had gone from me.

' "It can't be – it can't be!" I exclaimed.

' "What can't be?"

'I came back into the room and sat down by her. "This – this – " I hadn't any words. "Two weeks!" I said. "What's two weeks?"

'She answered vaguely, something about their thinking of Spain for the spring –

' "Two weeks – two weeks!" I repeated. "And the months we've lost – the days that belonged to us!"

' "Yes," she said, "I'm thankful it's settled."

'Our words seemed irrelevant, haphazard. It was as if each were answering a secret voice and not what the other was saying.

' "Don't you feel anything at all?" I remember bursting out at her. As I asked it the tears were streaming down her face. I felt angry with her, and was almost glad to note that her lids were red and that she didn't cry becomingly. I can't express my sensation to you except by saying that she seemed part of life's huge league against me. And suddenly I thought of an afternoon we had spent together in the country, on a ferny hillside, when we had sat under a beech tree, and her hand had lain palm upward in the moss, close to mine, and I had watched a little black-and-red beetle creeping over it . . .

'The bell rang, and we heard the voice of a visitor and the click of an umbrella in the umbrella-stand.

'She rose to go into the inner drawing-room, and I caught her suddenly by the wrist. "You understand," I said, "that we can't go on like this?"

' "I understand," she answered, and moved away to meet her visitor. As I went out I heard her saying in the other room, "Yes, we're really off on the twelfth."

4

'I wrote her a long letter that night, and waited two days for a reply.

'On the third day I had a brief line saying that she was going to spend Sunday with some friends who had a place near Riverdale, and that she would arrange to see me while she was there. That was all.

'It was on a Saturday that I received the note and I came out here the same night. The next morning was rainy, and I was in despair, for I had counted on her asking me to take her for a drive or a long walk. It was hopeless to try to say what I had to say to her in the drawing-room of a crowded country-house. And only eleven days were left!

'I stayed indoors all the morning, fearing to go out lest she should telephone me. But no sign came, and I grew more and more restless and anxious. She was too free and frank for coquetry, but her silence and evasiveness made me feel that, for some reason, she did not wish to hear what she knew I meant to say. Could it be that she was, after all, more conventional, less genuine, than I had thought? I went again and again over the whole maddening round of conjecture; but the only conclusion I could rest in was that, if she loved me as I loved her, she would be as determined as I was to let no obstacle come between us during the days that were left.

'The luncheon-hour came and passed, and there was no word from her. I had ordered my trap to be ready, so that I might drive over as soon as she summoned me; but the hours dragged on, the early twilight came, and I sat here in this very chair, or measured up and down, up and down, the length of this very rug – and still there was no message and no letter.

'It had grown quite dark, and I had ordered away, impatiently, the servant who came in with the lamps: I couldn't bear any definite sign that the day was over! And I was standing there on the rug, staring at the door, and noticing a bad crack in its panel, when I heard the sound of wheels on the gravel. A word at last, no doubt – a line to explain . . . I didn't seem to care much for her reasons, and I stood where I was and continued to stare at the door. And suddenly it opened and she came in.

'The servant followed her with a lamp, and then went out and closed the door. Her face looked pale in the lamplight, but her voice was as clear as a bell.

' "Well," she said, "you see I've come."

'I started towards her with hands outstretched. "You've come – you've come!" I stammered.

'Yes; it was like her to come in that way – without shame, without dissimulation, without explanations or excuses. It was like her, if she gave at all, to give not furtively or in haste, but openly, deliberately, without stinting the measure or counting the cost. But her quietness and serenity disconcerted me. She did not look like a woman who has yielded impetuously to an uncontrollable impulse. There was something almost solemn in her face.

'The awe of it stole over me as I looked at her, suddenly subduing the huge flush of gratified longing.

' "You're here, here, here!" I kept repeating, like a child singing over a happy word.

' "You said," she continued, in her grave clear voice, "that we couldn't go on as we were – "

' "Ah, it's divine of you!" I broke in, and held out my arms to her.

'She didn't draw back from them, but her faint smile said, "Wait," and lifting her hands she took the pins from her hat, and laid the hat on the table.

'As I saw her dear head bare in the lamplight, with the thick hair waving away from the parting, I forgot everything but the bliss and wonder of her being here – here, in my house, on my hearth – I can show you, yet, the exact spot where she was standing.

'I drew her over to the fire, and made her sit down in the chair where you're sitting, and knelt down by her, and hid my face on her knees. She put her hand on my head, and I was happy to the depths of my soul.

' "Oh, I forgot – " she exclaimed suddenly. I lifted my head and our eyes met. Hers were smiling.

'She reached out her hand, opened the little bag she had tossed down with her hat, and drew a small object from it. "I left my trunk at the station," she said. "Here's the check. Can you send for it?"

'Her trunk – she wanted me to send for her trunk! Oh, yes – I see your smile, your "lucky man!" Only, you see, I didn't love her in that way. I knew she couldn't come to my house without running a big risk of discovery, and my tenderness for her, my impulse to shield her, was stronger, even then, than masculine vanity or masculine desire. Judged from the point of view of those emotions I fell terribly short of my part. I hadn't any of the proper feelings. Such an act of romantic folly was so unlike her that it almost irritated me, and I found myself desperately wondering how I could get her to reconsider her plan without – well, without seeming to want her to.

'It's not the way a novel hero feels; it's probably not the way a man in real life ought to have felt. But it's the way I felt – and she saw it.

'She put her hands on my shoulders and looked at me with deep, deep eyes. "Then you didn't expect me to stay?" she asked, half-smiling.

'I caught her hands and pressed them close to me, stammering out that I hadn't dared to dream . . .

' "You thought I'd come – just for an hour?"

' "How could I dare think more? I adore you, you know, for what you've done! But it would be known if you – if you stayed on. My servants – everybody about here knows you. I've no right to expose you to the risk." She made no answer, and I went on tenderly: "Give me, if you will, the next few hours: there's a train that will get you to town by midnight. And then we'll arrange something – in town – where it's safer for you – easily managed . . . It's beautiful, it's glorious of you to have come; but I love you too much – I must take care of you and think for you – "

'I don't suppose it ever took me so long to say so few words, and though they were profoundly sincere they sounded unutterably shallow, irrelevant and grotesque. She made no effort to help me out, but sat silent, listening with her meditative smile. "It's my duty, dearest, as a man," I rambled on. "The more I love you the more I'm bound – "

' "Yes; but you don't understand," she interrupted.

'She rose as she spoke, and I got up also, and we stood and looked at each other.

' "I haven't come for a night; if you want me I've come for always," she said.

'Here again, if I give you an honest account of my feelings, I shall write myself down as the poor-spirited creature I suppose I am. There wasn't, I swear, at the moment, a gram of selfishness, of personal reluctance, in my feeling. I worshipped every hair of her head – when we were together I was happy, when I was away from her something was gone from every good thing; but I had always looked on our love for each other, our possible relation to each other, as such situations are looked on in what is called society. I had supposed her, for all her freedom and originality, to be just as tacitly subservient to that view as I was: ready to take what she wanted on the terms on which society concedes such taking, and to pay for it by the usual restrictions, concealments and hypocrisies. In short, I supposed that she would "play the game" – look out for her own safety and expect me to look out for it. It sounds cheap enough, put that way – but it's the rule we live under, all of us. And the amazement of finding her suddenly outside of it, oblivious of it, unconscious of it, left me, for an awful minute, stammering at her like a graceless dolt . . . Perhaps it wasn't even a minute; but in it she had gone the whole round of my thoughts.

' "It's raining," she said, very low. "I suppose you can telephone for a trap?"

'There was no irony or resentment in her voice. She walked slowly across the room and paused before the Brangwyn etching over there. "That's a good impression. Will you telephone, please?" she repeated.

'I found my voice again, and with it the power of movement. I followed her, and dropped at her feet. "You can't go like this!" I cried.

'She looked down on me from heights and heights. "I can't stay like this," she answered.

'I stood up and we faced each other like antagonists. "You don't know," I accused her passionately, "in the least what you're asking me to ask of you!"

' "Yes, I do: everything," she breathed.

' "And it's got to be that or nothing?"

' "Oh, on both sides," she reminded me.

' "Not on both sides. It isn't fair. That's why – "

' "Why you won't?"

' "Why I cannot – may not!"

' "Why you'll take a night and not a life?"

'The taunt, for a woman usually so sure of her aim, fell so short of the mark that its only effect was to increase my conviction of her helplessness. The very intensity of my longing for her made me tremble where she was fearless. I had to protect her first, and think of my own attitude afterwards.

'She was too discerning not to see this too. Her face softened, grew inexpressibly appealing, and she dropped again into that chair you're in, leaned forward, and looked up with her grave smile.

' "You think I'm beside myself – raving? (You're not thinking of yourself, I know.) I'm not: I never was saner. Since I've known you I've often thought that this might happen. This thing between us isn't an ordinary thing. If it had been we shouldn't, all these months, have drifted. We should have wanted to skip to the last page – and then throw down the book. We shouldn't have felt we could trust the future as we did. We were in no hurry because we knew we shouldn't get tired; and when two people feel that about each other they must live together – or part. I don't see what else they can do. A little trip along the coast won't answer. It's the high seas – or else being tied up to Lethe wharf. And I'm for the high seas, my dear!"

'Think of sitting here – here, in this room, in this chair – and listening to that, and seeing the light on her hair, and hearing the sound of her voice! I don't suppose there ever was a scene just like it . . .

'She was astounding – inexhaustible; through all my anguish of resistance I found a kind of fierce joy in following her. It was lucidity at white heat: the last sublimation of passion. She might have been an angel arguing a point in the empyrean if she hadn't been, so completely, a woman pleading for her life . . .

'Her life: that was the thing at stake! She couldn't do with less of it than she was capable of; and a woman's life is inextricably part of the man's she cares for.

'That was why, she argued, she couldn't accept the usual solution: couldn't enter into the only relation that society tolerates between people situated like ourselves. Yes: she knew all the arguments on that side: didn't I suppose she'd been over them and over them? She knew (for hadn't she often said it of others?) what is said of the woman who, by throwing in her lot with her lover's, binds him to a life-long duty which has the irksomeness without the dignity of marriage. Oh, she could talk on that side with the best of them: only she asked me to consider the other – the side of the man and woman who love each other deeply and completely enough to want their lives enlarged, and not diminished, by their love. What, in such a case – she reasoned – must be the inevitable effect of concealing, denying, disowning the central fact, the motive power of one's existence? She asked me to picture the course of such a love: first working as a fever in the blood, distorting and deflecting everything, making all other interests insipid, all other duties irksome, and then, as the acknowledged claims of life regained their hold, gradually dying – the poor starved passion! – for want of the wholesome necessary food of common living and doing, yet leaving life impoverished by the loss of all it might have been.

' "I'm not talking, dear – " I see her now, leaning towards me with shining eyes: "I'm not talking of the people who haven't enough to fill their days, and to whom a little mystery, a little manoeuvring, gives an illusion of importance that they can't afford to miss; I'm talking of you and me, with all our tastes and curiosities and activities; and I ask you what our love would become if we had to keep it apart from our lives, like a pretty useless animal that we went to peep at and feed with sweetmeats through its cage?"

'I won't, my dear fellow, go into the other side of our strange duel: the arguments I used were those that most men in my situation would have felt bound to use, and that most women in Paulina's accept instinctively, without even formulating them. The exceptionalness, the significance, of the case lay wholly in the fact that she had formulated them all and then rejected them . . .

'There was one point I didn't, of course, touch on, and that was the popular conviction (which I confess I shared) that when a man and a woman agree to defy the world together the man really sacrifices much more than the woman. I was not even conscious of thinking of this at the time, though it may have lurked somewhere in the shadow of my scruples for her; but she dragged it out into the daylight and held me face to face with it.

' "Remember, I'm not attempting to lay down any general rule," she insisted; "I'm not theorising about Man and Woman, I'm talking about you and me. How do I know what's best for the woman in the next house? Very likely she'll bolt when it would have been better for her to stay at home. And it's the same with the man: he'll probably do the wrong thing. It's generally the weak heads that commit follies, when it's the strong ones that ought to; and my point is that you and I are both strong enough to behave like fools if we want to . . .

' "Take your own case first – because, in spite of the sentimentalists, it's the man who stands to lose most. You'll have to give up the Iron Works: which you don't much care about – because it won't be particularly agreeable for us to live in New York: which you don't care much about either. But you won't be sacrificing what is called a 'career'. You made up your mind long ago that your best chance of self-development, and consequently of general usefulness, lay in thinking rather than doing, and, when we first met, you were already planning to sell out your business, and travel and write. Well! Those ambitions are of a kind that won't be harmed by your dropping out of your social setting. On the contrary, such work as you want to do ought to gain by it, because you'll be brought nearer to life-as-it-is, in contrast to life-as-a-visiting-list . . . "

'She threw back her head with a sudden laugh. "And the joy of not having any more visits to make! I wonder if you've ever thought of that? Just at first, I mean; for society's getting so deplorably lax that, little by little, it will edge up to us – you'll see! I don't want to idealise the situation, dearest, and I won't conceal from you that in time we shall be called on. But, oh, the fun we shall have had in the interval! And then, for the first time we shall be able to dictate our own terms, one of which will be that no bores need apply. Think of being cured of all one's chronic bores! We shall feel as jolly as people after a successful operation."

'I don't know why this nonsense sticks in my mind when some of the graver things we said are less distinct. Perhaps it's because of a certain iridescent quality of feeling that made her gaiety seem like sunshine through a shower . . .

' "You ask me to think of myself?" she went on. "But the beauty of our being together will be that, for the first time, I shall dare to! Now I have to think of all the tedious trifles I can pack the days with, because I'm afraid – I'm afraid – to hear the voice of the real me, down below, in the windowless underground hole where I keep her . . . "

' "Remember, again, please, it's not Woman, it's Paulina Trant, I'm talking of. The woman in the next house may have all sorts of reasons – honest reasons – for staying there. There may be someone there who needs her badly: for whom the light would go out if she went. Whereas to Philip I've been simply – well, what New York was before he decided to travel: the most important thing in life till he made up his mind to leave it; and now merely the starting-place of several lines of steamers. Oh, I didn't have to love you to know that! I only had to live with him . . . If he lost his eye-glasses he'd think it was the fault of the eye-glasses; he'd really feel that the eye-glasses had been careless. And he'd be convinced that no others would suit him quite as well. But at the optician's he'd probably be told that he needed something a little different, and after that he'd feel that the old eye-glasses had never suited him at all, and that that was their fault too . . . "

'At one moment – but I don't recall when – I remember she stood up with one of her quick movements, and came towards me, holding out her arms. "Oh, my dear, I'm pleading for my life; do you suppose I'll ever want for arguments?" she cried . . .

'After that, for a bit, nothing much remains with me except a sense of darkness and of conflict. The one spot of daylight in my whirling brain was the conviction that I couldn't – whatever happened – profit by the sudden impulse she had acted on, and allow her to take, in a moment of passion, a decision that was to shape her whole life. I couldn't so much as lift my little finger to keep her with me then, unless I were prepared to accept for her as well as for myself the full consequences of the future she had planned for us . . .

'Well – there's the point: I wasn't. I felt in her – poor fatuous idiot that I was! – that lack of objective imagination which had always seemed to me to account, at least in part, for many of the so-called heroic qualities in women. When their feelings are involved they simply can't look ahead. Her unfaltering logic notwithstanding, I felt this about Paulina as I listened. She had a specious air of knowing where she was going, but she didn't.

She seemed the genius of logic and understanding, but the demon of illusion spoke through her lips . . .

'I said just now that I hadn't, at the outset, given my own side of the case a thought. It would have been truer to say that I hadn't given it a separate thought. But I couldn't think of her without seeing myself as a factor – the chief factor – in her problem, and without recognising that whatever the experiment made of me, that it must fatally, in the end, make of her. If I couldn't carry the thing through she must break down with me: we should have to throw our separate selves into the melting-pot of this mad adventure and be 'one' in a terrible indissoluble completeness of which marriage is only an imperfect counterpart . . .

'There could be no better proof of her extraordinary power over me, and of the way she had managed to clear the air of sentimental illusion, than the fact that I presently found myself putting this to her with a merciless precision of touch.

' "If we love each other enough to do a thing like this, we must love each other enough to see just what it is we're going to do." '

'So I invited her to the dissecting-table, and I see now the fearless eye with which she approached the cadaver. "For that's what it is, you know," she flashed out at me, at the end of my long demonstration. "It's a dead body, like all the instances and examples and hypothetical cases that ever were! What do you expect to learn from that? The first great anatomist was the man who stuck his knife in a heart that was beating; and the only way to find out what doing a thing will be like is to do it!"

'She looked away from me suddenly, as if she were fixing her eyes on some vision on the outer rim of consciousness. "No: there's one other way," she exclaimed; "and that is, not to do it! To abstain and refrain; and then see what we become, or what we don't become, in the long run, and draw our inferences. That's the game that almost everybody about us is playing, I suppose; there's hardly one of the dull people one meets at dinner who hasn't had, just once, the chance of a berth on a ship that was off for the Happy Isles, and hasn't refused it for fear of sticking on a sand-bank!

' "I'm doing my best, you know," she continued, "to see the sequel as you see it, as you believe it's your duty to me to see it. I know the instances you're thinking of: the listless couples wearing out their lives in shabby watering places, and hanging on the favour of hotel acquaintances; or the proud quarrelling wretches shut up alone in a fine house because they're too good for the only society they can get, and trying to cheat their boredom by squabbling with their tradesmen and spying on their servants. No doubt there are such cases; but I don't recognise either of us in those dismal figures. Why, to do it would be to admit that our life, yours and mine, is in the people about us and not in ourselves; that we're parasites and not self-sustaining creatures; and that the lives we're leading now are so brilliant, full and satisfying that what we should have to give up would surpass even the blessedness of being together!"

'At that stage, I confess, the solid ground of my resistance began to give way under me. It was not that my convictions were shaken, but that she had swept me into a world whose laws were different, where one could reach out in directions that the slave of gravity hasn't pictured. But at the same time my opposition hardened from reason into instinct. I knew it was her voice, and not her logic, that was unsettling me. I knew that if she'd written out her thesis and sent it me by post I should have made short work of it; and again the part of me which I called by all the finest names: my chivalry, my unselfishness, my superior masculine experience, cried out with one voice: "You can't let a woman use her graces to her own undoing – you can't, for her own sake, let her eyes convince you when her reasons don't!"

'And then, abruptly, and for the first time, a doubt entered me: a doubt of her perfect moral honesty. I don't know how else to describe my feeling that she wasn't playing fair, that in coming to my house, in throwing herself at my head (I called things by their names), she had perhaps not so much obeyed an irresistible impulse as deeply, deliberately reckoned on the dissolvent effect of her generosity, her rashness and her beauty . . .

'From the moment that this mean doubt raised its head in me I was once more the creature of all the conventional scruples: I was repeating, before the looking-glass of my self-consciousness, all the stereotyped gestures of the "man of honour" . . . Oh, the sorry figure I must have cut! You'll understand my dropping the curtain on it as quickly as I can . . .

'Yet I remember, as I made my point, being struck by its impressiveness. I was suffering and enjoying my own suffering. I told her that, whatever step we decided to take, I owed it to her to insist on its being taken soberly, deliberately –

'("No: it's 'advisedly', isn't it? Oh, I was thinking of the Marriage Service," she interposed with a faint laugh.)

' – that if I accepted, there, on the spot, her headlong beautiful gift of herself, I should feel that I had taken an unmanly advantage of her, an advantage which she would be justified in reproaching me with ever afterward; that I was not afraid to tell her this because she was intelligent enough to know that my scruples were the surest proof of the quality of my love; that I refused to owe my happiness to an unconsidered impulse; that we must see each other again, in her own house, in less agitating circumstances, when she had had time to reflect on my words, to study her heart and look into the future . . .

'The factitious exhilaration produced by uttering these beautiful sentiments did not last very long, as you may imagine. It fell, little by little, under her quiet gaze, a gaze in which there was neither contempt nor irony nor wounded pride, but only a tender wistfulness of interrogation; and I think the acutest point in my suffering was reached when she said, as I ended: "Oh, yes, of course I understand."

' "If only you hadn't come to me here!" I blurted out in the torture of my soul.

'She was on the threshold when I said it, and she turned and laid her hand gently on mine. "There was no other way," she said; and at the moment it seemed to me like some hackneyed phrase in a novel that she had used without any sense of its meaning.

'I don't remember what I answered or what more we either of us said. At the end a desperate longing to take her in my arms and keep her with me swept aside everything else, and I went up to her, pleading, stammering, urging I don't know what . . . But she held me back with a quiet look, and went. I had ordered the carriage, as she asked me to; and my last definite recollection is of watching her drive off alone in the rain . . .

'I had her promise that she would see me, two days later, at her house in town, and that we should then have what I called "a decisive talk"; but I don't think that even at the moment I was the dupe of my phrase. I knew, and she knew, that the end had come . . .

5

'It was about that time,' Merrick went on after a long pause, 'that I definitely decided not to sell the Works, but to stick to my job and conform my life to it.

'I can't describe to you the rage of conformity that possessed me. Poetry, ideas – all the picture-making processes stopped. A kind of dull self-discipline seemed to me the only exercise worthy of a reflecting mind. I had to justify my great refusal, and I tried to do it by plunging myself up to the eyes into the very conditions I had been instinctively struggling to get away from. The only possible consolation would have been to find in a life of business routine and social submission such moral compensations as may reward the citizen if they fail the man; but to attain to these I should have had to accept the old delusion that the social and the individual man are two. Now, on the contrary, I found soon enough that I couldn't get one part of my machinery to work effectively while another wanted feeding; and that in rejecting what had seemed to me a negation of action I had made all my action negative.

'The best solution, of course, would have been to fall in love with another woman, but it was long before I could bring myself to wish that this might happen to me . . . Then, at length, I suddenly and violently desired it; and as such impulses are seldom without some kind of imperfect issue I contrived, a year or two later, to work myself up into the wished-for state . . . She was a woman in society, and with all the awe of that institution that Paulina lacked. Our relation was consequently one of those unavowed affairs in which triviality is the only alternative to tragedy. Luckily we had, on both sides, risked only as much as prudent people stake in a drawing-room game; and when the match was over I take it that we came out fairly even.

'My gain, at all events, was of an unexpected kind. The adventure had served only to make me understand Paulina's abhorrence of such experiments, and at every turn of the slight intrigue I had felt how exasperating and belittling such a relation was bound to be between two people who, had they been free, would have mated openly. And so from a brief phase of imperfect forgetting I was driven back to a deeper and more understanding remembrance . . .

'This second incarnation of Paulina was one of the strangest episodes of the whole strange experience. Things she had said during our extraordinary talk, things I had hardly heard at the time, came back to me with singular vividness and a fuller meaning. I hadn't any longer the cold consolation of believing in my own perspicacity: I saw that her insight had been deeper and keener than mine.

'I remember, in particular, starting up in bed one sleepless night as there flashed into my head the meaning of her last words: "There was no other way;" the phrase I had half-smiled at at the time, as a parrot-like echo of the novel-heroine's stock farewell. I had never, up to that moment, wholly understood why Paulina had come to my house that night. I had never been able to make that particular act – which could hardly, in the light of her subsequent conduct, be dismissed as a blind surge of passion – square with my conception of her character. She was at once the most spontaneous and the steadiest-minded woman I had ever known, and the last to wish to owe any advantage to surprise, to unpreparedness, to any play on the spring of sex. The better I came, retrospectively, to know her, the more sure I was of this, and the less intelligible her act appeared. And then, suddenly, after a night of hungry restless thinking, the flash of illumination came. She had come to my house, had brought her trunk with her, had thrown herself at my head with all possible violence and publicity, in order to give me a pretext, a loophole, an honourable excuse for doing and saying – why, precisely what I had said and done!

'As the idea came to me it was as if some ironic hand had touched an electric button, and all my fatuous phrases had leapt out on me in fire.

'Of course she had known all along just the kind of thing I should say if I didn't at once open my arms to her; and to save my pride, my dignity, my conception of the figure I was cutting in her eyes, she had recklessly and magnificently provided me with the decentest pretext a man could have for doing a pusillanimous thing . . .

'With that discovery the whole case took a different aspect. It hurt less to think of Paulina – and yet it hurt more. The tinge of bitterness, of doubt, in my thoughts of her had had a tonic quality. It was harder to go on persuading myself that I had done right as, bit by bit, my theories crumbled under the test of time. Yet, after all, as she herself had said, one could judge of results only in the long run.

'The Trants stayed away for two years; and about a year after they got back, you may remember, Trant was killed in a railway accident. You know fate's way of untying a knot after everybody has given up tugging at it!

'Well – there I was, completely justified: all my weaknesses turned into merits! I had "saved" a weak woman from herself, I had kept her to the path of duty, I had spared her the humiliation of scandal and the misery of self-reproach; and now I had only to put out my hand and take the reward I deserved.

'I had avoided Paulina since her return, and she had made no effort to see me. But after Trant's death I wrote her a few lines, to which she sent a friendly answer; and when a decent interval had elapsed, and I asked if I might call on her, she answered at once that she would see me.

'I went to her house with the fixed intention of asking her to marry me – and I left it without having done so. Why? I don't know that I can tell you. Perhaps you would have had to sit there opposite her, knowing what I did and feeling as I did, to understand why. She was kind, she was compassionate – I could see she didn't want to make it hard for me. Perhaps she even wanted to make it easy. But there, between us, was the memory of the gesture I hadn't made, forever parodying the one I was attempting! There wasn't a word I could think of that hadn't an echo in it of words of hers I had been deaf to; there wasn't an appeal I could make that didn't mock the appeal I had rejected. I sat there and talked of her husband's death; of her plans, of my sympathy; and I knew she understood; and knowing that, in a way, made it harder . . . The doorbell rang and the footman came in to ask if she would receive other visitors. She looked at me a moment and said, "Yes," and I stood up and shook hands with her and went away.

'A few days later she sailed for Europe, and the next time we met she had married Reardon . . . '

6

It was long past midnight, and the terrier's hints became imperious.

Merrick rose from his chair, pushed back a fallen log and put up the fender. He walked across the room and stared a moment at the Brangwyn etching before which Paulina Trant had paused at a memorable turn of their talk. Then he came back and laid his hand on my shoulder.

'She summed it all up, you know, when she said that one way of finding out whether a risk is worth taking is not to take it, and then to see what one becomes in the long run, and draw one's inferences. The long run – well, we've run it, she and I. I know what I've become, but that's nothing to the misery of knowing what she's become. She had to have some kind of life, and she married Reardon. Reardon's a very good fellow in his way; but the worst of it is that it's not her way . . .

'No: the worst of it is that now she and I meet as friends. We dine at the same houses, we talk about the same people, we play bridge together, and I lend her books. And sometimes Reardon slaps me on the back and says: "Come in and dine with us, old man! What you want is to be cheered up!" And I go and dine with them, and he tells me how jolly comfortable she makes him, and what an ass I am not to marry; and she presses on me a second helping of poulet Maryland, and I smoke one of Reardon's good cigars, and at half-past ten I get into my overcoat and goloshes, and walk back alone to my rooms . . . '

ROBERT LOUIS STEVENSON

Robert Louis Stevenson (1850–94) was born in Edinburgh, son of Thomas Stevenson the lighthouse engineer. He studied at Edinburgh, became a lawyer (1875), then turned to writing travel sketches, essays and short stories for magazines. The romantic adventure story *Treasure Island* (1883) brought him fame, and entered him on a course of romantic fiction which included *Kidnapped* (1886), *The Strange Case of Dr Jekyll and Mr Hyde* (1886), *The Master of Ballantrae* (1889), *Catriona* (1893) and the unfinished *Weir of Hermiston* (1896), considered his masterpiece. He suffered from a chronic bronchial condition and in 1888 he settled for health reasons at Vailima, Samoa, where he died of a cerebral haemorrhage six years later.

Olalla

'Now,' said the doctor, 'my part is done, and, I may say, with some vanity, well done. It remains only to get you out of this cold and poisonous city, and to give you two months of pure air and an easy conscience. The last is your affair. To the first I think I can help you. It falls indeed rather oddly; it was but the other day the padre came in from the country; and as he and I are old friends, although of contrary professions, he applied to me in a matter of distress among some of his parishioners. This was a family – but you are ignorant of Spain, and even the names of our grandees are hardly known to you; suffice it then, that they were once great people, and are now fallen to the brink of destitution. Nothing now belongs to them but the *residencia*, and certain leagues of desert mountain, in the greater part of which not even a goat could support life. But the house is a fine old place, and stands at a great height among the hills, and most salubriously; and I had no sooner heard my friend's tale than I remembered you. I told him I had a wounded officer, wounded in the good cause, who was now able to make a change; and I proposed that his friends should take you for a lodger. Instantly the padre's face grew dark, as I had maliciously foreseen it would. It was out of the question, he said. Then let them starve, said I, for I have no sympathy with tatterdemalion pride. Thereupon we separated, not very content with one another; but yesterday, to my wonder, the padre returned and made a submission: the difficulty, he said, he had found upon enquiry to be less than he had feared; or, in other words, these proud people had put their pride in their pocket. I closed with the offer; and, subject to your approval, I have taken rooms for you in the *residencia*. The air of these mountains will renew your blood; and the quiet in which you will there live is worth all the medicines in the world.'

'Doctor,' said I, 'you have been throughout my good angel, and your advice is a command. But tell me, if you please, something of the family with which I am to reside.'

'I am coming to that,' replied my friend; 'and, indeed, there is a difficulty in the way. These beggars are, as I have said, of very high descent and swollen with the most baseless vanity; they have lived for some generations in a growing isolation, drawing away, on either hand, from the rich who had now become too high for them, and from the poor, whom they still regarded as too low; and even today, when poverty forces them to unfasten their door to a guest, they cannot do so without a most ungracious stipulation. You are to remain, they say, a stranger; they will give you attendance, but they refuse from the first the idea of the smallest intimacy.'

I will not deny that I was piqued, and perhaps the feeling strengthened my desire to go, for I was confident that I could break down that barrier if I desired. 'There is nothing offensive in such a stipulation,' said I; 'and I even sympathise with the feeling that inspired it.'

'It is true they have never seen you,' returned the doctor politely; 'and if they knew you were the handsomest and the most pleasant man that ever came from England (where I am told that handsome men are common, but pleasant ones not so much so), they would doubtless make you welcome with a better grace. But since you take the thing so well, it matters not. To me, indeed, it seems discourteous. But you will find yourself the gainer. The family will not much tempt you. A mother, a son and a daughter: an old woman said to be half-witted, a country lout and a country girl, who stands very high with her confessor, and is, therefore,' chuckled the physician, 'most likely plain; there is not much in that to attract the fancy of a dashing officer.'

'And yet you say they are high born,' I objected.

'Well, as to that, I should distinguish,' returned the doctor. 'The mother is; not so the children. The mother was the last representative of a princely stock, degenerate both in parts and fortune. Her father was not only poor, he was mad; and the girl ran wild about the *residencia* till his death. Then, much of the fortune having died with him, and the family being quite extinct, the girl ran wilder than ever, until at last she married, heaven knows whom; a muleteer some say, others a smuggler; while there are some who upheld there was no marriage at all, and that Felipe and Olalla are bastards. The union, such as it was, was tragically dissolved some years ago; but they live in such seclusion, and the country at that time was in so much disorder, that the precise manner of the man's end is known only to the priest – if even to him.'

'I begin to think I shall have strange experiences,' said I.

'I would not romance, if I were you,' replied the doctor; 'you will find, I fear, a very grovelling and commonplace reality. Felipe, for instance, I have seen. And what am I to say? He is very rustic, very cunning, very loutish, and I should say, an innocent; the others are probably to match. No, no, Señor Commandante, you must seek congenial society among the great sights of our mountains; and in these at least, if you are at all a lover of the works of nature, I promise you will not be disappointed.'

The next day Felipe came for me in a rough country cart, drawn by a mule; and a little before the stroke of noon, after I had said farewell to the doctor, the innkeeper, and different good souls who had befriended me during my sickness, we set forth out of the city by the eastern gate, and began to ascend into the sierra. I had been so long a prisoner, since I was left behind for dying after the loss of the convoy, that the mere smell of the earth set me smiling. The country through which we went was wild and rocky, partially covered with rough woods, now of the cork tree, and now of the great Spanish chestnut, and frequently intersected by the beds of mountain torrents. The sun shone, the wind rustled joyously, and we had advanced some miles, and the city had already shrunk into an inconsiderable knoll upon the plain behind us, before my attention began to be diverted to the companion of my drive. To the eye, he seemed but a diminutive, loutish, well-made country lad, such as the doctor had described, mighty quick and active, but devoid of any culture; and this first impression was with most observers final. What began to strike me was his familiar, chattering talk, so strangely inconsistent with the terms on which I was to be received; and partly from his imperfect enunciation, partly from the sprightly incoherence of the matter, so very difficult to follow clearly without an effort of the mind. It is true I had before talked with persons of a similar mental constitution: persons who seemed to live (as he did) by the senses, taken and possessed by the visual object of the moment and unable to discharge their minds of that impression. His seemed to me (as I sat, distantly giving ear) a kind of conversation proper to drivers, who pass much of their time in a great vacancy of the intellect and threading the sights of a familiar country. But this was not the case with Felipe; by his own account, he was a homekeeper. 'I wish I was there now,' he said; and then, spying a tree by the wayside, he broke off to tell me that he had once seen a crow among its branches.

'A crow?' I repeated, struck by the ineptitude of the remark, and thinking I had heard imperfectly.

But by this time he was already filled with a new idea; hearkening with a rapt intentness, his head on one side, his face puckered; and he struck me rudely, to make me hold my peace. Then he smiled and shook his head.

'What did you hear?' I asked.

'Oh, it is all right,' he said; and began encouraging his mule with cries that echoed unhumanly up the mountain walls.

I looked at him more closely. He was superlatively well built, light, and lithe and strong; he was well-featured; his yellow eyes were very large, though, perhaps, not very expressive; take him altogether, he was a pleasant looking lad, and I had no fault to find with him, beyond that he was of a dusky hue, and inclined to hairiness; two characteristics that I disliked. It was his mind that puzzled and yet attracted me. The doctor's phrase – an innocent – came back to me; and I was wondering if that were, after all, the true description, when the road began to go down into the narrow and naked chasm of a torrent. The waters thundered tumultuously in the bottom; and the ravine was filled full of the sound, the thin spray and the claps of wind that accompanied their descent. The scene was certainly impressive; but the road was in that part very securely walled in; the mule went steadily forward; and I was astonished to perceive the paleness of terror in the face of my companion. The voice of that wild river was inconstant, now sinking lower as if in weariness, now doubling its hoarse tones; momentary freshets seemed to swell its volume, sweeping down the gorge, raving and booming against the barrier walls; and I observed it was at each of these accessions to the clamour that my driver more particularly winced and blanched. Some thoughts of Scottish superstition and the river Kelpie passed across my mind; I wondered if perchance the like were prevalent in that part of Spain; and turning to Felipe, sought to draw him out.

'What is the matter?' I asked.

'Oh, I am afraid,' he replied.

'Of what are you afraid?' I returned. 'This seems one of the safest places on this very dangerous road.'

'It makes a noise,' he said, with a simplicity of awe that set my doubts at rest.

The lad was but a child in intellect; his mind was like his body, active and swift, but stunted in development; and I began from that time to regard him with a measure of pity, and to listen at first with indulgence, and at last even with pleasure, to his disjointed babble.

By about four in the afternoon we had crossed the summit of the mountain line, said farewell to the western sunshine, and began to go down upon the other side, skirting the edge of many ravines and moving through the shadow of dusky woods. There rose upon all sides the voice of falling water, not condensed and formidable as in the gorge of the river, but scattered and sounding gaily and musically from glen to glen. Here, too, the spirits of my driver mended, and he began to sing aloud in a falsetto voice, and with a singular bluntness of musical perception, never true either to melody or key, but wandering at will, and yet somehow with an effect that was natural and pleasing, like that of the song of birds. As the dusk increased, I fell more and more under the spell of this artless warbling, listening and waiting for some articulate air, and still disappointed; and when at last I asked him what it was he sang – 'Oh,' cried he, 'I am just singing!' Above all, I was taken with a trick he had of unweariedly repeating the same note at little intervals; it was not so monotonous as you would think, or, at least, not disagreeable; and it seemed to breathe a wonderful contentment with what is, such as we love to fancy in the attitude of trees or the quiescence of a pool.

Night had fallen dark before we came out upon a plateau, and drew up a little after before a certain lump of superior blackness which I could only conjecture to be the *residencia*. Here, my guide, getting down from the cart, hooted and whistled for a long time in vain; until at last an old peasant man came towards us from somewhere in the surrounding dark, carrying a candle in his hand. By the light of this I was able to perceive a great arched doorway of a moorish character: it was closed by iron-studded gates, in one of the leaves of which Felipe opened a wicket. The peasant carried off the cart to some outbuilding; but my guide and I passed through the wicket, which was closed again behind us; and by the glimmer of the candle, passed through a court, up a stone stair, along a section of an open gallery, and up more stairs again, until we came at last to the door of a great and somewhat bare apartment. This room, which I understood was to be mine, was pierced by three windows, lined with some lustrous wood disposed in panels, and carpeted with the skins of many savage animals. A bright fire burned in the chimney, and shed abroad a changeful flicker; close up to the blaze there was drawn a table, laid for supper; and in the far end a bed stood ready. I was pleased by these preparations, and said so to Felipe; and he, with the same simplicity of disposition that I had already remarked in him, warmly re-echoed my praises. 'A fine room,' he said; 'a very fine room. And fire, too; fire is good; it melts out the pleasure in your bones. And the bed,' he continued, carrying over the candle in that direction – 'see what fine sheets – how soft, how smooth, smooth,' and he passed his hand again and again over their texture, and then laid down his head and rubbed his cheeks among them with a grossness of content that somehow offended me.

I took the candle from his hand (for I feared he would set the bed on fire) and walked back to the supper table, where, perceiving a measure of wine, I poured out a cup and called to him to come and drink of it. He started to his feet at once and ran to me with a strong expression of hope; but when he saw the wine, he visibly shuddered. 'Oh, no,' he said, 'not that, that is for you. I hate it.'

'Very well, señor,' said I; 'then I will drink to your good health, and to the prosperity of your house and family. Speaking of which,' I added, after I had drunk, 'shall I not have the pleasure of laying my salutations in person at the feet of the señora, your mother?'

But at these words all the childishness passed out of his face and was succeeded by a look of indescribable cunning and secrecy. He backed away from me at the same time, as though I were an animal about to leap or some dangerous fellow with a weapon, and when he had got near the door, glowered at me sullenly with contracted pupils. 'No,' he said at last, and the next moment was gone noiselessly out of the room; and I heard his footing die away downstairs as light as rainfall, and silence closed over the house.

After I had supped I drew up the table nearer to the bed and began to prepare for rest; but in the new position of the light, I was struck by a picture on the wall. It represented a woman, still young. To judge by her costume and the mellow unity which reigned over the canvas, she had long been dead; to judge by the vivacity of the attitude, the eyes and the features, I might have been beholding in a mirror the image of life. Her figure was very slim and strong, and of a just proportion; red tresses like a crown over her brow; her eyes, of a very golden brown, held mine with a look; and her face, which was perfectly shaped, was yet marred by a cruel, sullen, and sensual expression. Something in both face and figure, something exquisitely intangible, like the echo of an echo, suggested the features and bearing of my guide; and I stood awhile, unpleasantly attracted and wondering at the oddity of the resemblance. The common carnal stock of that race which had been originally designed for such high dames as the one now looking on me from the canvas had fallen to baser uses, wearing country clothes, sitting on the shaft and holding the reins of a mule cart, to bring home a lodger. Perhaps an actual link subsisted; perhaps some scruple of the delicate flesh that was once clothed upon with the satin and brocade of the dead lady now winced at the rude contact of Felipe's frieze.

The first light of the morning shone full upon the portrait, and, as I lay awake, my eyes continued to dwell upon it with growing complacency; its beauty crept about my heart insidiously, silencing my scruples one after another; and while I knew that to love such a woman were to sign and seal one's own sentence of degeneration, I still knew that, if she were alive, I should love her. Day after day the double knowledge of her wickedness and of my weakness grew clearer. She came to be the heroine of many daydreams, in which her eyes led on to, and sufficiently rewarded, crimes. She cast a dark shadow on my fancy; and when I was out in the free air of heaven, taking vigorous exercise and healthily renewing the current of my blood, it was often a glad thought to me that my enchantress was safe in the grave, her wand of beauty broken, her lips closed in silence, her philtre spilt. And yet I had a half-lingering terror that she might not be dead after all, but re-arisen in the body of some descendant.

Felipe served my meals in my own apartment; and his resemblance to the portrait haunted me. At times it was not; at times, upon some change of attitude or flash of expression, it would leap out upon me like a ghost. It was above all in his ill-tempers that the likeness triumphed. He certainly liked me; he was proud of my notice, which he sought to engage by many simple and childlike devices; he loved to sit close before my fire, talking his broken talk or singing his odd, endless, wordless songs, and sometimes drawing his hand over my clothes with an affectionate manner of caressing that never failed to cause in me an embarrassment of which I was ashamed. But for all that, he was capable of flashes of causeless anger and fits of sturdy sullenness. At a word of reproof, I have seen him upset the dish of which I was about to eat, and this not surreptitiously, but with defiance; and similarly at a hint of inquisition. I was not unnaturally curious, being in a strange place and surrounded by strange people; but at the shadow of a question, he shrank back, lowering and dangerous. Then it was that, for a fraction of a second, this rough lad might have been the brother of the lady in the frame. But these humours were swift to pass; and the resemblance died along with them.

In these first days I saw nothing of anyone but Felipe, unless the portrait is to be counted; and since the lad was plainly of weak mind, and had moments of passion, it may be wondered that I bore his dangerous neighbourhood with equanimity. As a matter of fact, it was for some time irksome; but it happened before long that I obtained over him so complete a mastery as set my disquietude at rest.

It fell in this way. He was by nature slothful, and much of a vagabond, and yet he kept by the house, and not only waited upon my wants, but laboured every day in the garden or small farm to the south of the *residencia*. Here he would be joined by the peasant whom I had seen on the night of my arrival, and who dwelt at the far end of the enclosure, about half a mile away, in a rude outhouse; but it was plain to me that, of these two, it was Felipe who did most; and though I would sometimes see him throw down his spade and go to sleep among the very plants he had been digging, his constancy and energy were admirable in themselves, and still more so since I was well assured they were foreign to his disposition and the fruit of an ungrateful effort. But while I admired, I wondered what had called forth in a lad so shuttle-witted this enduring sense of duty. How was it sustained? I asked myself, and to what length did it prevail over his instincts? The priest was possibly his inspirer. But the priest came one day to the *residencia*; I saw him both come and go after an interval of close upon an hour, from a knoll where I was sketching, and all that time Felipe continued to labour undisturbed in the garden.

At last, in a very unworthy spirit, I determined to debauch the lad from his good resolutions and, waylaying him at the gate, easily persuaded him to join me in a ramble. It was a fine day, and the woods to which I led him were green and pleasant and sweet-smelling and alive with the hum of insects. Here he discovered himself in a fresh character, mounting up to heights of gaiety that abashed me, and displaying an energy and grace of movement that delighted the eye. He leaped, he ran round me in a mere glee; he would stop, and look and listen, and seemed to drink in the world like a cordial; and then he would suddenly spring into a tree with one bound, and hang and gambol there like one at home. Little as he said to me, and that of not much import, I have rarely enjoyed more stirring company; the sight of his delight was a continual feast; the speed and accuracy of his movements pleased me to the heart; and I might have been so thoughtlessly unkind as to make a habit of these walks, had not chance prepared a very rude conclusion to my pleasure. By some swiftness or dexterity the lad captured a squirrel in a treetop. He was then some way ahead of me, but I saw him drop to the ground and crouch there, crying aloud for pleasure like a child. The sound stirred my sympathies, it was so fresh and innocent; but as I bettered my pace to draw near, the cry of the squirrel knocked upon my heart. I have heard and seen much of the cruelty of lads, and above all of peasants; but what I now beheld struck me into a passion of anger. I thrust the fellow aside, plucked the poor brute out of his hands, and with swift mercy killed it.

Then I turned upon the torturer, spoke to him long out of the heat of my indignation, calling him names at which he seemed to wither; and at length, pointing towards the *residencia*, bade him begone and leave me, for I chose to walk with men, not with vermin. He fell upon his knees and, the words coming to him with more clearness than usual, poured out a stream of the most touching supplications, begging me in mercy to forgive him, to forget what he had done, to look to the future. 'Oh, I try so hard,' he said. 'Oh, commandante, bear with Felipe this once, he will never be a brute again!'

Thereupon, much more affected than I cared to show, I suffered myself to be persuaded, and at last shook hands with him and made it up. But the squirrel, by way of penance, I made him bury; speaking of the poor thing's beauty, telling him what pains it had suffered, and how base a thing was the abuse of strength. 'See, Felipe,' said I, 'you are strong indeed, but in my hands you are as helpless as that poor thing of the trees. Give me your hand in mine. You cannot remove it. Now suppose that I were cruel like you, and took a pleasure in pain. I only tighten my hold, and see how you suffer.' He screamed aloud, his face stricken ashy and dotted with needle points of sweat; and when I set him free, he fell to the earth and nursed his hand and moaned over it like a baby. But he took the lesson in good part; and whether from that, or from what I had said to him, or the higher notion he now had of my bodily strength, his original affection was changed into a doglike, adoring fidelity.

Meanwhile I gained rapidly in health. The *residencia* stood on the crown of a stony plateau; on every side the mountains hemmed it about; only from the roof, where was a bartizan, there might be seen between two peaks, a small segment of plain, blue with extreme distance. The air in these altitudes moved freely and largely; great clouds congregated there, and were broken up by the wind and left in tatters on the hilltops; a hoarse, and yet faint rumbling of torrents rose from all round;

and one could there study all the ruder and more ancient characters of nature in something of their pristine force. I delighted from the first in the vigorous scenery and changeful weather; nor less in the antique and dilapidated mansion where I dwelt. This was a large oblong, flanked at two opposite corners by bastion-like projections, one of which commanded the door, while both were loopholed for musketry. The lower storey was, besides, naked of windows, so that the building, if garrisoned, could not be carried without artillery. It enclosed an open court planted with pomegranate trees. From this a broad flight of marble stairs ascended to an open gallery, running all round and resting, towards the court, on slender pillars. Thence again, several enclosed stairs led to the upper storeys of the house, which were thus broken up into distinct divisions. The windows, both within and without, were closely shuttered; some of the stonework in the upper parts had fallen; the roof in one place had been wrecked in one of the flurries of wind which were common in these mountains; and the whole house, in the strong, beating sunlight, and standing out above a grove of stunted cork trees, thickly laden and discoloured with dust, looked like the sleeping palace of the legend. The court, in particular, seemed the very home of slumber. A hoarse cooing of doves haunted about the eaves; the winds were excluded, but when they blew outside, the mountain dust fell here as thick as rain, and veiled the red bloom of the pomegranates; shuttered windows and the closed doors of numerous cellars, and the vacant arches of the gallery, enclosed it; and all day long the sun made broken profiles on the four sides, and paraded the shadow of the pillars on the gallery floor. At the ground level there was, however, a certain pillared recess, which bore the marks of human habitation. Though it was open in front upon the court, it was yet provided with a chimney, where a wood fire would be always prettily blazing; and the tile floor was littered with the skins of animals.

It was in this place that I first saw my hostess. She had drawn one of the skins forward and sat in the sun, leaning against a pillar. It was her dress that struck me first of all, for it was rich and brightly coloured, and shone out in that dusty courtyard with something of the same relief as the flowers of the pomegranates. At a second look it was her beauty of person that took hold of me. As she sat back – watching me, I thought, though with invisible eyes – and wearing at the same time an expression of almost imbecile good-humour and contentment, she showed a perfectness of feature and a quiet nobility of attitude that were beyond a statue's. I took off my hat to her in passing, and her face puckered with suspicion as swiftly and lightly as a pool ruffles in the breeze; but she paid no heed to my courtesy. I went forth on my customary walk a trifle daunted, her idol-like impassivity haunting me; and when I returned, although she was still in much the same posture, I was half surprised to see that she had moved as far as the next pillar, following the sunshine. This time, however, she addressed me with some trivial salutation, civilly enough conceived, and uttered in the same deep-chested, and yet indistinct and lisping tones, that had already baffled the utmost niceness of my hearing from her son. I answered rather at a venture; for not only did I fail to take her meaning with precision, but the sudden disclosure of her eyes disturbed me. They were unusually large, the iris golden like Felipe's, but the pupil at that moment so distended that they seemed almost black; and what affected me was not so much their size as (what was perhaps its consequence) the singular insignificance of their regard. A look more blankly stupid I have never met. My eyes dropped before it even as I spoke, and I went on my way upstairs to my own room, at once baffled and embarrassed. Yet, when I came there and saw the face of the portrait, I was again reminded of the miracle of family descent. My hostess was, indeed, both older and fuller in person; her eyes were of a different colour; her face, besides, was not only free from the ill-significance that offended and attracted me in the painting; it was devoid of either good or bad – a moral blank expressing literally naught. And yet there was a likeness, not so much speaking as immanent, nor so much in any particular feature as upon the whole. It should seem, I thought, as if when the master set his signature to that grave canvas, he had not only caught the image of one smiling and false-eyed woman, but stamped the essential quality of a race.

From that day forth, whether I came or went, I was sure to find the señora seated in the sun against a pillar, or stretched on a rug before the fire; only at times she would shift her station to the top round of the stone staircase, where she lay with the same nonchalance right across my path. In all these days, I never knew her to display the least spark of energy beyond what she expended in brushing and rebrushing her copious copper-coloured hair, or in lisping out, in the rich and broken hoarseness of her voice, her customary idle salutations to myself. These, I think, were her two chief pleasures, beyond that of mere quiescence. She seemed always proud of her remarks, as though they had been witticisms; and, indeed, though they were empty enough, like the conversation of many respectable persons, and turned on a very narrow range of subjects, they were never meaningless or incoherent; nay, they had a certain beauty of their own, breathing, as they did, of her entire contentment. Now she would speak of the warmth, in which (like her son) she greatly delighted; now of the flowers of the pomegranate trees, and now of the white doves and long-winged swallows that fanned the air of the court. The birds excited her. As they raked the eaves in their swift flight, or skimmed sidelong past her with a rush of wind, she would sometimes stir and sit up a little, and seem to awaken from her doze of satisfaction. But for the rest of her days she lay luxuriously folded on herself and sunk in sloth and pleasure. Her invincible content at first annoyed me, but I came gradually to find repose in the spectacle, until at last it grew to be my habit to sit down beside her four times in the day both coming and going, and to talk with her sleepily, I scarce knew of what. I had come to like her dull almost animal neighbourhood; her beauty and her stupidity soothed and amused me. I began to find a kind of transcendental good sense in her remarks, and her unfathomable good nature moved me to admiration and envy. The liking was returned; she enjoyed my presence half-consciously, as a man in deep meditation may enjoy the babbling of a brook. I can scarce say she brightened when I came, for satisfaction was written on her face eternally, as on some foolish statue's; but I was made conscious of her pleasure by some more intimate communication than the sight. And one day, as I sat within reach of her on the marble step, she suddenly shot forth one of her hands and patted mine. The thing was done, and she was back in her accustomed attitude, before my mind had received intelligence of the caress; and when I turned to look her in the face I could perceive no answerable sentiment. It was plain she attached no moment to the act, and I blamed myself for my own more uneasy consciousness.

The sight and (if I may so call it) the acquaintance of the mother confirmed the view I had already taken of the son. The family blood had been impoverished, perhaps by long inbreeding, which I knew to be a common error among the proud and the exclusive. No decline, indeed, was to be traced in the body, which had been handed down unimpaired in shapeliness and strength, and the faces of today were struck as sharply from the mint as the face of two centuries ago that smiled upon me from the portrait. But the intelligence (that more precious heirloom) was degenerate; the treasure of ancestral memory ran low; and it had required the potent, plebeian crossing of a muleteer or mountain *contrabandista* to raise what approached hebetude in the mother into the active oddity of the son. Yet of the two, it was the mother I preferred.

Of Felipe, vengeful and placable, full of starts and shyings, inconstant as a hare, I could even conceive as a creature possibly noxious. Of the mother I had no thoughts but those of kindness. And indeed, as spectators are apt ignorantly to take sides, I grew something of a partisan in the enmity which I perceived to smoulder between them. True, it seemed mostly on the mother's part. She would sometimes draw in her breath as he came near, and the pupils of her vacant eyes would contract as if with horror or fear. Her emotions, such as they were, were much upon the surface and readily shared; and this latent repulsion occupied my mind, and kept me wondering on what grounds it rested, and whether the son was certainly in fault.

I had been about ten days in the *residencia*, when there sprang up a high and harsh wind, carrying clouds of dust. It came out of malarious lowlands, and over several snowy sierras. The nerves of those on whom it blew were strung and jangled; their eyes smarted with the dust; their legs ached under the burden of their body; and the touch of one hand upon another grew to be odious. The wind, besides, came down the gullies of the hills and stormed about the house with a great, hollow buzzing and whistling that was wearisome to the ear and dismally depressing to the mind. It did not so much blow in gusts as
sweep of a waterfall, so that there was no
comfort while it blew. But higher upon
probably of a more variable strength, wit
there came down at times a far-off waili
to hear; and at times, on one of the hi
there would start up and then disperse a towe
smoke of an explosion.

I no sooner awoke in bed than I was conscious of the n
tension and depression of the weather, and the effect grew stronger as the day proceeded. It was in vain that I resisted; in vain that I set forth upon my customary morning's walk; the irrational, unchanging fury of the storm had soon beat down

my strength and wrecked my temper; and I returned to the *residencia* glowing with dry heat and foul and gritty with dust. The court had a forlorn appearance; now and then a glimmer of sun fled over it; now and then the wind swooped down upon the pomegranates and scattered the blossoms, and set the window shutters clapping on the wall. In the recess the señora was pacing to and fro with a flushed countenance and bright eyes; I thought, too, she was speaking to herself, like one in anger. And when I addressed her with my customary salutation she only replied by a sharp gesture and continued her walk. The weather had distempered even this impassive creature; and as I went on upstairs I was the less ashamed of my own discomposure.

All day the wind continued; and I sat in my room and made a feint of reading, or walked up and down and listened to the riot overhead. Night fell and I had not so much as a candle. I began to long for some society and stole down to the court. It was now plunged in the blue of the first darkness, but the recess was redly lighted by the fire. The wood had been piled high and was crowned by a shock of flames, which the draught of the chimney brandished to and fro. In this strong and shaken brightness the señora continued pacing from wall to wall with [illegible]tures, clasping her hands, stretching forth her [illegible]k her head as in appeal to heaven. In these [illegible]vements the beauty and grace of the woman [illegible]ore clearly; but there was a light in her eye that [illegible] on me unpleasantly; and when I had looked on awhile in silence, and seemingly unobserved, I turned tail as I had come, and groped my way back again to my own chamber.

By the time Felipe brought my supper and lights, my nerve was utterly gone; and, had the lad been such as I was used to seeing him, I should have kept him (even by force had that been necessary) to take off the edge from my distasteful solitude. But on Felipe, also, the wind had exercised its influence. He had been feverish all day; now that the night had come he was fallen into a low and tremulous humour that reacted on my own. The sight of his scared face, his starts and pallors and sudden hearkenings, unstrung me; and when he dropped and broke a dish, I fairly leaped out of my seat.

'I think we are all mad today,' said I, affecting to laugh.

'It is the black wind,' he replied dolefully. 'You feel as if you must do something, and you don't know what it is.'

I noted the aptness of the description; but, indeed, Felipe had sometimes a strange felicity in rendering into words the sensations of the body. 'And your mother, too,' said I, 'she seems to feel this weather much. Do you not fear she may be unwell?'

He stared at me a little, and then said, 'No,' almost defiantly, and the next moment, carrying his hand to his brow, cried out lamentably at the wind and the noise that made his head go round like a mill-wheel. 'Who can be well?' he cried; and indeed, I could only echo his question, for I was disturbed enough myself.

I went to bed early, wearied with daylong restlessness, but the poisonous nature of the wind, and its ungodly and unintermittent uproar, would not suffer me to sleep. I lay there and tossed, my nerves and senses on the stretch. At times I would doze, dream horribly, and wake again; and these snatches of oblivion confused me as to time. But it must have been late on in the night, when I was suddenly startled by an outbreak of pitiable and hateful cries. I leaped from my bed, supposing I had dreamed; but the cries still continued to fill the house, cries of pain, I thought, but certainly of rage also, and so savage and discordant that they shocked the heart. It was no illusion: some living thing, some lunatic or some wild animal, was being foully tortured. The thought of Felipe and the squirrel flashed into my mind, and I ran to the door, but it had been locked from the outside; and I might shake it as I pleased, I was a fast prisoner.

Still the cries continued. Now they would dwindle down into a moaning that seemed to be articulate, and at these times I made sure they must be human; and again they would break forth and fill the house with ravings worthy of hell. I stood at the door and gave ear to them, till at last they died away. Long after that I still lingered and still continued to hear them mingle in fancy with the storming of the wind; and when at last I crept to my bed, it was with a deadly sickness and a blackness of horror on my heart.

It was little wonder if I slept no more. Why had I been locked in? What had passed? Who was the author of these indescribable and shocking cries? A human being? It was inconceivable. A beast? The cries were scarce quite bestial; and what animal, short of a lion or a tiger, could thus shake the solid walls of the *residencia*? And while I was turning over the elements of the mystery, it came into my mind that I had not yet set eyes upon the daughter of the house. What was more probable than that the daughter of the señora, and the sister of Felipe, should be herself insane? Or, what more likely than that these ignorant and half-witted people should seek to manage an afflicted kinswoman by violence? Here was a solution; and yet when I called to mind the cries (which I never did without a shuddering chill), it seemed altogether insufficient: not even cruelty could wring such cries from madness. But of one thing I was sure: I could not live in a house where such a thing was half conceivable and not probe the matter home and, if necessary, interfere.

The next day came, the wind had blown itself out, and there was nothing to remind me of the business of the night. Felipe came to my bedside with obvious cheerfulness; as I passed through the court, the señora was sunning herself with her accustomed immobility; and when I issued from the gateway, I found the whole face of nature austerely smiling, the heavens of a cold blue, and sown with great cloud islands, and the mountainside mapped forth into provinces of light and shadow. A short walk restored me to myself, and renewed within me the resolve to plumb this mystery; and when, from the vantage of my knoll, I had seen Felipe pass forth to his labours in the garden, I returned at once to the *residencia* to put my design in practice. The señora appeared plunged in slumber; I stood awhile and marked her, but she did not stir; even if my design was indiscreet, I had little to fear from such a guardian; and turning away, I mounted to the gallery and began my explorations of the house.

All morning I went from one door to another, and entered spacious and faded chambers, some rudely shuttered, some receiving their full charge of daylight, all empty and unhomely. It was a rich house, on which Time had breathed his tarnish and dust had scattered disillusion. The spider swung there; the bloated tarantula scampered on the cornices; ants had their crowded highways on the floor of halls of audience; the big and foul fly, that lives on carrion and is often the messenger of death, had set up his nest in the rotten woodwork, and buzzed heavily about the rooms. Here and there a stool or two, a couch, a bed or a great carved chair remained behind, like islets on the bare floors, to testify to man's bygone habitation; and everywhere the walls were set with the portraits of the dead. I could judge, by these decaying effigies, in the house of what a great and what a handsome race I was then wandering. Many of the men wore orders on their breasts and had the port of noble offices; the women were all richly attired; the canvases most of them by famous hands. But it was not so much these evidences of greatness that took hold upon my mind, even contrasted, as they were, with the present depopulation and decay of that great house. It was rather the parable of family life that I read in this succession of fair faces and shapely bodies. Never before had I so realised the miracle of the continued race, the creation and recreation, the weaving and changing and handing down of fleshly elements. That a child should be born of its mother, that it should grow and clothe itself (we know not how) with humanity, and put on inherited looks, and turn its head with the manner of one ascendant, and offer its hand with the gesture of another, are wonders dulled for us by repetition. But in the singular unity of look, in the common features and common bearing, of all these painted generations on the walls of the *residencia*, the miracle started out and looked me in the face. And an ancient mirror falling opportunely in my way, I stood and read my own features a long while, tracing out on either hand the filaments of descent and the bonds that knit me with my family.

At last, in the course of these investigations, I opened the door of a chamber that bore the marks of habitation. It was of large proportions and faced to the north, where the mountains were most wildly figured. The embers of a fire smouldered and smoked upon the hearth, to which a chair had been drawn close. And yet the aspect of the chamber was ascetic to the degree of sternness; the chair was uncushioned; the floor and walls were naked; and beyond the books which lay here and there in some confusion, there was no instrument of either work or pleasure. The sight of books in the house of such a family exceedingly amazed me; and I began with a great hurry, and in momentary fear of interruption, to go from one to another and hastily inspect their character. They were of all sorts, devotional, historical and scientific, but mostly of a great age and in the Latin tongue. Some I could see to bear the marks of constant study; others had been torn across and tossed aside as if in petulance or disapproval. Lastly, as I cruised about that empty chamber, I espied some papers written upon with pencil on a table near the window. An unthinking curiosity led me to take one up. It bore a copy of verses, very roughly metred in the original Spanish, and which I may render somewhat thus:

Pleasure approached with pain and shame,
Grief with a wreath of lilies came.
Pleasure showed the lovely sun;
Jesu dear, how sweet it shone!
Grief with her worn hand pointed on,
Jesu dear, to thee!

Shame and confusion at once fell on me; and, laying down the paper, I beat an immediate retreat from the apartment. Neither Felipe nor his mother could have read the books nor written these rough but feeling verses. It was plain I had stumbled with sacrilegious feet into the room of the daughter of the house. God knows, my own heart most sharply punished me for my indiscretions. The thought that I had thus secretly pushed my way into the confidence of a girl so strangely situated, and the fear that she might somehow come to hear of it, oppressed me like guilt. I blamed myself besides for my suspicions of the night before; wondered that I should ever have attributed these shocking cries to one of whom I now conceived as of a saint, spectral of mien, wasted with maceration, bound up in the practices of a mechanical devotion, and dwelling in a great isolation of soul with her incongruous relatives; and as I leaned on the balustrade of the gallery and looked down into the bright close of pomegranates and at the gaily dressed and somnolent woman, who just then stretched herself and delicately licked her lips as in the very sensuality of sloth, my mind swiftly compared the scene with the cold chamber looking northward on the mountains, where the daughter dwelt.

That same afternoon, as I sat upon my knoll, I saw the padre enter the gates of the *residencia*. The revelation of the daughter's character had struck home to my fancy, and almost blotted out the horrors of the night before; but at sight of this worthy man the memory revived. I descended, then, from the knoll, and making a circuit among the woods, posted myself by the wayside to await his passage. As soon as he appeared I stepped forth and introduced myself as the lodger of the *residencia*. He had a very strong, honest countenance, on which it was easy to read the mingled emotions with which he regarded me: as a foreigner, a heretic, and yet one who had been wounded for the good cause. Of the family at the *residencia* he spoke with reserve, and yet with respect. I mentioned that I had not yet seen the daughter, whereupon he remarked that that was as it should be, and looked at me a little askance. Lastly, I plucked up courage to refer to the cries that had disturbed me in the night. He heard me out in silence, and then stopped and partly turned about, as though to mark beyond doubt that he was dismissing me.

'Do you take tobacco powder?' said he, offering his snuffbox; and then, when I had refused, 'I am an old man,' he added, 'and I may be allowed to remind you that you are a guest.'

'I have, then, your authority,' I returned, firmly enough, although I flushed at the implied reproof, 'to let things take their course, and not to interfere?'

He said, 'Yes,' and with a somewhat uneasy salute turned and left me where I was. But he had done two things: he had set my conscience at rest, and he had awakened my delicacy. I made a great effort, once more dismissed the recollection of the night, and fell once more to brooding on my saintly poetess. At the same time, I could not quite forget that I had been locked in, and that night when Felipe brought me my supper I attacked him warily on both points of interest.

'I never see your sister,' said I casually.

'Oh, no,' said he, 'she is a good, good girl,' and his mind instantly veered to something else.

'Your sister is pious, I suppose?' I asked in the next pause.

'Oh!' he cried, joining his hands with extreme fervour, 'a saint, it is she that keeps me up.'

'You are very fortunate,' said I, 'for the most of us, I am afraid, and myself among the number, are better at going down.'

'Señor,' said Felipe earnestly, 'I would not say that. You should not tempt your angel. If one goes down, where is he to stop?'

'Why, Felipe,' said I, 'I had no guess you were a preacher, and I may say a good one; but I suppose that is your sister's doing?'

He nodded at me with round eyes.

'Well, then,' I continued, 'she has doubtless reproved you for your sin of cruelty?'

'Twelve times!' he cried; for this was the phrase by which the odd creature expressed the sense of frequency. 'And I told her you had done so – I remembered that,' he added proudly – 'and she was pleased.'

'Then, Felipe,' said I, 'what were those cries that I heard last night? for surely they were cries of some creature in suffering.'

'The wind,' returned Felipe, looking in the fire.

I took his hand in mine, at which, thinking it to be a caress, he smiled with a brightness of pleasure that came near disarming my resolve. But I trod the weakness down. 'The wind,' I repeated; 'and yet I think it was this hand,' holding it up, 'that had first locked me in.' The lad shook visibly, but answered never a word. 'Well,' said I, 'I am a stranger and a guest. It is not my part either to meddle or to judge in your affairs; in these you shall take your sister's counsel, which I cannot doubt to be excellent. But in so far as concerns my own, I will be no man's prisoner, and I demand that key.' Half an hour later my door was suddenly thrown open, and the key tossed ringing on the floor.

A day or two after, I came in from a walk a little before the point of noon. The señora was lying lapped in slumber on the threshold of the recess; the pigeons dozed below the eaves like snowdrifts; the house was under a deep spell of noontide quiet; and only a wandering and gentle wind from the mountain stole round the galleries, rustled among the pomegranates and pleasantly stirred the shadows. Something in the stillness moved me to imitation, and I went very lightly across the court and up the marble staircase. My foot was on the topmost round, when a door opened, and I found myself face to face with Olalla. Surprise transfixed me; her loveliness struck to my heart; she glowed in the deep shadow of the gallery a gem of colour; her eyes took hold upon mine and clung there, and bound us together like the joining of hands; and the moments we thus stood face to face, drinking each other in, were sacramental and the wedding of souls. I know not how long it was before I awoke out of a deep trance, and, hastily bowing, passed on into the upper stair. She did not move, but followed me with her great thirsting eyes; and as I passed out of sight it seemed to me as if she paled and faded.

In my own room, I opened the window and looked out, and could not think what change had come upon that austere field of mountains that it should thus sing and shine under the lofty heaven. I had seen her – Olalla! And the stone crags answered, Olalla! and the dumb, unfathomable azure answered, Olalla! The pale saint of my dreams had vanished for ever; and in her place I beheld this maiden on whom God had lavished the richest colours and the most exuberant energies of life, whom He had made active as a deer, slender as a reed, and in whose great eyes He had lighted the torches of the soul. The thrill of her young life, strung like a wild animal's, had entered into me; the force of soul, that had looked out from her eyes and conquered mine, mantled about my heart and sprang to my lips in singing. She passed through my veins: she was one with me.

I will not say that this enthusiasm declined; rather my soul held out in its ecstasy as in a strong castle, and was there besieged by cold and sorrowful considerations. I could not doubt but that I loved her at first sight, and already with a quivering ardour that was strange to my experience. What then was to follow? She was the child of an afflicted house, the señora's daughter, the sister of Felipe; she bore it even in her beauty. She had the lightness and swiftness of the one, swift as an arrow, light as dew; like the other, she shone on the pale background of the world with the brillancy of flowers. I could not call by the name of brother that half-witted lad, nor by the name of mother that immovable and lovely thing of flesh, whose silly eyes and perpetual simper now recurred to my mind like something hateful. And if I could not marry, what then? She was helplessly unprotected; her eyes, in that single and long glance which had been all our intercourse, had confessed a weakness equal to my own; but in my heart I knew her for the student of the cold northern chamber, and the writer of the sorrowful lines; and this was a knowledge to disarm a brute. To flee was more than I could find courage for; but I registered a vow of unsleeping circumspection.

As I turned from the window, my eyes alighted on the portrait. It had fallen dead, like a candle after sunrise; it followed me with eyes of paint. I knew it to be like, and marvelled at the tenacity of type in that declining race; but the likeness was swallowed up in difference. I remembered how it had seemed to me a thing unapproachable in the life, a creature rather of the painter's craft than of the modesty of nature, and I marvelled at the thought, and exulted in the image of Olalla. Beauty I had seen before, and not been charmed, and I had been often drawn to women who were not beautiful except to me; but in Olalla all that I desired and had not dared to imagine was united.

I did not see her the next day, and my heart ached and my eyes longed for her, as men long for morning. But the day after, when I returned, about my usual hour, she was once more on the gallery, and our looks once more met and embraced. I would have spoken, I would have drawn near to her; but strongly as she plucked at my heart, drawing me like a magnet, something yet more imperious withheld me; and I could only bow and pass by;

and she, leaving my salutation unanswered, only followed me with her noble eyes.

I had now her image by rote, and as I conned the traits in memory it seemed as if I read her very heart. She was dressed with something of her mother's coquetry, and love of positive colour. Her robe, which I knew she must have made with her own hands, clung about her with a cunning grace. After the fashion of that country, besides, her bodice stood open in the middle, in a long slit, and here, in spite of the poverty of the house, a gold coin, hanging by a ribbon, lay on her brown bosom. These were proofs, had any been needed, of her inborn delight in life and her own loveliness. On the other hand, in her eyes that hung upon mine, I could read depth beyond depth of passion and sadness, lights of poetry and hope, blacknesses of despair, and thoughts that were above the earth. It was a lovely body, but the inmate, the soul, was more than worthy of that lodging. Should I leave this incomparable flower to wither unseen on these rough mountains? Should I despise the great gift offered me in the eloquent silence of her eyes? Here was a soul immured; should I not burst its prison? All side considerations fell off from me; were she the child of Herod I swore I should make her mine; and that very evening I set myself, with a mingled sense of treachery and disgrace, to captivate the brother. Perhaps I read him with more favourable eyes, perhaps the thought of his sister always summoned up the better qualities of that imperfect soul; but he had never seemed to be so amiable, and his very likeness to Olalla, while it annoyed, yet softened me.

A third day passed in vain – an empty desert of hours. I would not lose a chance, and loitered all afternoon in the court where (to give myself a countenance) I spoke more than usual with the señora. God knows it was with a most tender and sincere interest that I now studied her; and even as for Felipe, so now for the mother, I was conscious of a growing warmth of toleration. And yet I wondered. Even while I spoke with her, she would doze off into a little sleep, and presently awake again without embarrassment; and this composure staggered me. And again, as I marked her make infinitesimal changes in her posture, savouring and lingering on the bodily pleasure of the movement, I was driven to wonder at this depth of passive sensuality. She lived in her body; and her consciousness was all sunk into and disseminated through her members, where it luxuriously dwelt. Lastly, I could not grow accustomed to her eyes. Each time she turned on me these great beautiful and meaningless orbs, wide open to the day, but closed against human enquiry – each time I had occasion to observe the lively changes of her pupils which expanded and contracted in a breath – I know not what it was came over me, I can find no name for the mingled feeling of disappointment, annoyance and distaste that jarred along my nerves. I tried her on a variety of subjects, equally in vain; and at last led the talk to her daughter. But even there she proved indifferent; said she was pretty, which (as with children) was her highest word of commendation, but was plainly incapable of any higher thought and when I remarked that Olalla seemed silent, merely yawned in my face and replied that speech was of no great use when you had nothing to say. 'People speak much, very much,' she added, looking at me with expanded pupils; and then again yawned, and again showed me a mouth that was as dainty as a toy. This time I took the hint, and, leaving her to her repose, went up into my own chamber to sit by the open window, looking on the hills and not beholding them, sunk in lustrous and deep dreams, and hearkening in fancy to the note of a voice that I had never heard.

I awoke on the fifth morning with a brightness of anticipation that seemed to challenge fate. I was sure of myself, light of heart and foot, and resolved to put my love incontinently to the touch of knowledge. It should lie no longer under the bonds of silence, a dumb thing, living by the eye only, like the love of beasts; but should now put on the spirit, and enter upon the joys of the complete human intimacy. I thought of it with wild hopes, like a voyager to El Dorado; into that unknown and lovely country of her soul, I no longer trembled to adventure. Yet when I did encounter her, the same force of passion descended on me and at once submerged my mind; speech seemed to drop away from me like a childish habit; and I but drew near to her as the giddy man draws near to the margin of a gulf. She drew back from me a little as I came; but her eyes did not waver from mine, and these lured me forward. At last, when I was already within reach of her, I stopped. Words were denied me; if I advanced I could but clasp her to my heart in silence; and all that was sane in me, all that was still unconquered, revolted against the thought of such an accost. So we stood for a second, all our life in our eyes, exchanging salvos of attraction and yet each resisting; and then, with a great effort of the will, and conscious at the same time of a sudden bitterness of disappointment, I turned and went away in the same silence.

What power lay upon me that I could not speak? And she, why was she also silent? Why did she draw away before me dumbly, with fascinated eyes? Was this love? or was it a mere brute attraction, mindless and inevitable, like that of the magnet for the steel? We had never spoken, we were wholly strangers; and yet an influence, strong as the grasp of a giant, swept us silently together. On my side it filled me with impatience; and yet I was sure that she was worthy; I had seen her books, read her verses, and thus, in a sense, divined the soul of my mistress. But on her side it struck me almost cold. Of me she knew nothing but my bodily favour; she was drawn to me as stones fall to the earth; the laws that rule the earth conducted her, unconsenting, to my arms; and I drew back at the thought of such a bridal and began to be jealous for myself. It was not thus that I desired to be loved. And then I began to fall into a great pity for the girl herself. I thought how sharp must be her mortification, that she, the student, the recluse, Felipe's saintly monitress, should have thus confessed an overweening weakness for a man with whom she had never exchanged a word. And at the coming of pity, all other thoughts were swallowed up; and I longed only to find and console and reassure her; to tell her how wholly her love was returned on my side, and how her choice, even if blindly made, was not unworthy.

The next day it was glorious weather; depth upon depth of blue over-canopied the mountains; the sun shone wide; and the wind in the trees and the many falling torrents in the mountains filled the air with delicate and haunting music. Yet I was prostrated with sadness. My heart wept for the sight of Olalla, as a child weeps for its mother. I sat down on a boulder on the verge of the low cliffs that bound the plateau to the north. Thence I looked down into the wooded valley of a stream, where no foot came. In the mood I was in, it was even touching to behold the place untenanted; it lacked Olalla; and I thought of the delight and glory of a life passed wholly with her in that strong air, and among these rugged and lovely surroundings, at first with a whimpering sentiment, and then again with such a fiery joy that I seemed to grow in strength and stature, like a Samson.

And then suddenly I was aware of Olalla drawing near. She appeared out of a grove of cork trees, and came straight towards me; and I stood up and waited. She seemed in her walking a creature of such life and fire and lightness as amazed me; yet she came quietly and slowly. Her energy was in the slowness; but for inimitable strength, I felt she would have run, she would have flown to me. Still, as she approached, she kept her eyes lowered to the ground; and when she had drawn quite near, it was without one glance that she addressed me. At the first note of her voice I started. It was for this I had been waiting; this was the last test of my love. And lo, her enunciation was precise and clear, not lisping and incomplete like that of her family; and the voice, though deeper than usual with women, was still both youthful and womanly. She spoke in a rich chord; golden contralto strains mingled with hoarseness; as the red threads were mingled with the brown among her tresses. It was not only a voice that spoke to my heart directly, but it spoke to me of her. And yet her words immediately plunged me back upon despair.

'You will go away,' she said, 'today.'

Her example broke the bonds of my speech, I felt as lightened of a weight, or as if a spell had been dissolved. I know not in what words I answered; but, standing before her on the cliffs, I poured out the whole ardour of my love, telling her I lived upon the thought of her, slept only to dream of her loveliness, and would gladly forswear my country, my language and my friends, to live for ever by her side. And then, strongly commanding myself, I changed the note; I reassured, I comforted her: I told her I had divined in her a pious and heroic spirit, with which I was worthy to sympathise, and which I longed to share and lighten. 'Nature,' I told her, 'was the voice of God, which men disobey at peril; and if we were thus dumbly drawn together, ay, even as by a miracle of love, it must imply a divine fitness in our souls; we must be made,' I said – 'made for one another. We should be mad rebels,' I cried out – 'mad rebels against God, not to obey this instinct.'

She shook her head. 'You will go today,' she repeated, and then with a gesture, and in a sudden, sharp note – 'no, not today,' she cried, 'tomorrow!'

But at this sign of relenting, power came in upon me in a tide. I stretched out my arms and called upon her name; and she leaped to me and clung to me. The hills rocked about us, the earth quailed; a shock as of a blow went through me and left me blind and dizzy. And the next moment she had thrust me back, broken rudely from my arms, and fled with the speed of a deer among the cork trees.

I stood and shouted to the mountains; I turned and went back towards the *residencia*, walking upon air. She sent me away, and yet I had but to call upon her name and she came to me. These were but the weaknesses of girls, from which even she, the strangest of her sex, was not exempted. Go? Not I, Olalla – oh, not I, Olalla! A bird sang near by; and in that season birds were rare. It bade me be of good cheer. And once more the whole countenance of nature, from the ponderous and stable mountains down to the lightest leaf and the smallest darting fly in the shadow of the groves, began to stir before me and to put on the lineaments of life and wear a face of awful joy. The sunshine struck upon the hills, strong as a hammer on the anvil, and the hills shook; the earth, under that vigorous insolation, yielded up heady scents; the woods smouldered in the blaze. I felt the thrill of travail and delight run through the earth. Something elemental, something rude, violent, and savage, in the love that sang in my heart, was like a key to nature's secrets; and the very stones that rattled under my feet appeared alive and friendly. Olalla! Her touch had quickened, and renewed, and strung me up to the old pitch of concert with the rugged earth, to a swelling of the soul that men learned to forget in their polite assemblies. Love burned in me like rage; tenderness waxed fierce; I hated, I adored, I pitied, I revered her with ecstasy. She seemed the link that bound me in with dead things on the one hand, and with our pure and pitying God upon the other; a thing brutal and divine, and akin at once to the innocence and to the unbridled forces of the earth.

My head thus reeling, I came into the courtyard of the *residencia*, and the sight of the mother struck me like a revelation. She sat there, all sloth and contentment, blinking under the strong sunshine, branded with a passive enjoyment, a creature set quite apart, before whom my ardour fell away like a thing ashamed. I stopped a moment, and, commanding such shaken tones as I was able, said a word or two. She looked at me with her unfathomable kindness; her voice in reply sounded vaguely out of the realm of peace in which she slumbered, and there fell on my mind, for the first time, a sense of respect for one so uniformily innocent and happy, and I passed on in a kind of wonder at myself, that I should be so much disquieted.

On my table there lay a piece of the same yellow paper I had seen in the north room; it was written on with pencil in the same hand, Olalla's hand, and I picked it up with a sudden sinking of alarm, and read: 'If you have any kindness for Olalla, if you have any chivalry for a creature sorely wrought, go from here today; in pity, in honour, for the sake of Him who died, I supplicate that you shall go.' I looked at this awhile in mere stupidity, then I began to awaken to a weariness and horror of life; the sunshine darkened outside on the bare hills, and I began to shake like a man in terror. The vacancy thus suddenly opened in my life unmanned me like a physical void. It was not my heart, it was not my happiness, it was life itself that was involved. I could not lose her. I said so, and stood repeating it. And then, like one in a dream, I moved to the window, put forth my hand to open the casement and thrust it through the pane. The blood spurted from my wrist; and with an instantaneous quietude and command of myself, I pressed my thumb on the little leaping fountain and reflected what to do. In that empty room there was nothing to my purpose; I felt, besides, that I required assistance. There shot into my mind a hope that Olalla herself might be my helper, and I turned and went downstairs, still keeping my thumb upon the wound.

There was no sign of either Olalla or Felipe, and I addressed myself to the recess, whither the señora had now drawn quite back and sat dozing close before the fire, for no degree of heat appeared too much for her.

'Pardon me,' said I, 'if I disturb you, but I must apply to you for help.'

She looked up sleepily and asked me what it was, and with

the very words I thought she drew in her breath with a widening of the nostrils and seemed to come suddenly and fully alive.

'I have cut myself,' I said, 'and rather badly. See!' And I held out my two hands from which the blood was oozing and dripping.

Her great eyes opened wide, the pupils shrank into points; a veil seemed to fall from her face, and leave it sharply expressive and yet inscrutable. And as I still stood, marvelling a little at her disturbance, she came swiftly up to me, and stooped and caught me by the hand; and the next moment my hand was at her mouth, and she had bitten me to the bone. The pang of the bite, the sudden spurting of blood, and the monstrous horror of the act, flashed through me all in one, and I beat her back; and she sprang at me again and again, with bestial cries, cries that I recognised, such cries as had awakened me on the night of the high wind. Her strength was like that of madness; mine was rapidly ebbing with the loss of blood; my mind besides was whirling with the abhorrent strangeness of the onslaught, and I was already forced against the wall, when Olalla ran betwixt us, and Felipe, following at a bound, pinned down his mother on the floor.

A trancelike weakness fell upon me; I saw, heard and felt, but I was incapable of movement. I heard the struggle roll to and fro upon the floor, the yells of that catamount ringing up to heaven as she strove to reach me. I felt Olalla clasp me in her arms, her hair falling on my face, and, with the strength of a man, raise and half drag, half carry me upstairs into my own room, where she cast me down upon the bed. Then I saw her hasten to the door and lock it, and stand an instant listening to the savage cries that shook the *residencia*. And then, swift and light as a thought, she was again beside me, binding up my hand, laying it in her bosom, moaning and mourning over it with dovelike sounds. They were not words that came to her, they were sounds more beautiful than speech, infinitely touching, infinitely tender;

and yet as I lay there, a thought stung to my heart, a thought wounded me like a sword, a thought, like a worm in a flower, profaned the holiness of my love. Yes, they were beautiful sounds, and they were inspired by human tenderness; but was their beauty human?

All day I lay there. For a long time the cries of that nameless female thing, as she struggled with her half-witted whelp, resounded through the house, and pierced me with despairing sorrow and disgust. They were the death cry of my love; my love was murdered; it was not only dead, but an offence to me; and yet, think as I pleased, feel as I must, it still swelled within me like a storm of sweetness, and my heart melted at her looks and touch. This horror that had sprung out, this doubt upon Olalla, this savage and bestial strain that ran not only through the whole behaviour of her family, but found a place in the very foundations and story of our love – though it appalled, though it shocked and sickened me, was yet not of power to break the knot of my infatuation.

When the cries had ceased, there came a scraping at the door, by which I knew Felipe was without; and Olalla went and spoke to him – I know not what. With that exception, she stayed close beside me, now kneeling by my bed and fervently praying, now sitting with her eyes upon mine. So then, for these six hours I drank in her beauty, and silently perused the story in her face. I saw the golden coin hover on her breaths; I saw her eyes darken and brighten, and still speak no language but that of an unfathomable kindness; I saw the faultless face, and, through the robe, the lines of the faultless body. Night came at last, and in the growing darkness of the chamber, the sight of her slowly melted; but even then the touch of her smooth hand lingered in mine and talked with me. To lie thus in deadly weakness and drink in the traits of the beloved, is to re-awake to love from whatever shock of disillusion. I reasoned with myself, and I shut my eyes on horrors, and again I was very bold to accept the worst. What mattered it if that imperious sentiment survived; if her eyes still beckoned and attached me; if now, even as before, every fibre of my dull body yearned and turned to her? Late on in the night some strength revived in me, and I spoke: 'Olalla,' I said, 'nothing matters; I ask nothing; I am content; I love you.'

She knelt down awhile and prayed, and I devoutly respected her devotions. The moon had begun to shine in upon one side of each of the three windows, and make a misty clearness in the room, by which I saw her indistinctly. When she re-arose she made the sign of the cross.

'It is for me to speak,' she said, 'and for you to listen. I know; you can but guess. I prayed, how I prayed for you to leave this place. I begged it of you, and I know you would have granted me even this; or if not, oh, let me think so!'

'I love you,' I said.

'And yet you have lived in the world,' she said after a pause, 'you are a man and wise; and I am but a child. Forgive me, if I seem to teach, who am as ignorant as the trees of the mountain; but those who learn much do but skim the face of knowledge; they seize the laws, they conceive the dignity of the design – the horror of the living fact fades from their memory. It is we who sit at home with evil who remember, I think, and are warned and pity. Go, rather, go now, and keep me in mind. So I shall have a life in the cherished places of your memory: a life as much my own as that which I lead in this body.'

'I love you,' I said once more; and reaching out my weak hand, took hers, and carried it to my lips and kissed it. Nor did she resist, but winced a little, and I could see her look upon me with a frown that was not unkindly, only sad and baffled. And then it seemed she made a call upon her resolution; plucked my hand towards her, herself at the same time leaning somewhat forward, and laid it on the beating of her heart. 'There,' she cried, 'you feel the very footfall of my life. It only moves for you; it is yours. But is it even mine? It is mine indeed to offer you, as I might take the coin from my neck, as I might break a live branch from a tree and give it you. And yet not mine! I dwell, or I think I dwell (if I exist at all), somewhat apart, an impotent prisoner, and carried about and deafened by a mob that I disown. This capsule, such as throbs against the sides of animals, knows you at a touch for its master; ay, it loves you! But my soul, does my soul? I think not; I know not, fearing to ask. Yet when you spoke to me, your words were of the soul; it is of the soul that you ask – it is only from the soul that you would take me.'

'Olalla,' I said, 'the soul and the body are one, and mostly so in love. What the body chooses, the soul loves; where the body clings, the soul cleaves; body for body, soul to soul, they come together at God's signal; and the lower part (if we can call aught low) is only the footstool and foundation of the highest.'

'Have you,' she said, 'seen the portraits in the house of my fathers? Have you looked at my mother or at Felipe? Have your eyes never rested on that picture that hangs by your bed? She who sat for it died ages ago; and she did evil in her life. But, look again: there is my hand to the least line, there are my eyes and my hair. What is mine, then, and what am I? If not a curve in this poor body of mine (which you love, and for the sake of which you dotingly dream that you love me), not a gesture that I can frame, not a tone of my voice, not any look from my eyes, no, not even now when I speak to him I love, but has belonged to others? Others, ages dead, have wooed other men with my eyes; other men have heard the pleading of the same voice that now sounds in your ears. The hands of the dead are in my bosom; they move me, they pluck me, they guide me; I am a puppet at their command; and I but re-inform features and attributes that have long been laid aside from evil in the quiet of the grave. Is it me you love, friend? or the race that made me? The girl who does not know and cannot answer for the least portion of herself? or the stream of which she is a transitory eddy, the tree of which she is the passing fruit? The race exists; it is old, it is ever young, it carries its eternal destiny in its bosom; upon it, like waves upon the sea, individual succeeds to individual, mocked with a semblance of self-control, but they are nothing. We speak of the soul, but the soul is in the race.'

'You fret against the common law,' I said. 'You rebel against the voice of God, which He has made so winning to convince, so imperious to command. Hear it, and how it speaks between us! Your hand clings to mine, your heart leaps at my touch, the unknown elements of which we are compounded awake and run together at a look; the clay of the earth remembers its independent life and yearns to join us; we are drawn together as the stars are turned about in space, or as the tides ebb and flow, by things older and greater than we ourselves.'

'Alas!' she said, 'what can I say to you? My fathers, eight hundred years ago, ruled all this province: they were wise, great, cunning and cruel; they were a picked race of the Spanish; their flags led in war; the king called them his cousin; the people, when the rope was slung for them or when they returned and found their hovels smoking, blasphemed their name. Presently a change began. Man has risen; if he has sprung from the brutes, he can descend again to the same level. The breath of weariness blew on their humanity and cords relaxed; they began to go down; their minds fell on sleep, their passions awoke in gusts, heady and senseless like the wind in the gutters of the mountains; beauty was still handed down, but no longer the guiding wit nor the human heart; the seed passed on, it was wrapped in flesh, the flesh covered the bones, but they were the bones and the flesh of brutes, and their mind was as the mind of flies. I speak to you as I dare; but you have seen for yourself how the wheel has gone backwards with my doomed race. I stand, as it were, upon a little rising ground in this desperate descent, and see both before and behind, both what we have lost and to what we are condemned, to go farther downward. And shall I – I that dwell apart in the house of the dead, my body, loathing its ways – shall I repeat the spell? Shall I bind another spirit, reluctant as my own, into this bewitched and tempest-broken tenement that I now suffer in? Shall I hand down this cursed vessel of humanity, charge it with fresh life as with fresh poison, and dash it, like a fire, in the faces of posterity? But my vow has been given; the race shall cease from off the earth. At this hour my brother is making ready; his foot will soon be on the stair; and you will go with him and pass out of my sight for ever. Think of me sometimes as one to whom the lesson of life was very harshly told, but who heard it with courage; as one who loved you indeed, but who hated herself so deeply that her love was hateful to her; as one who sent you away and yet would have longed to keep you for ever; who had no dearer hope than to forget you, and no greater fear than to be forgotten.'

She had drawn towards the door as she spoke, her rich voice sounding softer and farther away; and with the last word she was gone, and I lay alone in the moonlit chamber. What I might have done had not I lain bound by my extreme weakness, I know not; but as it was there fell upon me a great and blank despair. It was not long before there shone in at the door the ruddy glimmer of a lantern, and Felipe coming, charged me without a word upon his shoulders, and carried me down to the great gate, where the cart was waiting. In the moonlight the hills stood out sharply, as if they were of cardboard; on the glimmering surface of the plateau, and from among the low trees which swung together and sparkled in the wind, the great black cube of the *residencia* stood out bulkily, its mass only broken by three dimly lighted windows in the northern front above the gate. They were Olalla's windows, and as the cart jolted onwards I kept my eyes fixed upon them till, where the road dipped into a valley, they were lost to my view for ever. Felipe walked in silence beside the shafts, but from time to time he would check the mule and seem to look back upon me; and at length drew quite near and laid his hand upon my head. There was such kindness in the touch, and such a simplicity, as of the brutes, that tears broke from me like the bursting of an artery.

'Felipe,' I said, 'take me where they will ask no questions.'

He said never a word, but he turned his mule about, end for end, retraced some part of the way we had gone, and, striking into another path, led me to the mountain village, which was, as we say in Scotland, the kirkton of that thinly peopled district. Some broken memories dwell in my mind of the day breaking over the plain, of the cart stopping, of arms that helped me down, of a bare room into which I was carried, and of a swoon that fell upon me like sleep.

The next day and the days following the old priest was often at my side with his snuffbox and prayer book, and after a while, when I began to pick up strength, he told me that I was now on a fair way to recovery, and must as soon as possible hurry my departure; whereupon, without naming any reason, he took snuff and looked at me sideways. I did not affect ignorance; I knew he must have seen Olalla. 'Sir,' said I, 'you know that I do not ask in wantonness. What of that family?'

He said they were very unfortunate; that it seemed a declining race, and that they were very poor and had been much neglected.

'But she has not,' I said. 'Thanks, doubtless, to yourself, she is instructed and wise beyond the use of women.'

'Yes,' he said, 'the señorita is well informed. But the family has been neglected.'

'The mother?' I queried.

'Yes, the mother too,' said the padre, taking snuff. 'But Felipe is a well-intentioned lad.'

'The mother is odd?' I asked.

'Very odd,' replied the priest.

'I think, sir, we beat about the bush,' said I. 'You must know more of my affairs than you allow. You must know my curiosity to be justified on many grounds. Will you not be frank with me?'

'My son,' said the old gentleman, 'I will be very frank with you on matters within my competence; on those of which I know nothing it does not require much discretion to be silent. I will not fence with you, I take your meaning perfectly; and what can I say, but that we are all in God's hands, and that His ways are not as our ways? I have even advised with my superiors in the Church, but they, too, were dumb. It is a great mystery.'

'Is she mad?' I asked.

'I will answer you according to my belief. She is not,' returned the padre, 'or she was not. When she was young – God help me, I fear I neglected that wild lamb – she was surely sane; and yet, although it did not run to such heights, the same strain was already notable; it had been so before her in her father, ay, and before him, and this inclined me, perhaps, to think too lightly of it. But these things go on growing, not only in the individual but in the race.'

'When she was young,' I began, and my voice failed me for a moment, and it was only with a great effort that I was able to go on, 'was she like Olalla?'

'Now God forbid!' exclaimed the padre. 'God forbid that any man should think so slightingly of my favourite penitent. No, no; the señorita (but for her beauty, which I wish most honestly she had less of) has not a hair's resemblance to what her mother was at the same age. I could not bear to have you think so; though, heaven knows, it were, perhaps, better that you should.'

At this, I raised myself in bed and opened my heart to the old man; telling him of our love and of her decision; owning my own horrors, my own passing fancies, but telling him that these were at an end, and with something more than a purely formal submission, appealing to his judgement.

He heard me very patiently and without surprise; and when I had done, he sat for some time silent. Then he began: 'The

Church,' and instantly broke off again to apologise. 'I had forgotten my child, that you are not a Christian,' said he. 'And indeed, upon a point so highly unusual, even the Church can scarce be said to have decided. But would you have my opinion? The señorita is, in a matter of this kind, the best judge; I would accept her judgement.'

On the back of that he went away, nor was he thenceforward so assiduous in his visits; indeed, even when I began to get about again, he plainly feared and deprecated my society, not as in distate but much as a man might be disposed to flee from the riddling sphinx. The villagers, too, avoided me; they were unwilling to be my guides upon the mountain. I thought they looked at me askance, and I made sure that the more superstitious crossed themselves on my approach. At first I set this down to my heretical opinions; but it began at length to dawn upon me that if I was thus redoubted it was because I had stayed at the *residencia*. All men despise the savage notions of such peasantry; and yet I was conscious of a chill shadow that seemed to fall and dwell upon my love. It did not conquer, but I may not deny that it restrained my ardour.

Some miles westward of the village there was a gap in the sierra, from which the eye plunged direct upon the *residencia*, and thither it became my daily habit to repair. A wood crowned the summit, and just where the pathway issued from its fringes, it was overhung by a considerable shelf of rock, and that, in its turn, was surmounted by a crucifix of the size of life and more than usually painful in design. This was my perch; thence, day after day, I looked down upon the plateau and the great old house, and could see Felipe, no bigger than a fly, going to and fro about the garden. Sometimes mists would draw across the view, and be broken up again by mountain winds; sometimes the plain slumbered below me in unbroken sunshine; it would sometimes be all blotted out by rain. This distant post, these interrupted sights of the place where my life had been so strangely changed, suited the indecision of my humour. I passed whole days there, debating with myself the various elements of our position; now leaning to the suggestions of love, now giving an ear to prudence, and in the end halting irresolute between the two.

One day, as I was sitting on my rock, there came by that way a somewhat gaunt peasant wrapped in a mantle. He was a stranger, and plainly did not know me even by repute; for, instead of keeping the other side, he drew near and sat down beside me, and we had soon fallen in talk. Among other things he told me he had been a muleteer, and in former years had much frequented these mountains; later on, he had followed the army with his mules, had realised a competence, and was now living retired with his family.

'Do you know that house?' I enquired at last, pointing to the *residencia*, for I readily wearied of any talk that kept me from the thought of Olalla.

He looked at me darkly and crossed himself.

'Too well,' he said, 'it was there that one of my comrades sold himself to Satan; the Virgin shield us from temptations! He has paid the price; he is now burning in the reddest place in Hell!'

A fear came upon me; I could answer nothing; and presently the man resumed, as if to himself: 'Yes,' he said, 'oh yes, I know it. I have passed its doors. There was snow upon the pass, the wind was driving it; sure enough there was death that night upon the mountains, but there was worse beside the hearth. I took him by the arm, señor, and dragged him to the gate; I conjured him, by all he loved and respected, to go forth with me; I went on my knees before him in the snow, and I could see he was moved by my entreaty. And just then she came out on the gallery and called him by his name; and he turned, and there was she standing with a lamp in her hand and smiling on him to come back. I cried out aloud to God, and threw my arms about him, but he put me by and left me alone. He had made his choice; God help us. I would pray for him, but to what end? There are sins that not even the Pope can loose.'

'And your friend,' I asked, 'what became of him?'

'Nay, God knows,' said the muleteer. 'If all be true that we hear, his end was like his sin, a thing to raise the hair.'

'Do you mean that he was killed?' I asked.

'Sure enough, he was killed,' returned the man. 'But how? Ay, how? But these are things that it is sin to speak of.'

'The people of that house . . . ' I began.

But he interrupted me with a savage outburst. 'The people?' he cried. 'What people? There are neither men nor women in that house of Satan's! What? have you lived here so long and never heard?' And here he put his mouth to my ear and whispered, as if even the fowls of the mountain might have overheard and been stricken with horror.

What he told me was not true, nor was it even original; being, indeed, but a new edition, vamped up again by village ignorance and superstition, of stories nearly as ancient as the race of man. It was rather the application that appalled me. In the old days, he said, the Church would have burned out that nest of basilisks; but the arm of the Church was now shortened; his friend Miguel had been unpunished by the hands of men, and left to the more awful judgement of an offended God. This was wrong; but it should be so no more. The padre was sunk in age; he was even bewitched himself; but the eyes of his flock were now awake to their own danger; someday – ay, and before long – the smoke of that house should go up to heaven.

He left me filled with horror and fear. Which way to turn I knew not; whether first to warn the padre, or to carry my ill news direct to the threatened inhabitants of the *residencia*. Fate was to decide for me, for, while I was still hesitating, I beheld the veiled figure of a woman drawing near to me up the path-way. No veil could deceive my penetration; by every line and every movement I recognised Olalla; and keeping hidden behind a corner of the rock, I suffered her to gain the summit. Then I came forward. She knew me and paused, but did not speak; I, too, remained silent, and we continued for some time to gaze upon each other with a passionate sadness.

'I thought you had gone,' she said at length. 'It is all that you can do for me – to go. It is all I ever asked of you. And you still stay. But do you know that every day heaps up the peril of death, not only on your head, but on ours? A report has gone about the mountain; it is thought you love me, and the people will not suffer it.'

I saw she was already informed of her danger, and I rejoiced at it. 'Olalla,' I said, 'I am ready to go this day, this very hour, but not alone.'

She stepped aside and knelt down before the crucifix to pray, and I stood by and looked now at her and now at the object of her adoration, now at the living figure of the penitent and now at the ghastly daubed countenance, the painted wounds and the projected ribs of the image. The silence was only broken by the wailing of some large birds that circled sidelong, as if in surprise or alarm, about the summit of the hills. Presently Olalla rose again, turned towards me, raised her veil, and, still leaning with one hand on the shaft of the crucifix, looked upon me with a pale and sorrowful countenance.

'I have laid my hand upon the cross,' she said. 'The padre says you are no Christian; but look up for a moment with my eyes, and behold the face of the Man of Sorrows. We are all such as He was – the inheritors of sin; we must all bear and expiate a past which was not ours; there is in all of us – ay, even in me – a sparkle of the divine. Like Him, we must endure for a little while, until morning returns bringing peace. Suffer me to pass on upon my way alone; it is thus that I shall be least lonely, counting for my friend Him who is the friend of all the distressed; it is thus that I shall be the most happy, having taken my farewell of earthly happiness, and willingly accepted sorrow for my portion.'

I looked at the face of the crucifix, and, though I was no friend to images, and despised that imitative and grimacing art of which it was a rude example, some sense of what the thing implied was carried home to my intelligence. The face looked down upon me with a painful and deadly contraction; but the rays of glory encircled it, and reminded me that the sacrifice was voluntary. It stood there, crowning the rock, as it still stands on so many highway sides, vainly preaching to passers-by, an emblem of sad and noble truths; that pleasure is not an end, but an accident; that pain is the choice of the magnanimous; that it is best to suffer all things and do well. I turned and went down the mountain in silence; and when I looked back for the last time before the wood closed about my path, I saw Olalla still leaning on the crucifix.

ARNOLD BENNETT

Arnold Bennett was born in 1867. He grew up in Hanley, Staffordshire, one of the pottery towns that later served as a backdrop to his celebrated *Five Towns* novels. The son of a solicitor, Bennett was forced to leave school at sixteen to be a clerk in his father's firm, but he escaped to London in 1889 to work in law offices. Gradually drawn into literary circles, he abandoned the law in 1894 and embarked on a writing career. In 1902 Bennett completed two highly popular works: *The Grand Babylon Hotel* and *Anna of the Five Towns.* He scored a triumphant success in 1908 with the publication of *The Old Wives' Tale,* a masterful portrayal of English provincial life, and enhanced his renown with the *Clayhanger* trilogy (1910–16). He also wrote celebrated plays for the stage. Bennett's prominence declined temporarily following World War I but he experienced a resurgence of popularity with *Riceyman Steps* (1923) and *Lord Raingo* (1926). His final novel, *Imperial Palace,* came out in 1930. Arnold Bennett died in London of typhoid fever in 1931.

The Box-Office Girl

1

The Rotunda Royal, as everyone who knows the world knows, lifts its immense mass of yellow masonry (not really masonry but iron thinly faced with stone) right in the middle of London. It is the largest music-hall in London, and the most successful music-hall in London, and it burns more electricity than any other place of amusement in London. Its upper parts are glitteringly outlined in green and yellow electricity, its high tower can be glimpsed from all manner of streets, and the rich glow of the whole affair illuminates a cloudy sky for the whole of central London to see. Though entirely respectable, it has an altar of its own in the hearts of the young and the old bloods of provincial cities who come to town strictly on business. It is the Mecca of suburban inhabitants with a dull afternoon in front of them and ten shillings in their pockets to squander. To have his, or her, name printed in fire on the façade of the Rotunda is the ambition of every music-hall artist in the world, and of many another artist besides. In brief, the Rotunda is a very important, grandiose and impressive organism, an organism which emphatically 'functions'. And it is a household word. Even judges of the High Court have heard of the Rotunda. No daily paper in London ever appears without some mention of it somewhere.

Now daily and nightly behind a counter on your left as you entered by the main entrance into the grand foyer stood, until lately, a girl named Elaine Edar. She was a blonde, with bright hair, an attractive, pretty and benevolent face, and a good figure – because these attributes were essential to her position. Her simple, smart dress was of black, but it had touches of fantasy and of colour – because Mr Walter King (managing director – risen from call-boy, as he openly stated about ten times every day) had said that he did not care for his girls to look like hotel clerks. Elaine's face and hair were known to tens of thousands of people. Often in the street such people would start at the sight of her and murmur something to a companion, and Elaine knew that they were saying: 'That's the box-office girl at the Rotunda.'

So she had a certain importance on earth, and assuredly at the Rotunda. For she gathered in money, and to Mr Walter King ('Old Wal', behind his back, to his employees, and 'Wally', without concealment, to those proud persons who had the great privilege of his intimacy) – to Mr Walter King the Rotunda was in the end nothing but a machine for gathering in more money than it paid out. Not that Elaine was the sole instrument for gathering in money. Far from it! Above her counter were displayed the words: 'Box-office for this performance only. Boxes. Royal *Fauteuils*. Royal Stalls. Stalls. Grand Balcony'. All advance booking was done in a special office up the street, and each of the unreserved parts of the house had its own entrance, with turnstile and money-taker. Still, Elaine took a goodish bit of money twice a day, and she was easily the most prominent of all the human machines that received silver coins and notes in exchange for bits of coloured paper or base-metal discs.

Twelve performances a week – and Elaine had to be on duty ten minutes before the doors opened and to remain on duty until one hour before the end of each performance. Then she had to check her money and prove to the cashier's department that the total was correct. An anxious job, especially during the 'rush' quarter of an hour, when she had to read with the glance of an eagle the numbers on the 'sheet' of the performance, treat every patron as a benefactor, return good for evil, give change like a flash of lightning, detect spurious coins in the tenth of a second and render sweet smiles to louts, curmudgeons and cads! Happily she was by nature profoundly and universally benevolent – and in this respect indeed a wonder to her assistant, who did the telephoning and lent a general hand. It was her benevolent air that had recommended her to Mr Walter King, who had sacked her predecessor for being hoity-toity to patrons whenever business was abnormally good. She was devoted to the theatre. Nobody thought of her apart from the theatre, and in fact she had little private life. Mr Walter King was himself passionately devoted to the theatre, and he expected all the staff to be passionately devoted to the theatre; but whereas his own devotion brought in a large share of the profits, Elaine's devotion brought in only a small fixed salary, which Mr King did not dream of passionately increasing when business grew fabulous. Elaine saw nothing odd in this arrangement.

It was a quarter to ten. The day's work was nearly over.

Elaine's assistant had gone. The entrance-hall and foyer blazed, deserted, with their super-lavish electricity. When an idle programme-girl swung open a door at the end of a vast corridor and peeped forth, Elaine could faintly catch the sound of clapping. She rarely got more of a performance than these brief distant rumours of applause. For her the Rotunda was not an auditorium but a foyer with box-office; and the artists were mere names on bills. She estimated the quality of the applause and glanced at the clock and the timetable to know who was being applauded, for she had to be in a position to inform patrons what artist was 'on' at any given moment. Then she proceeded with the secret counting of notes on a shelf beneath the counter. In view of the absence of a grille to protect the counter and of the prevalence of gangs of robbers in London, her situation with all that money for Mr Walter King might seem perilous. But it was not so in reality. Elaine and her treasure were well guarded by formidable giants and astute dwarfs in the shape of gorgeous doormen and pages. Though he disapproved of grilles, Mr Walter King took no chances with the night's receipts. Elaine was as safe as a priestess in a temple, dedicated, imprisoned, inviolate.

Then a dark and elegant young man in full evening panoply appeared from the street. The guardians saluted him. He saluted Elaine. This unidentified and mysterious gentleman came nearly every night towards ten o'clock. Elaine guessed that he came to witness the performance of the Russian dancer, the incomparably illustrious Feodora.

'Did you keep the *fauteuil* for me, Miss Edar?' (He had picked up her name from somewhere, it seemed.)

She nodded, kindly smiling. She liked the regular visitant, not in the least because he was regular, but because he was dark, elegant, slim, and had a sad, wistful smile. Yes, she had kept the stall for him, despite the fact that if he had not come to claim it she would have had to pay for it out of her own pocket. He usually telephoned just before the rush, and Elaine had accepted the risk of his not coming quite a dozen times. Occasionally, as tonight, he would try to get a box, and if successful would pay for both the box and the stall. And he would show amazing indecision. Tonight she had no box to sell; the sole empty seat in the house was the one she had retained for him; and yet in his rich, low voice he would keep talking about a box, and also she had to repeat to him several times precisely where the stall was in regard to the stage.

At length he paid, raised his hat again, and went off towards the auditorium, followed by her benedictory, sympathetic smile. The head-doorman, his pocket gaping for the harvest of sixpences which he would shortly garner for putting patrons into cars and taxis, winked at her rather broadly, as if to indicate that the dark gentleman was queer in the head. But Elaine gently deprecated the wink, seeing in the dark gentleman a victim of hopeless love for a Russian dancer. Silence fell upon the foyer, whose ceiling was upheld by the immobile figures of pink, nude girls.

Elaine had taken out the self-locking steel cash-drawer from its niche, detached and hidden the telephone, and was about to disappear through the little door behind the counter, when Rachel Gordon hurried up rather breathless from somewhere. 'I'm the publicity lady,' Rachel would introduce herself to the new artists in the wings and in dressing-rooms when she wanted material for piquant press-paragraphs. She did all the day-to-day publicity work for the Rotunda. A pretty Jewess, with full lips and eyes, waved hair, striking clothes, carefully tended complexion, and a general air of knowing all that was worth knowing; not quite young, but far from old! She spent every evening in the theatre, and little in it escaped her attention.

'Feo asked me to give you this note,' said she. 'I'm so glad I've caught you before you'd gone.'

She handed the note, with a characteristic, sparkling glance that was full of chicane and the spirit of plotting. 'Feo!' Thus she familiarly referred to the great, the unique Feodora! But then she managed to be very friendly with all, and she could be highly useful even to the greatest.

As Elaine read the note she showed extreme astonishment. It ran: 'My dear Miss Edar, I give a party tomorrow night at the Fantasy Club; some friends, dancing, fun. Will you come? I do hope. Your obliged Feo.' Indeed the thing was enough to astonish a box-office girl. 'Your obliged.' Elaine knew what that referred to. A fortnight earlier, when a not uncommon state of war existed between Feodora and Mr Walter King, Feodora had been unable to get two free seats for friends. She had most particularly wanted those seats, even if it should be necessary to pay for them. But she was too haughty to tell Mr King that she would pay for them, and so she had herself run round (furs and pearls and all – as described by Rachel for the press) to implore Elaine to allot seats to her even though all seats were sold. And Elaine, by methods known to box-office keepers only, had bestowed upon her the two desired seats – and Mr Walter King not a penny the wiser! Feodora, in the generosity of her impulsive, poetic heart, had not forgotten.

'Shall you come?' asked Rachel, who evidently knew what was in the scrawled note.

'I – I haven't a rag to wear,' answered Elaine, much flustered.

'Oh, stuff!' observed Rachel simply. 'You're always awfully well turned out. Everybody knows that.'

'But evening wear – ' protested Elaine, despite a secret mistrust of Rachel.

'Oh, stuff!' Rachel repeated.

Elaine could scarcely sleep that night. It was an incredible happening. She rose early to look through her wardrobe.

2

The Fantasy Club, scene of Feodora's party, was in Goodge Street, off Tottenham Court Road. Elaine had never heard of it, and indeed had some difficulty in finding it, since its portal was hidden at the end of a long covered passage and showed no signs of festivity. No wonder the conductor of the motor-bus by which she travelled could give her no information about it! In the lobby she saw a printed notice: 'Breakfasts served from 4 a.m.' This frightened her, but she was reassured by the sight of Rachel Gordon in the cloakroom.

Rachel gave the names of sundry high-brow novelists and painters and musicians who regularly frequented the club, and she said that in the art of turning night into day they were the greatest experts in London. Rachel laughed at the nocturnal pretensions of the more famous dancing-clubs – she scorned them as 'bourgeois'. Anyone could join them, but according to Rachel not anyone could join the Fantasy. You had to be someone or the approved friend of someone to be admitted to the Fantasy.

The dancing-room was large, low and very bare – compared to the ornate interiors of the Rotunda. It had no decorations except electric lights in Chinese lanterns, and the costumes of the ladies. These decorations, however, were extremely effective. The room was full; it was also noisy and torrid. Revellers were eating, drinking, dancing, chattering, laughing and giggling, with much gusto.

'There's Feo's table,' said Rachel, pointing to the biggest and busiest table in the place, and led Elaine towards it. Elaine was nervous.

'How sweet of you!' the slim and gorgeous Feo greeted her. 'How sweet you look! No! It is more than sweet. I understand now when Carly does say how you are *exotique*. It is so. Yes. Sit down. Have drink? Have chicken? Or soup? Yes. Soup first.

Rachel, occupy yourself with Miss Edar.' Feodora turned to two young men, who kissed her hand.

Elaine listened eagerly to the confused talk at the table, but, though all laughed or giggled, she heard nothing that struck her as amusing. No doubt the humour was being accomplished in French or Russian, of which languages Elaine had no knowledge. However, all the ladies looked either lovely or strange. She was still very shy, but she was mysteriously happy too – somehow uplifted.

'Who is Carly?' she murmured to Rachel, and Rachel by a discreet turn of the head indicated a young man who stood behind Feodora against the wall. Elaine started and flushed. It was the nightly visitant for whom she reserved stalls. The word 'exotic' in the tiny mouth of Feodora had already exercised Elaine, who could not comprehend how anybody could regard her as deserving of such an adjective. That the nightly visitant should deem her exotic, and should have said so to a high goddess like Feodora, almost disturbed her – while enchanting her! Rachel beckoned to the nightly visitant, who approached.

'Mr Lyeskov,' said Rachel. 'Miss Edar. I think you have met.'

She laughed. Mr Lyeskov blushed.

The next moment Elaine became aware that her hand had been kissed. A unique experience. Hand-kissing was of course 'foreign' and somewhat foolish, but it was surprisingly delicious, even flattering. So this was the young man who, while paying for stalls from which to worship Feodora, had found time to examine herself and to decide that she was exotic. Yes, disturbing! Disturbing!

He now asked her to dance. Could she refuse? How ridiculous! Unfortunately in the dance she could not think of a single thing to say to him. He was a fine dancer, but scarcely cleverer as a talker than Elaine. They just danced, yielded themselves to the music and the movement. It was exquisite.

'You are a natural dancer. You have the gift,' he remarked.

She smiled. She knew that she was a natural dancer. She had no more learnt to dance than she had learnt to breathe; she rarely danced – and only in suburban resorts with one or two dull acquaintances; yet she knew all the steps and never erred, never hesitated. They danced two consecutive dances. As he restored her to the table he asked if he might dance again with her very soon. Feodora called to him.

'How did you get on?' Rachel demanded of Elaine, with a peculiar glance.

'Oh, splendid! He's asked me for another dance.'

'And did you refuse?'

'Ought I?'

'Don't be silly. Can't you see he's mad about you? Why do you suppose he comes to get tickets off you every night? Why do you suppose he got Feo to ask you here tonight? And let me tell you – he may be a French-Russian, but he's very serious and very rich. *He* didn't lose anything in the Revolution, he didn't! Pity he's so shy, isn't it?'

Elaine's face burned again. The fact is, she was overwhelmed, absolutely overwhelmed, as she realised bit by bit that 'Carly' came nightly to the Rotunda not to worship Feodora but to worship her! It was staggering! She was glad when a male performer in Feodora's troupe invited her on to the floor. She did not care for his face nor for his coarse manners, nor yet for his dancing – how different from Carly's! – but he enabled her to escape from Rachel Gordon's enigmatic scrutiny. As she went round the room with the professional dancer something happened to her and she half stumbled and turned wholly pale. It was a night of sensations, blushes and pallors, such a night as she had never before known. The dancer looked at his faltering partner enquiringly, but said no word, and Elaine recovered herself. No one knew, no one could guess, what had happened to her. And after all it was naught. She had only caught sight of

Ned seated at a table with another man, and he had seemed to be somewhat unprosperous and defiant, in his shabby evening-dress. And he looked older, thinner, worn.

Ned was the one man who had entered into that private life of hers, the existence of which none of the patrons of the Rotunda could visualise. It was six years ago, when she was twenty-one, and before her connection with the life of music-halls. Ned was an advertising-agent and lots of things beside – he had had a hand in promoting one or two of the earlier dance clubs. He was up one month and down the next. He had defects, but he had made love to her, proposed to her, been accepted. She gave him all her heart; she learnt rapturously to love love. The world became magical. The date of the wedding was fixed. Then Ned came one day and said that candour was best, and that the sole manly course was to confess to her. What? What? That he had mistaken his feelings. That he had found that he did not care for her 'in that way'. Whereas he did care for Alice 'in that way' and Alice cared for him 'in that way'. That of course he was hers to command, but would it not be better for her sake and for the sake of them all, if she . . . ? He was extremely sorry. He did not and could not defend himself . . . Alice was a friend of hers, had but a few months before been congratulating her on her betrothal to nice Ned. Ned married Alice. And so that was that. Elaine's tragic grief softened gradually into vague regret, and vague regret changed into a vague feeling that perhaps she had done well to lose Ned. Such stories lie buried in the memory of numberless girls who go through life apparently as though butter had never melted in their mouths. And you dig up the stories with difficulty, with amazement . . .

Well, she had caught sight of Ned Haltright.

The next minute his table was empty. She hoped he had not seen her, and could not help thinking that he had. Undoubtedly she had had a shock. But when, after powdering herself anew and drinking some champagne, she put her hand once again in the hand of Carly Lyeskov, and felt his right hand lightly on her back, and resumed the dance with him, the effects of the shock soon disappeared. She glimpsed herself in a mirror and was satisfied with the vision. Idle to deny that she was pretty, had a good figure, or that her frock was not smart! She was as presentable as most, and more so than a lot of them, though her only trinket was a necklace of Chinese-dyed mother-of-pearl. Carly's worship of her blossomed like a flower. It was heavenly to be worshipped, to be able to confer a favour by merely consenting to exist. She had a sense of dominion which intoxicated. And then there was the band, the colours, the movement, the feeling of being surrounded by illustrious and witty artists – she wondered who was who! And Carly was so distinguished. His very shirt-front was a miracle. And he was so deferential.

'May I ask where you live?'

She told him Fulham.

'I suppose you would not let me drive you home in my car?'

Yes, she would – he was really too kind! Romance ! Romance! Soon she was thinking that Carly was unique in the whole world – so sympathetic he was! And he worshipped her. He had gone off his head about her. Triumph! Power! Dizziness! It was silently established between them that they would dance every dance together. And they did. The Fantasy faded to a dim background for their emotions. And Elaine looked with pity at her past life, at the horrid grind and daily work, at her loneliness – because behind her counter she was nearly as lonely as a bus-driver, and at home in her rooms she was terribly lonely. How had she supported it? Could she possibly continue to support it?

At three o'clock, when the gaiety was at its apogee, she said she thought she must go home. Not that she wanted to go home or had any reason for going home. She wanted simply to command him and to prove to the entire Fantasy Club that he was hers to command. She took leave of Feodora, who poured over her a delicious cascade of protests. And Carly did drive her to Fulham – Parson's Green it was. No little 'liberties' in the large, smooth-gliding car, such as are expected and condoned by the primmest maidens after such ecstasies, in such circumstances, at such an hour! Nothing but the deepest respect! Yes, he was 'serious . . .' She leaned forward suddenly and tapped on the window. The car stopped. Mr Lyeskov sprang to the pavement, handed her out, removed his hat, kissed her hand, and was richly rewarded by her smile under the lamp-post. He waited until she had found her latchkey and opened her door. Of course it was a poor little suburban house. But she knew that that didn't matter. It was where she lived. Her presence in it transformed it for him. Another smile from her; another bow from him. She shut the door. The car drove off.

3

Elaine went to bed in a state of ecstatic, blissful excitement. No sooner had she laid herself down than she heard the prolonged trill of the front-door bell in the back-room. She occupied the two rooms which constituted the third or top-floor of the old house. (In earlier days she had had only one room, but destiny had been fairly kind to her.) The front-room was a sort of bed-sitting-room; the back was a kitchen-scullery-dining-room. The floor was her home and held all that she possessed. Compared to many young and ageing women in her situation of life she was affluent and of luxurious habit. Now there were four bells on the front-door, each labelled. Sometimes, and especially at night, visitors got confused and rang the wrong bell. Elaine thought that on this occasion the wrong bell had been rung.

'They'll have to keep on ringing,' she said. After all, the bell did not make a great deal of noise. The bell continued to ring.

'Nobody can possibly be wanting me at this time of night,' she said.

Nevertheless she put on her dressing-gown and opened the

window and looked forth and down. But she could not see who was ringing because of the wide, leaded eave of the old-fashioned porch. She shut the window and shut out the invading chill of the dark night. At length the persistent bell began to exasperate her fatigued nerves, and with an annoyed, apprehensive shrug, she crept step by creaking step all the way downstairs and softly undid the front-door.

Ned Haltright was standing in the porch. She gave a start, and instinctively drew the thin peignoir more tightly round her shoulders. As she did so, she stiffened, looking at him. She was affronted, angered, by this inexcusable visitation. Nothing but sheer good-nature prevented her from shutting the door in Ned's face.

'I saw you at the club – ' he commenced.

'Not so loud, *please*!' She stopped him in a sharp whisper, thinking of her immaculate reputation in the crowded house that so often buzzed with gossip. To have come home at God knows what hour in a car was bad enough, but to receive male callers still later . . . !

'I want to see you. I must talk to you,' Ned whispered plaintively.

'Not now,' she whispered.

'Yes, now.'

She shook her head firmly. 'Fancy coming here now!' she whispered, in still colder reproof. 'And how on earth did you get here, at this time?'

'Walked,' he whispered.

'Walked?' she whispered.

'Yes.'

He must certainly have walked over six miles. The whispering seemed to render them intimate in spite of her aggrieved attitude towards him. It struck her as strange and affecting that she had once been his affianced sweetheart, that they used to kiss each other with long kisses, and that now they were nothing to each other . . . She made a sign for him to enter. She very gently and cautiously closed the door.

'I'm on the top-floor now,' she murmured, scarcely audible.

He nodded. The fanlight over the door let through the ray of the street-lamp, so that the first flight of stairs was fairly plain. The higher flights were dark. But Ned knew the staircase. Ned followed her on tiptoe, and every now and then a stair creaked with a thunderous sound that no prudence of tread could avoid. Elaine had the horrid illusion that behind every door as they passed it women with slanderous tongues were greedily listening.

At the summit of the perilous climb she led him into the kitchen-scullery-dining-room, and found the matches, lit the gas, lit the gas-stove. She put her finger to her lips. They must still exist and communicate without sound. No sound-proof floors in that house! She motioned him to the wicker easy-chair. He sank into it. She looked at him and looked round the room. Happily it was very tidy and cosy. He was pale, pathetic, with his pointed, exhausted, weak-charactered features. He wore a blue Burberry, strapped close at the waist and bulging out above and below over his evening clothes. In his hand he held an ordinary bowler hat. No style! What a contrast with Mr Lyeskov! He had the air of defeat, even of being a prisoner-of-war. And he had walked more than six miles in his madness. Without a word she turned away, lit the gas-ring, and began to make some tea. She had to do it from simple humanity. And there she was with him, sharing surreptitiously the room with him, in nightdress, peignoir and slippers. And their tender intimacy emerged towards them out of the past, indestructible. Somehow, what had been still was. How could she treat him as a stranger? She could not. Moreover, she felt far superior to him in moral force; she felt, despite her resentment, almost protective in a casual condescending way. She had the adoration of Carly Lyeskov at her back.

'Well?' she whispered.

Ned gazed at the rug under his feet. Silence. Hiss of the gas-stove; hiss of the gas-ring; fizzing of the blue-yellow gas-jet within its mantle.

'Well, how's Alice?' she whisperingly questioned, in a rather indifferent, half-quizzing tone, as if saying: 'Well, you got your Alice. How does it work now you've had her six years?'

He whispered solemnly: 'Poor Alice died two years ago, and the baby's two years old. Hadn't you heard?'

She shook her head. She could not speak; her throat was suddenly constricted; tears glittered in her eyes. At length: 'I'm sorry to hear it.' How poor the words! Then after a pause, while Ned stared at the inside of his hat: 'Is it a girl or a boy?'

'A girl.'

'What have you called her?'

'Alice.'

'And how do you manage about the poor little thing?'

'Ah! That's the trouble. How *do* I manage?' He looked up suddenly, and he was crying.

'Ellie' – nobody else had ever called her 'Ellie' – 'Ellie, I made a frightful mistake when I broke it off with you, and I've known it for years. And then when I saw you tonight . . . It was too much for me. Yes. I had to talk to you.' His whispered utterance was so obscure and feeble that she had to guess what he said; but she guessed right. The water boiled. She turned from him again to fill the teapot.

How weak he was! So impulsive! But so enterprising, too! Full of initiative as usual! He had had the wild idea of coming to her and he had come. He had arrived. He had wanted to talk to her, and he was talking to her.

'And how's business?' she asked, extinguishing the gas-ring. She was bound to say something – and something ordinary, banal, off the point.

'Oh, pretty fair,' he whispered. 'Not bad. Changeable, of course. But you rub along, you know.'

She was confirmed in her notion that he was out of luck. He drank the hot tea, which seemed to revive him – he was a man easy to revive and easy to deject. She took some tea herself. As an afterthought she cut some bread-and-butter; she gave him a slice with her hand, as there was no plate save the wooden bread-platter. He ate it savagely, and several more slices. The scene was domestic. The night, the enforced whispering, his trouble, her peignoir, the informality of the little meal, made it domestic. She stood near the fire in order to keep warm in her thin raiment.

'Ellie,' he said, rising vivaciously to put his cup and saucer on the table, and standing near to her, 'I've always been in love with you. I know there's no excuse for me. I didn't treat you right. But there it is. And when I saw you tonight –' He had raised his voice.

'Hsh!' she warned him.

She spoke gently, keeping resentment out of her voice, partly because she was flattered by the realisation of her power over him (and she had the same power over Carly Lyeskov), and partly because he was so wistful and she pitied him in his unhappiness. Nevertheless in her heart she was indignant. And she thought of her independence, of the stability of her position as a self-maintained woman beholden to none. She did not see Elaine Edar abandoning her independent situation for the status of the wife of a Ned Haltright, asking a Ned Haltright for money when she needed it, considering his wishes in regard to her own conduct, sacrificing herself to the baby of the girl who had supplanted her, sharing the material vicissitudes which must inevitably result from his character. He might love her, admire her, but that could not compensate. Moreover the whole idea was absurd, monstrous. His suggestion amounted to effrontery. And Carly Lyeskov existed and worshipped. However, she offered no reasoned reply. Her daily traffic with all sorts of human beings had taught her when to argue and when not to argue.

'Please don't say any more,' she murmured firmly. 'You can't burst out like this.'

'But I've had it on my mind for years, I tell you.'

'Please don't say any more.'

He seemed to wither.

'I'll go. Better go. Sorry I spoke.'

The wicker easy-chair, empty, complained with creakings of the burden which it had had to bear. The dawn began delicately to announce itself in silver-grey gleams through the interstice between the curtains of the window.

'You mustn't go yet,' Elaine whispered.

'Why not?'

'Because it's getting light, and the people on the first floor will be about, and I can't have a man, especially in evening-dress, leaving my rooms at this time. Besides, there's no buses or trams yet. You must wait till everyone's up and people have begun to go up and downstairs, and you must cover up your shirt-front properly. Then you can slip out.' She whispered soberly, with the sagacity of a young woman who has learnt her world. She added: 'I shall lie down. I'm frightfully tired, and you must be too. Try to sleep in the chair.' She left him for the front-room, and locked the door, and dropped on to her bed. She was indeed exhausted, but she could not sleep. Her eyes burned. She reflected that dancers were still dancing at the Fantasy. Then she slept.

4

When she woke the alarm-clock (which never alarmed) showed the hour of ten. The memory of the night gradually re-established itself in her mind. How fortunate that her char-woman came only at eleven-thirty! She thought gladly: 'Yesterday it was the day after tomorrow that I was to see Carly. Now it is tomorrow. Tea at the Regent Palace at five.' It was she who had chosen the Regent Palace. She arose, washed, dressed deliberately, gave particular attention to the toilette of her face. Cautiously she unlocked her door and cautiously went into the back-room. Ned was fast asleep, in a twisted, uncomfortable posture in the wicker-chair. His pallid face had the pathos of a corpse. He appeared tragically defenceless, so much so that she could have cried at the sight of him and at the thought of his weaknesses, his perils, his incompetency to deal with the responsibilities attached to little Alice the baby. Much gas had been burned, but she did not care. She drew the curtains back and the entire room became pathetic – the teacups, the teapot, crumbs on the floor. The image of Carly Lyeskov was obscured in her soul. She turned off the gas-jet. Ned awoke with a jump.

'You're all dressed. Shall I go now?'

'Where's little Alice?'

'She's with some people in Canonbury.'

'Who are they? Relations?'

'No. Not relations. I'm not strong in relations. *You* know that. I think they're very decent people. She seems to be pretty well looked after.'

'Oh, Ned! You must give me the address. I'll go and see her tomorrow morning. I'll have a look at things a bit.'

The images of Carly Lyeskov, automobiles, luxury, distinction, worship, adoration, passion, eternal romance, began to slip away from her. She clutched at them, drew them back, held them fast, hugged them, but the next moment they were wriggling away again like eels.

'Oh, Ellie! There's nobody like you, and there never was. You're an angel and nothing else.'

She wept. She let the tears fall – drop, drop; they slipped down her cheeks and fell into space. Perhaps she was sorry as much for herself as for little Alice and little Alice's father. She saw vistas of effort, struggle, reverses, obstinate recommencings, narrownesses, dependence, despairs, fluttering hopes, quarrels, reconciliations, disillusions and illusions. People would cease to stare at her in the streets of the West End because she would never be in the West End. She would be withdrawn from the vast world of pleasure and excitement and electricity, where tinted statues of nymphs supported heavily carved ceilings on their frail shoulders. Yet an immense peace took possession of her disturbed soul and stilled it.

'This is my fate,' she thought. 'I was born for it. I wasn't really born for the other thing.'

The immense peace in her was warmed and lighted with tenderness, and by the memory of far-off kisses. It was a strange sort of happiness, austere, purposeful, braced; but she was happy. She smiled kindly. Ned advanced towards her. She lifted her chin and stopped him. Did he suppose that things were as simple as all that, that the virgin fortress would yield like that at the first summons of the trumpet? Her smile changed to a look of self-possession and extreme gravity.

'Meet me this afternoon for tea at the Regent Palace, will you?' she said. 'After the matinée. Then you can tell me just how matters stand.'

And Carly Lyeskov went back to his Paris.

KATHERINE MANSFIELD

Kathleen Mansfield Beauchamp (1888–1923), who wrote short stories under the name Katherine Mansfield, was born in Wellington, New Zealand, daughter of a banker, who was later knighted. Her first story was published when she was nine, and later when at Queen's College, London, she edited the college magazine, but her plans then were for a musical career. In 1909 she married George Bowden, but left him after a few days. In 1911 she met John Middleton Murry, whom she married in 1918 when she obtained a divorce from her first husband. Ill-health due to lung trouble made her move about seeking a congenial climate, and she lived at different times in France and in Germany. In 1920 *Bliss and Other Stories* made her famous. Other collections were *The Garden Party* (1922), *The Dove's Nest* (1923), *Something Childish* (1924) and *The Aloe* (1930). In I922 she went to Paris for special treatment and died at Fontainebleau. Her *Poems* were published in 1923 and her autobiographical *Journal* (1927), *Letters* (1928) and *Scrapbook* (1940) were all edited by her husband after her death.

A Dill Pickle

And then, after six years, she saw him again. He was seated at one of those little bamboo tables decorated with a Japanese vase of paper daffodils. There was a tall plate of fruit in front of him, and very carefully, in a way she recognised immediately as his 'special' way, he was peeling an orange.

He must have felt that shock of recognition in her for he looked up and met her eyes. Incredible! He didn't know her! She smiled; he frowned. She came towards him. He closed his eyes an instant, but opening them his face lit up as though he had struck a match in a dark room. He laid down the orange and pushed back his chair, and she took her little warm hand out of her muff and gave it to him.

'Vera!' he exclaimed. 'How strange. Really, for a moment I didn't know you. Won't you sit down? You've had lunch? Won't you have some coffee?'

She hesitated, but of course she meant to.

'Yes, I'd like some coffee.' And she sat down opposite him.

'You've changed. You've changed very much,' he said, staring at her with that eager, lighted look. 'You look so well. I've never seen you look so well before.'

'Really?' She raised her veil and unbuttoned her high fur collar. 'I don't feel very well. I can't bear this weather, you know.'

'Ah, no. You hate the cold . . .'

'Loathe it.' She shuddered. 'And the worst of it is that the older one grows . . .'

He interrupted her. 'Excuse me,' and tapped on the table for the waitress. 'Please bring some coffee and cream.' To her: 'You are sure you won't eat anything? Some fruit, perhaps. The fruit here is very good.'

'No, thanks. Nothing.'

'Then that's settled.' And smiling just a hint too broadly he took up the orange again. 'You were saying – the older one grows – '

'The colder,' she laughed. But she was thinking how well she remembered that trick of his – the trick of interrupting her – and of how it used to exasperate her six years ago. She used to feel then as though he, quite suddenly, in the middle of what she was saying, put his hand over her lips, turned from her, attended to something different, and then took his hand away, and with just the same slightly too broad smile, gave her his attention again . . . Now we are ready. That is settled.

'The colder!' He echoed her words, laughing too. 'Ah, ah.

You still say the same things. And there is another thing about you that is not changed at all – your beautiful voice – your beautiful way of speaking.' Now he was very grave; he leaned towards her, and she smelled the warm, stinging scent of the orange peel. 'You have only to say one word and I would know your voice among all other voices. I don't know what it is – I've often wondered – that makes your voice such a – haunting memory . . . Do you remember that first afternoon we spent together at Kew Gardens? You were so surprised because I did not know the names of any flowers. I am still just as ignorant for all your telling me. But whenever it is very fine and warm, and I see some bright colours – it's awfully strange – I hear your voice saying: "Geranium, marigold and verbena." And I feel those three words are all I recall of some forgotten, heavenly language . . . You remember that afternoon?'

'Oh, yes, very well.' She drew a long, soft breath, as though the paper daffodils between them were almost too sweet to bear. Yet, what had remained in her mind of that particular afternoon was an absurd scene over the tea table. A great many people taking tea in a Chinese pagoda, and he behaving like a maniac about the wasps – waving them away, flapping at them with his straw hat, serious and infuriated out of all proportion to the occasion. How delighted the sniggering tea drinkers had been. And how she had suffered.

But now, as he spoke, that memory faded. His was the truer. Yes, it had been a wonderful afternoon, full of geranium and marigold and verbena, and – warm sunshine. Her thoughts lingered over the last two words as though she sang them.

In the warmth, as it were, another memory unfolded. She saw herself sitting on a lawn. He lay beside her, and suddenly, after a long silence, he rolled over and put his head in her lap.

'I wish,' he said, in a low, troubled voice, 'I wish that I had taken poison and were about to die – here now!'

At that moment a little girl in a white dress, holding a long, dripping water lily, dodged from behind a bush, stared at them, and dodged back again. But he did not see. She leaned over him.

'Ah, why do you say that? I could not say that.'

But he gave a kind of soft moan, and taking her hand he held it to his cheek. 'Because I know I am going to love you too much – far too much. And I shall suffer so terribly, Vera, because you never, never will love me.'

He was certainly far better looking now than he had been then. He had lost all that dreamy vagueness and indecision. Now he had the air of a man who has found his place in life, and fills it with a confidence and an assurance which was, to say the least, impressive. He must have made money, too. His clothes were admirable, and at that moment he pulled a Russian cigarette case out of his pocket.

'Won't you smoke?'

'Yes, I will.' She hovered over them. 'They look very good.'

'I think they are. I get them made for me by a little man in St James's Street. I don't smoke very much. I'm not like you – but when I do, they must be delicious, very fresh cigarettes. Smoking isn't a habit with me; it's a luxury – like perfume. Are you still so fond of perfumes? Ah, when I was in Russia . . . '

She broke in: 'You've really been to Russia?'

'Oh, yes. I was there for over a year. Have you forgotten how we used to talk of going there?'

'No, I've not forgotten.'

He gave a strange half-laugh and leaned back in his chair. 'Isn't it curious. I have really carried out all those journeys that we planned. Yes, I have been to all those places that we talked of, and stayed in them long enough to – as you used to say – "air oneself" in them. In fact, I have spent the last three years of my life travelling all the time. Spain, Corsica, Siberia, Russia, Egypt. The only country left is China, and I mean to go there, too, when the war is over.'

As he spoke, so lightly, tapping the end of his cigarette against the ashtray, she felt the strange beast that had slumbered so long within her bosom stir, stretch itself, yawn, prick up its ears and suddenly bound to its feet and fix its longing, hungry stare upon those faraway places. But all she said was, smiling gently: 'How I envy you.'

He accepted that. 'It has been,' he said, 'very wonderful – especially Russia. Russia was all that we had imagined, and far, far more. I even spent some days on a river boat on the Volga. Do you remember that boatman's song that you used to play?'

'Yes.' It began to play in her mind as she spoke.

'Do you ever play it now?'

'No, I've no piano.'

He was amazed at that. 'But what has become of your beautiful piano?'

She made a little grimace. 'Sold. Ages ago.'

'But you were so fond of music,' he wondered.

'I've no time for it now,' said she.

He let it go at that. 'That river life,' he went on, 'is something quite special. After a day or two you cannot realise that you have ever known another. And it is not necessary to know the language – the life of the boat creates a bond between you and the people that's more than sufficient. You eat with them, pass the day with them, and in the evening there is that endless singing.'

She shivered, hearing the boatman's song break out again loud and tragic, and seeing the boat floating on the darkening river with melancholy trees on either side . . . 'Yes, I should like that,' said she, stroking her muff.

'You'd like almost everything about Russian life,' he said warmly. 'It's so informal, so impulsive, so free without question. And then the peasants are so splendid. They are such human beings – yes, that is it. Even the man who drives your carriage has – has some real part in what is happening. I remember the evening a party of us, two friends of mine and the wife of one of them, went for a picnic by the Black Sea. We took supper and champagne and ate and drank on the grass. And while we were eating the coachman came up. "Have a dill pickle," he said. He wanted to share with us. That seemed to me so right, so – you know what I mean?'

And she seemed at that moment to be sitting on the grass beside the mysteriously Black Sea, black as velvet, and rippling against the banks in silent, velvet waves. She saw the carriage drawn up to one side of the road, and the little group on the grass, their faces and hands white in the moonlight. She saw the pale dress of the woman outspread and her folded parasol, lying on the grass like a huge pearl crochet hook. Apart from them, with his supper in a cloth on his knees, sat the coachman. 'Have a dill pickle,' said he, and although she was not certain what a dill pickle was, she saw the greenish glass jar with a red chilli like a parrot's beak glimmering through. She sucked in her cheeks: the dill pickle was terribly sour . . .

'Yes, I know perfectly what you mean,' she said.

In the pause that followed they looked at each other. In the past when they had looked at each other like that they had felt such a boundless understanding between them that their souls had, as it were, put their arms round each other and dropped into the same sea, content to be drowned, like mournful lovers. But now, the surprising thing was that it was he who held back. He who said: 'What a marvellous listener you are. When you look at me with those wild eyes I feel that I could tell you things that I would never breathe to another human being.'

Was there just a hint of mockery in his voice or was it her fancy? She could not be sure.

'Before I met you,' he said, 'I had never spoken of myself to anybody. How well I remember one night, the night that I brought you the little Christmas tree, telling you all about my childhood. And of how I was so miserable that I ran away and lived under a cart in our yard for two days without being discovered. And you listened, and your eyes shone, and I felt that you had even made the little Christmas tree listen too, as in a fairy story.'

But of that evening she had remembered a little pot of caviare. It had cost seven and sixpence. He could not get over it. Think of it – a tiny jar like that costing seven and sixpence. While she ate it he watched her, delighted and shocked.

'No, really, that is eating money. You could not get seven shillings into a little pot that size. Only think of the profit they must make . . . ' And he had begun some immensely complicated calculations . . . But now goodbye to the caviare. The Christmas tree was on the table, and the little boy lay under the cart with his head pillowed on the yard dog.

'The dog was called Bosun,' she cried delightedly.

But he did not follow. 'Which dog? Had you a dog? I don't remember a dog at all.'

'No, no. I mean the yard dog when you were a little boy.' He laughed and snapped the cigarette case to.

'Was he? Do you know I had forgotten that. It seems such ages ago. I cannot believe that it is only six years. After I had recognised you today – I had to take such a leap – I had to take a leap over my whole life to get back to that time. I was such a kid then.' He drummed on the table. 'I've often thought how I must have bored you. And now I understand so perfectly why you wrote to me as you did – although at the time that letter nearly finished my life. I found it again the other day, and I couldn't help laughing as I read it. It was so clever – such a true picture of me.' He glanced up. 'You're not going?'

She had buttoned her collar again and drawn down her veil.

'Yes, I am afraid I must,' she said, and managed a smile. Now she knew that he had been mocking.

'Ah, no, please,' he pleaded. 'Don't go just for a moment,' and he caught up one of her gloves from the table and clutched at it as if that would hold her. 'I see so few people to talk to nowadays that I have turned into a sort of barbarian,' he said. 'Have I said something to hurt you?'

'Not a bit,' she lied. But as she watched him draw her glove through his fingers, gently, gently, her anger really did die down, and besides, at the moment he looked more like himself of six years ago . . .

'What I really wanted then,' he said softly, 'was to be a sort of carpet – to make myself into a sort of carpet for you to walk on so that you need not be hurt by the sharp stones and the mud that you hated so. It was nothing more positive than that – nothing more selfish. Only I did desire, eventually, to turn into a magic carpet and carry you away to all those lands you longed to see.'

As he spoke she lifted her head as though she drank something; the strange beast in her bosom began to purr . . .

'I felt that you were more lonely than anybody else in the world,' he went on, 'and yet, perhaps, that you were the only person in the world who was really truly alive. Born out of your time,' he murmured, stroking the glove, 'fated.'

Ah, God! What had she done! How had she dared to throw away her happiness like this. This was the only man who had ever understood her. Was it too late? Could it be too late? She was that glove that he held in his fingers . . .

'And then the fact that you had no friends and never had made friends with people. How I understood that, for neither had I. Is it just the same now?'

'Yes,' she breathed. 'Just the same. I am as alone as ever.'

'So am I,' he laughed gently, 'just the same.'

Suddenly with a quick gesture he handed her back the glove and scraped his chair on the floor. 'But what seemed to me so mysterious then is perfectly plain to me now. And to you, too, of course . . . It simply was that we were such egoists, so self-engrossed, so wrapped up in ourselves that we hadn't a corner in our hearts for anybody else. Do you know,' he cried, naïve and hearty, and dreadfully like another side of that old self again, 'I began studying a Mind System when I was in Russia, and I found that we were not peculiar at all. It's quite a well-known form of . . . '

She had gone. He sat there, thunderstruck, astounded beyond words . . . And then he asked the waitress for his bill.

'But the cream has not been touched,' he said. 'Please do not charge me for it.'

MARK TWAIN

Samuel Langhorne Clemens was born in Missouri in 1835, the son of a lawyer. Early in his childhood, the family moved to Hannibal, Missouri – a town which would provide the inspiration for St Petersburg in *Tom Sawyer* and *Huckleberry Finn*. After a period spent as a travelling printer, Clemens became a river pilot on the Mississippi – a time he would look back upon as his happiest. When he turned to writing in his thirties, he adopted the pseudonym Mark Twain ('Mark Twain' is the cry of a Mississippi boatman taking depth measurements, and means 'two fathoms'), and a number of highly successful publications followed, including *The Prince and the Pauper* (1882), *Huckleberry Finn* (1884) and *A Connecticut Yankee* (1889). His later life, however, was marked by personal tragedy and sadness, as well as financial difficulty. In 1894, several businesses in which he had invested failed, and he was declared bankrupt. Over the next fifteen years – during which he managed to regain some measure of financial independence – he saw the deaths of two of his beloved daughters, and his wife. Increasingly bitter and depressed, Twain died in 1910, aged seventy-five.

The Eskimo Maiden's Romance

'Yes, I will tell you anything about my life that you would like to know, Mr Twain,' she said, in her soft voice, and letting her honest eyes rest placidly upon my face, 'for it is kind and good of you to like me and care to know about me.'

She had been absently scraping blubber-grease from her cheeks with a small bone-knife and transferring it to her fur sleeve, while she watched the aurora borealis swing its flaming streamers out of the sky and wash the lonely snow-plain and the templed icebergs with the rich hues of the prism, a spectacle of almost intolerable splendour and beauty; but now she shook off her reverie and prepared to give me the humble little history I had asked for.

She settled herself comfortably on the block of ice which we were using as a sofa, and I made ready to listen.

She was a beautiful creature. I speak from the Eskimo point of view. Others would have thought her a trifle over-plump. She was just twenty years old, and was held to be by far the most bewitching girl in her tribe. Even now, in the open air, with her cumbersome and shapeless fur coat and trousers and boots and vast hood, the beauty of her face at least was apparent; but her figure had to be taken on trust. Among all the guests who came and went, I had seen no girl at her father's hospitable trough who could be called her equal. Yet she was not spoiled. She was sweet and natural and sincere, and if she was aware that she was a belle, there was nothing about her ways to show that she possessed that knowledge.

She had been my daily comrade for a week now, and the better I knew her the better I liked her. She had been tenderly and carefully brought up, in an atmosphere of singularly rare refinement for the polar regions, for her father was the most important man of his tribe and ranked at the top of Eskimo cultivation. I made long dog-sledge trips across the mighty ice floes with Lasca – that was her name – and found her company always pleasant and her conversation agreeable. I went fishing with her, but not in her perilous boat: I merely followed along on the ice and watched her strike her game with her fatally accurate spear. We went sealing together; several times I stood by while she and the family dug blubber from a stranded whale; and once I went part of the way when she was hunting a bear, but turned back before the finish, because at bottom I am afraid of bears.

However, she was ready to begin her story now, and this is what she said: 'Our tribe had always been used to wander about from place to place over the frozen seas, like the other tribes, but my father got tired of that two years ago, and built this great mansion of frozen snow-blocks – look at it; it is seven feet high and three or four times as long as any of the others – and here we have stayed ever since. He was very proud of his house, and that was reasonable; for if you have examined it with care you must have noticed how much finer and completer it is than houses usually are. But if you have not, you must, for you will find it has luxurious appointments that are quite beyond the common. For instance, in that end of it which you have called the "parlour", the raised platform for the accommodation of guests and the family at meals is the largest you have ever seen in any house – is it not so?'

'Yes, you are quite right, Lasca; it is the largest; we have nothing resembling it in even the finest houses in the United States.' This admission made her eyes sparkle with pride and pleasure. I noted that, and took my cue.

'I thought it must have surprised you,' she said. 'And another thing: it is bedded far deeper in furs than is usual; all kinds of furs – seal, sea-otter, silver-grey fox, bear, marten, sable – every kind of fur in profusion; and the same with the ice-block sleeping-benches along the walls, which you call "beds". Are your platforms and sleeping-benches better provided at home?'

'Indeed, they are not, Lasca – they do not begin to be.' That pleased her again. All she was thinking of was the *number* of furs her aesthetic father took the trouble to keep on hand, not their value. I could have told her that those masses of rich furs constituted wealth – or would in my country – but she would not have understood that; those were not the kind of things that ranked as riches with her people. I could have told her that the clothes she had on, or the everyday clothes of the commonest person about her, were worth twelve or fifteen hundred dollars, and that I was not acquainted with anybody at home who wore twelve-hundred-dollar outfits to go fishing in; but she would not have understood it, so I said nothing. She resumed: 'And then the slop-tubs. We have two in the parlour, and two in the rest of the house. It is very seldom that one has two in the parlour. Have you two in the parlour at home?'

The memory of those tubs made me gasp, but I recovered myself before she noticed, and said with effusion: 'Why, Lasca, it is a shame of me to expose my country, and you must not let it go further, for I am speaking to you in confidence; but I give you my word of honour that not even the richest man in the city of New York has two slop-tubs in his drawing-room.'

She clapped her fur-clad hands in innocent delight, and exclaimed: 'Oh, but you cannot mean it, you cannot *mean* it!'

'Indeed, I am in earnest, dear. There is Vanderbilt. Vanderbilt is almost the richest man in the whole world. Now, if I were on my dying bed, I could say to you that not even he has two in his drawing-room. Why, he hasn't even *one* – I wish I may die in my tracks if it isn't true.'

Her lovely eyes stood wide with amazement, and she said, slowly, and with a sort of awe in her voice: 'How strange – how incredible – one is not able to realise it. Is he penurious?'

'No – it isn't that. It isn't the expense he minds, but – er – well, you know, it would look like showing off. Yes, that is it, that is the idea; he is a plain man in his way, and shrinks from display.'

'Why, that humility is right enough,' said Lasca, 'if one does not carry it too far – but what does the place *look* like?'

'Well, necessarily it looks pretty barren and unfinished, but – '

'I should think so! I never heard anything like it. Is it a fine house – that is, otherwise?'

'Pretty fine, yes. It is very well thought of.'

The girl was silent awhile, and sat dreamily gnawing a candle-end, apparently trying to think the thing out. At last she gave her head a little toss and spoke out her opinion with decision: 'Well, to my mind there's a breed of humility which is *itself* a species of showing-off, when you get down to the marrow of it; and when a man is able to afford two slop-tubs in his parlour, and don't do it, it *may* be that he is truly humble-minded, but it's a hundred times more likely that he is just trying to strike the public eye. In my judgement, your Mr Vanderbilt knows what he is about.'

I tried to modify this verdict, feeling that a double slop-tub standard was not a fair one to try everybody by, although a sound enough one in its own habitat; but the girl's head was set, and she was not to be persuaded. Presently she said: 'Do the rich people, with you, have as good sleeping-benches as ours, and made out of as nice broad ice-blocks?'

'Well, they are pretty good – good enough – but they are not made of ice-blocks.'

'I want to know! *Why* aren't they made of ice-blocks?'

I explained the difficulties in the way, and the expensiveness of ice in a country where you have to keep a sharp eye on your ice man or your ice bill will weigh more than your ice. Then she cried out: 'Dear me, do you *buy* your ice?'

'We most surely do, dear.'

She burst into a gale of guileless laughter, and said: 'Oh, I *never* heard of anything so silly! My, there's plenty of it – it isn't worth anything. Why, there is a hundred miles of it in sight, right now. I wouldn't give a fish bladder for the whole of it.'

'Well, it's because you don't know how to value it, you little provincial muggins. If you had it in New York in midsummer, you could buy all the whales in the market with it.'

She looked at me doubtfully, and said: 'Are you speaking true?'

'Absolutely. I take my oath to it.'

This made her thoughtful. Presently she said, with a little sigh: 'I wish *I* could live there.'

I had merely meant to furnish her a standard of values which she could understand; but my purpose had miscarried. I had only given her the impression that whales were cheap and plenty in New York, and set her mouth to watering for them. It seemed best to try to mitigate the evil which I had done, so I said: 'But you wouldn't care for whale meat if you lived there. Nobody does.'

'What!'

'Indeed they don't.'

'*Why* don't they?'

'Wel-l-l, I hardly know. It's prejudice, I think. Yes, that is it – just prejudice. I reckon somebody that hadn't anything better to do started a prejudice against it, some time or other, and once you get a caprice like that fairly going, you know, it will last no end of time.'

'That is true – *perfectly* true,' said the girl, reflectively. 'Like our prejudice against soap, here – our tribes had a prejudice against soap at first, you know.'

I glanced at her to see if she was in earnest. Evidently she was. I hesitated, then said, cautiously: 'But pardon me. They *had* a prejudice against soap? Had?' – with falling inflection.

'Yes – but that was only at first; nobody would eat it.'

'Oh – I understand. I didn't get your idea before.'

She resumed: 'It was just a prejudice. The first time soap came here from the foreigners, nobody liked it; but as soon as it got to be fashionable, everybody liked it, and now everybody has it that can afford it. Are you fond of it?'

'Yes, indeed! I should die if I couldn't have it – especially here. Do you like it?'

'I just *adore* it! Do you like candles?'

'I regard them as an absolute necessity. Are you fond of them?'

Her eyes fairly danced, and she exclaimed: 'Oh! Don't mention it! Candles! – and soap! – '

'And fish-interiors! – '

'And train-oil! – '

'And slush! – '

'And whale-blubber! – '

'And carrion! and sour-krout! and beeswax! and tar! and turpentine! and molasses! and – '

'Don't – oh, don't – I shall expire with ecstasy! – '

'And then serve it all up in a slush-bucket, and invite the neighbours and sail in!'

But this vision of an ideal feast was too much for her, and she swooned away, poor thing. I rubbed snow in her face and brought her to, and after a while got her excitement cooled down. By and by she drifted into her story again: 'So we began to live here, in the fine house. But I was not happy. The reason was this: I was born for love; for me there could be no true happiness without it. I wanted to be loved for myself alone. I wanted an idol, and I wanted to be my idol's idol; nothing less than mutual idolatry would satisfy my fervent nature. I had suitors in plenty – in over-plenty, indeed – but in each and every case they had a fatal defect; sooner or later I discovered that defect – not one of them failed to betray it – it was not me they wanted, but my wealth.'

'Your wealth?'

'Yes; for my father is much the richest man in this tribe – or in any tribe in these regions.'

I wondered what her father's wealth consisted of. It couldn't be the house – anybody could build its mate. It couldn't be the furs – they were not valued. It couldn't be the sledge, the dogs, the harpoons, the boat, the bone fish-hooks and needles, and such things – no, these were not wealth. Then what could it be that made this man so rich and brought this swarm of sordid suitors to his house? It seemed to me, finally, that the best way to find out would be to ask. So I did it. The girl was so manifestly gratified by the question that I saw she had been aching to have me ask it. She was suffering fully as much to tell as I was to know. She snuggled confidentially up to me and said: 'Guess how much he is worth – you never can!'

I pretended to consider the matter deeply, she watching my anxious and labouring countenance with a devouring and delighted interest; and when, at last, I gave it up and begged her to appease my longing by telling me herself how much this polar Vanderbilt was worth, she put her mouth close to my ear and whispered, impressively: '*Twenty-two fish-hooks* – not bone, but foreign – *made out of real iron!*'

Then she sprang back dramatically, to observe the effect. I did my level best not to disappoint her.

I turned pale and murmured: 'Great Scott!'

'It's as true as you live, Mr Twain!'

Lasca, you are deceiving me – you cannot mean it.'

She was frightened and troubled. She exclaimed: 'Mr Twain, every word of it is true – every word. You believe me – you *do* believe me, now *don't* you? *Say* you believe me – *do* say you believe me!'

'I – well, yes, I do – I am *trying* to. But it was all so *sudden*. So sudden and prostrating. You shouldn't do such a thing in that sudden way. It – '

'Oh, I'm *so* sorry! If I had only thought – '

'Well, it's all right, and I don't blame you any more, for you are young and thoughtless, and of course you couldn't foresee what an effect – '

'But oh, dear, I ought certainly to have *known* better. Why – '

'You see, Lasca, if you had said five or six hooks, to start with, and then gradually – '

'Oh, I see, I see – then gradually added one, and then two, and then – ah, why couldn't I have thought of that!'

'Never mind, child, it's all right – I am better now – I shall be over it in a little while. *But* – to spring the whole twenty-two on a person unprepared and not very strong anyway – '

'Oh, it *was* a crime! But you forgive me – say you forgive me. Do!'

After harvesting a good deal of very pleasant coaxing and petting and persuading, I forgave her and she was happy again, and by and by she got under way with her narrative once more. I presently discovered that the family treasury contained still another feature – a jewel of some sort, apparently – and that she was trying to get around speaking squarely about it, lest I get paralysed again. But I wanted to know about that thing, too, and urged her to tell me what it was. She was afraid. But I insisted, and said I would brace myself this time and be prepared, then the shock would not hurt me. She was full of misgivings, but the temptation to reveal that marvel to me and enjoy my astonishment and admiration was too strong for her, and she confessed that she had it on her person, and said that if I was *sure* I was prepared – and so on and so on – and with that she reached into her bosom and brought out a battered square of brass, watching my eyes anxiously the while. I fell over against her in a quite well-acted faint, which delighted her heart and nearly frightened it out of her, too, at the same time. When I came to and got calm, she was eager to know what I thought of her jewel.

'What do I think of it? I think it is the most exquisite thing I ever saw.'

'Do you really? How nice of you to say that! But it *is* a love, now isn't it?'

'Well, I should say so! I'd rather own it than the equator.'

'I thought you would admire it,' she said. 'I think it is *so* lovely. And there isn't another one in all these latitudes. People have come all the way from the Open Polar Sea to look at it. Did you ever see one before?'

I said no, this was the first one I had ever seen. It cost me a pang to tell that generous lie, for I had seen a million of them in my time, this humble jewel of hers being nothing but a battered old New York Central baggage check.

'Land!' said I, 'you don't go about with it on your person this way, alone and with no protection, not even a dog?'

'Ssh! not so loud,' she said. 'Nobody knows I carry it with me. They think it is in papa's treasury. That is where it generally is.'

'Where is the treasury?'

It was a blunt question, and for a moment she looked startled and a little suspicious, but I said: 'Oh, come, don't you be afraid about me. At home we have seventy millions of people, and although I say it myself that shouldn't, there is not one person among them all but would trust me with untold fish-hooks.'

This reassured her, and she told me where the hooks were hidden in the house. Then she wandered from her course to brag a little about the size of the sheets of transparent ice that formed the windows of the mansion, and asked me if I had ever seen their like at home, and I came right out frankly and confessed that I hadn't, which pleased her more than she could find words to dress her gratification in. It was so easy to please her, and such a pleasure to do it, that I went on and said: 'Ah, Lasca, you *are* a fortunate girl! – this beautiful house, this dainty jewel, that rich treasure, all this elegant snow, and sumptuous icebergs and limitless sterility, and public bears and walruses, and noble freedom and largeness, and everybody's admiring eyes upon you, and everybody's homage and respect at your command without the asking; young, rich, beautiful, sought, courted, envied, not a requirement unsatisfied, not a desire ungratified, nothing to wish for that you cannot have – it is immeasurable good fortune! I have seen myriads of girls, but none of these extraordinary things could be truthfully said of any but you alone. And you are worthy – worthy of it all, Lasca – I believe it in my heart.'

It made her infinitely proud and happy to hear me say this, and she thanked me over and over again for that closing remark, and her voice and eyes showed that she was touched. Presently she said: 'Still, it is not all sunshine – there is a cloudy side. The burden of wealth is a heavy one to bear. Sometimes I have doubted if it were not better to be poor – at least not inordinately rich. It pains me to see neighbouring tribesmen stare as they pass by, and overhear them say, reverently, one to another, "There – that is she – the millionaire's daughter!" And sometimes they say sorrowfully, "She is rolling in fish-hooks, and I – I have nothing." It breaks my heart. When I was a child and we were poor, we slept with the door open, if we chose, but now – now we have to have a night watchman. In those days my father was gentle and courteous to all; but now he is austere and haughty, and cannot abide familiarity. Once his family were his sole thought, but now he goes about thinking of his fish-hooks all the time. And his wealth makes everybody cringing and obsequious to him. Formerly nobody laughed at his jokes, they being always stale and far-fetched and poor, and destitute of the one element that can really justify a joke – the element of humour; but now everybody laughs and cackles at those dismal things, and if any fails to do it my father is deeply displeased, and shows it. Formerly his opinion was not sought upon any matter and was not valuable when he volunteered it; it has that infirmity yet, but nevertheless it is sought by all and applauded by all – and he helps do the applauding himself, having no true delicacy and a plentiful want of tact. He has lowered the tone of all our tribe. Once they were a frank and manly race, now they are measly hypocrites, and sodden with servility. In my heart of hearts I hate all the ways of millionaires! Our tribe was once plain, simple folk, and content with the bone fish-hooks of their fathers; now they are eaten up with avarice and would sacrifice every sentiment of honour and honesty to possess themselves of the debasing iron fish-hooks of the foreigner. However, I must not dwell on these sad things. As I have said, it was my dream to be loved for myself alone.

'At last, this dream seemed about to be fulfilled. A stranger came by, one day, who said his name was Kalula. I told him my name, and he said he loved me. My heart gave a great bound of gratitude and pleasure, for I had loved him at sight, and now I said so. He took me to his breast and said he would not wish to be happier than he was now. We went strolling together far over the ice floes, telling all about each other, and planning, oh, the loveliest future! When we were tired at last we sat down and ate, for he had soap and candles and I had brought along some blubber. We were hungry, and nothing was ever so good.

'He belonged to a tribe whose haunts were far to the north, and I found that he had never heard of my father, which rejoiced me exceedingly. I mean he had heard of the millionaire, but had never heard his name – so, you see, he could not know that I was the heiress. You may be sure that I did not tell him. I was loved for myself at last, and was satisfied. I was so happy – oh, happier than you can think!

'By and by it was towards supper time, and I led him home. As we approached our house he was amazed, and cried out: "How splendid! Is *that* your father's?"

'It gave me a pang to hear that tone and see that admiring light in his eye, but the feeling quickly passed away, for I loved him so, and he looked so handsome and noble. All my family of aunts and uncles and cousins were pleased with him, and many guests were called in, and the house was shut up tight and the rag-lamps lighted, and when everything was hot and comfortable and suffocating, we began a joyous feast in celebration of my betrothal.

'When the feast was over, my father's vanity overcame him, and he could not resist the temptation to show off his riches and let Kalula see what grand good fortune he had stumbled into – and mainly, of course, he wanted to enjoy the poor man's amazement. I could have cried – but it would have done no good to try to dissuade my father, so I said nothing, but merely sat there and suffered.

'My father went straight to the hiding place, in full sight of everybody, and got out the fish-hooks and brought them and flung them scatteringly over my head, so that they fell in glittering confusion on the platform at my lover's knee.

'Of course, the astounding spectacle took the poor lad's breath away. He could only stare in stupid astonishment, and wonder how a single individual could possess such incredible riches. Then presently he glanced brilliantly up and exclaimed: "Ah, it is *you* who are the renowned millionaire!"

'My father and all the rest burst into shouts of happy laughter, and when my father gathered the treasure carelessly up as if it might be mere rubbish and of no consequence, and carried it back to its place, poor Kalula's surprise was a study. He said: "Is it possible that you put such things away without counting them?"

'My father delivered a vainglorious horse-laugh, and said: "Well, truly, a body may know *you* have never been rich, since a mere matter of a fish-hook or two is such a mighty matter in your eyes."

'Kalula was confused, and hung his head, but said: "Ah, indeed, sir, I was never worth the value of the barb of one of those precious things, and I have never seen any man before who was so rich in them as to render the counting of his hoard worthwhile, since the wealthiest man I have ever known, till now, was possessed of but three."

'My foolish father roared again with jejune delight, and allowed the impression to remain that he was not accustomed to count his hooks and keep sharp watch over them. He was showing off, you see. Count them? Why, he counted them every day!

'I had met and got acquainted with my darling just at dawn; I had brought him home just at dark, three hours afterwards – for the days were shortening towards the six-months night at that time. We kept up the festivities many hours; then, at last, the guests departed and the rest of us distributed ourselves along the walls on sleeping-benches, and soon all were steeped in dreams but me. I was too happy, too excited, to sleep. After I had lain quiet a long, long time, a dim form passed by me and was swallowed up in the gloom that pervaded the farther end of the house. I could not make out who it was, or whether it was man or woman. Presently that figure or another one passed me going the other way. I wondered what it all meant, but wondering did no good; and while I was still wondering, I fell asleep.

'I do not know how long I slept, but at last I came suddenly broad awake and heard my father say in a terrible voice, "By the great Snow God, there's a fish-hook gone!" Something told me that that meant sorrow for me, and the blood in my veins turned cold. The presentiment was confirmed in the same instant: my father shouted, "Up, everybody, and seize the stranger!" Then there was an outburst of cries and curses from all sides, and a wild rush of dim forms through the obscurity. I flew to my beloved's help, but what could I do but wait and wring my hands? – he was already fenced away from me by a living wall and he was being bound hand and foot. Not until he was secured would they let me get to him. I flung myself upon his poor insulted form and cried my grief out upon his breast, while my father and all my family scoffed at me and heaped threats and shameful epithets upon him. He bore his ill usage with a tranquil dignity which endeared him to me more than ever, and made me proud and happy to suffer with him and for him. I heard my father order that the elders of the tribe be called together to try my Kalula for his life.

' "What?" I said, "before any search has been made for the lost hook?"

' "Lost hook!" they all shouted, in derision; and my father added, mockingly, "Stand back, everybody, and be properly serious – she is going to hunt up that *lost* hook; oh, without doubt she will find it!" – whereat they all laughed again.

'I was not disturbed – I had no fears, no doubts. I said: "It is for you to laugh now; it is your turn. But ours is coming; wait and see."

'I got a rag-lamp. I thought I should find that miserable thing in one little moment; and I set about the matter with such confidence that those people grew grave, beginning to suspect that perhaps they had been too hasty. But, alas and alas! – oh, the bitterness of that search! There was deep silence while one might count his fingers ten or twelve times, then my heart began to sink, and around me the mockings began again, and grew steadily louder and more assured, until at last, when I gave up, they burst into volley after volley of cruel laughter.

'None will ever know what I suffered then. But my love was my support and my strength, and I took my rightful place at my Kalula's side, and put my arm about his neck, and whispered in his ear, saying: "You are innocent, my own – that I know; but say it to me yourself, for my comfort, then I can bear whatever is in store for us.'

'He answered: "As surely as I stand upon the brink of death at this moment, I am innocent. Be comforted, then, O bruised heart; be at peace, O thou breath of my nostrils, life of my life!"

' "Now, then, let the elders come!" – and as I said the words there was a gathering sound of crunching snow outside, and then a vision of stooping forms filing in at the door – the elders.

'My father formally accused the prisoner, and detailed the happenings of the night. He said that the watchman was outside the door, and that in the house were none but the family and the stranger. "Would the family steal their own property?"

'He paused. The elders sat silent many minutes; at last, one after another said to his neighbour, "This looks bad for the stranger" – sorrowful words for me to hear. Then my father sat down. Oh, miserable, miserable me! at that very moment I could have proved my darling innocent, but I did not know it!

'The chief of the court asked: "Is there any here to defend the prisoner?"

'I rose and said: "Why should *he* steal that hook, or any or all of them? In another day he would have been heir to the whole!"

'I stood waiting. There was a long silence, the steam from the many breaths rising about me like a fog. At last, one elder after another nodded his head slowly several times and muttered, "There is force in what the child has said." Oh, the heartlift that was in those words! – so transient, but oh, so precious! I sat down.

' "If any would say further, let him speak now, or after hold his peace," said the chief of the court.

'My father rose and said: "In the night a form passed by me in the gloom, going towards the treasury, and presently returned. I think, now, it was the stranger."

'Oh, I was like to swoon! I had supposed that that was my secret; not the grip of the great Ice God himself could have dragged it out of my heart.

The chief of the court said sternly to my poor Kalula: "Speak!"

'Kalula hesitated, then answered: "It was I. I could not sleep for thinking of the beautiful hooks. I went there and kissed them and fondled them, to appease my spirit and drown it in a harmless joy, then I put them back. I may have dropped one, but I stole none."

'Oh, a fatal admission to make in such a place! There was an awful hush. I knew he had pronounced his own doom, and that all was over. On every face you could see the words hieroglyphed: "It is a confession! – and paltry, lame and thin."

'I sat drawing in my breath in faint gasps – and waiting. Presently, I heard the solemn words I knew were coming; and each word, as it came, was a knife in my heart: "It is the command of the court that the accused be subjected to the *trial by water*."

'Oh, curses be upon the head of him who brought "trial by

water" to our land! It came, generations ago, from some far country that lies none knows where. Before that, our fathers used augury and other unsure methods of trial, and doubtless some poor, guilty creatures escaped with their lives sometimes; but it is not so with trial by water, which is an invention by wiser men than we poor, ignorant savages are. By it the innocent are proved innocent, without doubt or question, for they drown; and the guilty are proven guilty with the same certainty, for they do not drown. My heart was breaking in my bosom, for I said, "He is innocent, and he will go down under the waves and I shall never see him more."

'I never left his side after that. I mourned in his arms all the precious hours, and he poured out the deep stream of his love upon me, and oh, I was so miserable and so happy! At last, they tore him from me, and I followed sobbing after them, and saw them fling him into the sea – then I covered my face with my hands. Agony? Oh, I know the deepest deeps of that word!

'The next moment the people burst into a shout of malicious joy, and I took away my hands, startled. Oh, bitter sight – he was *swimming*!

'My heart turned instantly to stone, to ice. I said, "He was guilty, and he lied to me!"

'I turned my back in scorn and went my way homeward.

'They took him far out to sea and set him on an iceberg that was drifting southward in the great waters. Then my family came home, and my father said to me: "Your thief sent his dying message to you, saying, 'Tell her I am innocent, and that all the days and all the hours and all the minutes while I starve and perish I shall love her and think of her and bless the day that gave me sight of her sweet face.' Quite pretty, even poetical!"

'I said, "He is dirt – let me never hear mention of him again." And oh, to think – he *was* innocent all the time!

'Nine months – nine dull, sad months – went by, and at last

came the day of the Great Annual Sacrifice, when all the maidens of the tribe wash their faces and comb their hair. With the first sweep of my comb, out came the fatal fish-hook from where it had been all those months nestling, and I fell fainting into the arms of my remorseful father! Groaning, he said, "We murdered him, and I shall never smile again!" He has kept his word. Listen: from that day to this not a month goes by that I do not comb my hair. But oh, where is the good of it all now!'

So ended the poor maid's humble little tale – whereby we learn that, since a hundred million dollars in New York and twenty-two fish-hooks on the border of the Arctic Circle represent the same financial supremacy, a man in straitened circumstances is a fool to stay in New York when he can buy ten cents' worth of fish-hooks and emigrate.

EDGAR ALLAN POE

Edgar Poe was born in Boston in 1809 to travelling actors David Poe and Elizabeth Arnold Hopkins. His mother died in December 1811 and his father died or disappeared soon afterwards, leading to Edgar's being brought up by John Allan, a prosperous Virginian merchant. Five of his formative years were spent with the Allans in England. On their return to the States, Edgar attended the University of Virginia before enlisting as a private soldier. He published his first poems in 1827 but it was not until he was discharged from the army and won a literary prize for his tale 'MS Found in a Bottle' that he started to achieve fame as a short-story writer. He gained the position of editor at the *Southern Literary Messenger* and distinguished himself writing journalism, literary criticism, stories and poems. Poe had his greatest successes in 1845 when 'The Raven' and a new collection of his *Tales* were published to national acclaim. His wife Virginia, a cousin whom he had married when she was only thirteen, died early and this led to the depression and reliance on drink that have scarred his reputation and dominated the interpretation of his work. He himself died in mysterious circumstances in 1849 and the details of his biography remain controversial and disputed.

The Assignation

VENICE

Stay for me there! I will not fail
To meet thee in that hollow vale.

HENRY KING, Bishop of Chichester
Exequy on the death of his wife

Ill-fated and mysterious man! – bewildered in the brilliancy of thine own imagination and fallen in the flames of thine own youth! Again in fancy I behold thee! Once more thy form hath risen before me! – not – oh, not as thou art – in the cold valley and shadow – but as thou *shouldst be* – squandering away a life of magnificent meditation in that city of dim visions, thine own Venice – which is a star-beloved Elysium of the sea, and the wide windows of whose Palladian palaces look down with a deep and bitter meaning upon the secrets of her silent waters. Yes! I repeat it – as thou *shouldst be*. There are surely other worlds than this – other thoughts than the thoughts of the multitude – other speculations than the speculations of the sophist. Who then shall call thy conduct into question? who blame thee for thy visionary hours, or denounce those occupations as a wasting away of life, which were but the overflowings of thine everlasting energies?

It was at Venice, beneath the covered archway there called the Ponte di Sospiri, that I met for the third or fourth time the person of whom I speak. It is with a confused recollection that I bring to mind the circumstances of that meeting. Yet I remember – ah! how should I forget? – the deep midnight, the Bridge of Sighs, the beauty of a woman, and the Genius of Romance that stalked up and down the narrow canal.

It was a night of unusual gloom. The great clock of the Piazza had sounded the fifth hour of the Italian evening. The square of the Campanile lay silent and deserted, and the lights in the old Ducal Palace were dying fast away. I was returning home from the Piazetta, by way of the Grand Canal. But as my gondola arrived opposite the mouth of the canal San Marco, a female voice from its recesses broke suddenly upon the night in one wild, hysterical and long continued shriek. Startled at the sound, I sprang upon my feet, while the gondolier, letting slip his single oar, lost it in the pitchy darkness beyond a chance of recovery, and we were consequently left to the guidance of the current which here sets from the greater into the smaller channel. Like some huge and sable-feathered condor, we were slowly drifting down towards the Bridge of Sighs, when a thousand flambeaux, flashing from the windows and down the staircases of the Ducal Palace, turned all at once that deep gloom into livid and preternatural day.

A child, slipping from the arms of its own mother, had fallen from an upper window of the lofty structure into the deep and dim canal. The quiet waters had closed placidly over their victim; and, although my own gondola was the only one in sight, many a stout swimmer, already in the stream, was seeking in vain upon the surface the treasure which was to be found, alas! only within the abyss. Upon the broad black marble flagstones at the entrance of the palace, and a few steps above the water, stood a figure which none who then saw can have ever since forgotten. It was the Marchesa Aphrodite – the adoration of all Venice – the gayest of the gay – the most lovely where all were beautiful – but still the young wife of the old and intriguing Mentoni, and the mother of that fair child, her first and only one, who now deep beneath the murky water was thinking in bitterness of heart upon her sweet caresses, and exhausting its little life in struggles to call upon her name.

She stood alone. Her small, bare and silvery feet gleamed in the black mirror of marble beneath her. Her hair, not as yet more than half loosened for the night from its ballroom array, clustered, amid a shower of diamonds, round and round her classical head, in curls like those of the young hyacinth. A snowy-white and gauze-like drapery seemed to be nearly the sole covering to her delicate form; but the midsummer and midnight air was hot, sullen and still, and no motion in the statue-like form itself stirred even the folds of that raiment of very vapour which hung around it as the heavy marble hangs around the Niobe. Yet – strange to say! – her large lustrous eyes were not turned downwards upon that grave wherein her brightest hope lay buried – but riveted in a widely different direction! The prison of the Old Republic is, I think, the stateliest building in all Venice – but how could that lady gaze so fixedly upon it, when beneath her lay stifling her only child? Yon dark, gloomy niche, too, yawns right opposite her chamber window – what, then, *could* there be in its shadows – in its architecture – in its ivy-wreathed and solemn cornices – that the Marchesa di Mentoni had not wondered at a thousand times before? Nonsense! – Who does not remember that, at such a time as this, the eye, like a shattered mirror, multiplies the images of its sorrow, and sees in innumerable far off places, the woe which is close at hand?

Many steps above the Marchesa, and within the arch of the water-gate, stood, in full dress, the Satyr-like figure of Mentoni himself. He was occasionally occupied in thrumming a guitar, and seemed ennuyé to the very death, as at intervals he gave directions for the recovery of his child. Stupefied and aghast, I had myself no power to move from the upright position I had assumed upon first hearing the shriek, and must have presented to the eyes of the agitated group a spectral and ominous appearance, as with pale countenance and rigid limbs, I floated down among them in that funereal gondola.

All efforts proved in vain. Many of the most energetic in the search were relaxing their exertions and yielding to a gloomy sorrow. There seemed but little hope for the child; (how much less than for the mother!) but now, from the interior of that dark niche which has been already mentioned as forming a part of the Old Republican prison, and as fronting the lattice of the Marchesa, a figure muffled in a cloak, stepped out within reach of the light, and, pausing a moment upon the verge of the giddy descent, plunged headlong into the canal. As, in an instant afterwards, he stood with the still living and breathing child within his grasp upon the marble flagstones by the side of the Marchesa, his cloak, heavy with the drenching water, became unfastened, and, falling in folds about his feet, discovered to the wonder-stricken spectators the graceful person of a very young man, with the sound of whose name the greater part of Europe was then ringing.

No word spoke the deliverer. But the Marchesa! She will now receive her child – she will press it to her heart – she will cling to its little form, and smother it with her caresses. Alas! *another's* arms have taken it from the stranger – *another's* arms have taken it away, and borne it afar off, unnoticed, into the palace! And the Marchesa! Her lip – her beautiful lip trembles: tears are gathering in her eyes – those eyes which, like Pliny's acanthus, are 'soft and almost liquid'. Yes! tears are gathering in those eyes – and see! the entire woman thrills throughout the soul, and the statue has started into life! The pallor of the marble countenance, the swelling of the marble bosom, the very purity of the marble feet, we behold suddenly flushed over with a tide of ungovernable crimson; and a slight shudder quivers about her delicate frame, as a gentle air at Napoli about the rich silver lilies in the grass.

Why should that lady blush! To this demand there is no answer – except that, having left, in the eager haste and terror of a mother's heart, the privacy of her own boudoir, she has neglected to enthrall her tiny feet in their slippers, and utterly forgotten to throw over her Venetian shoulders that drapery which is their due. What other possible reason could there have been for her so blushing? – for the glance of those wild appealing eyes? for the unusual tumult of that throbbing bosom? – for the convulsive pressure of that trembling hand? – that hand which fell, as Mentoni turned into the palace, accidentally, upon the hand of the stranger. What reason could there have been for the low, the singularly low, tone of those unmeaning words which the lady uttered hurriedly in bidding him adieu? 'Thou hast conquered – ' she said, or the murmurs of the water deceived me – 'thou hast conquered – one hour after sunrise – we shall meet – so let it be!'

* * *

The tumult had subsided, the lights had died away within the palace, and the stranger, whom I now recognised, stood alone upon the flags. He shook with inconceivable agitation, and his eye glanced around in search of a gondola. I could not do less than offer him the service of my own; and he accepted the civility. Having obtained an oar at the water-gate, we proceeded together to his residence, while he rapidly recovered his self-possession, and spoke of our former slight acquaintance in terms of great apparent cordiality.

There are some subjects upon which I take pleasure in being minute. The person of the stranger – let me call him by this title, who to all the world was still a stranger – the person of the stranger is one of these subjects. In height he might have been below rather than above the medium size: although there were moments of intense passion when his frame actually *expanded* and belied the assertion. The light, almost slender symmetry of his figure, promised more of that ready activity which he evinced at the Bridge of Sighs, than of that Herculean strength which he has been known to wield without an effort, upon occasions of more dangerous emergency. With the mouth and chin of a deity – singular, wild, full, liquid eyes, whose shadows varied from pure hazel to intense and brilliant jet – and a profusion of curling, black hair, from which a forehead of unusual breadth gleamed forth at intervals all light and ivory – his were features than which I have seen none more classically regular, except, perhaps, the marble ones of the Emperor Commodus. Yet his countenance was, nevertheless, one of those which all men have seen at some period of their lives, and have never afterwards seen again. It had no peculiar – it had no settled predominant expression to be fastened upon the memory; a countenance seen and instantly forgotten – but forgotten with a vague and never-ceasing desire of recalling it to mind. Not that the spirit of each rapid passion failed, at any time, to throw its own distinct image upon the mirror of that face – but that the mirror, mirror-like, retained no vestige of the passion, when the passion had departed.

Upon my leaving him on the night of our adventure, he solicited me, in what I thought an urgent manner, to call upon him *very* early the next morning. Shortly after sunrise, I found myself accordingly at his Palazzo, one of those huge structures of gloomy, yet fantastic pomp, which tower above the waters of the Grand Canal in the vicinity of the Rialto. I was shown up a broad winding staircase of mosaics, into an apartment whose unparalleled splendour burst through the opening door with an actual glare, making me blind and dizzy with luxuriousness.

I knew my acquaintance to be wealthy. Report had spoken of his possessions in terms which I had even ventured to call terms of ridiculous exaggeration. But as I gazed about me, I could not bring myself to believe that the wealth of any subject in Europe could have supplied the princely magnificence which burned and blazed around.

Although, as I say, the sun had arisen, yet the room was still brilliantly lighted up. I judged from this circumstance, as well as from an air of exhaustion in the countenance of my friend, that he had not retired to bed during the whole of the preceding night. In the architecture and embellishments of the chamber, the evident design had been to dazzle and astound. Little attention had been paid to the *decora* of what is technically called *keeping*, or to the proprieties of nationality. The eye wandered from object to object, and rested upon none – neither the *grotesques* of the Greek painters, nor the sculptures of the best Italian days, nor the huge carvings of untutored Egypt. Rich draperies in every part of the room trembled to the vibration of low, melancholy music, whose origin was not to be discovered. The senses were oppressed by mingled and conflicting perfumes, reeking up from strange convolute censers, together with multitudinous flaring and flickering tongues of emerald and violet fire. The rays of the newly risen sun poured in upon the whole, through windows formed each of a single pane of crimson-tinted glass. Glancing to and fro, in a thousand reflections, from curtains which rolled from their cornices like cataracts of molten silver, the beams of natural glory mingled at length fitfully with the artificial light, and lay weltering in subdued masses upon a carpet of rich, liquid-looking cloth of Chile gold.

'Ha! ha! ha! – ha! ha! ha!' – laughed the proprietor, motioning me to a seat as I entered the room, and throwing himself back at full length upon an ottoman. 'I see,' said he, perceiving that I could not immediately reconcile myself to the *bienséance* of so singular a welcome – 'I see you are astonished at my apartment – at my statues – my pictures – my originality of conception in architecture and upholstery – absolutely drunk, eh? with my magnificence? But pardon me, my dear sir' (here his tone of voice dropped to the very spirit of cordiality), 'pardon me for my uncharitable laughter. You appeared so *utterly* astonished. Besides, some things are so completely ludicrous that a man *must* laugh or die. To die laughing must be the most glorious of all glorious deaths! Sir Thomas More – a very fine man was Sir Thomas More – Sir Thomas More died laughing, you remember. Also in the *Absurdities* of Ravisius Textor, there is a long list of characters who came to the same magnificent end.

Do you know, however,' continued he musingly, 'that at Sparta (which is now Palaeochori), at Sparta, I say, to the west of the citadel, among a chaos of scarcely visible ruins, is a kind of *socle*, upon which are still legible the letters ΛΑΣΜ. They are undoubtedly part of ΓΕΛΑΣΜΑ. Now at Sparta were a thousand temples and shrines to a thousand different divinities. How exceedingly strange that the altar of Laughter should have survived all the others! But in the present instance,' he resumed, with a singular alteration of voice and manner, 'I have no right to be merry at your expense. You might well have been amazed. Europe cannot produce anything so fine as this, my little regal cabinet. My other apartments are by no means of the same order; mere *ultras* of fashionable insipidity. This is better than fashion – is it not? Yet this has but to be seen to become the rage – that is, with those who could afford it at the cost of their entire patrimony. I have guarded, however, against any such profanation. With one exception you are the only human being, besides myself and my valet, who has been admitted within the mysteries of these imperial precincts since they have been bedizened as you see!'

I bowed in acknowledgement; for the overpowering sense of splendour and perfume and music, together with the unexpected eccentricity of his address and manner, prevented me from expressing, in words, my appreciation of what I might have construed into a compliment.

'Here,' he resumed, arising and leaning on my arm as he sauntered around the apartment, 'here are paintings from the Greeks to Cimabue, and from Cimabue to the present hour. Many are chosen, as you see, with little deference to the opinions of Virtû. They are all, however, fitting tapestry for a chamber such as this. Here too, are some *chefs d'œuvre* of the unknown great – and here unfinished designs by men, celebrated in their day, whose very names the perspicacity of the academies has left to silence and to me. What think you,' said he, turning abruptly as he spoke – 'what think you of this Madonna della Pietà?'

'It is Guido's own!' I said with all the enthusiasm of my nature, for I had been poring intently over its surpassing loveliness. 'It is Guido's own! – how *could* you have obtained it? – she is undoubtedly in painting what the Venus is in sculpture.'

'Ha!' said he thoughtfully, 'the Venus – the beautiful Venus – the Venus of the Medici? – she of the diminutive head and the gilded hair? Part of the left arm' (here his voice dropped so as to be heard with difficulty) 'and all the right are restorations, and in the coquetry of that right arm lies, I think, the quintessence of all affectation. Give *me* the Canova! The Apollo, too! – is a copy – there can be no doubt of it – blind fool that I am, who cannot behold the boasted inspiration of the Apollo! I cannot help – pity me! – I cannot help preferring the Antinous. Was it not Socrates who said that the statuary found his statue in the block of marble? Then Michelangelo was by no means original in his couplet –

> Non ha l'ottimo artista alcun concetto
> Che un marmo solo in se non circonscriva.'

It has been, or should be remarked, that, in the manner of the true gentleman, we are always aware of a difference from the bearing of the vulgar, without being at once precisely able to determine in what such difference consists. Allowing the remark to have applied in its full force to the outward demeanor of my acquaintance, I felt it, on that eventful morning, still more fully applicable to his moral temperament and character. Nor can I better define that peculiarity of spirit which seemed to place him so essentially apart from all other human beings than by calling it a *habit* of intense and continual thought, pervading even his most trivial actions – intruding upon his moments of dalliance – and interweaving itself with his very flashes of merriment – like adders which writhe from out the eyes of the grinning masks in the cornices around the temples of Persepolis.

I could not help, however, repeatedly observing, through the mingled tone of levity and solemnity with which he rapidly descanted upon matters of little importance, a certain air of trepidation – a degree of nervous *unction* in action and in speech – an unquiet excitability of manner which appeared to me at all times unaccountable, and upon some occasions even filled me with alarm. Frequently, too, pausing in the middle of a sentence whose commencement he had apparently forgotten, he seemed to be listening in the deepest attention, as if either in momentary expectation of a visiter, or to sounds which must have had existence in his imagination alone.

It was during one of these reveries or pauses of apparent abstraction that, in turning over a page of the poet and scholar Politian's beautiful tragedy *The Orfeo* (the first native Italian tragedy), which lay near me upon an ottoman, I discovered a passage underlined in pencil. It was a passage towards the end of the third act – a passage of the most heart-stirring excitement – a passage which, although tainted with impurity, no man shall read without a thrill of novel emotion – no woman without a sigh. The whole page was blotted with fresh tears, and upon the opposite interleaf were the following English lines, written in a hand so very different from the peculiar characters of my acquaintance that I had some difficulty in recognising it as his own.

Thou wast that all to me, love,
  For which my soul did pine –
A green isle in the sea, love,
  A fountain and a shrine,
All wreathed with fairy fruits and flowers;
  And all the flowers were mine.

Ah, dream too bright to last;
  Ah, starry Hope that didst arise
But to be overcast!
  A voice from out the Future cries,

'On! On!' – but o'er the Past
 (Dim gulf!) my spirit hovering lies,
Mute, motionless, aghast!

For alas! alas! with me
 The light of life is o'er.
'No more – no more – no more'
 (Such language holds the solemn sea
To the sands upon the shore)
 Shall bloom the thunder-blasted tree,
Or the stricken eagle soar!

Now all my hours are trances;
 And all my nightly dreams
Are where thy grey eye glances,
 And where thy footstep gleams,
In what ethereal dances,
 By what Italian streams.

Alas! for that accursed time
 They bore thee o'er the billow,
From Love to titled age and crime,
 And an unholy pillow –
From me, and from our misty clime,
 Where weeps the silver willow!

That these lines were written in English – a language with which I had not believed their author acquainted – afforded me little matter for surprise. I was too well aware of the extent of his acquirements, and of the singular pleasure he took in concealing them from observation, to be astonished at any similar discovery; but the place of date, I must confess, occasioned me no little amazement. It had been originally written *London*, and afterwards carefully overscored – not, however, so effectually as to conceal the word from a scrutinising eye. I say this occasioned me no little amazement; for I well remember that, in a former conversation with my friend, I particularly enquired if he had at any time met in London the Marchesa di Mentoni (who for some years previous to her marriage had resided in that city), when his answer, if I mistake not, gave me to understand that he had never visited the metropolis of Great Britain. I might as well here mention that I have more than once heard (without of course giving credit to a report involving so many improbabilities) that the person of whom I speak was not only by birth, but in education, an *Englishman*.

'There is one painting,' said he, without being aware of my notice of the tragedy – 'there is still one painting which you have not seen.' And throwing aside a drapery, he discovered a full-length portrait of the Marchesa Aphrodite.

Human art could have done no more in the delineation of her superhuman beauty. The same ethereal figure which stood before me the preceding night upon the steps of the Ducal Palace stood before me once again. But in the expression of the countenance, which was beaming all over with smiles, there still lurked (incomprehensible anomaly!) that fitful stain of melancholy which will ever be found inseparable from the perfection of the beautiful. Her right arm lay folded over her bosom. With her left she pointed downward to a curiously fashioned vase. One small, fairy foot, alone visible, barely touched the earth – and, scarcely discernible in the brilliant atmosphere which seemed to encircle and enshrine her loveliness, floated a pair of the most delicately imagined wings. My glance fell from the painting to the figure of my friend, and the vigorous words of Chapman's *Bussy D'Ambois* quivered instinctively upon my lips:

> 'He is up
> There like a Roman statue! He will stand
> Till Death hath made him marble!'

'Come!' he said at length, turning towards a table of richly enamelled and massive silver, upon which were a few goblets fantastically stained, together with two large Etruscan vases, fashioned in the same extraordinary model as that in the foreground of the portrait, and filled with what I supposed to be Johannisberger. 'Come!' he said abruptly, 'let us drink! It is early – but let us drink. It is *indeed* early,' he continued, musingly, as a cherub with a heavy golden hammer made the apartment ring with the first hour after sunrise – 'It is *indeed* early, but what matters it? let us drink! Let us pour out an offering to yon solemn sun which these gaudy lamps and censers are so eager to subdue!' And, having made me pledge him in a bumper, he swallowed in rapid succession several goblets of the wine.

'To dream,' he continued, resuming the tone of his desultory conversation, as he held up to the rich light of a censer one of the magnificent vases – 'to dream has been the business of my life. I have therefore framed for myself, as you see, a bower of dreams. In the heart of Venice could I have erected a better? You behold around you, it is true, a medley of architectural embellishments. The chastity of Ionia is offended by antediluvian devices, and the sphynxes of Egypt are outstretched upon carpets of gold. Yet the effect is incongruous to the timid alone. Proprieties of place, and especially of time, are the bugbears which terrify mankind from the contemplation of the magnificent. Once I was myself a decorist; but that sublimation of folly has palled upon my soul. All this is now the fitter for my purpose. Like these arabesque censers, my spirit is writhing in fire, and the delirium of this scene is fashioning me for the wilder visions of that land of real dreams whither I am now rapidly departing.' He here paused abruptly, bent his head to his bosom, and seemed to listen to a sound which I could not hear. At length, erecting his frame, he looked upwards and ejaculated the lines of the Bishop of Chichester:

Stay for me there! I will not fail
To meet thee in that hollow vale.

In the next instant, confessing the power of the wine, he threw himself at full length upon an ottoman.

A quick step was now heard upon the staircase, and a loud knock at the door rapidly succeeded. I was hastening to anticipate a second disturbance, when a page of Mentoni's household burst into the room, and faltered out, in a voice choking with emotion, the incoherent words, 'My mistress! – my mistress! – poisoned! – poisoned! Oh beautiful – oh beautiful Aphrodite!'

Bewildered, I flew to the ottoman, and endeavored to arouse the sleeper to a sense of the startling intelligence. But his limbs were rigid – his lips were livid – his lately beaming eyes were riveted in *death*. I staggered back towards the table – my hand fell upon a cracked and blackened goblet – and a consciousness of the entire and terrible truth flashed suddenly over my soul.

KATE CHOPIN

Kate O'Flaherty Chopin (1851–1904) was a short-story writer and novelist. Though living most of her life in St Louis, Missouri, she is principally known for regional fiction focused on the Louisiana Creole and Cajun society that she knew through her marriage and residence in Louisiana before her husband's death in 1882. She was the foremost woman writing about this region. Her collections *Bayou Folk* (1894) and *A Night in Acadie* (1897) contain searingly human, memorable and ironic treatments of sex, love, class and race in Louisiana society. An equally consistent theme in Chopin's writing is women's oppression and suppression of self. While her last novel, *The Awakening* (1899), is the most sustained, famous and infamous treatment of this theme, earlier work like 'The Story of an Hour' shows Chopin's habitual exploration of what women would feel and do in the absence of their husbands' (and society's) oppressive expectations and dictates. She died of a brain haemorrhage at the age of fifty-three.

The Kiss

It was still quite light out of doors, but inside with the curtains drawn and the smouldering fire sending out a dim, uncertain glow, the room was full of deep shadows.

Brantain sat in one of these shadows; it had overtaken him and he did not mind. The obscurity lent him courage to keep his eyes fastened as ardently as he liked upon the girl who sat in the firelight.

She was very handsome, with a certain fine, rich colouring that belongs to the healthy brune type. She was quite composed, as she idly stroked the satiny coat of the cat that lay curled in her lap, and she occasionally sent a slow glance into the shadow where her companion sat. They were talking low, of indifferent things which plainly were not the things that occupied their thoughts. She knew that he loved her – a frank, blustering fellow without guile enough to conceal his feelings, and no desire to do so. For two weeks past he had sought her society eagerly and persistently. She was confidently waiting for him to declare himself and she meant to accept him. The rather insignificant and unattractive Brantain was enormously rich; and she liked and required the entourage which wealth could give her.

During one of the pauses between their talk of the last tea and the next reception the door opened and a young man entered whom Brantain knew quite well. The girl turned her face towards him. A stride or two brought him to her side, and bending over her chair – before she could suspect his intention, for she did not realise that he had not seen her visitor – he pressed an ardent, lingering kiss upon her lips.

Brantain slowly arose; so did the girl arise, but quickly, and the newcomer stood between them, a little amusement and some defiance struggling with the confusion in his face.

'I believe,' stammered Brantain, 'I see that I have stayed too long. I – I had no idea – that is, I must wish you goodbye.' He was clutching his hat with both hands, and probably did not perceive that she was extending her hand to him, her presence of mind had not completely deserted her; but she could not have trusted herself to speak.

'Hang me if I saw him sitting there, Nattie! I know it's deuced awkward for you. But I hope you'll forgive me this once – this very first break. Why, what's the matter?'

'Don't touch me; don't come near me,' she returned angrily. 'What do you mean by entering the house without ringing?'

'I came in with your brother, as I often do,' he answered coldly, in self-justification. 'We came in the side way. He went upstairs and I came in here hoping to find you. The explanation is simple enough and ought to satisfy you that the misadventure was unavoidable. But do say that you forgive me, Nathalie,' he entreated, softening.

'Forgive you! You don't know what you are talking about. Let me pass. It depends upon – a good deal whether I ever forgive you.'

At that next reception which she and Brantain had been talking about she approached the young man with a delicious frankness of manner when she saw him there.

'Will you let me speak to you a moment or two, Mr Brantain?' she asked with an engaging but perturbed smile. He seemed extremely unhappy; but when she took his arm and walked away with him, seeking a retired corner, a ray of hope mingled with the almost comical misery of his expression. She was apparently very outspoken.

'Perhaps I should not have sought this interview, Mr Brantain; but – but, oh, I have been very uncomfortable, almost miserable since that little encounter the other afternoon. When I thought how you might have misinterpreted it, and believed things' – hope was plainly gaining the ascendancy over misery in Brantain's round, guileless face – 'of course, I know it is nothing to you, but for my own sake I do want you to understand that Mr Harvy is an intimate friend of long standing. Why, we have always been like cousins – like brother and sister, I may say. He is my brother's most intimate associate and often fancies that he is entitled to the same privileges as the family. Oh, I know it is absurd, uncalled for, to tell you this; undignified even,' she was almost weeping, 'but it makes so much difference to me what you think of – of me.' Her voice had grown very low and agitated. The misery had all disappeared from Brantain's face.

'Then you do really care what I think, Miss Nathalie? May I call you Miss Nathalie?' They turned into a long, dim corridor that was lined on either side with tall, graceful plants. They walked slowly to the very end of it. When they turned to retrace their steps Brantain's face was radiant and hers was triumphant.

Harvy was among the guests at the wedding; and he sought her out in a rare moment when she stood alone.

'Your husband,' he said, smiling, 'has sent me over to kiss you.'

A quick blush suffused her face and round polished throat. 'I suppose it's natural for a man to feel and act generously on an occasion of this kind. He tells me he doesn't want his marriage to interrupt wholly that pleasant intimacy which has existed between you and me. I don't know what you've been telling him,' with an insolent smile, 'but he has sent me here to kiss you.'

She felt like a chess player who, by the clever handling of his pieces, sees the game taking the course intended. Her eyes were bright and tender with a smile as they glanced up into his; and her lips looked hungry for the kiss which they invited.

'But, you know,' he went on quietly, 'I didn't tell him so it would have seemed ungrateful, but I can tell you. I've stopped kissing women; it's dangerous.'

Well, she had Brantain and his million left. A person can't have everything in this world; and it was a little unreasonable of her to expect it.

SAKI

Hector Hugh Munro (1870–1916), a novelist who wrote under the name Saki, was born at Akyab, Burma, son of a police official of Scottish extraction, and was brought up by aunts at Pilton in Devon. Educated at Exmouth and Bedford Grammar School, he travelled with his father in France, Germany and Switzerland, then was for a time in the police service in Burma but suffered badly from malaria. Returning to England, he wrote for the *Westminster Gazette,* and from 1902 to 1908 was a foreign correspondent for the *Morning Post.* In the First World War he served as a private with the Royal Fusiliers and was killed at Beaumont-Hamel. His books of humorous short stories include *Reginald* (1904), *Reginald in Russia* (1910), *The Chronicles of Clovis* (1912) and *Beasts and Super-Beasts* (1914); *The Unbearable Bassington* (1912) and *When William Came* (1914) are novels. His pseudonym Saki is the name of the cup-bearer in *The Rubáiyát* of Omar Khayyám.

The Open Window

'My aunt will be down presently, Mr Nuttel,' said a very self-possessed young lady of fifteen; 'in the meantime you must try and put up with me.'

Framton Nuttel endeavoured to say the correct something which should duly flatter the niece of the moment without unduly discounting the aunt that was to come. Privately he doubted more than ever whether these formal visits on a succession of total strangers would do much towards helping the nerve cure which he was supposed to be undergoing.

'I know how it will be,' his sister had said when he was preparing to migrate to this rural retreat; 'you will bury yourself down there and not speak to a living soul, and your nerves will be worse than ever from moping. I shall just give you letters of introduction to all the people I know there. Some of them, as far as I can remember, were quite nice.'

Framton wondered whether Mrs Sappleton, the lady to whom he was presenting one of the letters of introduction, came into the nice division.

'Do you know many of the people round here?' asked the niece, when she judged that they had had sufficient silent communion.

'Hardly a soul,' said Framton. 'My sister was staying here, at the rectory, you know, some four years ago, and she gave me letters of introduction to some of the people here.'

He made the last statement in a tone of distinct regret.

'Then you know practically nothing about my aunt?' pursued the self-possessed young lady.

'Only her name and address,' admitted the caller. He was wondering whether Mrs Sappleton was in the married or widowed state. An undefinable something about the room seemed to suggest masculine habitation.

'Her great tragedy happened just three years ago,' said the child; 'that would be since your sister's time.'

'Her tragedy?' asked Framton; somehow in this restful country spot tragedies seemed out of place.

'You may wonder why we keep that window wide open on an October afternoon,' said the niece, indicating a large French window that opened on to a lawn.

'It is quite warm for the time of the year,' said Framton; 'but has that window got anything to do with the tragedy?'

'Out through that window, three years ago to the day, her husband and her two young brothers went off for their day's shooting. They never came back. In crossing the moor to their favourite snipe-shooting ground they were all three engulfed in a treacherous piece of bog. It had been that dreadful wet summer, you know, and places that were safe in other years gave way suddenly without warning. Their bodies were never recovered. That was the dreadful part of it.' Here the child's voice lost its self-possessed note and became falteringly human. 'Poor aunt always thinks that they will come back someday, they and the little brown spaniel that was lost with them, and walk in at that window just as they used to do. That is why the window is kept open every evening till it is quite dusk. Poor dear aunt, she has often told me how they went out, her husband with his white waterproof coat over his arm, and Ronnie, her youngest brother, singing, "Bertie, why do you bound?" as he always did to tease her, because she said it got on her nerves. Do you know, sometimes on still, quiet evenings like this, I almost get a creepy feeling that they will all walk in through that window – '

She broke off with a little shudder. It was a relief to Framton when the aunt bustled into the room with a whirl of apologies for being late in making her appearance.

'I hope Vera has been amusing you?' she said.

'She has been very interesting,' said Framton.

'I hope you don't mind the open window,' said Mrs Sappleton briskly; 'my husband and brothers will be home directly from shooting, and they always come in this way. They've been out for snipe in the marshes today, so they'll make a fine mess over my poor carpets. So like you menfolk, isn't it?'

She rattled on cheerfully about the shooting and the scarcity of birds, and the prospects for duck in the winter. To Framton, it was all purely horrible. He made a desperate but only partially successful effort to turn the talk on to a less ghastly topic; he was conscious that his hostess was giving him only a fragment of her attention, and her eyes were constantly straying past him to the open window and the lawn beyond. It was certainly an unfortunate coincidence that he should have paid his visit on this tragic anniversary.

'The doctors agree in ordering me complete rest, an absence of mental excitement, and avoidance of anything in the nature of violent physical exercise,' announced Framton, who laboured under the tolerably widespread delusion that total strangers and chance acquaintances are hungry for the least detail of one's ailments and infirmities, their cause and cure. 'On the matter of diet they are not so much in agreement,' he continued.

'No?' said Mrs Sappleton, in a voice which only replaced a yawn at the last moment. Then she suddenly brightened into alert attention – but not to what Framton was saying.

'Here they are at last!' she cried. 'Just in time for tea, and don't they look as if they were muddy up to the eyes!'

Framton shivered slightly and turned towards the niece with a look intended to convey sympathetic comprehension. The child was staring out through the open window with dazed horror in her eyes. In a chill shock of nameless fear Framton swung round in his seat and looked in the same direction.

In the deepening twilight three figures were walking across the lawn towards the window; they all carried guns under their arms, and one of them was additionally burdened with a white coat hung over his shoulders. A tired brown spaniel kept close at their heels. Noiselessly they neared the house, and then a hoarse young voice chanted out of the dusk: 'I said, Bertie, why do you bound?'

Framton grabbed wildly at his stick and hat; the hall-door, the gravel-drive, and the front gate were dimly noted stages in his headlong retreat. A cyclist coming along the road had to run into the hedge to avoid imminent collision.

'Here we are, my dear,' said the bearer of the white mackintosh, coming in through the window; 'fairly muddy, but most of it's dry. Who was that who bolted out as we came up?'

'A most extraordinary man, a Mr Nuttel,' said Mrs Sappleton;

'could only talk about his illnesses, and dashed off without a word of goodbye or apology when you arrived. One would think he had seen a ghost.'

'I expect it was the spaniel,' said the niece calmly; 'he told me he had a horror of dogs. He was once hunted into a cemetery somewhere on the banks of the Ganges by a pack of pariah dogs, and had to spend the night in a newly dug grave with the creatures snarling and grinning and foaming just above him. Enough to make anyone lose their nerve.'

Romance at short notice was her speciality.

JOSEPH CONRAD

Joseph Conrad was born in the Ukraine in 1857 to Polish parents who died while he was still a child. He longed for a life at sea from an early age and in 1874 began a twenty-year career as a sailor. In 1886 he became a British subject and eight years later devoted himself to being a full-time writer. He married Jessie George – the mother of his two sons – in 1895. Publication of his first novel, *Almayer's Folly*, when he was thirty-eight, marked the beginning of a career as a novelist that was to produce such classics as *Lord Jim* (1900), *Nostromo* (1904) and *Under Western Eyes* (1911). Conrad died in 1924 at a point when his stature as a writer of considerable significance was firmly established.

Amy Foster

Kennedy is a country doctor, and lives in Colebrook, on the shores of Eastbay. The high ground rising abruptly behind the red roofs of the little town crowds the quaint High Street against the wall which defends it from the sea. Beyond the sea-wall there curves for miles in a vast and regular sweep the barren beach of shingle, with the village of Brenzett standing out darkly across the water, a spire in a clump of trees; and still farther out the perpendicular column of a lighthouse, looking in the distance no bigger than a lead-pencil, marks the vanishing-point of the land. The country at the back of Brenzett is low and flat; but the bay is fairly well sheltered from the seas, and occasionally a big ship, windbound or through stress of weather, makes use of the anchoring ground a mile and a half due north from you as you stand at the back door of the Ship Inn in Brenzett. A dilapidated windmill near by lifting its shattered arms from a mound no loftier than a rubbish-heap, and a Martello tower squatting at the water's edge half a mile to the south of the coastguard cottages, are familiar to the skippers of small craft. These are the official sea marks for the patch of trustworthy bottom represented on the Admiralty charts by an irregular oval of dots enclosing several figures six, with a tiny anchor engraved among them, and the legend 'mud and shells' over all.

The brow of the upland overtops the square tower of the Colebrook Church. The slope is green and looped by a white road. Ascending along this road, you open a valley broad and shallow, a wide green trough of pastures and hedges merging inland into a vista of purple tints and flowing lines closing the view.

In this valley down to Brenzett and Colebrook and up to Darnford, the market town fourteen miles away, lies the practice of my friend Kennedy. He had begun life as a surgeon in the navy, and afterwards had been the companion of a famous traveller, in the days when there were continents with unexplored interiors. His papers on the fauna and flora made him known to scientific societies. And now he had come to a country practice – from choice. The penetrating power of his mind, acting like a corrosive fluid, had destroyed his ambition, I fancy. His intelligence is of a scientific order, of an investigating habit, and of that unappeasable curiosity which believes that there is a particle of a general truth in every mystery.

A good many years ago now, on my return from abroad, he invited me to stay with him. I came readily enough, and as he could not neglect his patients to keep me company, he took me on his rounds – thirty miles or so of an afternoon, sometimes. I waited for him on the roads; the horse reached after the leafy twigs, and, sitting high in the dogcart, I could hear Kennedy's laugh through the half-open door of some cottage. He had a big, hearty laugh that would have fitted a man twice his size, a brisk manner, a bronzed face, and a pair of grey, profoundly attentive eyes. He had the talent of making people talk to him freely, and an inexhaustible patience in listening to their tales.

One day, as we trotted out of a large village into a shady bit of road, I saw on our left hand a low, black cottage, with diamond panes in the windows, a creeper on the end wall, a roof of shingle, and some roses climbing on the rickety trelliswork of the tiny porch. Kennedy pulled up to a walk. A woman, in full sunlight, was throwing a dripping blanket over a line stretched between two old apple trees. And as the bobtailed, long-necked chestnut, trying to get his head, jerked the left hand, covered by a thick dogskin glove, the doctor raised his voice over the hedge: 'How's your child, Amy?'

I had the time to see her dull face, red, not with a mantling blush, but as if her flat cheeks had been vigorously slapped, and to take in the squat figure, the scanty, dusty brown hair drawn into a tight knot at the back of the head. She looked quite young. With a distinct catch in her breath, her voice sounded low and timid.

'He's well, thank you.'

We trotted again. 'A young patient of yours,' I said; and the doctor, flicking the chestnut absently, muttered, 'Her husband used to be.'

'She seems a dull creature,' I remarked listlessly.

'Precisely,' said Kennedy. 'She is very passive. It's enough to look at the red hands hanging at the end of those short arms, at those slow, prominent brown eyes, to know the inertness of her mind – an inertness that one would think made it everlastingly safe from all the surprises of imagination. And yet which of us is safe? At any rate, such as you see her, she had enough imagination to fall in love. She's the daughter of one Isaac Foster, who from a small farmer has sunk into a shepherd; the beginning of his misfortunes dating from his runaway marriage with the cook of his widowed father – a well-to-do, apoplectic grazier, who passionately struck his name off his will, and had been heard to utter threats against his life. But this old affair, scandalous enough to serve as a motive for a Greek tragedy, arose from the similarity of their characters. There are other tragedies, less scandalous and of a subtler poignancy, arising from irreconcilable differences and from that fear of the incomprehensible that hangs over all our heads – over all our heads . . .'

The tired chestnut dropped into a walk; and the rim of the sun, all red in a speckless sky, touched familiarly the smooth top of a ploughed rise near the road as I had seen it times innumerable touch the distant horizon of the sea. The uniform brownness of the harrowed field glowed with a rosy tinge, as though the powdered clods had sweated out in minute pearls of blood the toil of uncounted ploughmen. From the edge of a copse a waggon with two horses was rolling gently along the ridge. Raised above our heads upon the skyline, it loomed up against the red sun, triumphantly big, enormous, like a chariot of giants drawn by two slow-stepping steeds of legendary proportions. And the clumsy figure of the man plodding at the head of the leading horse projected itself on the background of the Infinite with a heroic uncouthness. The end of his carter's whip quivered high up in the blue.

Kennedy discoursed. 'She's the eldest of a large family. At the age of fifteen they put her out to service at the New Barns Farm. I attended Mrs Smith, the tenant's wife, and saw that girl there for the first time. Mrs Smith, a genteel person with a sharp nose, made her put on a black dress every afternoon. I don't know what induced me to notice her at all. There are faces that call your attention by a curious want of definiteness in their whole aspect, as, walking in a mist, you peer attentively at a vague shape which, after all, may be nothing more curious or strange than a signpost. The only peculiarity I perceived in her was a slight hesitation in her utterance, a sort of preliminary stammer which passes away with the first word. When sharply spoken to, she was apt to lose her head at once; but her heart was of the kindest. She had never been heard to express a dislike for a single human being, and she was tender to every living creature. She was devoted to Mrs Smith, to Mr Smith, to their dogs, cats, canaries; and as to Mrs Smith's grey parrot, its peculiarities exercised upon her a positive fascination. Nevertheless, when that outlandish bird, attacked by the cat, shrieked for help in human accents, she ran out into the yard stopping her ears, and did not prevent the crime. For Mrs Smith this was another evidence of her stupidity; on the other hand, her want of charm, in view of Smith's well-known frivolousness, was a great recommendation. Her short-sighted eyes would swim with pity for a poor mouse in a trap, and she had been seen once by some boys on her knees in the wet grass helping a toad in difficulties. If it's true, as some German fellow has said, that without phosphorus there is no thought, it is still more true that there is no kindness of heart without a certain amount of imagination. She had some. She had even more than is necessary to understand suffering and to be moved by pity. She fell in love under circumstances that leave no room for doubt in the matter; for you need imagination to form a notion of beauty at all, and still more to discover your ideal in an unfamiliar shape.

'How this aptitude came to her, what it did feed upon, is an inscrutable mystery. She was born in the village, and had never been farther away from it than Colebrook or perhaps Darnford. She lived for four years with the Smiths. New Barns is an isolated farmhouse a mile away from the road, and she was content to look day after day at the same fields, hollows, rises; at the trees and the hedgerows; at the faces of the four men about the farm, always the same – day after day, month after month, year after year. She never showed a desire for conversation, and, as it seemed to me, she did not know how to smile. Sometimes of a fine Sunday afternoon she would put on her best dress, a pair of stout boots, a large grey hat trimmed with a black feather (I've seen her in that finery), seize an absurdly slender parasol, climb over two stiles, tramp over three fields and along two hundred yards of road – never farther. There stood Foster's cottage. She would help her mother to give their tea to the younger children, wash up the crockery, kiss the little ones, and go back to the farm. That was all. All the rest, all the change, all the relaxation. She never seemed to wish for anything more. And then she fell in love. She fell in love silently, obstinately – perhaps helplessly. It came slowly, but when it came it worked like a powerful spell; it was love as the Ancients understood it: an irresistible and fateful impulse – a possession! Yes, it was in her to become haunted and possessed by a face, by a presence, fatally, as though she had been a pagan worshipper of form under a joyous sky – and to be awakened at last from that mysterious forgetfulness of self, from that enchantment, from that transport, by a fear resembling the unaccountable terror of a brute . . .'

With the sun hanging low on its western limit, the expanse of the grasslands framed in the counterscarps of the rising ground took on a gorgeous and sombre aspect. A sense of penetrating sadness, like that inspired by a grave strain of music, disengaged itself from the silence of the fields. The men we met walked past, slow, unsmiling, with downcast eyes, as if the melancholy of an over-burdened earth had weighted their feet, bowed their shoulders, borne down their glances.

'Yes,' said the doctor to my remark, 'one would think the earth is under a curse, since of all her children these that cling to her the closest are uncouth in body and as leaden of gait as if their very hearts were loaded with chains. But here on this same road you might have seen among these heavy men a being lithe, supple and long-limbed, straight like a pine, with something striving upwards in his appearance as though the heart within him had been buoyant. Perhaps it was only the force of the contrast, but when he was passing one of these villagers here, the soles of his feet did not seem to me to touch the dust of the road. He vaulted over the stiles, paced these slopes with a long elastic stride that made him noticeable at a great distance, and had lustrous black eyes. He was so different from the mankind around that, with his freedom of movement, his soft – a little startled – glance, his olive complexion and graceful bearing, his humanity suggested to me the nature of a woodland creature. He came from there.'

The doctor pointed with his whip, and from the summit of the descent seen over the rolling tops of the trees in a park by the side of the road, appeared the level sea far below us, like the floor of an immense edifice inlaid with bands of dark ripple, with still trails of glitter, ending in a belt of glassy water at the foot of the sky. The light blur of smoke, from an invisible steamer, faded on the great clearness of the horizon like the mist of a breath on a mirror; and, inshore, the white sails of a coaster, with the appearance of disentangling themselves slowly from under the branches, floated clear of the foliage of the trees.

'Shipwrecked in the bay?' I said.

'Yes; he was a castaway. A poor emigrant from central Europe bound to America and washed ashore here in a storm. And for him, who knew nothing of the earth, England was an undiscovered country. It was some time before he learned its name; and for all I know he might have expected to find wild beasts or wild men here, when, crawling in the dark over the sea-wall, he rolled down the other side into a dyke, where it was another miracle he didn't get drowned. But he struggled instinctively like an animal under a net, and this blind struggle threw him out into a field. He must have been, indeed, of a tougher fibre than he looked to withstand without expiring such buffetings, the violence of his exertions, and so much fear. Later on, in his broken English that resembled curiously the speech of a young child, he told me himself that he put his trust in God, believing he was no longer in this world. And truly – he would add – how was he to know? He fought his way against the rain and the gale on all fours, and crawled at last among some sheep huddled close under the lee of a hedge. They ran off in all directions, bleating in the darkness, and he welcomed the first familiar sound he heard on these shores. It must have been two in the morning then. And this is all we know of the manner of his landing, though he did not arrive unattended by any means. Only his grisly company did not begin to come ashore till much later in the day . . .'

The doctor gathered the reins, clicked his tongue; we trotted down the hill. Then turning, almost directly, a sharp corner into the High Street, we rattled over the stones and were home.

Late in the evening Kennedy, breaking a spell of moodiness that had come over him, returned to the story. Smoking his pipe, he paced the long room from end to end. A reading-lamp concentrated all its light upon the papers on his desk; and, sitting by the open window, I saw, after the windless, scorching day, the frigid splendour of a hazy sea lying motionless under the moon. Not a whisper, not a splash, not a stir of the shingle, not a footstep, not a sigh came up from the earth below – never a sign of life but the scent of climbing jasmine; and Kennedy's voice, speaking behind me, passed through the wide casement, to vanish outside in a chill and sumptuous stillness.

'. . . The relations of shipwrecks in the olden time tell us of much suffering. Often the castaways were only saved from drowning to die miserably from starvation on a barren coast; others suffered violent death or else slavery, passing through years of precarious existence with people to whom their strangeness was an object of suspicion, dislike or fear. We read about these things, and they are very pitiful. It is indeed hard upon a man to find himself a lost stranger, helpless, incomprehensible, and of a mysterious origin, in some obscure corner of the earth.

Yet among all the adventurers shipwrecked in all the wild parts of the world, there is not one, it seems to me, that ever had to suffer a fate so simply tragic as the man I am speaking of, the most innocent of adventurers cast out by the sea in the bight of this bay, almost within sight from this very window.

'He did not know the name of his ship. Indeed, in the course of time we discovered he did not even know that ships had names – 'like Christian people'; and when, one day, from the top of the Talfourd Hill, he beheld the sea lying open to his view, his eyes roamed afar, lost in an air of wild surprise, as though he had never seen such a sight before. And probably he had not. As far as I could make out, he had been hustled together with many others on board an emigrant ship lying at the mouth of the Elbe, too bewildered to take note of his surroundings, too weary to see anything, too anxious to care. They were driven below into the 'tween-deck and battened down from the very start. It was a low timber dwelling – he would say – with wooden beams overhead, like the houses in his country, but you went into it down a ladder. It was very large, very cold, damp and sombre, with places in the manner of wooden boxes where people had to sleep one above another, and it kept on rocking all ways at once all the time. He crept into one of these boxes and lay down there in the clothes in which he had left his home many days before, keeping his bundle and his stick by his side. People groaned, children cried, water dripped, the lights went out, the walls of the place creaked, and everything was being shaken so that in one's little box one dared not lift one's head. He had lost touch with his only companion (a young man from the same valley, he said), and all the time a great noise of wind went on outside and heavy blows fell – boom! boom! An awful sickness overcame him, even to the point of making him neglect his prayers. Besides, one could not tell whether it was morning or evening. It seemed always to be night in that place.

'Before that he had been travelling a long, long time on the iron track. He looked out of the window, which had a wonderfully clear glass in it, and the trees, the houses, the fields and the long roads seemed to fly round and round about him till his head swam. He gave me to understand that he had on his passage beheld uncounted multitudes of people – whole nations – all dressed in such clothes as the rich wear. Once he was made to get out of the carriage, and slept through a night on a bench in a house of bricks with his bundle under his head; and once for many hours he had to sit on a floor of flat stones dozing, with his knees up and with his bundle between his feet. There was a roof over him, which seemed made of glass, and was so high that the tallest mountain-pine he had ever seen would have had room to grow under it. Steam-machines rolled in at one end and out at the other. People swarmed more than you can see on a feast-day round the miraculous Holy Image in the yard of the Carmelite Convent down in the plains where, before he left his home, he drove his mother in a wooden cart – a pious old woman who wanted to offer prayers and make a vow for his safety. He could not give me an idea of how large and lofty and full of noise and smoke and gloom, and clang of iron, the place was, but someone had told him it was called Berlin. Then they rang a bell, and another steam-machine came in, and again he was taken on and on through a land that wearied his eyes by its flatness without a single bit of a hill to be seen anywhere. One more night he spent shut up in a building like a good stable with a litter of straw on the floor, guarding his bundle among a lot of men, of whom not one could understand a single word he said. In the morning they were all led down to the stony shores of an extremely broad muddy river, flowing not between hills but between houses that seemed immense. There was a steam-machine that went on the water, and they all stood upon it packed tight, only now there were with them many women and children who made much noise. A cold rain fell, the wind blew in his face; he was wet through, and his teeth chattered. He and the young man from the same valley took each other by the hand.

'They thought they were being taken to America straight away, but suddenly the steam-machine bumped against the side of a thing like a great house on the water. The walls were smooth and black, and there uprose, growing from the roof as it were, bare trees in the shape of crosses, extremely high. That's how it appeared to him then, for he had never seen a ship before. This was the ship that was going to swim all the way to America. Voices shouted, everything swayed; there was a ladder dipping up and down. He went up on his hands and knees in mortal fear of falling into the water below, which made a great splashing. He got separated from his companion, and when he descended into the bottom of that ship his heart seemed to melt suddenly within him.

'It was then also, as he told me, that he lost contact for good and all with one of those three men who the summer before had been going about through all the little towns in the foothills of his country. They would arrive on market-days driving in a peasant's cart, and would set up an office in an inn or some other Jew's house. There were three of them, of whom one with a long beard looked venerable; and they had red cloth collars round their necks and gold lace on their sleeves like government officials. They sat proudly behind a long table; and in the next room, so that the common people shouldn't hear, they kept a cunning telegraph machine, through which they could talk to the Emperor of America. The fathers hung about the door, but the young men of the mountains would crowd up to the table asking many questions, for there was work to be got all the year round at three dollars a day in America, and no military service to do.

'But the American Kaiser would not take everybody. Oh no! He himself had great difficulty in getting accepted, and the venerable man in uniform had to go out of the room several times to work the telegraph on his behalf. The American Kaiser engaged him at last at three dollars, he being young and strong. However, many able young men backed out, afraid of the great distance; besides, those only who had some money could be taken. There were some who had sold their huts and their land because it cost a lot of money to get to America; but then, once there, you had three dollars a day, and if you were clever you could find places where true gold could be picked up on the ground. His father's house was getting over full. Two of his brothers were married and had children. He promised to send money home from America by post twice a year. His father sold an old cow, a pair of piebald mountain ponies of his own raising, and a cleared plot of fair pasture land on the sunny slope of a pine-clad pass to a Jew innkeeper, in order to pay the people of the ship that took men to America to get rich in a short time.

'He must have been a real adventurer at heart, for how many of the greatest enterprises in the conquest of the earth had for their beginning just such a bargaining away of the paternal cow for the mirage of true gold far away! I have been telling you more or less in my own words what I learned fragmentarily in the course of two or three years, during which I seldom missed an opportunity of a friendly chat with him. He told me this story of his adventure with many flashes of white teeth and lively glances of black eyes, at first in a sort of anxious baby-talk, then, as he acquired the language, with great fluency, but always with that singing, soft, and at the same time vibrating intonation that instilled a strangely penetrating power into the sound of the most familiar English words, as if they had been the words of an unearthly language. And he always would come to an end, with many emphatic shakes of his head, upon that awful sensation of his heart melting within him directly he set foot on board that ship. Afterwards there seemed to come for him a period of blank ignorance, at any rate as to facts. No doubt he must have been abominably seasick and abominably unhappy – this soft and passionate adventurer, taken thus out of his knowledge, and feeling bitterly as he lay in his emigrant bunk his utter loneliness; for his was a highly sensitive nature. The next thing we know of him for certain is that he had been hiding in Hammond's pig-pound by the side of the road to Norton, six miles, as the crow flies, from the sea. Of these experiences he was unwilling to speak: they seemed to have seared into his soul a sombre sort of wonder and indignation. Through the rumours of the countryside, which lasted for a good many days after his arrival, we know that the fishermen of West Colebrook had been disturbed and startled by heavy knocks against the walls of weatherboard cottages, and by a voice crying piercingly strange words in the night. Several of them turned out even, but, no doubt, he had fled in sudden alarm at their rough angry tones hailing each other in the darkness. A sort of frenzy must have helped him up the steep Norton Hill. It was he, no doubt, who early the following morning had been seen lying (in a swoon, I should say) on the roadside grass by the Brenzett carrier, who actually got down to have a nearer look, but drew back, intimidated by the perfect immobility, and by something queer in the aspect of that tramp, sleeping so still under the showers. As the day advanced, some children came dashing into school at Norton in such a fright that the schoolmistress went out and spoke indignantly to a "horrid-looking man" on the road. He edged away, hanging his head, for a few steps, and then suddenly ran off with extraordinary fleetness. The driver of Mr Bradley's milk-cart made no secret of it that he had lashed with his whip at a hairy sort of gypsy fellow who, jumping up at a turn of the road by the Vents, made a snatch at the pony's bridle. And he caught him a good one too, right over the face, he said, that made him drop down in the mud a jolly sight quicker than he had jumped up; but it was a good half a mile before he could stop the pony. Maybe that in his desperate endeavours to get help, and in his need to get in touch with someone, the poor devil had tried to stop the cart. Also three boys confessed afterwards to throwing stones at a funny tramp, knocking about all wet and muddy, and, it seemed, very drunk, in the narrow deep lane by the limekilns. All this was the talk of three villages for days; but we have Mrs Finn's (the wife of Smith's waggoner) unimpeachable testimony that she saw him get over the low wall of Hammond's pig-pound and lurch straight at her, babbling aloud in a voice that was enough to make one die of fright. Having the baby with her in a perambulator, Mrs Finn called out to him to go away, and as he persisted in coming nearer, she hit him courageously with her umbrella over the head, and, without once looking back, ran like the wind with the perambulator as far as the first house in the village. She stopped then, out of breath, and spoke to old Lewis, hammering there at a heap of stones; and the old chap, taking off his immense black wire goggles, got up on his shaky legs to look where she pointed. Together they followed with their eyes the figure of the man running over a field; they saw him fall down, pick himself up, and run on again, staggering and waving his long arms above his head, in the direction of the New Barns Farm. From that moment he is plainly in the toils of his obscure and touching destiny. There is no doubt after this of what happened to him. All is certain now: Mrs Smith's intense terror; Amy Foster's stolid conviction held against the other's nervous attack, that the man "meant no harm"; Smith's exasperation (on his return from Darnford Market) at finding the dog barking himself into a fit, the back-door locked, his wife in hysterics; and all for an unfortunate dirty tramp, supposed to be even then lurking in his stackyard. Was he? He would teach him to frighten women.

'Smith is notoriously hot-tempered, but the sight of some nondescript and miry creature sitting cross-legged among a lot of loose straw, and swinging itself to and fro like a bear in a cage, made him pause. Then this tramp stood up silently before him, one mass of mud and filth from head to foot. Smith, alone among his stacks with this apparition, in the stormy twilight ringing with the infuriated barking of the dog, felt the dread of an inexplicable strangeness. But when that being, parting with his black hands the long matted locks that hung before his face, as you part the two halves of a curtain, looked out at him with glistening, wild, black-and-white eyes, the weirdness of this silent encounter fairly staggered him. He has admitted since (for the story has been a legitimate subject of conversation about here for years) that he made more than one step backwards. Then a sudden burst of rapid, senseless speech persuaded him at once that he had to do with an escaped lunatic. In fact, that impression never wore off completely. Smith has not in his heart given up his secret conviction of the man's essential insanity to this very day.

'As the creature approached him, jabbering in a most discomposing manner, Smith (unaware that he was being addressed as "gracious lord", and adjured in God's name to afford food and shelter) kept on speaking firmly but gently to it, and retreating all the time into the other yard. At last, watching his chance, by a sudden charge he bundled him headlong into the wood-lodge, and instantly shot the bolt. Thereupon he wiped his brow, though the day was cold. He had done his duty to the community by shutting up a wandering and probably dangerous maniac. Smith isn't a hard man at all, but he had room in his brain only for that one idea of lunacy. He was not imaginative enough to ask himself whether the man might not be perishing with cold and hunger. Meantime, at first, the maniac made a great deal of noise in the lodge. Mrs Smith was screaming upstairs, where she had locked herself in her bedroom; but Amy Foster sobbed piteously at the kitchen-door, wringing her hands and muttering, "Don't! don't!" I dare say Smith had a rough time of it that evening with one noise and another, and this insane, disturbing voice crying obstinately through the door only added to his irritation. He couldn't possibly have connected this troublesome lunatic with the sinking of a ship in Eastbay, of which there had been a rumour in the Darnford market-place. And I dare say the man inside had been very near to insanity on that night. Before his excitement collapsed and he became unconscious he was throwing himself violently about in the dark, rolling on some dirty sacks and biting his fists with rage, cold, hunger, amazement and despair.

'He was a mountaineer of the eastern range of the Carpathians, and the vessel sunk the night before in Eastbay was the Hamburg emigrant ship *Herzogin Sophia-Dorothea*, of appalling memory.

'A few months later we could read in the papers the accounts of the bogus "Emigration Agencies" among the Sclavonian peasantry in the more remote provinces of Austria. The object of these scoundrels was to get hold of the poor ignorant people's homesteads, and they were in league with the local usurers. They exported their victims through Hamburg mostly. As to the ship, I had watched her out of this very window, reaching close-hauled under short canvas into the bay on a dark, threatening afternoon. She came to an anchor, correctly by the chart, off the Brenzett coastguard station. I remember before the night fell looking out again at the outlines of her spars and rigging that stood out dark and pointed on a background of ragged, slaty clouds like another and a slighter spire to the left of the Brenzett church-tower. In the evening the wind rose. At midnight I could hear in my bed the terrific gusts and the sounds of a driving deluge.

'About that time the coastguardmen thought they saw the lights of a steamer over the anchoring-ground. In a moment they vanished; but it is clear that another vessel of some sort had tried for shelter in the bay on that awful, blind night, had rammed the German ship amidships (a breach – as one of the divers told me afterwards – 'that you could sail a Thames barge through'), and then had gone out either scathless or damaged, who shall say; but had gone out, unknown, unseen, and fatal, to perish mysteriously at sea. Of her nothing ever came to light, and yet the hue and cry that was raised all over the world would have found her out if she had been in existence anywhere on the face of the waters.

'A completeness without a clue, and a stealthy silence as of a neatly executed crime, characterise this murderous disaster, which, as you may remember, had its gruesome celebrity. The wind would have prevented the loudest outcries from reaching the shore; there had been evidently no time for signals of distress. It was death without any sort of fuss. The Hamburg ship, filling all at once, capsized as she sank, and at daylight there was not even the end of a spar to be seen above water. She was missed, of course, and at first the coastguardmen surmised that she had either dragged her anchor or parted her cable some time during the night, and had been blown out to sea. Then, after the tide turned, the wreck must have shifted a little and released some of the bodies, because a child – a little fair-haired child in a red frock – came ashore abreast of the Martello tower. By the afternoon you could see along three miles of beach dark figures with bare legs dashing in and out of the tumbling foam, and rough-looking men, women with hard faces, children, mostly fair-haired, were being carried, stiff and dripping, on stretchers, on wattles, on ladders, in a long procession past the door of the Ship Inn, to be laid out in a row under the north wall of the Brenzett Church.

'Officially, the body of the little girl in the red frock is the first thing that came ashore from that ship. But I have patients among the seafaring population of West Colebrook, and, unofficially, I am informed that very early that morning two brothers, who went down to look after their cobble hauled up on the beach, found, a good way from Brenzett, an ordinary ship's hencoop lying high and dry on the shore, with eleven drowned ducks inside. Their families ate the birds, and the hencoop was split into firewood with a hatchet. It is possible that a man (supposing he happened to be on deck at the time of the accident) might have floated ashore on that hencoop. He might. I admit it is improbable, but there was the man – and for days, nay, for weeks – it didn't enter our heads that we had among us the only living soul that had escaped from that disaster. The man himself, even when he learned to speak intelligibly, could tell us very little. He remembered he had felt better (after the ship had anchored, I suppose), and that the darkness, the wind and the rain took his breath away. This looks as if he had been on deck some time during that night. But we mustn't forget he had been taken out of his knowledge, that he had been sea-sick and battened down below for four days, that he had no general notion of a ship or of the sea, and therefore could have no definite idea of what was happening to him. The rain, the wind, the darkness he knew; he understood the bleating of the sheep, and he remembered the pain of his wretchedness and misery, his heartbroken astonishment that it was neither seen nor understood, his dismay at finding all the men angry and all the women fierce. He had approached them as a beggar, it is true, he said; but in his country, even if they gave nothing, they spoke gently to beggars. The children in his country were not taught to throw stones at those who asked for compassion. Smith's strategy overcame him completely. The wood-lodge presented the horrible aspect of a dungeon. What would be done to him next? . . . No wonder that Amy Foster appeared to his eyes with the aureole of an angel of light. The girl had not been able to sleep for thinking of the poor man, and in the morning, before the Smiths were up, she slipped out across the back yard. Holding the door of the wood-lodge ajar, she looked in and extended to him half a loaf of white bread – "such bread as the rich eat in my country," he used to say.

'At this he got up slowly from among all sorts of rubbish, stiff, hungry, trembling, miserable, and doubtful. "Can you eat this?" she asked in her soft and timid voice. He must have taken her for a "gracious lady". He devoured ferociously, and tears were falling on the crust. Suddenly he dropped the bread, seized her wrist, and imprinted a kiss on her hand. She was not frightened. Through his forlorn condition she had observed that he was good-looking. She shut the door and walked back slowly to the kitchen. Much later on, she told Mrs Smith, who shuddered at the bare idea of being touched by that creature.

'Through this act of impulsive pity he was brought back again within the pale of human relations with his new surroundings. He never forgot it – never.

'That very same morning old Mr Swaffer (Smith's nearest neighbour) came over to give his advice, and ended by carrying him off. He stood, unsteady on his legs, meek, and caked over in half-dried mud, while the two men talked around him in an incomprehensible tongue. Mrs Smith had refused to come downstairs till the madman was off the premises; Amy Foster, from far within the dark kitchen, watched through the open back door; and he obeyed the signs that were made to him to the best of his ability. But Smith was full of mistrust. "Mind, sir! It may be all his cunning," he cried repeatedly in a tone of warning. When Mr Swaffer started the mare, the deplorable being sitting humbly by his side, through weakness, nearly fell out over the back of the high two-wheeled cart. Swaffer took him straight home. And it is then that I come upon the scene.

'I was called in by the simple process of the old man beckoning to me with his forefinger over the gate of his house as I happened to be driving past. I got down, of course.

' "I've got something here," he mumbled, leading the way to an outhouse at a little distance from his other farm-buildings.

'It was there that I saw him first, in a long low room taken upon the space of that sort of coach-house. It was bare and whitewashed, with a small square aperture glazed with one cracked, dusty pane at its farther end. He was lying on his back upon a straw pallet; they had given him a couple of horse-blankets, and he seemed to have spent the remainder of his strength in the exertion of cleaning himself. He was almost speechless; his quick breathing under the blankets pulled up to his chin, his glittering, restless black eyes reminded me of a wild bird caught in a snare. While I was examining him, old Swaffer stood silently by the door, passing the tips of his fingers along his shaven upper lip. I gave some directions, promised to send a bottle of medicine, and naturally made some enquiries.

' "Smith caught him in the stackyard at New Barns," said the old chap in his deliberate, unmoved manner, and as if the other had been indeed a sort of wild animal, "That's how I came by him. Quite a curiosity, isn't he? Now tell me, doctor – you've been all over the world – don't you think that's a bit of a Hindu we've got hold of here?"

'I was greatly surprised. His long black hair scattered over the straw bolster contrasted with the olive pallor of his face. It occurred to me he might be a Basque. It didn't necessarily follow that he should understand Spanish; but I tried him with the few words I know, and also with some French. The whispered sounds I caught by bending my ear to his lips puzzled me utterly. That afternoon the young ladies from the rectory (one of them read Goethe with a dictionary, and the other had struggled with Dante for years), coming to see Miss Swaffer, tried their German and Italian on him from the doorway. They retreated, just the least bit scared by the flood of passionate speech which, turning on his pallet, he let out at them. They admitted that the sound was pleasant, soft, musical – but, in conjunction with his looks perhaps, it was startling – so excitable, so utterly unlike anything one had ever heard. The village boys climbed up the bank to have a peep through the little square aperture. Everybody was wondering what Mr Swaffer would do with him.

'He simply kept him.

'Swaffer would be called eccentric were he not so much respected. They will tell you that Mr Swaffer sits up as late as ten o'clock at night to read books, and they will tell you also that he can write a cheque for two hundred pounds without thinking twice about it. He himself would tell you that the Swaffers have owned land between this and Darnford for these three hundred years. He must be eighty-five today, but he does not look a bit older than when I first came here. He is a great breeder of sheep, and deals extensively in cattle. He attends market days for miles around in every sort of weather, and drives sitting bowed low over the reins, his lank grey hair curling over the collar of his warm coat, and with a green plaid rug round his legs. The calmness of advanced age gives a solemnity to his manner. He is clean-shaved; his lips are thin and sensitive; something rigid and monarchal in the set of his features lends a certain elevation to the character of his face. He has been known to drive miles in the rain to see a new kind of rose in somebody's garden, or a monstrous cabbage grown by a cottager. He loves to hear tell of or to be shown something that he calls "outlandish". Perhaps it was just that outlandishness of the man which influenced old Swaffer. Perhaps it was only an inexplicable caprice. All I know is that at the end of three weeks I caught sight of Smith's lunatic digging in Swaffer's kitchen garden. They had found out he could use a spade. He dug barefooted.

'His black hair flowed over his shoulders. I suppose it was Swaffer who had given him the striped old cotton shirt; but he wore still the national brown cloth trousers (in which he had been washed ashore) fitting to the leg almost like tights; was belted with a broad leathern belt studded with little brass discs; and had never yet ventured into the village. The land he looked upon seemed to him kept neatly, like the grounds round a landowner's house; the size of the cart-horses struck him with astonishment; the roads resembled garden walks, and the aspect of the people, especially on Sundays, spoke of opulence. He wondered what made them so hard-hearted and their children so bold. He got his food at the back door, carried it in both hands, carefully, to his outhouse, and, sitting alone on his pallet, would make the sign of the cross before he began. Beside the same pallet, kneeling in the early darkness of the short days, he recited aloud the Lord's Prayer before he slept. Whenever he saw old Swaffer he would bow with veneration from the waist, and stand erect while the old man, with his fingers over his upper lip, surveyed him silently. He bowed also to Miss Swaffer, who kept house frugally for her father – a broad-shouldered, big-boned woman of forty-five, with the pocket of her dress full of keys, and a grey, steady eye. She was Church – as people said (while her father was one of the trustees of the Baptist Chapel) – and wore a little steel cross at her waist. She dressed severely in black, in memory of one of the innumerable Bradleys of the neighbourhood, to whom she had been engaged some twenty-five years ago – a young farmer who broke his neck out hunting on the eve of the wedding-day. She had the unmoved countenance of the deaf, spoke very seldom, and her lips, thin like her father's, astonished one sometimes by a mysteriously ironic curl.

'These were the people to whom he owed allegiance, and an overwhelming loneliness seemed to fall from the leaden sky of that winter without sunshine. All the faces were sad. He could talk to no one, and had no hope of ever understanding anybody. It was as if these had been the faces of people from the other world – dead people – he used to tell me years afterwards. Upon my word, I wonder he did not go mad. He didn't know where he was. Somewhere very far from his mountains – somewhere over the water. Was this America, he wondered?

'If it hadn't been for the steel cross at Miss Swaffer's belt he would not, he confessed, have known whether he was in a Christian country at all. He used to cast stealthy glances at it, and feel comforted. There was nothing here the same as in his country! The earth and the water were different; there were no images of the Redeemer by the roadside. The very grass was different, and the trees. All the trees but the three old Norway pines on the bit of lawn before Swaffer's house, and these reminded him of his country. He had been detected once, after dusk, with his forehead against the trunk of one of them, sobbing, and talking to himself. They had been like brothers to him at that time, he affirmed. Everything else was strange. Conceive you the kind of an existence overshadowed, oppressed, by the everyday material appearances, as if by the visions of a nightmare. At night, when he could not sleep, he kept on thinking of the girl who gave him the first piece of bread he had eaten in this foreign land. She had been neither fierce nor angry, nor frightened. Her face he remembered as the only comprehensible face among all these faces that were as closed, as mysterious and as mute as the faces of the dead who are possessed of a knowledge beyond the comprehension of the living. I wonder whether the memory of her compassion prevented him from cutting his throat. But there! I suppose I am an old sentimentalist, and forget the instinctive love of life which it takes all the strength of an uncommon despair to overcome.

'He did the work which was given him with an intelligence which surprised old Swaffer. By and by it was discovered that he could help at the ploughing, could milk the cows, feed the bullocks in the cattle-yard, and was of some use with the sheep. He began to pick up words, too, very fast; and suddenly, one fine morning in spring, he rescued from an untimely death a grandchild of old Swaffer.

'Swaffer's younger daughter is married to Willcox, a solicitor and the Town Clerk of Colebrook. Regularly twice a year they come to stay with the old man for a few days. Their only child, a little girl not three years old at the time, ran out of the house alone in her little white pinafore, and, toddling across the grass of a terraced garden, pitched herself over a low wall head first into the horsepond in the yard below.

'Our man was out with the waggoner and the plough in the field nearest to the house, and as he was leading the team round to begin a fresh furrow, he saw, through the gap of a gate, what for anybody else would have been a mere flutter of something white. But he had straight-glancing, quick, far-reaching eyes, that only seemed to flinch and lose their amazing power before the immensity of the sea. He was barefooted, and looking as outlandish as the heart of Swaffer could desire. Leaving the horses on the turn, to the inexpressible disgust of the waggoner he bounded off, going over the ploughed ground in long leaps, and suddenly appeared before the mother, thrust the child into her arms, and strode away.

'The pond was not very deep; but still, if he had not had such good eyes, the child would have perished – miserably suffocated in the foot or so of sticky mud at the bottom. Old Swaffer walked out slowly into the field, waited till the plough came over to his side, had a good look at him, and without saying a word went back to the house. But from that time they laid out his meals on the kitchen table; and at first, Miss Swaffer, all in black and with an inscrutable face, would come and stand in the doorway of the living-room to see him make a big sign of the cross before he fell to. I believe that from that day, too, Swaffer began to pay him regular wages.

'I can't follow step by step his development. He cut his hair short, was seen in the village and along the road going to and fro his work like any other man. Children ceased to shout after him. He became aware of social differences, but remained for a long time surprised at the bare poverty of the churches among so much wealth. He couldn't understand either why they were kept shut up on weekdays. There was nothing to steal in them. Was it to keep people from praying too often? The rectory took much notice of him about that time, and I believe the young ladies attempted to prepare the ground for his conversion. They could not, however, break him of his habit of crossing himself, but he went so far as to take off the string with a couple of brass medals the size of a sixpence, a tiny metal cross, and a square sort of scapulary which he wore round his neck. He hung them on the wall by the side of his bed, and he was still to be heard every evening reciting the Lord's Prayer, in incomprehensible words and in a slow, fervent tone, as he had heard his old father do at the head of all the kneeling family, big and little, on every evening of his life. And though he wore corduroys at work, and a slop-made pepper-and-salt suit on Sundays, strangers would turn round to look after him on the road. His foreignness had a peculiar and indelible stamp. At last people became used to seeing him. But they never became used to him. His rapid, skimming walk; his swarthy complexion; his hat cocked on the left ear; his habit, on warm evenings, of wearing his coat over one shoulder, like a hussar's dolman; his manner of leaping over the stiles, not as a feat of agility, but in the ordinary course of progression – all these peculiarities were, as one may say, so many causes of scorn and offence to the inhabitants of the village. *They* wouldn't in their dinner hour lie flat on their backs on the grass to stare at the sky. Neither did they go about the fields screaming dismal tunes. Many times have I heard his high-pitched voice from behind the ridge of some sloping sheep-walk, a voice light and soaring, like a lark's, but with a melancholy human note, over our fields that hear only the song of birds. And I would be startled myself. Ah! He was different: innocent of heart, and full of good will, which nobody wanted, this castaway, that, like a man transplanted into another planet, was separated by an immense space from his past and by an immense ignorance from his future. His quick, fervent utterance positively shocked everybody. "An excitable devil", they called him. One evening, in the tap-room of the Coach and Horses (having drunk some whisky), he upset them all by singing a love-song of his country. They hooted him down, and he was pained; but Preble, the lame wheelwright, and Vincent, the fat blacksmith, and the other notables too, wanted to drink their evening beer in peace. On another occasion he tried to show them how to dance. The dust rose in clouds from the sanded floor; he leaped straight up among the deal tables, struck his heels together, squatted on one heel in front of old Preble, shooting out the other leg, uttered wild and exulting cries, jumped up to whirl on one foot, snapping his fingers above his head – and a strange carter who was having a drink in there began to swear, and cleared out with his half-pint in his hand into the bar. But when suddenly he sprang upon a table and continued to dance among the glasses, the landlord interfered. He didn't want any "acrobat tricks in the tap-room". They laid their hands on him. Having had a glass or two, Mr Swaffer's foreigner tried to expostulate: was ejected forcibly: got a black eye.

'I believe he felt the hostility of his human surroundings. But he was tough – tough in spirit, too, as well as in body. Only the memory of the sea frightened him, with that vague terror that is left by a bad dream. His home was far away; and he did not want now to go to America. I had often explained to him that there is no place on earth where true gold can be found lying ready and to be got for the trouble of the picking up. How then, he asked, could he ever return home with empty hands when there had been sold a cow, two ponies and a bit of land to pay for his going? His eyes would fill with tears, and, averting them from the immense shimmer of the sea, he would throw himself face down on the grass. But sometimes, cocking his hat with a little conquering air, he would defy my wisdom. He had found his bit of true gold. That was Amy Foster's heart; which was "a golden heart, and soft to people's misery", he would say in the accents of overwhelming conviction.

'He was called Yanko. He had explained that this meant Little John; but as he would also repeat very often that he was a mountaineer (some word sounding in the dialect of his country like Goorall) he got it for his surname. And this is the only trace of him that the succeeding ages may find in the marriage register of the parish. There it stands – Yanko Goorall – in the rector's handwriting. The crooked cross made by the castaway, a cross whose tracing no doubt seemed to him the most solemn part of the whole ceremony, is all that remains now to perpetuate the memory of his name.

'His courtship had lasted some time – ever since he got his precarious footing in the community. It began by his buying for Amy Foster a green satin ribbon in Darnford. This was what you did in his country. You bought a ribbon at a Jew's stall on a fair-day. I don't suppose the girl knew what to do with it, but he seemed to think that his honourable intentions could not be mistaken.

'It was only when he declared his purpose to get married that I fully understood how, for a hundred futile and inappreciable reasons, how – shall I say odious? – he was to all the countryside. Every old woman in the village was up in arms. Smith, coming upon him near the farm, promised to break his head for him if he found him about again. But he twisted his little black moustache with such a bellicose air and rolled such big, black fierce eyes at Smith that this promise came to nothing. Smith, however, told the girl that she must be mad to take up with a man who was surely wrong in his head. All the same, when she heard him in the gloaming whistle from beyond the orchard a couple of bars of a weird and mournful tune, she would drop whatever she had in her hand – she would leave Mrs Smith in the middle of a sentence – and she would run out to his call. Mrs Smith called her a shameless hussy. She answered nothing. She said nothing at all to anybody, and went on her way as if she had been deaf. She and I alone in all the land, I fancy, could see his very real beauty. He was very good-looking, and most graceful in his bearing, with that something wild as of a woodland creature in his aspect. Her mother moaned over her dismally whenever the girl came to see her on her day out. The father was surly, but pretended not to know; and Mrs Finn once told her plainly that "this man, my dear, will do you some harm someday yet". And so it went on. They could be seen on the roads, she tramping stolidly in her finery – grey dress, black feather, stout boots, prominent white cotton gloves that caught your eye a hundred yards away; and he, his coat slung picturesquely over one shoulder, pacing by her side, gallant of bearing and casting tender glances upon the girl with the golden heart. I wonder whether he saw how plain she was. Perhaps, among types so different from what he had ever seen, he had not the power to judge; or perhaps he was seduced by the divine quality of her pity.

'Yanko was in great trouble meantime. In his country you get an old man for an ambassador in marriage affairs. He did not know how to proceed. However, one day in the midst of sheep in a field (he was now Swaffer's under-shepherd with Foster), he took off his hat to the father and declared himself humbly. "I dare say she's fool enough to marry you," was all Foster said. "And then," he used to relate, "he puts his hat on his head, looks black at me as if he wanted to cut my throat, whistles the dog, and off he goes, leaving me to do the work." The Fosters, of course, didn't like to lose the wages the girl earned: Amy used to give all her money to her mother. But there was in Foster a very genuine aversion to that match. He contended that the fellow was very good with sheep, but was not fit for any girl to marry. For one thing, he used to go along the hedges muttering to himself like a dam' fool; and then, these foreigners behave very queerly to women sometimes. And perhaps he would want to carry her off somewhere – or run off himself. It was not safe. He preached it to his daughter that the fellow might ill-use her in some way. She made no answer. It was, they said in the village, as if the man had done something to her. People discussed the matter. It was quite an excitement, and the two went on "walking out" together in the face of opposition. Then something unexpected happened.

'I don't know whether old Swaffer ever understood how much he was regarded in the light of a father by his foreign retainer. Anyway the relation was curiously feudal. So when Yanko asked formally for an interview – "and the Miss too" (he called the severe, deaf Miss Swaffer simply *Miss*) – it was to obtain their permission to marry. Swaffer heard him unmoved, dismissed him by a nod, and then shouted the intelligence into Miss Swaffer's best ear. She showed no surprise, and only remarked grimly, in a veiled blank voice, "He certainly won't get any other girl to marry him."

'It is Miss Swaffer who has all the credit of the munificence: but in a very few days it came out that Mr Swaffer had presented Yanko with a cottage (the cottage you've seen this morning) and something like an acre of ground – had made it over to him in absolute property. Willcox expedited the deed, and I remember him telling me he had a great pleasure in making it ready. It recited: "In consideration of saving the life of my beloved grandchild, Bertha Willcox."

'Of course, after that no power on earth could prevent them from getting married.

'Her infatuation endured. People saw her going out to meet him in the evening. She stared with unblinking, fascinated eyes up the road where he was expected to appear, walking freely, with a swing from the hip, and humming one of the love-tunes of his country. When the boy was born, he got elevated at the Coach and Horses, essayed again a song and a dance, and was again ejected. People expressed their commiseration for a woman married to that Jack-in-the-box. He didn't care. There was a man now (he told me boastfully) to whom he could sing and talk in the language of his country, and show how to dance by and by.

'But I don't know. To me he appeared to have grown less springy of step, heavier in body, less keen of eye. Imagination, no doubt; but it seems to me now as if the net of fate had been drawn closer round him already.

'One day I met him on the footpath over the Talfourd Hill. He told me that "women were funny". I had heard already of domestic differences. People were saying that Amy Foster was beginning to find out what sort of man she had married. He looked upon the sea with indifferent, unseeing eyes. His wife had snatched the child out of his arms one day as he sat on the doorstep crooning to it a song such as the mothers sing to babies in his mountains. She seemed to think he was doing it some harm. Women are funny. And she had objected to him praying aloud in the evening. Why? He expected the boy to repeat the prayer aloud after him by and by, as he used to do after his old father when he was a child – in his own country. And I discovered he longed for their boy to grow up so that he could have a man to talk with in that language that to our ears sounded so disturbing, so passionate and so bizarre. Why his wife should dislike the idea he couldn't tell. But that would pass, he said. And tilting his head knowingly, he tapped his breastbone to indicate that she had a good heart: not hard, not fierce, open to compassion, charitable to the poor!

'I walked away thoughtfully; I wondered whether his difference, his strangeness, were not penetrating with repulsion that dull nature they had begun by irresistibly attracting. I wondered . . .'

The doctor came to the window and looked out at the frigid splendour of the sea, immense in the haze, as if enclosing all the earth with all the hearts lost among the passions of love and fear.

'Physiologically, now,' he said, turning away abruptly, 'it was possible. It was possible.'

He remained silent. Then went on – 'At all events, the next time I saw him he was ill – lung trouble. He was tough, but I dare say he was not acclimatised as well as I had supposed. It was a bad winter; and, of course, these mountaineers do get fits of home sickness; and a state of depression would make him vulnerable. He was lying half dressed on a couch downstairs.

'A table covered with a dark oilcloth took up all the middle of the little room. There was a wicker cradle on the floor, a kettle spouting steam on the hob, and some child's linen lay drying on the fender. The room was warm, but the door opens right into the garden, as you noticed perhaps.

'He was very feverish, and kept on muttering to himself. She sat on a chair and looked at him fixedly across the table with her brown, blurred eyes. "Why don't you have him upstairs?" I asked. With a start and a confused stammer she said, "Oh! ah! I couldn't sit with him upstairs, sir."

'I gave her certain directions; and going outside, I said again that he ought to be in bed upstairs. She wrung her hands. "I couldn't. I couldn't. He keeps on saying something – I don't know what." With the memory of all the talk against the man that had been dinned into her ears, I looked at her narrowly. I looked into her short-sighted eyes, at her dumb eyes that once in her life had seen an enticing shape, but seemed, staring at me, to see nothing at all now. But I saw she was uneasy.

' "What's the matter with him?" she asked in a sort of vacant trepidation. "He doesn't look very ill. I never did see anybody look like this before . . . "

' "Do you think," I asked indignantly, "he is shamming?"

' "I can't help it, sir," she said stolidly. And suddenly she clapped her hands and looked right and left. "And there's the baby. I am so frightened. He wanted me just now to give him the baby. I can't understand what he says to it."

' "Can't you ask a neighbour to come in tonight?" I asked.

' "Please, sir, nobody seems to care to come," she muttered, dully resigned all at once.

'I impressed upon her the necessity of the greatest care, and then had to go. There was a good deal of sickness that winter. "Oh, I hope he won't talk!" she exclaimed softly just as I was going away.

'I don't know how it is I did not see – but I didn't. And yet, turning in my trap, I saw her lingering before the door, very still, and as if meditating a flight up the miry road.

'Towards the night his fever increased.

'He tossed, moaned, and now and then muttered a complaint. And she sat with the table between her and the couch, watching every movement and every sound, with the terror, the unreasonable terror, of that man she could not understand creeping over her. She had drawn the wicker cradle close to her feet. There was nothing in her now but the maternal instinct and that unaccountable fear.

'Suddenly coming to himself, parched, he demanded a drink of water. She did not move. She had not understood, though he may have thought he was speaking in English. He waited, looking at her, burning with fever, amazed at her silence and immobility, and then he shouted impatiently, "Water! Give me water!"

'She jumped to her feet, snatched up the child, and stood still. He spoke to her, and his passionate remonstrances only increased her fear of that strange man. I believe he spoke to her for a long time, entreating, wondering, pleading, ordering, I suppose. She says she bore it as long as she could. And then a gust of rage came over him.

'He sat up and called out terribly one word – some word. Then he got up as though he hadn't been ill at all, she says. And as in fevered dismay, indignation and wonder he tried to get to her round the table, she simply opened the door and ran out with the child in her arms. She heard him call twice after her down the road in a terrible voice – and fled. . . . Ah! but you should have seen stirring behind the dull, blurred glance of those eyes the spectre of the fear which had hunted her on that night three miles and a half to the door of Foster's cottage! I did the next day.

'And it was I who found him lying face down and his body in a puddle, just outside the little wicket-gate.

'I had been called out that night to an urgent case in the village, and on my way home at daybreak passed by the cottage. The door stood open. My man helped me to carry him in. We laid him on the couch. The lamp smoked, the fire was out, the chill of the stormy night oozed from the cheerless yellow paper on the wall. "Amy!" I called aloud, and my voice seemed to lose itself in the emptiness of this tiny house as if I had cried in a desert. He opened his eyes. "Gone!" he said distinctly. "I had only asked for water – only for a little water . . ."

'He was muddy. I covered him up and stood waiting in silence, catching a painfully gasped word now and then. They were no longer in his own language. The fever had left him, taking with it the heat of life. And with his panting breast and lustrous eyes he reminded me again of a wild creature under the net; of a bird caught in a snare. She had left him. She had left him – sick – helpless – thirsty. The spear of the hunter had entered his very soul. "Why?" he cried in the penetrating and indignant voice of a man calling to a responsible Maker. A gust of wind and a swish of rain answered.

'And as I turned away to shut the door he pronounced the word "Merciful!" and expired.

'Eventually I certified heart-failure as the immediate cause of death. His heart must have indeed failed him, or else he might have stood this night of storm and exposure, too. I closed his eyes and drove away. Not very far from the cottage I met Foster walking sturdily between the dripping hedges with his collie at his heels.

' "Do you know where your daughter is?" I asked.

' "Don't I!" he cried. "I am going to talk to him a bit. Frightening a poor woman like this."

' "He won't frighten her any more," I said. "He is dead."

'He struck with his stick at the mud.

' "And there's the child."

'Then, after thinking deeply for a while – "I don't know that it isn't for the best."

'That's what he said. And she says nothing at all now. Not a word of him. Never. Is his image as utterly gone from her mind as his lithe and striding figure, his carolling voice are gone from our fields? He is no longer before her eyes to excite her imagination into a passion of love or fear; and his memory seems to have vanished from her dull brain as a shadow passes away upon a white screen. She lives in the cottage and works for Miss Swaffer. She is Amy Foster for everybody, and the child is "Amy Foster's boy". She calls him Johnny – which means Little John.

'It is impossible to say whether this name recalls anything to her. Does she ever think of the past? I have seen her hanging over the boy's cot in a very passion of maternal tenderness. The little fellow was lying on his back, a little frightened at me, but very still, with his big black eyes, with his fluttered air of a bird in a snare. And looking at him I seemed to see again the other one – the father, cast out mysteriously by the sea to perish in the supreme disaster of loneliness and despair.'

RUDYARD KIPLING

Rudyard Kipling (1865–1936) was named after the Staffordshire reservoir near Leek beside which his parents became engaged. He was born in India, and spent the first six years of his life there, acquiring Hindustani as a second language and living in an idyllic childhood world. In 1871 he was taken with his sister Alice to England to board at Lorne Lodge in Southsea and there had a miserable time before being sent to the United Services College at Westward Ho! in Devon, the model he drew on for *Stalky & Co.* He left school at sixteen to return to India and work on the *Civil and Military Gazette* in Lahore, and his familiarity with all classes of society provided him with material for *Barrack Room Ballads* and *Plain Tales from the Hills*. In 1889 he returned to England and in 1891 published his novel *The Light That Failed*. He married Caroline (Carrie) Balestier the following year and they returned to her home at Brattleboro, Vermont, where Kipling wrote *The Jungle Book*, *The Second Jungle Book* and *Captains Courageous*. In 1896 the family returned to England, where Kipling continued to write prolifically. In 1907 he was the first Englishman to receive the Nobel Prize for Literature. His later years were darkened by the death of his son John at the Battle of Loos in 1915.

The Bronckhorst Divorce Case

In the daytime, when she moved about me,
In the night, when she was sleeping at my side,
I was wearied, I was wearied of her presence;
Day by day and night by night I grew to hate her –
Would to God that she or I had died!

Confessions

There was a man called Bronckhorst – a three-cornered, middle-aged man in the army – grey as a badger, and, some people said, with a touch of country-blood in him. That, however, cannot be proved. Mrs Bronckhorst was not exactly young, though fifteen years younger than her husband. She was a large, pale, quiet woman, with heavy eyelids over weak eyes, and hair that turned red or yellow as the lights fell on it.

Bronckhorst was not nice in any way. He had no respect for the pretty public and private lies that make life a little less nasty than it is. His manner towards his wife was coarse. There are many things – including actual assault with the clenched fist – that a wife will endure; but seldom can a wife bear – as Mrs Bronckhorst bore – with a long course of brutal, hard chaff, making light of her weaknesses, her headaches, her small fits of gaiety, her dresses, her queer little attempts to make herself attractive to her husband when she knows that she is not what she has been, and – worst of all – the love that she spends on her children. That particular sort of heavy-handed jest was specially dear to Bronckhorst. I suppose that he had first slipped into it, meaning no harm, on the honeymoon, when folk find their ordinary stock of endearments run short, and so go to the other extreme to express their feelings. A similar impulse makes a man say, '*Hutt*, you old beast!' when a favourite horse nuzzles his coat-front. Unluckily, when the reaction of marriage sets in, the form of speech remains, and, the tenderness having died out, hurts the wife more than she cares to say. But Mrs Bronckhorst was devoted to her 'Teddy' as she called him. Perhaps that was why he objected to her. Perhaps – this is only a theory to account for his infamous behaviour later on – he gave way to the queer, savage feeling that sometimes takes by the throat a husband twenty years married, when he sees, across the table, the same, same face of his wedded wife, and knows that, as he has sat facing it, so must he continue to sit until the day of its death or his own. Most men and all women know the spasm. It only lasts for three breaths as a rule, must be a 'throw-back' to times when men and women were rather worse than they are now, and is too unpleasant to be discussed.

Dinner at the Bronckhorsts' was an infliction few men cared to undergo. Bronckhorst took a pleasure in saying things that made his wife wince. When their little boy came in at dessert Bronckhorst used to give him half a glass of wine, and, naturally enough, the poor little mite got first riotous, next miserable, and was removed screaming. Bronckhorst asked if that was the way Teddy usually behaved, and whether Mrs Bronckhorst could not spare some of her time 'to teach the little beggar decency'. Mrs Bronckhorst, who loved the boy more than her own life, tried not to cry – her spirit seemed to have been broken by her marriage. Lastly, Bronckhorst used to say, 'There! That'll do, that'll do. For God's sake try to behave like a rational woman. Go into the drawing-room.' Mrs Bronckhorst would go, trying to carry it all off with a smile; and the guest of the evening would feel angry and uncomfortable.

After three years of this cheerful life – for Mrs Bronckhorst had no women-friends to talk to – the station was startled by the news that Bronckhorst had instituted proceedings *in the criminal count* against a man called Biel, who certainly had been rather attentive to Mrs Bronckhorst whenever she had appeared in public. The utter want of reserve with which Bronckhorst treated his own dishonour helped us to know that the evidence against Biel would be entirely circumstantial and native. There were no letters; but Bronckhorst said openly that he would rack heaven and earth until he saw Biel superintending the manufacture of carpets in the Central Jail. Mrs Bronckhorst kept entirely to her house, and let charitable folks say what they pleased. Opinions were divided. Some two-thirds of the station jumped at once to the conclusion that Biel was guilty; but a dozen men who knew and liked him held by him. Biel was furious and surprised. He denied the whole thing, and vowed that he would thrash Bronckhorst within an inch of his life. No jury, we knew, would convict a man on the criminal count on native evidence in a land where you can buy a murder charge, including the corpse, all complete for fifty-four rupees; but Biel did not care to scrape through by the benefit of a doubt. He wanted the whole thing cleared; but, as he said one night, 'He can prove anything with servants' evidence, and I've only my bare word.' This was almost a month before the case came on; and beyond agreeing with Biel, we could do little. All that we could be sure of was that the native evidence would be bad enough to blast Biel's character for the rest of his service; for when a native begins perjury he perjures himself thoroughly. He does not boggle over details.

Some genius at the end of the table whereat the affair was being talked over, said, 'Look here! I don't believe lawyers are any good. Get a man to wire to Strickland, and beg him to come down and pull us through.'

Strickland was about a hundred and eighty miles up the line. He had not long been married to Miss Youghal, but he scented in the telegram a chance of return to the old detective work that his soul lusted after, and he came down and heard our story. He finished his pipe and said oracularly, 'We must get at the evidence. Oorya bearer, Mussulman *khit* and sweeper *ayah*,

I suppose, are the pillars of the charge. I am on in this piece; but I'm afraid I'm getting rusty in my talk.'

He rose and went into Biel's bedroom, where his trunk had been put, and shut the door. An hour later, we heard him say, 'I hadn't the heart to part with my old make-ups when I married. Will this do?' There was a loathly *fakir* salaaming in the doorway.

'Now lend me fifty rupees,' said Strickland, 'and give me your words of honour that you won't tell my wife.'

He got all that he asked for, and left the house while the table drank his health. What he did only he himself knows. A *fakir* hung about Bronckhorst's compound for twelve days. Then a sweeper appeared, and when Biel heard of *him*, he said that Strickland was an angel full-fledged. Whether the sweeper made love to Janki, Mrs Bronckhorst's *ayah*, is a question which concerns Strickland exclusively.

He came back at the end of three weeks, and said quietly, 'You spoke the truth, Biel. The whole business is put up from beginning to end. Jove! It almost astonishes *me*! That Bronckhorst beast isn't fit to live.'

There was uproar and shouting, and Biel said, 'How are you going to prove it? You can't say that you've been trespassing on Bronckhorst's compound in disguise!'

'No,' said Strickland. 'Tell your lawyer-fool, whoever he is, to get up something strong about "inherent improbabilities" and "discrepancies of evidence". He won't have to speak, but it will make him happy. *I*'m going to run this business.'

Biel held his tongue, and the other men waited to see what would happen. They trusted Strickland as men trust quiet men. When the case came off the court was crowded. Strickland hung about in the veranda of the court, till he met the Mohammedan *khitmutgar*. Then he murmured a *fakir*'s blessing in his ear, and asked him how his second wife did. The man spun round, and, as he looked into the eyes of 'Estreekin Sahib', his jaw dropped. You must remember that before Strickland was married, he was, as I have told you already, a power among natives. Strickland whispered a rather coarse vernacular proverb to the effect that he was abreast of all that was going on, and went into the court armed with a gut trainer's-whip.

The Mohammedan was the first witness, and Strickland beamed upon him from the back of the court. The man moistened his lips with his tongue and, in his abject fear of 'Estreekin Sahib' the *fakir*, went back on every detail of his evidence – said he was a poor man, and God was his witness that he had forgotten everything that Bronckhorst Sahib had told him to say. Between his terror of Strickland, the judge, and Bronckhorst he collapsed weeping.

Then began the panic among the witnesses. Janki, the *ayah*, leering chastely behind her veil, turned grey, and the bearer left the court. He said that his mamma was dying, and that it was not wholesome for any man to lie unthriftily in the presence of 'Estreekin Sahib'.

Biel said politely to Bronckhorst, 'Your witnesses don't seem to work. Haven't you any forged letters to produce?' But Bronckhorst was swaying to and fro in his chair, and there was a dead pause after Biel had been called to order.

Bronckhorst's counsel saw the look on his client's face, and without more ado pitched his papers on the little green-baize table, and mumbled something about having been misinformed. The whole court applauded wildly, like soldiers at a theatre, and the judge began to say what he thought.

* * *

Biel came out of the court, and Strickland dropped a gut trainer's-whip in the veranda. Ten minutes later, Biel was cutting Bronckhorst into ribbons behind the old court cells, quietly and without scandal. What was left of Bronckhorst was sent home in a carriage; and his wife wept over it and nursed it into a man again. Later on, after Biel had managed to hush up the counter-charge against Bronckhorst of fabricating false evidence, Mrs Bronckhorst, with her faint, watery smile, said that there had been a mistake, but it wasn't her Teddy's fault altogether. She would wait till her Teddy came back to her. Perhaps he had grown tired of her, or she had tried his patience, and perhaps we wouldn't cut her any more, and perhaps the mothers would let their children play with 'little Teddy' again. He was so lonely. Then the station invited Mrs Bronckhorst everywhere, until Bronckhorst was fit to appear in public, when he went home and took his wife with him. According to latest advices, her Teddy did come back to her, and they are moderately happy. Though, of course, he can never forgive her the thrashing that she was the indirect means of getting for him.

* * *

What Biel wants to know is, 'Why didn't I press home the charge against the Bronckhorst brute, and have him run in?'

What Mrs Strickland wants to know is, 'How *did* my husband bring such a lovely, lovely Waler* from your station? I know *all* his money affairs; and I'm *certain* he didn't *buy* it.'

What I want to know is, 'How do women like Mrs Bronckhorst come to marry men like Bronckhorst?'

And my conundrum is the most unanswerable of the three.

* a riding horse bred in Australia, specifically in New South Wales

O. HENRY

William Sydney Porter (1862–1910), a short-story writer who used the pen name O. Henry, was born at Greensboro, North Carolina, son of a doctor. After leaving school he worked for five years in his father's dispensary, then went to Texas and was successively a ranch hand, a bank teller and editor and publisher of the humorous magazine *The Rolling Stone*. In 1896 he was charged with having embezzled bank funds, and though he seems to have been only technically guilty he cleared off to South America, where he associated with law breakers and refugees. In 1897 he returned to Texas because of the illness of his wife and was arrested and sentenced to five years in the penitentiary, where he is thought to have taken the pseudonym of O. Henry from the name of a French pharmacist, Etienne-Ossian Henry, he found in the *U.S. Dispensatory*. Set at liberty in 1901, he roamed New York, living from hand to mouth and consuming an average of a quart of whiskey a day. He supported himself by his short stories, of which he wrote some six hundred, and eventually died in hospital of cirrhosis of the liver. With their use of ironical coincidence and unexpected endings they set a fashion in American literature. In 1918 the American Society of Arts and Sciences founded the O. Henry Memorial Award for the best American short story of each year.

The Lost Blend

Since the bar has been blessed by the clergy, and cocktails open the dinners of the elect, one may speak of the saloon. Teetotalers need not listen, if they choose; there is always the slot restaurant, where a dime dropped into the cold bouillon aperture will bring forth a dry Martini.

Con Lantry worked on the sober side of the bar in Kenealy's Café. You and I stood, one-legged like geese, on the other side and went into voluntary liquidation with our week's wages. Opposite danced Con, clean, temperate, clear-headed, polite, white-jacketed, punctual, trustworthy, young, responsible, and took our money.

The saloon (whether blessed or cursed) stood in one of those little 'places' which are parallelograms instead of streets, and are inhabited by laundries, decayed Knickerbocker families and Bohemians who have nothing to do with either.

Over the café lived Kenealy and his family. His daughter Katherine had eyes of dark Irish – but why should you be told? Be content with your Geraldine or your Eliza Ann. For Con dreamed of her; and when she called softly at the foot of the back stairs for the pitcher of beer for dinner, his heart went up and down like a milk punch in the shaker. Orderly and fit are the rules of Romance; and if you hurl the last shilling of your fortune upon the bar for whiskey, the bartender shall take it, and marry his boss's daughter, and good will grow out of it.

But not so Con. For in the presence of women he was tongue-tied and scarlet. He who would quell with his eye the sonorous youth whom the claret punch made loquacious, or smash with lemon squeezer the obstreperous, or hurl gutterward the cantankerous without a wrinkle coming to his white lawn tie, when he stood before a woman he was voiceless, incoherent, stuttering, buried beneath a hot avalanche of bashfulness and misery. What, then, was he before Katherine? A trembler, with no word to say for himself, a stone without blarney, the dumbest lover that ever babbled of the weather in the presence of his divinity.

There came to Kenealy's two sunburned men, Riley and McQuirk. They had conference with Kenealy; and then they took possession of a back room which they filled with bottles and siphons and jugs and druggist's measuring glasses. All the appurtenances and liquids of a saloon were there, but they dispensed no drinks. All day long the two sweltered in there, pouring and mixing unknown brews and decoctions from the liquors in their store. Riley had the education, and he figured on reams of paper, reducing gallons to ounces and quarts to fluid drams. McQuirk, a morose man with a red eye, dashed each unsuccessful completed mixture into the waste pipes with curses gentle, husky and deep. They laboured heavily and untiringly to achieve some mysterious solution, like two alchemists striving to resolve gold from the elements.

Into this back room one evening when his watch was done sauntered Con. His professional curiosity had been stirred by these occult bartenders at whose bar none drank, and who daily drew upon Kenealy's store of liquors to follow their consuming and fruitless experiments.

Down the backstairs came Katherine with her smile like sunrise on Gweebarra Bay.

'Good-evening, Mr Lantry,' says she. 'And what is the news today, if you please?'

It looks like r–rain,' stammered the shy one, backing to the wall.

'It couldn't do better,' said Katherine. 'I'm thinking there's nothing the worse off for a little water.'

In the back room Riley and McQuirk toiled like bearded witches over their strange compounds. From fifty bottles they drew liquids carefully measured after Riley's figures, and shook the whole together in a great glass vessel. Then McQuirk would dash it out, with gloomy profanity, and they would begin again.

'Sit down,' said Riley to Con, 'and I'll tell you.

'Last summer me and Tim concludes that an American bar in this nation of Nicaragua would pay. There was a town on the coast where there's nothing to eat but quinine and nothing to drink but rum. The natives and foreigners lay down with chills and get up with fevers; and a good mixed drink is nature's remedy for all such tropical inconveniences.

'So we lays in a fine stock of wet goods in New York, and bar fixtures and glassware, and we sails for that Santa Palma town on a line steamer. On the way me and Tim sees flying fish and plays seven-up with the captain and steward, and already begins to feel like the high-ball kings of the Tropic of Capricorn.

'When we gets to within five hours of the country that we was going to introduce to long drinks and short change the captain calls us over to the starboard binnacle and recollects a few things.

' "I forgot to tell you, boys," says he, "that Nicaragua slapped an import duty of forty-eight per cent *ad valorem* on all bottled goods last month. The President took a bottle of Cincinnati hair tonic by mistake for tabasco sauce, and he's getting even. Barrelled goods is free."

' "Sorry you didn't mention it sooner," says we. And we bought two forty-two gallon casks from the captain, and opened every bottle we had and dumped the stuff all together in the casks. That forty-eight per cent would have ruined us; so we took the chances on making that $1,200 cocktail rather than throw the stuff away.

'Well, when we landed we tapped one of the barrels. The mixture was something heart-rending. It was the colour of a plate of Bowery pea-soup, and it tasted like one of those coffee substitutes your aunt makes you take for the heart trouble you get by picking losers. We gave a nigger four fingers of it to try it, and he lay under a coconut tree three days beating the sand with his heels and refused to sign a testimonial.

'But the other barrel! Say, bartender, did you ever put on a straw hat with a yellow band around it and go up in a balloon with a pretty girl with eight million dollars in your pocket all at the same time? That's what thirty drops of it would make you feel like. With two fingers of it inside you you would bury your face in your hands and cry because there wasn't anything more worth while around for you to lick than little Jim Jeffries. Yes, sir, the stuff in that second barrel was distilled elixir of battle money and high life. It was the colour of gold and as clear as glass, and it shone after dark like the sunshine was still in it. A thousand years from now you'll get a drink like that across the bar.

'Well, we started up business with that one line of drinks, and it was enough. The piebald gentry of that country stuck to it like a hive of bees. If that barrel had lasted that country would have become the greatest on earth. When we opened up of mornings we had a line of generals and colonels and ex-presidents and revolutionists a block long waiting to be served. We started in at fifty cents silver a drink. The last ten gallons went easy at five dollars a gulp. It was wonderful stuff. It gave a man courage and ambition and nerve to do anything; at the same time he didn't care whether his money was tainted or fresh from the Ice Trust. When that barrel was half gone Nicaragua had repudiated the National Debt, removed the duty on cigarettes and was about to declare war on the United States and England.

' 'Twas by accident we discovered this king of drinks, and 'twill be by good luck if we strike it again. For ten months we've been trying. Small lots at a time, we've mixed barrels of all the harmful ingredients known to the profession of drinking. Ye could have stocked ten bars with the whiskies, brandies, cordials, bitters, gins and wines me and Tim have wasted. A glorious drink like that to be denied to the world! 'tis a sorrow and a loss of money. The United States as a nation would welcome a drink of the sort, and pay for it.'

All the while McQuirk had been carefully measuring and pouring together small quantities of various spirits, as Riley called them, from his latest pencilled prescription. The completed mixture was of a vile, mottled chocolate colour. McQuirk tasted it, and hurled it, with appropriate epithets, into the waste sink.

' 'Tis a strange story, even if true,' said Con. 'I'll be going now along to my supper.'

'Take a drink,' said Riley. 'We've all kinds except the lost blend.'

'I never drink,' said Con, 'anything stronger than water. I am just after meeting Miss Katherine by the stairs. She said a true word. "There's not anything," says she, "but is better off for a little water." '

When Con had left them Riley almost felled McQuirk by a blow on the back.

'Did ye hear that?' he shouted. 'Two fools are we. The six dozen bottles of 'pollinaris we had on the ship – ye opened them yourself – which barrel did ye pour them in – which barrel, ye mud-head?'

'I mind,' said McQuirk, slowly, ' 'twas in the second barrel we opened. I mind the blue piece of paper pasted on the side of it.'

'We've got it now,' cried Riley. ' 'Twas that we lacked. 'Tis the water that does the trick. Everything else we had right. Hurry, man, and get two bottles of 'pollinaris from the bar, while I figure out the proportionments with me pencil.'

An hour later Con strolled down the sidewalk towards Kenealy's Café. Thus faithful employees haunt, during their recreation hours, the vicinity where they labour, drawn by some mysterious attraction.

A police patrol waggon stood at the side door. Three able cops were half carrying, half hustling Riley and McQuirk up its rear steps. The eyes and faces of each bore the bruises and cuts of sanguinary and assiduous conflict. Yet they whooped with strange joy, and directed upon the police the feeble remnants of their pugnacious madness.

'Began fighting each other in the back room,' explained Kenealy to Con. 'And singing! That was worse. Smashed everything pretty much up. But they're good men. They'll pay for everything. Trying to invent some new kind of cocktail, they was. I'll see they come out all right in the morning.'

Con sauntered into the back room to view the battlefield. As he went through the hall Katherine was just coming down the stairs.

'Good-evening again, Mr Lantry,' said she. 'And is there no news from the weather yet?'

'Still threatens r–rain,' said Con, slipping past with red in his smooth, pale cheek.

Riley and McQuirk had indeed waged a great and friendly battle. Broken bottles and glasses were everywhere. The room was full of alcohol fumes; the floor was variegated with spirituous puddles.

On the table stood a 32-ounce glass graduated measure. In the bottom of it were two tablespoonfuls of liquid – a bright golden liquid that seemed to hold the sunshine a prisoner in its auriferous depths.

Con smelled it. He tasted it. He drank it.

As he returned through the hall Katherine was just going up the stairs.

'No news yet, Mr Lantry?' she asked, with her teasing laugh.

Con lifted her clear from the floor and held her there. 'The news is,' he said, 'that we're to be married.'

'Put me down, sir!' she cried indignantly, 'or I will – Oh, Con, where, oh, wherever did you get the nerve to say it?'

WILKIE COLLINS

The eldest son of the landscape painter William Collins, Wilkie Collins was born in London in 1824. Educated for a few years at private schools in London, he moved with his family to Italy when he was thirteen and it was there that he gained his real education. Rebelling against his father's strict religious code and conservative values, Wilkie Collins refused to settle into life in either the tea business or as a barrister and remained adamant that he wanted to write. He went on to become one of the most popular novelists of his day. His reputation now rests on his novels *The Woman in White* and *The Moonstone*. Because in his work he explored the realms of mystery, suspense and crime, he is often regarded as the inventor of the detective story. Collins never married and his private life remains a mixture of the romantic and the raffish. Living with his mother until he was thirty-two, Collins then left to set up home with a young woman, Caroline Graves, and her daughter by another man. Remaining with Caroline on and off for the rest of his life, he also fathered three illegitimate children by Martha Rudd. This scandalous arrangement led to Collins being ostracised by smart Victorian society. Plagued by gout from his thirties, Collins was often in great pain, which he attempted to dull with increasing amounts of opium. He died in 1889.

Mr Lismore and the Widow

Late in the autumn, not many years since, a public meeting was held at the Mansion House, London, under the direction of the Lord Mayor.

The list of gentlemen invited to address the audience had

been chosen with two objects in view. Speakers of celebrity, who would rouse public enthusiasm, were supported by speakers connected with commerce, who would be practically useful in explaining the purpose for which the meeting was convened. Money wisely spent in advertising had produced the customary result: every seat was occupied before the proceedings began.

Among the late arrivals, who had no choice but to stand or to leave the hall, were two ladies. One of them at once decided on leaving the hall.

'I shall go back to the carriage,' she said, 'and wait for you at the door.'

Her friend answered, 'I shan't keep you long. He is advertised to support the second resolution; I want to see him, and that is all.'

An elderly gentleman, seated at the end of a bench, rose and offered his place to the lady who remained. She hesitated to take advantage of his kindness, until he reminded her that he had heard what she said to her friend. Before the third resolution was proposed his seat would be at his own disposal again. She thanked him, and without further ceremony took his place. He was provided with an opera-glass, which he more than once offered to her when famous orators appeared on the platform. She made no use of it until a speaker, known in the City as a ship-owner, stepped forward to support the second resolution.

His name (announced in the advertisements) was Ernest Lismore.

The moment he rose the lady asked for the opera-glass. She kept it to her eyes for such a length of time, and with such evident interest in Mr Lismore, that the curiosity of her neighbours was aroused. Had he anything to say in which a lady (evidently a stranger to him) was personally interested? There was nothing in the address that he delivered which appealed to the enthusiasm of women. He was undoubtedly a handsome man, whose appearance proclaimed him to be in the prime of life, midway, perhaps, between thirty and forty years of age. But why a lady should persist in keeping an opera-glass fixed on him all through his speech was a question which found the general ingenuity at a loss for a reply.

Having returned the glass with an apology, the lady ventured on putting a question next. 'Did it strike you, sir, that Mr Lismore seemed to be out of spirits?' she asked.

'I can't say it did, ma'am.'

'Perhaps you noticed that he left the platform the moment he had done?'

This betrayal of interest in the speaker did not escape the notice of a lady seated on the bench in front. Before the old gentleman could answer she volunteered an explanation. 'I am afraid Mr Lismore is troubled by anxieties connected with his business,' she said. 'My husband heard it reported in the City yesterday that he was seriously embarrassed by the failure – '

A loud burst of applause made the end of the sentence inaudible. A famous Member of Parliament had risen to propose the third resolution. The polite old man took his seat, and the lady left the hall to join her friend.

'Well, Mrs Callender, has Mr Lismore disappointed you?'

'Far from it! But I have heard a report about him which has alarmed me: he is said to be seriously troubled about money matters. How can I find out his address in the City?'

'We can stop at the first stationer's shop we pass, and ask to look at the directory. Are you going to pay Mr Lismore a visit?'

'I am going to think about it.'

The next day a clerk entered Mr Lismore's private room at the office, and presented a visiting-card. Mrs Callender had reflected, and had arrived at a decision. Underneath her name she had written these explanatory words: 'An important business.'

'Does she look as if she wanted money?' Mr Lismore enquired.

'Oh dear, no! She comes in her carriage.'

'Is she young or old?'

'Old, sir.'

To Mr Lismore, conscious of the disastrous influence occasionally exercised over busy men by youth and beauty, this was a recommendation in itself. He said, 'Show her in.'

Observing the lady as she approached him with the momentary curiosity of a stranger, he noticed that she still preserved the remains of beauty. She had also escaped the misfortune, common to persons at her time of life, of becoming too fat. Even to a man's eye, her dressmaker appeared to have made the most of that favourable circumstance. Her figure had its defects concealed, and its remaining merits set off to advantage. At the same time she evidently held herself above the common deceptions by which some women seek to conceal their age. She wore her own grey hair, and her complexion bore the test of daylight. On entering the room, she made her apologies with some embarrassment. Being the embarrassment of a stranger (and not of a youthful stranger), it failed to impress Mr Lismore favourably.

'I am afraid I have chosen an inconvenient time for my visit,' she began.

'I am at your service,' he answered, a little stiffly, 'especially if you will be so kind as to mention your business with me in few words.'

She was a woman of some spirit, and that reply roused her.

'I will mention it in one word,' she said, smartly. 'My business is – gratitude.'

He was completely at a loss to understand what she meant, and he said so plainly. Instead of explaining herself she put a question.

'Do you remember the night of the 11th of March, between five and six years since?'

He considered for a moment.

'No,' he said, 'I don't remember it. Excuse me, Mrs Callender, I have affairs of my own to attend to which cause me some anxiety – '

'Let me assist your memory, Mr Lismore, and I will leave you to your affairs. On the date that I have referred to you were on your way to the railway station at Bexmore to catch the night express from the north to London.'

As a hint that his time was valuable the ship-owner had hitherto remained standing. He now took his customary seat, and began to listen with some interest. Mrs Callender had produced her effect on him already.

'It was absolutely necessary,' she proceeded, 'that you should be on board your ship in the London docks at nine o'clock the next morning. If you had lost the express the vessel would have sailed without you.'

The expression of his face began to change to surprise.

'Who told you that?' he asked.

'You shall hear directly. On your way into the town your carriage was stopped by an obstruction on the high road. The people of Bexmore were looking at a house on fire.'

He started to his feet.

'Good heavens! are you the lady?'

She held up her hand in satirical protest.

'Gently, sir! You suspected me just now of wasting your valuable time. Don't rashly conclude that I am the lady until you find that I am acquainted with the circumstances.'

'Is there no excuse for my failing to recognise you?' Mr Lismore asked. 'We were on the dark side of the burning house; you were fainting, and I – '

'And you,' she interposed, 'after saving me at the risk of your own life, turned a deaf ear to my poor husband's entreaties when he asked you to wait till I had recovered my senses.'

'Your poor husband? Surely, Mrs Callender, he received no serious injury from the fire?'

'The firemen rescued him under circumstances of peril,' she answered, 'and at his great age he sank under the shock. I have lost the kindest and best of men. Do you remember how you parted from him – burned and bruised in saving me? He liked to talk of it in his last illness. "At least," he said to you, "tell me the name of the man who preserved my wife from a dreadful death." You threw your card to him out of the carriage window, and away you went at a gallop to catch your train. In all the years that have passed I have kept that card, and have vainly enquired for my brave sea-captain. Yesterday I saw your name on the list of speakers at the Mansion House. Need I say that I attended the meeting? Need I tell you now why I come here and interrupt you in business hours?'

She held out her hand. Mr Lismore took it in silence, and pressed it warmly.

'You have not done with me yet,' she resumed, with a smile. 'Do you remember what I said of my errand when I first came in?'

'You said it was an errand of gratitude.'

'Something more than the gratitude which only says "thank you",' she added. 'Before I explain myself, however, I want to know what you have been doing, and how it was that my enquiries failed to trace you after that terrible night.' The appearance of depression which Mrs Callender had noticed at the public meeting showed itself again in Mr Lismore's face. He sighed as he answered her.

'My story has one merit,' he said: 'it is soon told. I cannot wonder that you failed to discover me. In the first place, I was not captain of my ship at that time; I was only mate. In the second place, I inherited some money, and ceased to lead a sailor's life, in less than a year from the night of the fire. You will now understand what obstacles were in the way of your tracing me. With my little capital I started successfully in business as a ship-owner. At the time I naturally congratulated myself on my own good fortune. We little know, Mrs Callender, what the future has in store for us.'

He stopped. His handsome features hardened, as if he were suffering (and concealing) pain. Before it was possible to speak to him there was a knock at the door. Another visitor without an appointment had called; the clerk appeared again with a card and a message.

'The gentleman begs you will see him, sir. He has something to tell you which is too important to be delayed.'

Hearing the message, Mrs Callender rose immediately.

'It is enough for today that we understand each other,' she said. 'Have you any engagement tomorrow after the hours of business?'

'None.'

She pointed to her card on the writing-table. 'Will you come to me tomorrow evening at that address? I am like the gentleman who has just called: I too have my reason for wishing to see you.'

He gladly accepted the invitation. Mrs Callender stopped him as he opened the door for her.

'Shall I offend you,' she said, 'if I ask a strange question before I go? I have a better motive, mind, than mere curiosity. Are you married?'

'No.'

'Forgive me again,' she resumed. 'At my age you cannot possibly misunderstand me; and yet – '

She hesitated. Mr Lismore tried to give her confidence. 'Pray don't stand on ceremony, Mrs Callender. Nothing that *you* can ask me need be prefaced by an apology.'

Thus encouraged, she ventured to proceed. 'You may be engaged to be married?' she suggested. 'Or you may be in love?'

He found it impossible to conceal his surprise, but he answered without hesitation.

'There is no such bright prospect in *my* life,' he said. 'I am not even in love.'

She left him with a little sigh. It sounded like a sigh of relief.

Ernest Lismore was thoroughly puzzled. What could be the old lady's object in ascertaining that he was still free from a matrimonial engagement? If the idea had occurred to him in time he might have alluded to her domestic life, and might have asked if she had children. With a little tact he might have discovered more than this. She had described her feeling towards him as passing the ordinary limits of gratitude, and she was evidently rich enough to be above the imputation of a mercenary motive. Did she propose to brighten those dreary prospects to which he had alluded in speaking of his own life? When he presented himself at her house the next evening would she introduce him to a charming daughter?

He smiled as the idea occurred to him. 'An appropriate time to be thinking of my chances of marriage!' he said to himself. 'In another month I may be a ruined man.'

The gentleman who had so urgently requested an interview was a devoted friend who had obtained a means of helping Ernest at a serious crisis in his affairs.

It had been truly reported that he was in a position of pecuniary embarrassment, owing to the failure of a mercantile house with which he had been intimately connected. Whispers affecting his own solvency had followed on the bankruptcy of the firm. He had already endeavoured to obtain advances of money on the usual conditions, and had been met by excuses for delay. His friend had now arrived with a letter of introduction to a capitalist, well known in commercial circles for his daring speculations and for his great wealth.

Looking at the letter, Ernest observed that the envelope was sealed. In spite of that ominous innovation on established usage in cases of personal introduction, he presented the letter. On this occasion he was not put off with excuses. The capitalist flatly declined to discount Mr Lismore's bills unless they were backed by responsible names.

Ernest made a last effort.

He applied for help to two mercantile men whom he had assisted in *their* difficulties, and whose names would have satisfied the money-lender. They were most sincerely sorry, but they too refused.

The one security that he could offer was open, it must be owned, to serious objections on the score of risk. He wanted an advance of twenty thousand pounds, secured on a homeward-bound ship and cargo. But the vessel was not insured, and at that stormy season she was already more than a month overdue. Could grateful colleagues be blamed if they forgot their obligations when they were asked to offer pecuniary help to a merchant in this situation? Ernest returned to his office without money and without credit.

A man threatened by ruin is in no state of mind to keep an engagement at a lady's tea-table. Ernest sent a letter of apology to Mrs Callender, alleging extreme pressure of business as the excuse for breaking his engagement.

'Am I to wait for an answer, sir?' the messenger asked.

'No; you are merely to leave the letter.'

In an hour's time, to Ernest's astonishment, the messenger returned with a reply.

'The lady was just going out, sir, when I rang at the door,' he explained, 'and she took the letter from me herself. She didn't appear to know your handwriting, and she asked me who I came from. When I mentioned your name I was ordered to wait.'

Ernest opened the letter.

DEAR MR LISMORE – One of us must speak out, and your letter of apology forces me to be that one. If you are really so proud and so distrustful as you seem to be, I shall offend you; if not, I shall prove myself to be your friend.

Your excuse is 'pressure of business'; the truth (as I have good reason to believe) is 'want of money'. I heard a stranger at that public meeting say that you were seriously embarrassed by some failure in the City.

Let me tell you what my own pecuniary position is in two words: I am the childless widow of a rich man – '

Ernest paused. His anticipated discovery of Mrs Callender's 'charming daughter' was in his mind for the moment. 'That little romance must return to the world of dreams,' he thought, and went on with the letter.

After what I owe to you, I don't regard it as repaying an obligation; I consider myself as merely performing a duty when I offer to assist you by a loan of money.

Wait a little before you throw my letter into the waste-paper basket.

Circumstances (which it is impossible for me to mention before we meet) put it out of my power to help you – unless I attach to my most sincere offer of service a very unusual and very embarrassing condition. If you are on the brink of ruin that misfortune will plead my excuse – and your excuse too, if you accept the loan on my terms. In any case, I rely on the sympathy and forbearance of the man to whom I owe my life.

After what I have now written, there is only one thing to add: I beg to decline accepting your excuses, and I shall expect to see you tomorrow evening, as we arranged. I am an obstinate old woman, but I am also your faithful friend and servant,

MARY CALLENDER

Ernest looked up from the letter. 'What can this possibly mean?' he wondered.

But he was too sensible a man to be content with wondering; he decided on keeping his engagement.

What Dr Johnson called 'the insolence of wealth' appears

far more frequently in the houses of the rich than in the manners of the rich. The reason is plain enough. Personal ostentation is, in the very nature of it, ridiculous; but the ostentation which exhibits magnificent pictures, priceless china and splendid furniture can purchase good taste to guide it, and can assert itself without affording the smallest opening for a word of depreciation or a look of contempt. If I am worth a million of money, and if I am dying to show it, I don't ask you to look at me, I ask you to look at my house.

Keeping his engagement with Mrs Callender, Ernest discovered that riches might be lavishly and yet modestly used.

In crossing the hall and ascending the stairs, look where he might, his notice was insensibly won by proofs of the taste which is not to be purchased, and the wealth which uses, but never exhibits, its purse. Conducted by a manservant to the landing on the first floor, he found a maid at the door of the boudoir waiting to announce him. Mrs Callender advanced to welcome her guest, in a simple evening dress, perfectly suited to her age. All that had looked worn and faded in her fine face by daylight was now softly obscured by shaded lamps. Objects of beauty surrounded her, which glowed with subdued radiance from their background of sober colour. The influence of appearances is the strongest of all outward influences, while it lasts. For the moment the scene produced its impression on Ernest, in spite of the terrible anxieties which consumed him. Mrs Callender in his office was a woman who had stepped out of her appropriate sphere. Mrs Callender in her own house was a woman who had risen to a new place in his estimation.

'I am afraid you don't thank me for forcing you to keep your engagement,' she said, with her friendly tones and her pleasant smile.

'Indeed I do thank you,' he replied. 'Your beautiful house and your gracious welcome have persuaded me into forgetting my troubles – for a while.'

The smile passed away from her face. 'Then it is true,' she said, gravely.

'Only too true.'

She led him to a seat beside her, and waited to speak again until her maid had brought in the tea.

'Have you read my letter in the same friendly spirit in which I wrote it?' she asked, when they were alone again.

'I have read your letter gratefully, but – '

'But you don't know yet what I have to say. Let us understand each other before we make any objections on either side. Will you tell me what your present position is – at its worst? I can, and will, speak plainly when my turn comes, if you will honour me with your confidence. Not if it distresses you,' she added, observing him attentively. He was ashamed of his hesitation, and he made amends for it.

'Do you thoroughly understand me?' he asked, when the whole truth had been laid before her without reserve.

She summed up the result in her own words: 'If your overdue ship returns safely within a month from this time, you can borrow the money you want without difficulty. If the ship is lost, you have no alternative, when the end of the month comes, but to accept a loan from me or to suspend payment. Is that the hard truth?'

'It is.'

'And the sum you require is – twenty thousand pounds?'

'Yes.'

'I have twenty times as much money as that, Mr Lismore, at my sole disposal – on one condition.'

'The condition alluded to in your letter?'

'Yes.'

'Does the fulfilment of the condition depend in some way on any decision of mine?'

'It depends entirely on you.'

That answer closed his lips.

With a composed manner and a steady hand, she poured herself out a cup of tea. 'I conceal it from you,' she said, 'but I want confidence. Here' (she pointed to the cup) 'is the friend of women, rich or poor, when they are in trouble. What I have now to say obliges me to speak in praise of myself. I don't like it; let me get it over as soon as I can. My husband was very fond of me; he had the most absolute confidence in my discretion, and in my sense of duty to him and to myself. His last words before he died were words that thanked me for making the happiness of his life. As soon as I had in some degree recovered after the affliction that had fallen on me, his lawyer and executor produced a copy of his will, and said there were two clauses in it which my husband had expressed a wish that I should read. It is needless to say that I obeyed.'

She still controlled her agitation – but she was now unable to conceal it. Ernest made an attempt to spare her.

'Am I concerned in this?' he asked.

'Yes. Before I tell you why, I want to know what you would do – in a certain case which I am unwilling even to suppose. I have heard of men, unable to pay the demands made on them, who began business again, and succeeded, and in course of time paid their creditors.'

'And you want to know if there is any likelihood of my following their example?' he said. 'Have you also heard of men who have made that second effort – who have failed again – and who have doubled the debts they owed to their brethren in business who trusted them? I knew one of those men myself. He committed suicide.'

She laid her hand for a moment on his.

'I understand you,' she said. 'If ruin comes – '

'If ruin comes,' he interposed, 'a man without money and without credit can make but one last atonement. Don't speak of it now.'

She looked at him with horror.

'I didn't mean that!' she said.

'Shall we go back to what you read in the will?' he suggested.

'Yes – if you will give me a minute to compose myself.'

In less than the minute she had asked for, Mrs Callender was calm enough to go on.

'I now possess what is called a life-interest in my husband's fortune,' she said. 'The money is to be divided, at my death, among charitable institutions; excepting a certain event – '

'Which is provided for in the will?' Ernest added, helping her to go on.

'Yes. I am to be absolute mistress of the whole of the four hundred thousand pounds – ' her voice dropped, and her eyes looked away from him as she spoke the next words – 'on this one condition, that I marry again.'

He looked at her in amazement.

'Surely I have mistaken you,' he said. 'You mean on this one condition, that you do *not* marry again?'

'No, Mr Lismore; I mean exactly what I have said. You now know that the recovery of your credit and your peace of mind rests entirely with yourself.'

After a moment of reflection he took her hand and raised it respectfully to his lips. 'You are a noble woman!' he said.

She made no reply. With drooping head and downcast eyes she waited for his decision. He accepted his responsibility.

'I must not, and dare not, think of the hardship of my own position,' he said; 'I owe it to you to speak without reference to the future that may be in store for me. No man can be worthy of the sacrifice which your generous forgetfulness of yourself is willing to make. I respect you; I admire you; I thank you with my whole heart. Leave me to my fate, Mrs Callender – and let me go.'

He rose. She stopped him by a gesture.

'A young woman,' she answered, 'would shrink from saying what I, as an old woman, mean to say now. I refuse to leave you to your fate. I ask you to prove that you respect me, admire me, and thank me with your whole heart. Take one day to think – and let me hear the result. You promise me this?'

He promised. 'Now go,' she said.

Next morning Ernest received a letter from Mrs Callender. She wrote to him as follows:

There are some considerations which I ought to have mentioned yesterday evening, before you left my house.

I ought to have reminded you – if you consent to reconsider your decision – that the circumstances do not require you to pledge yourself to me absolutely.

At my age, I can with perfect propriety assure you that I regard our marriage simply and solely as a formality which we must fulfill, if I am to carry out my intention of standing between you and ruin.

Therefore – if the missing ship appears in time, the only reason for the marriage is at an end. We shall be as good friends as ever; without the encumbrance of a formal tie to bind us.

In the other event, I should ask you to submit to certain restrictions, which, remembering my position, you will understand and excuse.

'We are to live together, it is unnecessary to say, as mother and son. The marriage ceremony is to be strictly private, and you are so to arrange our affairs that, immediately afterwards, we leave England for any foreign place which you prefer. Some of my friends, and (perhaps) some of your friends, will certainly misinterpret our motives, if we stay in our own country, in a manner which would be unendurable to a woman like me.

As to our future lives, I have the most perfect confidence in you, and I should leave you in the same position of independence which you occupy now. When you wish for my company you will always be welcome. At other times you are your own master. I live on my side of the house, and you live on yours; and I am to be allowed my hours of solitude every day in the pursuit of musical occupations, which have been happily associated with all my past life, and which I trust confidently to your indulgence.

A last word, to remind you of what you may be too kind to think of yourself.

At my age, you cannot, in the course of nature, be troubled by the society of a grateful old woman for many years. You are young enough to look forward to another marriage, which shall be something more than a mere form. Even if you meet with the happy woman in my lifetime, honestly tell me of it, and I promise to tell her that she has only to wait.

In the meantime, don't think, because I write composedly, that I write heartlessly. You pleased and interested me when I first saw you at the public meeting. I don't think I could have proposed what you call this sacrifice of myself to a man who had personally repelled me, though I had felt my debt of gratitude as sincerely as ever. Whether your ship is safe or whether your ship is lost, old Mary Callender likes you, and owns it without false shame.

Let me have your answer this evening, either personally or by letter, whichever you like best.

Mrs Callender received a written answer long before the evening. It said much in few words:

A man impenetrable to kindness might be able to resist your letter. I am not that man. Your great heart has conquered me.

The few formalities which precede marriage by special licence were observed by Ernest. While the destiny of their future lives was still in suspense, an unacknowledged feeling of embarrassment on either side kept Ernest and Mrs Callender apart. Every day brought the lady her report of the state of affairs in the City, written always in the same words: 'No news of the ship.'

On the day before the ship-owner's liabilities became due the terms of the report from the City remained unchanged, and the special licence was put to its contemplated use. Mrs Callender's lawyer and Mrs Callender's maid were the only persons trusted with the secret. Leaving the chief clerk in charge of the business, with every pecuniary demand on his employer satisfied in full, the strangely married pair quitted England.

They arranged to wait for a few days in Paris, to receive any letters of importance which might have been addressed to Ernest in the interval. On the evening of their arrival a telegram from London was waiting at their hotel. It announced that the missing ship had passed up channel – undiscovered in a fog until she reached the Downs – on the day before Ernest's liabilities fell due.

'Do you regret it?' Mrs Lismore said to her husband.

'Not for a moment!' he answered.

They decided on pursuing their journey as far as Munich.

Mrs Lismore's taste for music was matched by Ernest's taste for painting. In his leisure hours he cultivated the art, and delighted in it. The picture-galleries of Munich were almost the only galleries in Europe which he had not seen. True to the engagements to which she had pledged herself, his wife was willing to go wherever it might please him to take her. The one suggestion she made was that they should hire furnished apartments. If they lived at a hotel friends of the husband or the wife (visitors like themselves to the famous city) might see their names in the book or might meet them at the door.

They were soon established in a house large enough to provide them with every accommodation which they required. Ernest's days were passed in the galleries, Mrs Lismore remaining at home, devoted to her music, until it was time to go out with her husband for a drive. Living together in perfect amity and concord, they were nevertheless not living happily. Without any visible reason for the change, Mrs Lismore's spirits were depressed. On the one occasion when Ernest noticed it she made an effort to be cheerful, which it distressed him to see. He allowed her to think that she had relieved him of any further anxiety. Whatever doubts he might feel were doubts delicately concealed from that time forth.

But when two people are living together in a state of artificial tranquillity, it seems to be a law of nature that the element of disturbance gathers unseen, and that the outburst comes inevitably with the lapse of time.

In ten days from the date of their arrival at Munich the crisis came. Ernest returned later than usual from the picture-gallery, and, for the first time in his wife's experience, shut himself up in his own room.

He appeared at the dinner hour with a futile excuse. Mrs Lismore waited until the servant had withdrawn.

'Now, Ernest,' she said, 'it's time to tell me the truth.'

Her manner, when she said those few words, took him by surprise. She was unquestionably confused, and, instead of looking at him, she trifled with the fruit on her plate. Embarrassed on his side, he could only answer: 'I have nothing to tell.'

'Were there many visitors at the gallery?' she asked.

'About the same as usual.'

'Any that you particularly noticed?' she went on. 'I mean among the ladies.'

He laughed uneasily.

'You forget how interested I am in the pictures,' he said.

There was a pause. She looked up at him, and suddenly looked away again; but – he saw it plainly – there were tears in her eyes.

'Do you mind turning down the gas?' she said. 'My eyes have been weak all day.'

He complied with her request the more readily, having his own reasons for being glad to escape the glaring scrutiny of the light.

'I think I will rest a little on the sofa,' she resumed. In the position which he occupied his back would have been now turned on her. She stopped him when he tried to move his chair. 'I would rather not look at you, Ernest,' she said, 'when you have lost confidence in me.'

Not the words, but the tone, touched all that was generous and noble in his nature. He left his place and knelt beside her, and opened to her his whole heart.

'Am I not unworthy of you?' he asked, when it was over.

She pressed his hand in silence.

'I should be the most ungrateful wretch living,' he said, 'if I did not think of you, and you only, now that my confession is made. We will leave Munich tomorrow, and, if resolution can help me, I will only remember the sweetest woman my eyes ever looked on as the creature of a dream.'

She hid her face on his breast, and reminded him of that letter of her writing which had decided the course of their lives.

'When I thought you might meet the happy woman in my lifetime I said to you, "Tell me of it, and I promise to tell her that she has only to wait." Time must pass, Ernest, before it can be needful to perform my promise, but you might let me see her. If you find her in the gallery tomorrow you might bring her here.'

Mrs Lismore's request met with no refusal. Ernest was only at a loss to know how to grant it.

'You tell me she is a copyist of pictures,' his wife reminded him. 'She will be interested in hearing of the portfolio of drawings by the great French artists which I bought for you in Paris. Ask her to come and see them, and to tell you if she can make some copies; and say, if you like, that I shall be glad to become acquainted with her.'

He felt her breath beating fast on his bosom. In the fear that she might lose all control over herself, he tried to relieve her by speaking lightly.

'What an invention yours is!' he said. 'If my wife ever tries to deceive me, I shall be a mere child in her hands.'

She rose abruptly from the sofa, kissed him on the forehead, and said wildly, 'I shall be better in bed!' Before he could move or speak she had left him.

The next morning he knocked at the door of his wife's room, and asked how she had passed the night.

'I have slept badly,' she answered, 'and I must beg you to excuse my absence at breakfast-time.' She called him back as he was about to withdraw. 'Remember,' she said, 'when you return from the gallery today I expect that you will not return alone.'

Three hours later he was at home again. The young lady's services as a copyist were at his disposal; she had returned with him to look at the drawings.

The sitting-room was empty when they entered it. He rang for his wife's maid, and was informed that Mrs Lismore had gone out. Refusing to believe the woman, he went to his wife's apartments. She was not to be found.

When he returned to the sitting-room the young lady was not unnaturally offended. He could make allowances for her being a little out of temper at the slight that had been put on her; but he was inexpressibly disconcerted by the manner – almost the coarse manner – in which she expressed herself.

'I have been talking to your wife's maid while you have been away,' she said. 'I find you have married an old lady for her money. She is jealous of me, of course?'

'Let me beg you to alter your opinion,' he answered. 'You are wronging my wife; she is incapable of any such feeling as you attribute to her.'

The young lady laughed. 'At any rate, you are a good husband,' she said, satirically. 'Suppose you own the truth: wouldn't you like her better if she was young and pretty like me?'

He was not merely surprised, he was disgusted. Her beauty had so completely fascinated him when he first saw her that the idea of associating any want of refinement and good breeding with such a charming creature never entered his mind. The disenchantment to him was already so complete that he was even disagreeably affected by the tone of her voice; it was almost as repellent to him as this exhibition of unrestrained bad temper which she seemed perfectly careless to conceal.

'I confess you surprise me,' he said, coldly.

The reply produced no effect on her. On the contrary, she became more insolent than ever.

'I have a fertile fancy,' she went on, 'and your absurd way of taking a joke only encourages me! Suppose you could transform this sour old wife of yours, who has insulted me, into the sweetest young creature that ever lived by only holding up your finger, wouldn't you do it?'

This passed the limits of his endurance. 'I have no wish,' he said, 'to forget the consideration which is due to a woman. You leave me but one alternative.' He rose to go out of the room.

She ran to the door as he spoke, and placed herself in the way of his going out.

He signed to her to let him pass.

She suddenly threw her arms round his neck, kissed him passionately, and whispered, with her lips at his ear, 'Oh Ernest, forgive me! Could I have asked you to marry me for my money if I had not taken refuge in a disguise?'

When he had sufficiently recovered to think he put her back from him. 'Is there an end of the deception now?' he asked, sternly. 'Am I to trust you in your new character?'

'You are not to be harder on me than I deserve,' she answered, gently. 'Did you ever hear of an actress named Miss Max?'

He began to understand her. 'Forgive me if I spoke harshly,' he said. 'You have put me to a severe trial.'

She burst into tears. 'Love,' she murmured, 'is my only excuse.'

From that moment she had won her pardon. He took her hand and made her sit by him.

'Yes,' he said, 'I have heard of Miss Max, and of her wonderful powers of personation; and I have always regretted not having seen her while she was on the stage.'

'Did you hear anything more of her, Ernest?'

'Yes; I heard that she was a pattern of modesty and good conduct, and that she gave up her profession at the height of her success to marry an old man.'

'Will you come with me to my room?' she asked. 'I have something there which I wish to show you.'

It was the copy of her husband's will.

'Read the lines, Ernest, which begin at the top of the page. Let my dead husband speak for me.'

The lines ran thus:

My motive in marrying Miss Max must be stated in this place, in justice to her, and, I will venture to add, in justice to myself. I felt the sincerest sympathy for her position. She was without father, mother, or friends, one of the poor forsaken children whom the mercy of the foundling hospital provides with a home. Her afterlife on the stage was the life of a virtuous woman, persecuted by profligates, insulted by some of the baser creatures associated with her, to whom she was an object of envy. I offered her a home and the protection of a father, on the only terms which the world would recognise as worthy of us. My experience of her since our marriage has been the experience of unvarying goodness, sweetness, and sound sense. She has behaved so nobly in a trying position that I wish her (even in this life) to have her reward. I entreat her to make a second choice in marriage, which shall not be a mere form. I firmly believe that she will choose well and wisely, that she will make the happiness of a man who is worthy of her, and that, as wife and mother, she will set an example of inestimable value in the social sphere that she occupies. In proof of the heartfelt sincerity with which I pay my tribute to her virtues, I add to this, my will, the clause that follows.

With the clause that followed Ernest was already acquainted.

'Will you now believe that I never loved till I saw your face for the first time?' said his wife. 'I had no experience to place me on my guard against the fascination – the madness, some people might call it – which possesses a woman when all her heart is given to a man. Don't despise me, my dear! Remember that I had to save you from disgrace and ruin. Besides, my old stage remembrances tempted me. I had acted in a play in which the heroine did – what I have done. It didn't end with me as it did with her in the story. *She* was represented as rejoicing in the success of her disguise. I have known some miserable hours of doubt and shame since our marriage. When I went to meet you in my own person at the picture-gallery, oh, what relief, what joy I felt when I saw how you admired me! It was not because I could no longer carry on the disguise; I was able to get hours of rest from the effort, not only at night, but in the daytime, when I was shut up in my retirement in the music-room, and when my maid kept watch against discovery. No, my love! I hurried on the disclosure because I could no longer endure the hateful triumph of my own deception. Ah, look at that witness against me! I can't bear even to see it.'

She abruptly left him. The drawer that she had opened to take out the copy of the will also contained the false grey hair which she had discarded. It had only that moment attracted her notice. She snatched it up and turned to the fireplace.

Ernest took it from her before she could destroy it. 'Give it to me,' he said.

'Why?'

He drew her gently to his bosom, and answered, 'I must not forget my old wife.'

MARY ELEANOR WILKINS FREEMAN

Mary Eleanor Wilkins Freeman was born in Randolph, Massachusetts in 1852. She passed the greater part of her life in Massachusetts and Vermont and for many years was the private secretary of Oliver Wendell Holmes. Freeman began writing stories and verse for children while still a teenager to help support her family and was quickly successful. Her best known work was written in the 1880s and 1890s while she lived in Randolph. She produced more than two dozen volumes of published short stories and novels. She is best known for two collections of stories, *A Humble Romance and Other Stories* (1887) and *A New England Nun and Other Stories* (1891), which deal mostly with New England life and are among the best of their kind. Freeman is also remembered for her novel *Pembroke* (1894), and she contributed a notable chapter to the collaborative novel *The Whole Family* (1908). In 1902 she married Dr Charles M. Freeman of Metuchen, New Jersey. In April 1926, Freeman became the first recipient of the William Dean Howells Medal for Distinction in Fiction from the American Academy of Arts and Letters. She died in 1930 and was interred in Hillside Cemetery in Scotch Plains, New Jersey.

The Amethyst Comb

Miss Jane Carew was at the railroad station waiting for the New York train. She was about to visit her friend, Mrs Viola Longstreet. With Miss Carew was her maid, Margaret, a middle-aged New England woman, attired in the stiffest and most correct of maid-uniforms. She carried an old, large sole-leather bag, and also a rather large sole-leather jewel-case. The jewel-case, carried openly, was rather an unusual sight at a New England railroad station, but few knew what it was. They concluded it to be Margaret's special handbag. Margaret was a very tall, thin woman, unbending as to carriage and expression. The one thing out of absolute plumb about Margaret was her little black bonnet. That was askew. Time had bereft the woman of so much hair that she could fasten no headgear with security, especially when the wind blew, and that morning there was a stiff gale. Margaret's bonnet was cocked over one eye.

Miss Carew noticed it. 'Margaret, your bonnet is crooked,' she said.

Margaret straightened her bonnet, but immediately the bonnet veered again to the side, weighted by a stiff jet aigrette. Miss Carew observed the careen of the bonnet, realised that it was inevitable, and did not mention it again. Inwardly she resolved upon the removal of the jet aigrette later on. Miss Carew was slightly older than Margaret, and dressed in a style somewhat beyond her age. Jane Carew had been alert upon the situation of departing youth. She had eschewed gay colours and extreme cuts, and had her bonnets made to order, because there were no longer anything but hats in the millinery shop. The milliner in Wheaton, where Miss Carew lived, had objected, for Jane Carew inspired reverence.

'A bonnet is too old for you. Miss Carew,' she said. 'Women much older than you wear hats.'

'I trust that I know what is becoming to a woman of my years, thank you, Miss Waters,' Jane had replied, and the milliner had meekly taken her order.

After Miss Carew had left, the milliner told her girls that she had never seen a woman so perfectly crazy to look her age as Miss Carew. 'And she a pretty woman, too,' said the milliner; 'as straight as an arrer, and slim, and with all that hair, scarcely turned at all.'

Miss Carew, with all her haste to assume years, remained a pretty woman, softly slim, with an abundance of dark hair, showing little grey. Sometimes Jane reflected, uneasily, that it ought at her time of life to be entirely grey. She hoped nobody would suspect her of dyeing it. She wore it parted in the middle, folded back smoothly, and braided in a compact mass on the top of her head. The style of her clothes was slightly behind the fashion, just enough to suggest conservatism and age. She carried a little silver-bound bag in one nicely gloved hand; with the other she held daintily out of the dust of the platform her dress-skirt. A glimpse of a silk frilled petticoat, of slender feet, and ankles delicately slim, was visible before the onslaught of the wind. Jane Carew made no futile effort to keep her skirts down before the wind-gusts. She was so much of the gentlewoman that she could be gravely oblivious to the exposure of her ankles. She looked as if she had never heard of ankles when her black silk skirts lashed about them. She rose superbly above the situation. For some abstruse reason Margaret's skirts were not affected by the wind. They might have been weighted with buckram, although it was no longer in general use. She stood, except for her veering bonnet, as stiffly immovable as a wooden doll.

Miss Carew seldom left Wheaton. This visit to New York was an innovation. Quite a crowd gathered about Jane's sole-leather trunk when it was dumped on the platform by the local expressman. 'Miss Carew is going to New York,' one said to another, with much the same tone as if he had said, 'The great elm on the common is going to move into Dr Jones's front yard.'

When the train arrived, Miss Carew, followed by Margaret, stepped aboard with a majestic disregard of ankles. She sat beside a window, and Margaret placed the bag on the floor and held the jewel-case in her lap. The case contained the Carew jewels. They were not especially valuable, although they were rather numerous. There were cameos in brooches and heavy gold bracelets; corals which Miss Carew had not worn since her young girlhood. There were a set of garnets, some badly cut diamonds in earrings and rings, some seed-pearl ornaments, and a really beautiful set of amethysts. There were a necklace, two brooches – a bar and a circle – earrings, a ring and a comb. Each piece was charming, set in filigree gold with seed-pearls, but perhaps of them all the comb was the best. It was a very large comb. There was one great amethyst in the centre of the top; on either side was an intricate pattern of plums in small amethysts, and seed-pearl grapes, with leaves and stems of gold. Margaret in charge of the jewel-case was imposing. When they arrived in New York she confronted everybody whom she met with a stony stare, which was almost accusative and convictive of guilt, in spite of entire innocence on the part of the person stared at. It was inconceivable that any mortal would have dared lay violent hands upon that jewel-case under that stare. It would have seemed to partake of the nature of grand larceny from providence.

When the two reached the up-town residence of Viola Longstreet, Viola gave a little scream at the sight of the case.

'My dear Jane Carew, here you are with Margaret carrying that jewel-case out in plain sight. How dare you do such a thing? I really wonder you have not been held up a dozen times.'

Miss Carew smiled her gentle but almost stern smile – the Carew smile, which consisted in a widening and slightly upward curving of tightly closed lips.

'I do not think,' said she, 'that anybody would be apt to interfere with Margaret.'

Viola Longstreet laughed, the ringing peal of a child, although she was as old as Miss Carew. 'I think you are right, Jane,' said she. 'I don't believe a crook in New York would dare face that maid of yours. He would as soon encounter Plymouth Rock. I am glad you have brought your delightful old jewels, although you never wear anything except those lovely old pearl sprays and dull diamonds.'

'Now,' stated Jane, with a little toss of pride, 'I have Aunt Felicia's amethysts.'

'Oh, sure enough! I remember you did write me last summer that she had died and you had the amethysts at last. She must have been very old.'

'Ninety-one.'

'She might have given you the amethysts before. You, of course, will wear them; and I – am going to borrow the corals!'

Jane Carew gasped.

'You do not object, do you, dear? I have a new dinner-gown which clamours for corals, and my bank-account is strained, and I could buy none equal to those of yours, anyway.'

'Oh, I do not object,' said Jane Carew; still she looked aghast.

Viola Longstreet shrieked with laughter. 'Oh, I know. You think the corals too young for me. You have not worn them since you left off dotted muslin. My dear, you insisted upon growing old – I insisted upon remaining young. I had two new dotted muslins last summer. As for corals, I would wear them in the face of an opposing army! Do not judge me by yourself, dear. You laid hold of Age and held him, although you had your complexion and your shape and hair. As for me, I had my complexion and kept it. I also had my hair and kept it. My shape has been a struggle, but it was worth while. I, my dear, have held Youth so tight that he has almost choked to death, but held him I have. You cannot deny it. Look at me, Jane Carew, and tell me if, judging by my looks, you can reasonably state that I have no longer the right to wear corals.'

Jane Carew looked. She smiled the Carew smile. 'You *do* look very young, Viola,' said Jane, 'but you are not.'

'Jane Carew,' said Viola, 'I am young. May I wear your corals at my dinner tomorrow night?'

'Why, of course, if you think – '

'If I think them suitable. My dear, if there were on this earth ornaments more suitable to extreme youth than corals, I would borrow them if you owned them, but, failing that, the corals will answer. Wait until you see me in that taupe dinner-gown and the corals!'

Jane waited. She visited with Viola, whom she loved, although they had little in common, partly because of leading widely different lives, partly because of constitutional variations. She was dressed for dinner fully an hour before it was necessary, and she sat in the library reading when Viola swept in.

Viola was really entrancing. It was a pity that Jane Carew had such an unswerving eye for the essential truth that it could not be appeased by actual effect. Viola had doubtless, as she had said, struggled to keep her slim shape, but she had kept it, and, what was more, kept it without evidence of struggle. If she was in the least hampered by tight lacing and length of under-garment, she gave no evidence of it as she curled herself up in a big chair and (Jane wondered how she could bring herself to do it) crossed her legs, revealing one delicate foot and ankle, silk-stockinged with taupe, and shod with a coral satin slipper with a silver heel and a great silver buckle. On Viola's fair round neck the Carew corals lay bloomingly; her beautiful arms were clasped with them; a great coral brooch with wonderful carving confined a graceful fold of the taupe over one hip, a coral comb surmounted the shining waves of Viola's hair. Viola was an ash-blonde, her complexion was as roses, and the corals were ideal for her. As Jane regarded her friend's beauty, however, the fact that Viola was not young, that she was as old as herself, hid it and overshadowed it.

'Well, Jane, don't you think I look well in the corals, after all?' asked Viola, and there was something pitiful in her voice.

When a man or a woman holds fast to youth, even if successfully, there is something of the pitiful and the tragic involved. It is the everlasting struggle of the soul to retain the joy of earth, whose fleeting distinguishes it from heaven, and whose retention is not accomplished without an inner knowledge of its futility.

'I suppose you do, Viola,' replied Jane Carew, with the inflexibility of fate, 'but I really think that only very young girls ought to wear corals.'

Viola laughed, but the laugh had a minor cadence. 'But I *am* a young girl, Jane,' she said. 'I *must* be a young girl. I never had any girlhood when I should have had. You know that.'

Viola had married, when very young, a man old enough to be her father, and her wedded life had been a sad affair, to which, however, she seldom alluded. Viola had much pride with regard to the inevitable past.

'Yes,' agreed Jane. Then she added, feeling that more might be expected, 'Of course I suppose that marrying so very young does make a difference.'

'Yes,' said Viola, 'it does. In fact, it makes of one's girlhood an anticlimax, of which many dispute the wisdom, as you do. But have it I will. Jane, your amethysts are beautiful.'

Jane regarded the clear purple gleam of a stone on her arm. 'Yes,' she agreed, 'Aunt Felicia's amethysts have always been considered very beautiful.'

'And such a full set,' said Viola.

'Yes,' said Jane. She coloured a little, but Viola did not know why. At the last moment Jane had decided not to wear the amethyst comb, because it seemed to her altogether too decorative for a woman of her age, and she was afraid to mention it to Viola. She was sure that Viola would laugh at her and insist upon her wearing it.

'The earrings are lovely,' said Viola. 'My dear, I don't see how you ever consented to have your ears pierced.'

'I was very young, and my mother wished me to,' replied Jane, blushing.

The doorbell rang. Viola had been covertly listening for it all the time. Soon a very beautiful young man came with a curious dancing step into the room. Harold Lind always gave the effect of dancing when he walked. He always, moreover, gave the effect of extreme youth and of the utmost joy and mirth in life itself. He regarded everything and everybody with a smile as of humorous appreciation, and yet the appreciation was so good-natured that it offended nobody.

'Look at me – I am absurd and happy; look at yourself, also absurd and happy; look at everybody else likewise; look at life – a jest so delicious that it is quite worth one's while dying to be made acquainted with it.' That is what Harold Lind seemed to say. Viola Longstreet became even more youthful under his gaze; even Jane Carew regretted that she had not worn her amethyst comb and began to doubt its unsuitability. Viola very soon called the young man's attention to Jane's amethysts, and Jane always wondered why she did not then mention the comb. She removed a brooch and a bracelet for him to inspect.

'They are really wonderful,' he declared. 'I have never seen greater depth of colour in amethysts.'

'Mr Lind is an authority on jewels,' declared Viola. The young man shot a curious glance at her, which Jane remembered long afterwards. It was one of those glances which are as keystones to situations.

Harold looked at the purple stones with the expression of a child with a toy. There was much of the child in the young man's whole appearance, but of a mischievous and beautiful child, of whom his mother might observe, with adoration and ill-concealed boastfulness, 'I can never tell what that child will do next!'

Harold returned the bracelet and brooch to Jane, and smiled at her as if amethysts were a lovely purple joke between her and himself, uniting them by a peculiar bond of fine understanding. 'Exquisite, Miss Carew,' he said. Then he looked at Viola. 'Those corals suit you wonderfully, Mrs Longstreet,' he observed, 'but amethysts would also suit you.'

'Not with this gown,' replied Viola, rather pitifully. There was something in the young man's gaze and tone which she did not understand, but which she vaguely quivered before.

Harold certainly thought the corals were too young for Viola. Jane understood, and felt an unworthy triumph. Harold, who was young enough in actual years to be Viola's son, and was younger still by reason of his disposition, was amused by the sight of her in corals, although he did not intend to betray his amusement. He considered Viola in corals as too rude a jest to share with her. Had poor Viola once grasped Harold Lind's estimation of her she would have as soon gazed upon herself in her coffin. Harold's comprehension of the essentials was beyond Jane Carew's. It was fairly ghastly, partaking of the nature of X-rays, but it never disturbed Harold Lind. He went along his dance-track undisturbed, his blue eyes never losing their high lights of glee, his lips never losing their inscrutable smile at some happy understanding between life and himself. Harold had fair hair, which was very smooth and glossy. His skin was like a girl's. He was so beautiful that he showed cleverness in an affectation of carelessness in dress. He did not like to wear evening clothes, because they had necessarily to be immaculate. That evening Jane regarded him with an inward criticism that he was too handsome for a man. She told Viola so when the dinner was over and he and the other guests had gone.

'He is very handsome,' she said, 'but I never like to see a man quite so handsome.'

'You will change your mind when you see him in tweeds,' returned Viola. 'He loathes evening clothes.'

Jane regarded her anxiously. There was something in Viola's tone which disturbed and shocked her. It was inconceivable that Viola should be in love with that youth, and yet – 'He looks very young,' said Jane in a prim voice.

'He *is* young,' admitted Viola; 'still, not quite so young as he looks. Sometimes I tell him he will look like a boy if he lives to be eighty.'

'Well, he must be very young,' persisted Jane.

'Yes,' said Viola, but she did not say how young. Viola herself, now that the excitement was over, did not look so young as at the beginning of the evening. She removed the corals, and Jane considered that she looked much better without them.

'Thank you for your corals, dear,' said Viola. 'Where is Margaret?'

Margaret answered for herself by a tap on the door. She and Viola's maid, Louisa, had been sitting on an upper landing, out of sight, watching the guests downstairs. Margaret took the corals and placed them in their nest in the jewel-case, also the amethysts, after Viola had gone. The jewel-case was a curious old affair with many compartments. The amethysts required two. The comb was so large that it had one for itself. That was the reason why Margaret did not discover that evening that it was gone. Nobody discovered it for three days, when Viola had a little card-party. There was a whist-table for Jane, who had never given up the reserved and stately game. There were six tables in Viola's pretty living-room, with a little conservatory at one end and a leaping hearth fire at the other. Jane's partner was a stout old gentleman whose wife was shrieking with merriment at an auction-bridge table. The other whist-players were a stupid, very small young man who was aimlessly willing to play anything, and an amiable young woman who believed in self-denial. Jane played conscientiously. She returned trump leads, and played second hand low, and third high, and it was not until the third rubber was over that she saw. It had been in full evidence from the first. Jane would have seen it before the guests arrived, but Viola had not put it in her hair until the last moment. Viola was wild with delight, yet shamefaced and a trifle uneasy. In a soft, white gown, with violets at her waist, she was playing with Harold Lind, and in her ash-blonde hair was Jane Carew's amethyst comb. Jane gasped and paled.

The amiable young woman who was her opponent stared at her. Finally she spoke in a low voice. 'Aren't you well, Miss Carew?' she asked.

The men, in their turn, stared. The stout one rose fussily. 'Let me get a glass of water,' he said. The stupid small man stood up and waved his hands with nervousness.

'Aren't you well?' asked the amiable young lady again.

Then Jane Carew recovered her poise. It was seldom that she lost it. 'I am quite well, thank you, Miss Murdock,' she replied. 'I believe diamonds are trumps.'

They all settled again to the play, but the young lady and the two men continued glancing at Miss Carew. She had recovered her dignity of manner, but not her colour. Moreover, she had a bewildered expression. Resolutely she abstained from glancing again at her amethyst comb in Viola Longstreet's ash-blonde hair, and gradually, by a course of subconscious reasoning as she carefully played her cards, she arrived at a conclusion which caused her colour to return and the bewildered expression to disappear.

When refreshments were served, the amiable young lady said, kindly: 'You look quite yourself, now, dear Miss Carew, but at one time while we were playing I was really alarmed. You were very pale.'

'I did not feel in the least ill,' replied Jane Carew. She smiled her Carew smile at the young lady. Jane had settled it with herself that of course Viola had borrowed that amethyst comb, appealing to Margaret. Viola ought not to have done that; she should have asked her, Miss Carew; and Jane wondered, because Viola was very well bred; but of course that was what had happened. Jane had come down before Viola, leaving Margaret in her room, and Viola had asked her. Jane did not then remember that Viola had not even been told that there was an amethyst comb in existence. She remembered when Margaret, whose face was as pale and bewildered as her own, mentioned it, when she was brushing her hair.

'I saw it, first thing, Miss Jane,' said Margaret. 'Louisa and I were on the landing, and I looked down and saw your amethyst comb in Mrs Longstreet's hair.'

'She had asked you for it, because I had gone downstairs?' asked Jane, feebly.

'No, Miss Jane. I had not seen her. I went out right after you did. Louisa had finished Mrs Longstreet, and she and I went down to the mail-box to post a letter, and then we sat on the landing, and – I saw your comb.'

'Have you,' asked Jane, 'looked in the jewel-case?'

'Yes, Miss Jane.'

'And it is not there?'

'It is not there, Miss Jane.' Margaret spoke with a sort of solemn intoning. She recognised what the situation implied, and she, who fitted squarely and entirely into her humble state, was aghast before a hitherto unimagined occurrence. She could not, even with the evidence of her senses against a lady and her mistress's old friend, believe in those senses. Had Jane told her firmly that she had not seen that comb in that ash-blonde hair she might have been hypnotised into agreement. But Jane simply stared at her, and the Carew dignity was more shaken than she had ever seen it.

'Bring the jewel-case here, Margaret,' ordered Jane in a gasp.

Margaret brought the jewel-case, and everything was taken out; all the compartments were opened, but the amethyst comb was not there. Jane could not sleep that night. At dawn she herself doubted the evidence of her senses. The jewel-case was thoroughly overlooked again, and still Jane was incredulous that she would ever see her comb in Viola's hair again. But that evening, although there were no guests except Harold Lind, who dined at the house, Viola appeared in a pink-tinted gown, with a knot of violets at her waist, and – she wore the amethyst comb. She said not one word concerning it; nobody did. Harold Lind was in wild spirits. The conviction grew upon Jane that the irresponsible, beautiful youth was covertly amusing himself at her, at Viola's, at everybody's expense. Perhaps he included himself. He talked incessantly, not in reality brilliantly, but with an effect of sparkling effervescence which was fairly dazzling. Viola's servants restrained with difficulty their laughter at his sallies. Viola regarded Harold with ill-concealed tenderness and admiration. She herself looked even younger than usual, as if the innate youth in her leaped to meet this charming comrade.

Jane felt sickened by it all. She could not understand her friend. Not for one minute did she dream that there could be any serious outcome of the situation: that Viola would marry this mad youth, who, she knew, was making such covert fun at her expense; but she was bewildered and indignant. She wished that she had not come. That evening when she went to her room she directed Margaret to pack, as she intended to return home the next day. Margaret began folding gowns with alacrity. She was as conservative as her mistress and she severely disapproved of many things. However, the matter of the amethyst comb was uppermost in her mind. She was wild with curiosity. She hardly dared enquire, but finally she did.

'About the amethyst comb, ma'am?' she said, with a delicate cough.

'What about it, Margaret?' returned Jane, severely.

'I thought perhaps Mrs Longstreet had told you how she happened to have it.'

Poor Jane Carew had nobody in whom to confide. For once she spoke her mind to her maid. 'She has not said one word. And, oh, Margaret, I don't know what to think of it.'

Margaret pursed her lips.

'What do *you* think, Margaret?'

'I don't know, Miss Jane.'

'I don't.'

'I did not mention it to Louisa,' said Margaret.

'Oh, I hope not!' cried Jane.

'But she did to me,' said Margaret. 'She asked had I seen Miss Viola's new comb, and then she laughed, and I thought from the way she acted that – ' Margaret hesitated.

'That what?'

'That she meant Mr Lind had given Miss Viola the comb.'

Jane started violently. 'Absolutely impossible!' she cried. 'That, of course, is nonsense. There must be some explanation. Probably Mrs Longstreet will explain before we go.'

Mrs Longstreet did not explain. She wondered and expostulated when Jane announced her firm determination to leave, but she seemed utterly at a loss for the reason. She did not mention the comb.

When Jane Carew took leave of her old friend she was entirely sure in her own mind that she would never visit her again – might never even see her again.

Jane was unutterably thankful to be back in her own peaceful home, over which no shadow of absurd mystery brooded; only a calm afternoon light of life, which disclosed gently but did not conceal or betray. Jane settled back into her pleasant life, and the days passed, and the weeks, and the months, and the years. She heard nothing whatever from or about Viola Longstreet for three years. Then, one day, Margaret returned from the city, and she had met Viola's old maid Louisa in a department store, and she had news. Jane wished for strength to refuse to listen, but she could not muster it. She listened while Margaret brushed her hair.

'Louisa has not been with Miss Viola for a long time,' said Margaret. 'She is living with somebody else. Miss Viola lost her money, and had to give up her house and her servants, and Louisa said she cried when she said goodbye.'

Jane made an effort. 'What became of – ' she began.

Margaret answered the unfinished sentence. She was excited by gossip as by a stimulant. Her thin cheeks burned, her eyes blazed. 'Mr Lind,' said Margaret, 'Louisa told me, had turned out to be real bad. He got into some money trouble, and then' – Margaret lowered her voice – 'he was arrested for taking a lot of money which didn't belong to him. Louisa said he had been in some business where he handled a lot of other folks' money, and he cheated the men who were in the business with him, and he was tried, and Miss Viola, Louisa thinks, hid away somewhere so they wouldn't call her to testify, and then he had to go to prison; but – ' Margaret hesitated.

'What is it?' asked Jane.

'Louisa thinks he died about a year and a half ago. She heard the lady where she lives now talking about it. The lady used to know Miss Viola, and she heard the lady say Mr Lind had died in prison, that he couldn't stand the hard life, and that Miss Viola had lost all her money through him, and then' – Margaret hesitated again, and her mistress prodded sharply – 'Louisa said that she heard the lady say that she had thought Miss Viola would marry him, but she hadn't, and she had more sense than she had thought.'

'Mrs Longstreet would never for one moment have entertained the thought of marrying Mr Lind; he was young enough to be her grandson,' said Jane, severely.

'Yes, ma'am,' said Margaret.

It so happened that Jane went to New York that day week, and at a jewellery counter in one of the shops she discovered the amethyst comb. There were on sale a number of bits of antique jewellery, the precious flotsam and jetsam of old and wealthy families which had drifted, nobody knew before what currents of adversity, into that harbour of sale for all the world to see. Jane made no enquiries; the saleswoman volunteered simply the information that the comb was a real antique, and the stones were real amethysts and pearls, and the setting was solid gold, and the price was thirty dollars; and Jane bought it. She carried her old amethyst comb home, but she did not show it to anybody. She replaced it in its old compartment in her jewel-case and thought of it with wonder, with a hint of joy at regaining it, and with much sadness. She was still fond of Viola Longstreet. Jane did not easily part with her loves. She did not know where Viola was. Margaret had enquired of Louisa, who did not know. Poor Viola had probably drifted into some obscure harbour of life wherein she was hiding until life was over.

And then Jane met Viola one spring day on Fifth Avenue.

'It is a very long time since I have seen you,' said Jane with a reproachful accent, but her eyes were tenderly enquiring.

'Yes,' agreed Viola. Then she added, 'I have seen nobody. Do you know what a change has come in my life?' she asked.

'Yes, dear,' replied Jane, gently. 'My Margaret met Louisa once and she told her.'

'Oh yes – Louisa,' said Viola. 'I had to discharge her. My money is about gone. I have only just enough to keep the wolf from entering the door of a hall bedroom in a respectable boarding-house. However, I often hear him howl, but I do not mind at all. In fact, the howling has become company for me. I rather like it. It is queer what things one can learn to like. There are a few left yet, like the awful heat in summer, and the food, which I do not fancy, but that is simply a matter of time.'

Viola's laugh was like a bird's song – a part of her – and nothing except death could silence it for long.

'Then,' said Jane, 'you stay in New York all summer?'

Viola laughed again. 'My dear,' she replied, 'of course. It is all very simple. If I left New York, and paid board anywhere, I would never have enough money to buy my return fare, and certainly not to keep that wolf from my hall-bedroom door.'

'Then,' said Jane, 'you are going home with me.'

'I cannot consent to accept charity, Jane,' said Viola. 'Don't ask me.'

Then, for the first time in her life, Viola Longstreet saw Jane Carew's eyes blaze with anger. 'You dare to call it charity coming from me to you?' she said, and Viola gave in.

When Jane saw the little room where Viola lived, she marvelled, with the exceedingly great marvelling of a woman to whom love of a man has never come, at a woman who could give so much and with no return.

Little enough to pack had Viola. Jane understood with a shudder of horror that it was almost destitution, not poverty, to which her old friend was reduced.

'You shall have that north-east room which you always liked,' she told Viola when they were on the train.

'The one with the old-fashioned peacock paper, and the pine tree growing close to one window?' said Viola, happily.

Jane and Viola settled down to life together, and Viola, despite the tragedy which she had known, realised a peace and happiness beyond her imagination. In reality, although she still looked so youthful, she was old enough to enjoy the pleasures of later life. Enjoy them she did to the utmost. She and Jane made calls together, entertained friends at small and stately dinners, and gave little teas. They drove about in the old Carew carriage. Viola had some new clothes. She played very well on Jane's old piano. She embroidered, she gardened. She lived the sweet, placid life of an older lady in a little village, and loved it. She never mentioned Harold Lind.

Not among the vicious of the earth was poor Harold Lind; rather among those of such beauty and charm that the earth spoils them, making them, in their own estimation, free guests at all its tables of bounty. Moreover, the young man had, deeply rooted in his character, the traits of a mischievous child, rejoicing in his mischief more from a sense of humour so keen that it verged on cruelty than from any intention to harm others. Over that affair of the amethyst comb, for instance, his irresponsible, selfish, childish soul had fairly revelled in glee. He had not been fond of Viola, but he liked her fondness for himself. He had made sport of her, but only for his own entertainment – never for the entertainment of others. He was a beautiful creature, seeking out paths of pleasure and folly for himself alone, which ended as do all paths of earthly pleasure and folly. Harold had admired Viola, but from the same point of view as Jane Carew's. Viola had, when she looked her youngest and best, always seemed so old as to be venerable to him. He had at times compunctions, as if he were making a jest of his grandmother. Viola never knew the truth about the amethyst comb. He had considered that one of the best frolics of his life. He had simply purloined it and presented it to Viola, and merrily left matters to settle themselves.

Viola and Jane had lived together a month before the comb was mentioned. Then one day Viola was in Jane's room and the jewel-case was out, and she began examining its contents. When she found the amethyst comb she gave a little cry. Jane, who had been seated at her desk and had not seen what was going on, turned around.

Viola stood holding the comb, and her cheeks were burning. She fondled the trinket as if it had been a baby. Jane watched her. She began to understand the bare facts of the mystery of the disappearance of her amethyst comb, but the subtlety of it was for ever beyond her. Had the other woman explained what was in her mind, in her heart – how that reckless young man whom she had loved had given her the treasure because he had heard her admire Jane's amethysts, and she, all unconscious of any wrongdoing, had ever regarded it as the one evidence of his thoughtful tenderness, it being the one gift she had ever received from him; how she parted with it, as she had parted with her other jewels, in order to obtain money to purchase comforts for him while he was in prison – Jane could not have understood. The fact of an older woman being fond of a young man, almost a boy, was beyond her mental grasp. She had no imagination with which to comprehend that innocent, pathetic, almost terrible love of one who has trodden the earth long for one who has just set dancing feet upon it. It was noble of Jane Carew that, lacking all such imagination, she acted as she did: that, although she did not, could not, formulate it to herself, she would no more have deprived the other woman and the dead man of that one little unscathed bond of tender goodness than she would have robbed his grave of flowers.

Viola looked at her. 'I cannot tell you all about it; you would laugh at me,' she whispered; 'but this was mine once.'

'It is yours now, dear,' said Jane.

JAMES JOYCE

James Joyce was born in Dublin on 2 February 1882. He was one of a large family described by his father as consisting of 'sixteen or seventeen children'. He was educated by the Jesuits at Clongowes Wood College and later at Belvedere College, Dublin. He did well at school, being interested in poetry, Latin and modern languages. In 1898 he entered University College, Dublin, where he studied philosophy and languages. He was interested in the theatre and in April 1900 wrote in the *Fortnightly Review* an essay on 'Ibsen's New Drama'. In October 1902 Joyce went to Paris, but returned to Dublin in 1903 as his mother was dying. He taught at a school in Dalkey until, following his marriage in 1904, he and his wife went to Zurich and later Trieste, where he taught languages in the Berlitz school.

Joyce returned to Dublin in 1912 when he made an unsuccessful attempt to publish *Dubliners* privately. He spent the First World War in Zurich with his wife and two children in great poverty, but was helped by a modest grant from the Privy Purse. He lived in Paris from 1920, publishing *Ulysses* in 1922 and *Finnegan's Wake* in 1939. He died in January 1941.

The Boarding House

Mrs Mooney was a butcher's daughter. She was a woman who was quite able to keep things to herself: a determined woman. She had married her father's foreman and opened a butcher's shop near Spring Gardens. But as soon as his father-in-law was dead Mr Mooney began to go to the devil. He drank, plundered the till, ran headlong into debt. It was no use making him take the pledge: he was sure to break out again a few days after. By fighting his wife in the presence of customers and by buying bad meat he ruined his business. One night he went for his wife with the cleaver and she had to sleep in a neighbour's house.

After that they lived apart. She went to the priest and got a separation from him with care of the children. She would give him neither money nor food nor house-room; and so he was obliged to enlist himself as a sheriff's man. He was a shabby stooped little drunkard with a white face and a white moustache and white eyebrows, pencilled above his little eyes, which were pink-veined and raw; and all day long he sat in the bailiff's room, waiting to be put on a job. Mrs Mooney, who had taken what remained of her money out of the butcher business and set up a boarding house in Hardwicke Street, was a big imposing woman. Her house had a floating population made up of tourists from Liverpool and the Isle of Man and, occasionally, *artistes* from the music halls. Its resident population was made up of clerks from the city. She governed the house cunningly and firmly, knew when to give credit, when to be stern and when to let things pass. All the resident young men spoke of her as *the Madam*.

Mrs Mooney's young men paid fifteen shillings a week for board and lodgings (beer or stout at dinner excluded). They shared in common tastes and occupations and for this reason they were very chummy with one another. They discussed with one another the chances of favourites and outsiders. Jack Mooney, the Madam's son, who was clerk to a commission agent in Fleet Street, had the reputation of being a hard case. He was fond of using soldiers' obscenities: usually he came home in the small hours. When he met his friends he had always a good one to tell them and he was always sure to be on to a good thing – that is to say, a likely horse or a likely *artiste*. He was also handy with the mits and sang comic songs. On Sunday nights there would often be a reunion in Mrs Mooney's front drawing-room. The music-hall *artistes* would oblige; and Sheridan played waltzes and polkas and vamped accompaniments. Polly Mooney, the Madam's daughter, would also sing. She sang:

'I'm a . . . naughty girl.
You needn't sham:
You know I am.'

Polly was a slim girl of nineteen; she had light soft hair and a small full mouth. Her eyes, which were grey with a shade of green through them, had a habit of glancing upwards when she spoke with anyone, which made her look like a little perverse madonna. Mrs Mooney had first sent her daughter to be a typist in a corn-factor's office, but as a disreputable sheriff's man used to come every other day to the office, asking to be allowed to say a word to his daughter, she had taken her daughter home again and set her to do housework. As Polly was very lively the intention was to give her the run of the young men. Besides, young men like to feel that there is a young woman not very far away. Polly, of course, flirted with the young men but Mrs Mooney, who was a shrewd judge, knew that the young men were only passing the time away: none of them meant business. Things went on so for a long time and Mrs Mooney began to think of sending Polly back to typewriting when she noticed that something was going on between Polly and one of the young men. She watched the pair and kept her own counsel.

Polly knew that she was being watched, but still her mother's persistent silence could not be misunderstood. There had been no open complicity between mother and daughter, no open understanding, but, though people in the house began to talk of the affair, still Mrs Mooney did not intervene. Polly began to grow a little strange in her manner and the young man was evidently perturbed. At last, when she judged it to be the right moment, Mrs Mooney intervened. She dealt with moral problems as a cleaver deals with meat: and in this case she had made up her mind. It was a bright Sunday morning of early summer, promising heat, but with a fresh breeze blowing. All the windows of the boarding house were open and the lace curtains ballooned gently towards the street beneath the raised sashes. The belfry of George's Church sent out constant peals and worshippers, singly or in groups, traversed the little circus before the church, revealing their purpose by their self-contained demeanour no less than by the little volumes in their gloved hands. Breakfast was over in the boarding house and the table of the breakfast-room was covered with plates on which lay yellow streaks of eggs with morsels of bacon-fat and bacon-rind. Mrs Mooney sat in the straw armchair and watched the servant Mary remove the breakfast things. She made Mary collect the crusts and pieces of broken bread to help to make Tuesday's bread-pudding. When the table was cleared, the broken bread collected, the sugar and butter safe under lock and key, she began to reconstruct the interview which she had had the night before with Polly. Things were as she had suspected: she had been frank in her questions and Polly had been frank in her answers. Both had been somewhat awkward, of course. She had been made awkward by her not wishing to receive the news in too cavalier a fashion or to seem to have connived and Polly had been made awkward not merely because allusions of that kind always made her awkward but also because she did not wish it to be thought that in her wise innocence she had divined the intention behind her mother's tolerance.

Mrs Mooney glanced instinctively at the little gilt clock on the mantelpiece as soon as she had become aware through her reverie that the bells of George's Church had stopped ringing. It was seventeen minutes past eleven: she would have lots of time to have the matter out with Mr Doran and then catch short twelve at Marlborough Street. She was sure she would win. To begin with she had all the weight of social opinion on her side: she was an outraged mother. She had allowed him to live beneath her roof, assuming that he was a man of honour, and he had simply abused her hospitality. He was thirty-four or thirty-five years of age, so that youth could not be pleaded as his excuse; nor could ignorance be his excuse since he was a man who had seen something of the world. He had simply taken advantage of Polly's youth and inexperience: that was evident. The question was: What reparation would he make?

There must be reparation made in such case. It is all very well for the man: he can go his ways as if nothing has happened, having had his moment of pleasure, but the girl has to bear the brunt. Some mothers would be content to patch up such an affair for a sum of money; she had known cases of it. But she would not do so. For her only one reparation could make up for the loss of her daughter's honour: marriage.

She counted all her cards again before sending Mary up to Mr Doran's room to say that she wished to speak with him. She felt sure she would win. He was a serious young man, not rakish or loud-voiced like the others. If it had been Mr Sheridan or Mr Meade or Bantam Lyons her task would have been much harder. She did not think he would face publicity. All the lodgers in the house knew something of the affair; details had been invented by some. Besides, he had been employed for thirteen years in a great Catholic wine-merchant's office and publicity would mean for him, perhaps, the loss of his job. Whereas if he agreed all might be well. She knew he had a good screw for one thing and she suspected he had a bit of stuff put by.

Nearly the half-hour! She stood up and surveyed herself in the pier-glass. The decisive expression of her great florid face satisfied her and she thought of some mothers she knew who could not get their daughters off their hands.

Mr Doran was very anxious indeed this Sunday morning. He had made two attempts to shave but his hand had been so unsteady that he had been obliged to desist. Three days' reddish beard fringed his jaws and every two or three minutes a mist gathered on his glasses so that he had to take them off and polish them with his pocket-handkerchief. The recollection of his confession of the night before was a cause of acute pain to him; the priest had drawn out every ridiculous detail of the affair and in the end had so magnified his sin that he was almost thankful at being afforded a loophole of reparation. The harm was done. What could he do now but marry her or run away? He could not brazen it out. The affair would be sure to be talked of and his employer would be certain to hear of it. Dublin is such a small city: everyone knows everyone else's business. He felt his heart leap warmly in his throat as he heard in his excited imagination old Mr Leonard calling out in his rasping voice: 'Send Mr Doran here, please.'

All his long years of service gone for nothing! All his industry and diligence thrown away! As a young man he had sown his wild oats, of course; he had boasted of his free-thinking and denied the existence of God to his companions in public-houses. But that was all passed and done with . . . nearly. He still bought a copy of *Reynolds's Newspaper* every week but he attended to his religious duties and for nine-tenths of the year lived a regular life. He had money enough to settle down on; it was not that. But the family would look down on her. First of all there was her disreputable father and then her mother's boarding house was beginning to get a certain fame. He had a notion that he was being had. He could imagine his friends talking of the affair and laughing. She *was* a little vulgar; sometimes she said 'I seen' and 'If I had've known.' But what would grammar matter if he really loved her? He could not make up his mind whether to like her or despise her for what she had done. Of course he had done it too. His instinct urged him to remain free, not to marry. Once you are married you are done for, it said.

While he was sitting helplessly on the side of the bed in shirt and trousers she tapped lightly at his door and entered. She told him all, that she had made a clean breast of it to her mother and that her mother would speak with him that morning. She cried and threw her arms round his neck, saying: 'Oh, Bob! Bob! What am I to do? What am I to do at all?'

She would put an end to herself, she said.

He comforted her feebly, telling her not to cry, that it would be all right, never fear. He felt against his shirt the agitation of her bosom.

It was not altogether his fault that it had happened. He remembered well, with the curious patient memory of the celibate, the first casual caresses her dress, her breath, her fingers had given him. Then late one night as he was undressing for bed she had tapped at his door, timidly. She wanted to relight her candle at his for hers had been blown out by a gust. It was her bath night. She wore a loose open combing-jacket of printed flannel. Her white instep shone in the opening of her furry slippers and the blood glowed warmly behind her perfumed skin. From her hands and wrists too as she lit and steadied her candle a faint perfume arose.

On nights when he came in very late it was she who warmed up his dinner. He scarcely knew what he was eating feeling her beside him alone, at night, in the sleeping house. And her thoughtfulness! If the night was anyway cold or wet or windy there was sure to be a little tumbler of punch ready for him. Perhaps they could be happy together . . .

They used to go upstairs together on tiptoe, each with a candle, and on the third landing exchange reluctant good-nights. They used to kiss. He remembered well her eyes, the touch of her hand and his delirium . . .

But delirium passes. He echoed her phrase, applying it to himself: '*What am I to do?*' The instinct of the celibate warned him to hold back. But the sin was there; even his sense of honour told him that reparation must be made for such a sin.

While he was sitting with her on the side of the bed Mary

came to the door and said that the missus wanted to see him in the parlour. He stood up to put on his coat and waistcoat, more helpless than ever. When he was dressed he went over to her to comfort her. It would be all right, never fear. He left her crying on the bed and moaning softly: '*Oh my God!*'

Going down the stairs his glasses became so dimmed with moisture that he had to take them off and polish them. He longed to ascend through the roof and fly away to another country where he would never hear again of his trouble, and yet a force pushed him downstairs step by step. The implacable faces of his employer and of the Madam stared upon his discomfiture. On the last flight of stairs he passed Jack Mooney who was coming up from the pantry nursing two bottles of Bass. They saluted coldly; and the lover's eyes rested for a second or two on a thick bulldog face and a pair of thick short arms. When he reached the foot of the staircase he glanced up and saw Jack regarding him from the door of the return-room.

Suddenly he remembered the night when one of the music-hall *artistes*, a little blond Londoner, had made a rather free allusion to Polly. The reunion had been almost broken up on account of Jack's violence. Everyone tried to quiet him. The music-hall artiste, a little paler than usual, kept smiling and saying that there was no harm meant, but Jack kept shouting at him that if any fellow tried that sort of a game on with his sister he'd bloody well put his teeth down his throat, so he would.

Polly sat for a little time on the side of the bed, crying. Then she dried her eyes and went over to the looking-glass. She dipped the end of the towel in the water-jug and refreshed her eyes with the cool water. She looked at herself in profile and readjusted a hairpin above her ear. Then she went back to the bed again and sat at the foot. She regarded the pillows for a long time and the sight of them awakened in her mind secret, amiable memories. She rested the nape of her neck against the cool iron bed-rail and fell into a reverie. There was no longer any perturbation visible on her face.

She waited on patiently, almost cheerfully, without alarm, her memories gradually giving place to hopes and visions of the future. Her hopes and visions were so intricate that she no longer saw the white pillows on which her gaze was fixed or remembered that she was waiting for anything.

At last she heard her mother calling. She started to her feet and ran to the banisters.

'Polly! Polly!'

'Yes, mamma?'

'Come down, dear. Mr Doran wants to speak to you.'

Then she remembered what she had been waiting for.

GEORGE GISSING

George Robert Gissing was born in 1857 in Yorkshire. His father, who died when he was thirteen, was a chemist from a family of Suffolk shoemakers. Gissing won a scholarship to Owens College (now the University of Manchester), and in 1874 he took his BA at the University of London where he was placed first in England for both English and Latin. In 1875 he fell in love with a woman of ill-repute, Marianne Helen Harrison, 'Nell'. Trying to support her financially, he was caught stealing money from other students and sentenced to one month's hard labour at Bellevue Prison in Manchester. Gissing's mother sent him to the United States to start anew. It was a difficult period, full of the hard work and misery so often reflected in his novels. In Chicago, Gissing was barely able to provide for himself with his writing. His first fiction, *The Sins of the Fathers*, was published in the *Chicago Tribune* in 1877. The same year Gissing returned to England and again met Nell whom he married in 1879; in 1888 she died in a Lambeth slum. In 1891 he married another uneducated young woman, Edith Alice Underwood, who was committed to an insane asylum in 1902. Estranged from her, Gissing had moved to France in 1898 with a young French writer, Gabrielle Fleury. Gissing's literary output was prodigious but he is best remembered as the author of *New Grub Street* (1891). He died in France in 1903.

The Scrupulous Father

It was market day in the little town; at one o'clock a rustic company besieged the table of the Greyhound, lured by savoury odours and the frothing of amber ale. Apart from three frequenters of the ordinary, in a small room prepared for overflow sat two persons of a different stamp – a middle-aged man, bald, meagre, unimpressive, but wholly respectable in bearing and apparel, and a girl, evidently his daughter, who had the look of the latter twenties, her plain dress harmonising with a subdued charm of features and a timidity of manner not ungraceful. While waiting for their meal they conversed in an undertone; their brief remarks and ejaculations told of a long morning's ramble from the seaside resort some miles away; in their quiet fashion they seemed to have enjoyed themselves, and dinner at an inn evidently struck them as something of an escapade. Rather awkwardly the girl arranged a handful of wild flowers which she had gathered, and put them for refreshment into a tumbler of water; when a woman entered with viands, silence fell upon the two; after hesitations and mutual glances, they began to eat with nervous appetite.

Scarcely was their modest confidence restored when in the doorway sounded a virile voice, gaily humming, and they became aware of a tall young man, red-headed, anything but handsome, flushed and perspiring from the sunny road; his open jacket showed a blue cotton shirt without waistcoat, in his hand was a shabby straw hat, and thick dust covered his boots. One would have judged him a tourist of the noisier class, and his rather loud 'Good-morning!' as he entered the room seemed a serious menace to privacy; on the other hand, the rapid buttoning of his coat, and the quiet choice of a seat as far as possible from the two guests whom his arrival disturbed, indicated a certain tact. His greeting had met with the merest murmur of reply; their eyes on their plates, father and daughter resolutely disregarded him; yet he ventured to speak again.

'They're busy here today. Not a seat to be had in the other room.'

It was apologetic in intention, and not rudely spoken. After a moment's delay the bald, respectable man made a curt response.

'This room is public, I believe.'

The intruder held his peace. But more than once he glanced at the girl, and after each furtive scrutiny his plain visage manifested some disturbance, a troubled thoughtfulness. His one look at the mute parent was from beneath contemptuous eyebrows.

Very soon another guest appeared, a massive agricultural man, who descended upon a creaking chair and growled a remark about the hot weather. With him the red-haired pedestrian struck into talk. Their topic was beer. Uncommonly good, they agreed, the local brew, and each called for a second pint. What, they asked in concert, would England be without her ale? Shame on the base traffickers who enfeebled or poisoned this noble liquor! And how cool it was – ah! The right sort of cellar! He of the red hair hinted at a third pewter.

These two were still but midway in their stout attack on meat and drink, when father and daughter, having exchanged a few whispers, rose to depart. After leaving the room, the girl remembered that she had left her flowers behind; she durst not return for them, and, knowing her father would dislike to do so, said nothing about the matter.

'A pity!' exclaimed Mr Whiston (that was his respectable name) as they strolled away. 'It looked at first as if we should have such a nice quiet dinner.'

'I enjoyed it all the same,' replied his companion, whose name was Rose.

'That abominable habit of drinking!' added Mr Whiston austerely. He himself had quaffed water, as always. 'Their ale, indeed! See the coarse, gross creatures it produces!'

He shuddered. Rose, however, seemed less consentient than usual. Her eyes were on the ground; her lips were closed with a certain firmness. When she spoke, it was on quite another subject.

They were Londoners. Mr Whiston held the position of draughtsman in the office of a geographical publisher; though his income was small, he had always practised a rigid economy, and the possession of a modest private capital put him beyond fear of reverses. Profoundly conscious of social limits, he felt it a subject for gratitude that there was nothing to be ashamed of in his calling, which he might fairly regard as a profession, and he nursed this sense of respectability as much on his daughter's behalf as on his own. Rose was an only child; her mother had been dead for years; her kinsfolk on both sides laid claim to the title of gentlefolk, but supported it on the narrowest margin of independence. The girl had grown up in an atmosphere unfavourable to mental development, but she had received a fairly good education, and nature had dowered her with intelligence. A sense of her father's conscientiousness and of his true affection forbade her to criticise openly the principles on which he had directed her life; hence a habit of solitary meditation, which half fostered, yet half opposed, the gentle diffidence of Rose's character.

Mr Whiston shrank from society, ceaselessly afraid of receiving less than his due; privately, meanwhile, he deplored the narrowness of the social opportunities granted to his daughter, and was forever forming schemes for her advantage – schemes which never passed beyond the stage of nervous speculation. They inhabited a little house in a western suburb, a house illumined with every domestic virtue; but scarcely a dozen persons crossed the threshold within a twelvemonth. Rose's two or three friends were, like herself, mistrustful of the world. One of them had lately married after a very long engagement, and Rose still trembled from the excitement of that occasion, still debated fearfully with herself on the bride's chances of happiness. Her own marriage was an event so inconceivable that merely to glance at the thought appeared half immodest and wholly irrational.

Every winter Mr Whiston talked of new places which he and Rose would visit when the holidays came round; every summer he shrank from the thought of adventurous novelty, and ended by proposing a return to the same western seaside-town, to the familiar lodgings. The climate suited neither him nor his daughter, who both needed physical as well as moral bracing; but they only thought of this on finding themselves at home again, with another long year of monotony before them. And it was so good to feel welcome, respected; to receive the smiling reverences of tradesfolk; to talk with just a little well-bred condescension, sure that it would be appreciated. Mr Whiston savoured these things, and Rose in this respect was not wholly unlike him.

Today was the last of their vacation. The weather had been magnificent throughout; Rose's cheeks were more than touched by the sun, greatly to the advantage of her unpretending comeliness. She was a typical English maiden, rather tall, shapely rather than graceful, her head generally bent, her movements always betraying the diffidence of solitary habit. The lips were her finest feature, their perfect outline indicating sweetness without feebleness of character. Such a girl is at her best towards the stroke of thirty. Rose had begun to know herself; she needed only opportunity to act upon her knowledge.

A train would take them back to the seaside. At the railway station Rose seated herself on a shaded part of the platform, while her father, who was exceedingly short of sight, peered over publications on the bookstall. Rather tired after her walk, the girl was dreamily tracing a pattern with the point of her parasol, when someone advanced and stood immediately in front of her. Startled, she looked up, and recognised the red-haired stranger of the inn.

'You left these flowers in a glass of water on the table. I hope I'm not doing a rude thing in asking whether they were left by accident.'

He had the flowers in his hand, their stems carefully protected by a piece of paper. For a moment Rose was incapable of replying; she looked at the speaker; she felt her cheeks burn; in utter embarrassment she said she knew not what.

'Oh! – thank you! I forgot them. It's very kind.'

Her hand touched his as she took the bouquet from him. Without another word the man turned and strode away.

Mr Whiston had seen nothing of this. When he approached, Rose held up the flowers with a laugh.

'Wasn't it kind? I forgot them, you know, and someone from the inn came looking for me.'

'Very good of them, very,' replied her father graciously. 'A very nice inn, that. We'll go again – someday. One likes to encourage such civility; it's rare nowadays.'

He of the red hair travelled by the same train, though not in the same carriage. Rose caught sight of him at the seaside station. She was vexed with herself for having so scantily acknowledged his kindness; it seemed to her that she had not really thanked him at all; how absurd, at her age, to be incapable of common self-command! At the same time she kept thinking of her father's phrase, 'coarse, gross creatures', and it vexed her even more than her own ill behaviour. The stranger was certainly not coarse, far from gross. Even his talk about beer (she remembered every word of it) had been amusing rather than offensive. Was he a 'gentleman'? The question agitated her; it involved so technical a definition, and she felt so doubtful as to the reply. Beyond doubt he had acted in a gentlemanly way; but his voice lacked something. Coarse? Gross? No, no, no! Really, her father was very severe, not to say uncharitable. But perhaps he was thinking of the heavy agricultural man; oh, he must have been!

Of a sudden she felt very weary. At the lodgings she sat down in her bedroom, and gazed through the open window at the sea. A sense of discouragement, hitherto almost unknown, had fallen upon her; it spoilt the blue sky and the soft horizon. She thought rather drearily of the townward journey tomorrow, of her home in the suburbs, of the endless monotony that awaited her. The flowers lay on her lap; she smelt them, dreamed over them. And then – strange incongruity – she thought of beer!

Between tea and supper she and her father rested on the beach. Mr Whiston was reading. Rose pretended to turn the leaves of a book. Of a sudden, as unexpectedly to herself as to her companion, she broke silence.

'Don't you think, father, that we are too much afraid of talking with strangers?'

'Too much afraid?'

Mr Whiston was puzzled. He had forgotten all about the incident at the dinner-table.

'I mean – what harm is there in having a little conversation when one is away from home? At the inn today, you know, I can't help thinking we were rather – perhaps a little too silent.'

'My dear Rose, did you want to talk about beer?'

She reddened, but answered all the more emphatically.

'Of course not. But, when the first gentleman came in, wouldn't it have been natural to exchange a few friendly words? I'm sure he wouldn't have talked of beer to *us*.

'The *gentleman*? I saw no gentleman, my dear. I suppose he was a small clerk, or something of the sort, and he had no business whatever to address us.'

'Oh, but he only said good-morning, and apologised for sitting at our table. He needn't have apologised at all.'

'Precisely. That is just what I mean,' said Mr Whiston with self-satisfaction. 'My dear Rose, if I had been alone, I might perhaps have talked a little, but with you it was impossible. One cannot be too careful. A man like that will take all sorts of liberties. One has to keep such people at a distance.'

A moment's pause, then Rose spoke with unusual decision – 'I feel quite sure, father, that he would not have taken liberties. It seems to me that he knew quite well how to behave himself.'

Mr Whiston grew still more puzzled. He closed his book to meditate this new problem.

'One has to lay down rules,' fell from him at length, sententiously. 'Our position, Rose, as I have often explained, is a delicate one. A lady in circumstances such as yours cannot exercise too much caution. Your natural associates are in the world of wealth; unhappily, I cannot make you wealthy. We have to guard our self-respect, my dear child. Really, it is not *safe* to talk with strangers – least of all at an inn. And you have only to remember that disgusting conversation about beer!'

Rose said no more. Her father pondered a little, felt that he had delivered his soul, and resumed the book.

The next morning they were early at the station to secure good places for the long journey to London. Up to almost the last moment it seemed that they would have a carriage to themselves. Then the door suddenly opened, a bag was flung on to the seat, and after it came a hot, panting man, a red-haired man, recognised immediately by both the travellers.

'I thought I'd missed it!' ejaculated the intruder merrily.

Mr Whiston turned his head away, disgust transforming his countenance. Rose sat motionless, her eyes cast down. And the stranger mopped his forehead in silence.

He glanced at her; he glanced again and again; and Rose was aware of every look. It did not occur to her to feel offended. On the contrary, she fell into a mood of tremulous pleasure, enhanced by every turn of the stranger's eyes in her direction. At him she did not look, yet she saw him. Was it a coarse face? she asked herself. Plain, perhaps, but decidedly not vulgar. The red hair, she thought, was not disagreeably red; she didn't dislike that shade of colour. He was humming a tune; it seemed to be his habit, and it argued healthy cheerfulness. Meanwhile Mr Whiston sat stiffly in his corner, staring at the landscape, a model of respectable muteness.

At the first stop another man entered. This time, unmistakably, a commercial traveller. At once a dialogue sprang up between him and Rufus. The traveller complained that all the smoking compartments were full.

'Why,' exclaimed Rufus, with a laugh, 'that reminds me that

I wanted a smoke. I never thought about it till now; jumped in here in a hurry.'

The traveller's 'line' was tobacco; they talked tobacco – Rufus with much gusto. Presently the conversation took a wider scope.

'I envy you,' cried Rufus, 'always travelling about. I'm in a beastly office, and get only a fortnight off once a year. I enjoy it, I can tell you! Time's up today, worse luck! I've a good mind to emigrate. Can you give me a tip about the colonies?'

He talked of how he had spent his holiday. Rose missed not a word, and her blood pulsed in sympathy with the joy of freedom which he expressed. She did not mind his occasional slang; the tone was manly and right-hearted; it evinced a certain simplicity of feeling by no means common in men, whether gentle or other. At a certain moment the girl was impelled to steal a glimpse of his face. After all, was it really so plain? The features seemed to her to have a certain refinement which she had not noticed before.

'I'm going to try for a smoker,' said the man of commerce, as the train slackened into a busy station.

Rufus hesitated. His eye wandered.

'I think I shall stay where I am,' he ended by saying.

In that same moment, for the first time, Rose met his glance. She saw that his eyes did not at once avert themselves; they had a singular expression, a smile which pleaded pardon for its audacity. And Rose, even while turning away, smiled in response.

The train stopped. The commercial traveller alighted. Rose, leaning towards her father, whispered that she was thirsty; would he get her a glass of milk or of lemonade? Though little disposed to rush on such errands, Mr Whiston had no choice but to comply; he sped at once for the refreshment-room.

And Rose knew what would happen; she knew perfectly. Sitting rigid, her eyes on vacancy, she felt the approach of the young man, who for the moment was alone with her. She saw him at her side: she heard his voice.

'I can't help it. I want to speak to you. May I?'

Rose faltered a reply. 'It was so kind to bring the flowers. I didn't thank you properly.'

'It's now or never,' pursued the young man in rapid, excited tones. 'Will you let me tell you my name? Will you tell me yours?'

Rose's silence consented. The daring Rufus rent a page from a pocket-book, scribbled his name and address, gave it to Rose. He rent out another page, offered it to Rose with the pencil, and in a moment had secured the precious scrap of paper in his pocket. Scarce was the transaction completed when a stranger jumped in. The young man bounded to his own corner, just in time to see the return of Mr Whiston, glass in hand.

During the rest of the journey Rose was in the strangest state of mind. She did not feel in the least ashamed of herself. It seemed to her that what had happened was wholly natural and simple. The extraordinary thing was that she must sit silent and with cold countenance at the distance of a few feet from a person with whom she ardently desired to converse. Sudden illumination had wholly changed the aspect of life. She seemed to be playing a part in a grotesque comedy rather than living in a world of grave realities. Her father's dignified silence struck her as intolerably absurd. She could have burst into laughter; at moments she was indignant, irritated, tremulous with the spirit of revolt. She detected a glance of frigid superiority with which Mr Whiston chanced to survey the other occupants of the compartment. It amazed her. Never had she seen her father in such an alien light. He bent forward and addressed to her some commonplace remark; she barely deigned a reply. Her views of conduct, of character, had undergone an abrupt and extraordinary change. Having justified without shadow of argument her own incredible proceeding, she judged everything and everybody by some new standard, mysteriously attained. She was no longer the Rose Whiston of yesterday. Her old self seemed an object of compassion. She felt an unspeakable happiness, and at the same time an encroaching fear.

The fear predominated; when she grew aware of the streets of London looming on either hand it became a torment, an anguish. Small-folded, crushed within her palm, the piece of paper with its still unread inscription seemed to burn her. Once, twice, thrice she met the look of her friend. He smiled cheerily, bravely, with evident purpose of encouragement. She knew his face better than that of any oldest acquaintance; she saw in it a manly beauty. Only by a great effort of self-control could she refrain from turning aside to unfold and read what he had written. The train slackened speed, stopped. Yes, it was London. She must arise and go. Once more their eyes met. Then, without recollection of any interval, she was on the Metropolitan Railway, moving towards her suburban home.

A severe headache sent her early to bed. Beneath her pillow lay a scrap of paper with a name and address she was not likely to forget. And through the night of broken slumbers Rose suffered a martyrdom. No more self-glorification! All her courage gone, all her new vitality! She saw herself with the old eyes, and was shame-stricken to the very heart.

Whose the fault? Towards dawn she argued it with the bitterness of misery. What a life was hers in this little world of choking respectabilities! Forbidden this, forbidden that; permitted – the pride of ladyhood. And she was not a lady, after all. What lady would have permitted herself to exchange names and addresses with a strange man in a railway carriage – furtively, too, escaping her father's observation? If not a lady, what *was* she? It meant the utter failure of her breeding and education. The sole end for which she had lived was frustrate. A common, vulgar young woman – well mated, doubtless, with an impudent clerk, whose noisy talk was of beer and tobacco!

This arrested her. Stung to the defence of her friend, who, clerk though he might be, was neither impudent nor vulgar, she found herself driven back upon self-respect. The battle went on for hours; it exhausted her; it undid all the good effects of sun and sea, and left her flaccid, pale.

'I'm afraid the journey yesterday was too much for you,' remarked Mr Whiston, after observing her as she sat mute the next evening.

'I shall soon recover,' Rose answered coldly.

The father meditated with some uneasiness. He had not forgotten Rose's singular expression of opinion after their dinner at the inn. His affection made him sensitive to changes in the girl's demeanour. Next summer they must really find a more bracing resort. Yes, yes; clearly Rose needed bracing. But she was always better when the cool days came round.

On the morrow it was his daughter's turn to feel anxious. Mr Whiston all at once wore a face of indignant severity. He was absent-minded; he sat at table with scarce a word; he had little nervous movements, and subdued mutterings as of wrath. This continued on a second day, and Rose began to suffer an intolerable agitation. She could not help connecting her father's strange behaviour with the secret which tormented her heart.

Had something happened? Had her friend seen Mr Whiston, or written to him?

She had awaited with tremors every arrival of the post. It was probable – more than probable – that *he* would write to her; but as yet no letter came. A week passed, and no letter came. Her father was himself again; plainly she had mistaken the cause of his perturbation. Ten days, and no letter came.

It was Saturday afternoon. Mr Whiston reached home at teatime. The first glance showed his daughter that trouble and anger once more beset him. She trembled, and all but wept, for suspense had overwrought her nerves.

'I find myself obliged to speak to you on a very disagreeable subject' – thus began Mr Whiston over the teacups – 'a very unpleasant subject indeed. My one consolation is that it will probably settle a little argument we had down at the seaside.'

As his habit was when expressing grave opinions (and Mr Whiston seldom expressed any other), he made a long pause and ran his fingers through his thin beard. The delay irritated Rose to the last point of endurance.

'The fact is,' he proceeded at length, 'a week ago I received a most extraordinary letter – the most impudent letter I ever read in my life. It came from that noisy, beer-drinking man who intruded upon us at the inn – you remember. He began by explaining who he was, and – if you can believe it – had the impertinence to say that he wished to make my acquaintance! An amazing letter! Naturally, I left it unanswered – the only dignified thing to do. But the fellow wrote again, asking if I had received his proposal. I now replied, briefly and severely, asking him how he came to know my name; secondly, what reason I had given him for supposing that I desired to meet him again. His answer to this was even more outrageous than the first offence. He bluntly informed me that in order to discover my name and address he had followed us home that day from Paddington Station! As if this was not bad enough, he went on to – really, Rose, I feel I must apologise to you, but the fact is I seem to have no choice but to tell you what he said. The fellow tells me, really, that he wants to know *me* only that he may come to know *you*! My first idea was to go with this letter to the police. I am not sure that I shan't do so even yet; most certainly I shall if he writes again. The man may be crazy – he may be dangerous. Who knows but he may come lurking about the house? I felt obliged to warn you of this unpleasant possibility.'

Rose was stirring her tea; also she was smiling. She continued to stir and to smile, without consciousness of either performance.

'You make light of it?' exclaimed her father solemnly.

'Oh, father, of course I am sorry you have had this annoyance.'

So little was there of manifest sorrow in the girl's tone and countenance that Mr Whiston gazed at her rather indignantly. His pregnant pause gave birth to one of those admonitory axioms which had hitherto ruled his daughter's life.

'My dear, I advise you never to trifle with questions of propriety. Could there possibly be a better illustration of what I have so often said – that in self-defence we are bound to keep strangers at a distance?'

'Father – '

Rose began firmly, but her voice failed.

'You were going to say, Rose?'

She took her courage in both hands. 'Will you allow me to see the letters?'

'Certainly. There can be no objection to that.' He drew from his pocket the envelopes and held them out to his daughter.

With shaking hand Rose unfolded the first letter; it was written in clear commercial character, and was signed 'Charles James Burroughs'. When she had read all, the girl said quietly, 'Are you quite sure, father, that these letters are impertinent?'

Mr Whiston stopped in the act of finger-combing his beard. 'What doubt can there be of it?'

'They seem to me,' proceeded Rose nervously, 'to be very respectful and very honest.'

'My dear, you astound me! Is it respectful to force one's acquaintance upon an unwilling stranger? I really don't understand you. Where is your sense of propriety, Rose? A vulgar, noisy fellow, who talks of beer and tobacco – a petty clerk! And he has the audacity to write to me that he wants to – to make friends with my daughter! Respectful? Honest? Really!'

When Mr Whiston became sufficiently agitated to lose his decorous gravity, he began to splutter, and at such moments he was not impressive. Rose kept her eyes cast down. She felt her strength once more, the strength of a wholly reasonable and half-passionate revolt against that tyrannous propriety which Mr Whiston worshipped.

'Father – '

'Well, my dear?'

'There is only one thing I dislike in these letters – and that is a falsehood.'

'I don't understand.'

Rose was flushing. Her nerves grew tense; she had wrought herself to a simple audacity which overcame small embarrassments.

'Mr Burroughs says that he followed us home from Paddington to discover our address. That is not true. He asked me for my name and address in the train, and gave me his.'

The father gasped.

'He *asked* – ? You *gave* – ?'

'It was while you were away in the refreshment-room,' proceeded the girl, with singular self-control, in a voice almost matter-of-fact. 'I ought to tell you, at the same time, that it was Mr Burroughs who brought me the flowers from the inn, when I forgot them. You didn't see him give them to me in the station.'

The father stared.

'But, Rose, what does all this mean? You – you overwhelm me! Go on, please. What next?'

'Nothing, father.'

And of a sudden the girl was so beset with confusing emotions that she hurriedly quitted her chair and vanished from the room.

Before Mr Whiston returned to his geographical drawing on Monday morning, he had held long conversations with Rose, and still longer with himself. Not easily could he perceive the justice of his daughter's quarrel with propriety; many days were to pass, indeed, before he would consent to do more than make enquiries about Charles James Burroughs, and to permit that aggressive young man to give a fuller account of himself in writing. It was by silence that Rose prevailed. Having defended herself against the charge of immodesty, she declined to urge her own inclination or the rights of Mr Burroughs; her mute patience did not lack its effect with the scrupulous but tender parent.

'I am willing to admit, my dear,' said Mr Whiston one evening, *à propos* of nothing at all, 'that the falsehood in that young man's letter gave proof of a certain delicacy.'

'Thank you, father,' replied Rose, very quietly and simply.

It was next morning that the father posted a formal, proper, self-respecting note of invitation, which bore results.

D. H. LAWRENCE

David Herbert Lawrence was born in 1885 in Eastwood, a small mining village in Nottinghamshire in the Midlands. Despite ill health as a child and a comparatively disadvantaged position in society, he studied at Nottingham University and became a schoolmaster. His first novel, *The White Peacock*, was published in 1911. In 1912 he eloped with Frieda Weekley, the wife of his professor at Nottingham, and from then until his death he wrote feverishly, producing poetry, novels, essays, plays, travel books and short stories, while travelling around the world, settling for periods in Italy, New Mexico and Mexico. Lawrence's greatest novels, *The Rainbow* and *Women in Love*, were completed in 1915 and 1916. His last novel, *Lady Chatterley's Lover*, was banned in 1928 and his paintings confiscated in 1929. He died of tuberculosis in France in 1930.

The Lovely Lady

At seventy-two, Pauline Attenborough could still sometimes be mistaken, in the half-light, for thirty. She really was a wonderfully-preserved woman, of perfect chic. Of course it helps a great deal to have the right frame. She would be an exquisite skeleton, and her skull would be an exquisite skull, like that of some Etruscan woman with feminine charm still in the swerve of the bone and the pretty, naïve teeth.

Mrs Attenborough's face was of the perfect oval and slightly flat type that wears best. There is no flesh to sag. Her nose rode serenely, in its finely-bridged curve. Only the big grey eyes were a tiny bit prominent, on the surface of her face, and they gave her away most. The bluish lids were heavy, as if they ached sometimes with the strain of keeping the eyes beneath them arch and bright; and at the corners of the eyes were fine little wrinkles which would slacken into haggardness, then be pulled up tense again to that bright, gay look like a Leonardo woman who really could laugh outright.

Her niece Cecilia was perhaps the only person in the world who was aware of the invisible little wire which connected Pauline's eye-wrinkles with Pauline's willpower. Only Cecilia consciously watched the eyes go haggard and old and tired, and remain so, for hours; until Robert came home. Then ping! – the mysterious little wire that worked between Pauline's will and her face went taut, the weary, haggard, prominent eyes suddenly began to gleam, the eyelids arched, the queer, curved eyebrows which floated in such frail arches on Pauline's forehead began to gather a mocking significance, and you had the *real* lovely lady, in all her charm.

She really had the secret of everlasting youth; that is to say, she could don her youth again like an eagle. But she was sparing of it. She was wise enough not to try being young for too many people. Her son Robert, in the evenings, and Sir Wilfrid Knipe sometimes in the afternoon to tea; then occasional visitors on Sunday, when Robert was home – for these she was her lovely and changeless self, that age could not wither, nor custom stale; so bright and kindly and yet subtly mocking, like Mona Lisa, who knew a thing or two. But Pauline knew more, so she needn't be smug at all. She could laugh that lovely, mocking Bacchante laugh of hers, which was at the same time never malicious, always good-naturedly tolerant, both of virtues and vices – the former, of course, taking much more tolerating. So she suggested, roguishly.

Only with her niece Cecilia she did not trouble to keep up the glamour. Ciss was not very observant, anyhow; and, more than that, she was plain; more still, she was in love with Robert;

and most of all, she was thirty, and dependent on her aunt Pauline. Oh, Cecilia – why make music for her?

Cecilia, called by her aunt and by her cousin Robert just Ciss, like a cat spitting, was a big, dark-complexioned, pug-faced young woman who very rarely spoke, and when she did couldn't get it out. She was the daughter of a poor Congregational clergyman who had been, while he lived, brother to Ronald, Aunt Pauline's husband. Ronald and the Congregational minister were both well dead, and Aunt Pauline had had charge of Ciss for the last five years.

They lived all together in a quite exquisite though rather small Queen Anne house some twenty-five miles out of town, secluded in a little dale, and surrounded by small but very quaint and pleasant grounds. It was an ideal place and an ideal life for Aunt Pauline, at the age of seventy-two. When the kingfishers flashed up the little stream in her garden, going under the alders, something still flashed in her heart. She was that kind of woman.

Robert, who was two years older than Ciss, went every day to town, to his chambers in one of the Inns. He was a barrister, and, to his secret but very deep mortification, he earned about a hundred pounds a year. He simply *couldn't* get above that figure, though it was rather easy to get below it. Of course, it didn't matter. Pauline had money. But then, what was Pauline's was Pauline's, and though she could give almost lavishly, still, one was always aware of having a *lovely* and *undeserved* present made to one. Presents are so much nicer when they're undeserved, Aunt Pauline would say.

Robert, too, was plain, and almost speechless. He was medium sized, rather broad and stout, though not fat. Only his creamy, clean-shaven face was rather fat, and sometimes suggestive of an Italian priest in its silence and its secrecy. He had grey eyes like his mother, but very shy and uneasy, not bold like hers. Perhaps Ciss was the only person who fathomed his awful shyness and malaise, his habitual feeling that he was in the wrong place: almost like a soul that has got into a wrong body. But he never did anything about it. He went up to Chambers, and read law. It was, however, all the weird old processes that interested him. He had, unknown to everybody but his mother, a quite extraordinary collection of old Mexican legal documents – reports of processes and trials, pleas, accusations: the weird and awful mixture of ecclesiastical law and common law in seventeenth-century Mexico. He had started a study in this direction through coming across the report of a trial of two English sailors, for murder, in Mexico, in 1620, and he had gone on, when the next document was an accusation against a Don Miguel Estrada for seducing one of the nuns of the Sacred Heart Convent in Oaxaca in 1680.

Pauline and her son Robert had wonderful evenings with these old papers. The lovely lady knew a little Spanish. She even looked a trifle Spanish herself, with a high comb and a marvellous dark-brown shawl embroidered in thick silvery silk embroidery. So she would sit at the perfect old table, soft as velvet in its deep brown surface, a high comb in her hair, ear-rings with dropping pendants in her ears, her arms bare and still beautiful, a few strings of pearls round her throat, a puce velvet dress on and this or another beautiful shawl, and by candlelight she looked, yes, a Spanish high-bred beauty of thirty-two or three. She set the candles to give her face just the chiaroscuro she knew suited her; her high chair that rose behind her face was done in old green brocade, against which her face emerged like a Christmas rose.

They were always three at table, and they always drank a bottle of champagne: Pauline two glasses, Ciss two glasses, Robert the rest. The lovely lady sparkled and was radiant. Ciss, her black hair bobbed, her broad shoulders in a very nice and becoming dress that Aunt Pauline had helped her to make, stared from her aunt to her cousin and back again, with rather confused, mute hazel eyes, and played the part of an audience suitably impressed. She *was* impressed, somewhere, all the time. And even rendered speechless by Pauline's brilliancy, even after five years. But at the bottom of her consciousness was the data of as weird a document as Robert ever studied: all the things she knew about her aunt and her cousin.

Robert was always a gentleman, with an old-fashioned, punctilious courtesy that covered his shyness quite completely. He was, and Ciss knew it, more confused than shy. He was worse than she was. Cecilia's own confusion dated from only five years back. Robert's must have started before he was born. In the lovely lady's womb he must have felt *very* confused.

He paid all his attention to his mother, drawn to her as a humble flower to the sun. And yet, priest-like, he was all the time aware, with the tail of his consciousness, that Ciss was there, and that she was a bit shut out of it, and that something wasn't right. He was aware of the third consciousness in the room. Whereas to Pauline, her niece Cecilia was an appropriate part of her own setting, rather than a distinct consciousness.

Robert took coffee with his mother and Ciss in the warm drawing-room, where all the furniture was so lovely, all collectors' pieces – Mrs Attenborough had made her own money, dealing privately in pictures and furniture and rare things from barbaric countries – and the three talked desultorily till about eight or half-past. It was very pleasant, very cosy, very homely even; Pauline made a real home cosiness out of so much elegant material. The chat was simple, and nearly always bright. Pauline was her *real* self, emanating a friendly mockery and an odd, ironic gaiety – till there came a little pause.

At which Ciss always rose and said good-night, and carried out the coffee-tray, to prevent Burnett from intruding any more.

And then! ah, then, the lovely, glowing intimacy of the evening, between mother and son, when they deciphered manuscripts and discussed points, Pauline with that eagerness of a girl for which she was famous. And it was quite genuine. In some mysterious way she had *saved up* her power for being thrilled, in connection with a man. Robert, solid, rather quiet and subdued, seemed like the elder of the two – almost like a priest with a young girl pupil. And that was rather how he felt.

Ciss had a flat for herself just across the courtyard, over the old coach-house and stables. There were no horses. Robert kept his car in the coach-house. Ciss had three very nice rooms up there, stretching along in a row one after the other, and she had got used to the ticking of the stable clock.

But sometimes she did not go to her rooms. In the summer she would sit on the lawn, and from the open window of the drawing-room upstairs she would hear Pauline's wonderful, heart-searching laugh. And in winter the young woman would put on a thick coat and walk slowly to the little balustraded bridge over the stream, and then look back at the three lighted windows of that drawing-room where mother and son were so happy together.

Ciss loved Robert, and she believed that Pauline intended the two of them to marry – when she was dead. But poor Robert, he was so convulsed with shyness already, with man or woman. What would he be when his mother was dead? – in a dozen more years. He would be just a shell, the shell of a man who had never lived.

The strange, unspoken sympathy of the young with one another, when they are overshadowed by the old, was one of the bonds between Robert and Ciss. But another bond, which Ciss did not know how to draw tight, was the bond of passion. Poor Robert was by nature a passionate man. His silence and his agonised, though hidden, shyness were both the result of a secret physical passionateness. And how Pauline could play on this! Ah, Ciss was not blind to the eyes which he fixed on his mother – eyes fascinated yet humiliated, full of shame. He was ashamed that he was not a man. And he did not love his mother. He was fascinated by her. Completely fascinated. And for the rest, paralysed in a life-long confusion.

Ciss stayed in the garden till the lights leapt up in Pauline's bedroom – about ten o'clock. The lovely lady had retired. Robert would now stay another hour or so, alone. Then he, too, would retire. Ciss, in the dark outside, sometimes wished she could creep up to him and say: 'Oh, Robert! It's all wrong!' But Aunt Pauline would hear. And, anyhow, Ciss couldn't do it. She went off to her own rooms, once more, once more, and so for ever.

In the morning coffee was brought up on a tray to each of the rooms of the three relatives. Ciss had to be at Sir Wilfrid Knipe's at nine o'clock, to give two hours of lessons to his little granddaughter. It was her sole serious occupation, except that she played the piano for the love of it. Robert set off to town about nine. And as a rule, Aunt Pauline appeared to lunch, though sometimes not till tea-time. When she appeared, she looked fresh and young. But she was inclined to fade rather rapidly, like a flower without water, in the daytime. Her hour was the candle hour.

So she always rested in the afternoon. When the sun shone, if possible she took a sun-bath. This was one of her secrets. Her lunch was very light; she could take her sun-and-air-bath before noon or after, as it pleased her. Often it was in the afternoon, when the sun shone very warmly into a queer little yew-walled square just behind the stables. Here Ciss stretched out the lying-chair and rugs, and put the light parasol handy in the silent little enclosure of thick dark yew hedges beyond the old red walls of the unused stables. And hither came the lovely lady with her book. Ciss then had to be on guard in one of her own rooms, should her aunt, who was very keen-eared, hear a footstep.

One afternoon it occurred to Cecilia that she herself might while away this rather long afternoon hour by taking a sun-bath. She was growing restive. The thought of the flat roof of the stable buildings, to which she could climb from a loft at the end, started her on a new adventure. She often went on to the roof; she had to, to wind up the stable clock, which was a job she had assumed to herself. Now she took a rug, climbed out under the heavens, looked at the sky and the great elm-tops, looked at the sun, then took off her things and lay down perfectly securely, in a corner of the roof under the parapet, full in the sun.

It was rather lovely, to bask all one's length like this in warm sun and air. Yes, it was very lovely! It even seemed to melt some of the hard bitterness of her heart, some of that core of unspoken resentment which never dissolved. Luxuriously, she spread herself, so that the sun should touch her limbs fully, fully. If she had no other lover, she should have the sun! She rolled over voluptuously.

And suddenly her heart stood still in her body, and her hair almost rose on end as a voice said very softly, musingly, in her ear: 'No, Henry dear! It was not my fault you died instead of marrying that Claudia. No, darling. I was quite, quite willing for you to marry her, unsuitable though she was.'

Cecilia sank down on her rug, powerless and perspiring with dread. That awful voice, so soft, so musing, yet so unnatural. Not a human voice at all. Yet there must, there *must* be someone on the roof! Oh, how unspeakably awful!

She lifted her weak head and peeped across the sloping leads. Nobody! The chimneys were too narrow to shelter anybody. There was nobody on the roof. Then it must be someone in the trees, in the elms. Either that, or – terror unspeakable – a bodiless voice! She reared her head a little higher.

And as she did so, came the voice again: 'No, darling! I told you you would tire of her in six months. And you see it was true, dear. It was true, true, true! I wanted to spare you that. So it wasn't I who made you feel weak and disabled, wanting that very silly Claudia – poor thing, she looked so woebegone afterwards! – wanting her and not wanting her. You got yourself into that perplexity, my dear. I only warned you. What else could I do? And you lost your spirit and died without ever knowing me again. It was bitter, bitter – '

The voice faded away. Cecilia subsided weakly on to her rug, after the anguished tension of listening. Oh, it was awful. The sun shone, the sky was blue, all seemed so lovely and afternoony and summery. And yet, oh, horror! – she was going to be forced to believe in the supernatural! And she loathed the supernatural, ghosts and voices and rappings and all the rest.

But that awful, creepy, bodiless voice, with its rusty sort of whispers of an overtone! It had something so fearfully familiar in it, too! And yet was so utterly uncanny. Poor Cecilia could only lie there unclothed, and so all the more agonisingly helpless, inert, collapsed in sheer dread.

And then she heard the thing sigh! – a deep sigh that seemed weirdly familiar, yet was not human. 'Ah well, ah well! the heart must bleed. Better it should bleed than break. It is grief, grief! But it wasn't my fault, dear. And Robert could marry our poor, dull Ciss tomorrow, if he wanted her. But he doesn't care about it, so why force him into anything?' The sounds were very uneven, sometimes only a husky sort of whisper. Listen! Listen!

Cecilia was about to give vent to loud and piercing screams of hysteria, when the last two sentences arrested her. All her caution and her cunning sprang alert. It was Aunt Pauline! It *must* be Aunt Pauline, practising ventriloquism, or something like that. What a devil she was!

Where was she? She must be lying down there, right below where Cecilia herself was lying. And it was either some fiend's trick of ventriloquism, or else thought-transference. The sounds were very uneven; sometimes quite inaudible, sometimes only a brushing sort of noise. Ciss listened intently. No, it could not be ventriloquism. It was worse: some form of thought-transference that conveyed itself like sound. Some horror of that sort! Cecilia still lay weak and inert, too terrified to move; but she was growing calmer with suspicion. It was some diabolic trick of that unnatural woman.

But *what* a devil of a woman! She even knew that she, Cecilia, had mentally accused her of killing her son Henry. Poor Henry was Robert's elder brother, twelve years older than Robert. He had died suddenly when he was twenty-two, after an awful struggle with himself, because he was passionately in love with a young and very good-looking actress, and his mother had humorously despised him for the attachment. So he had caught some sudden ordinary disease, but the poison had gone to his brain and killed him before he ever regained consciousness. Ciss knew the few facts from her own father. And lately she had been thinking that Pauline was going to kill Robert as she had killed Henry. It was clear murder: a mother murdering her sensitive sons, who were fascinated by her: the Circe!

'I suppose I may as well get up,' murmured the dim, unbreathing voice. 'Too much sun is as bad as too little. Enough sun, enough love-thrill, enough proper food, and not too much of any of them, and a woman might live for ever. I verily believe, for ever. If she absorbs as much vitality as she expends. Or perhaps a trifle more!'

It was certainly Aunt Pauline! How – how terrible! She, Ciss, was hearing Aunt Pauline's thoughts. Oh, how ghastly! Aunt Pauline was sending out her thoughts in a sort of radio, and she, Ciss, had to *hear* what her aunt was thinking. How ghastly! How insufferable! One of them would surely have to die.

She twisted and lay inert and crumpled, staring vacantly in front of her. Vacantly! Vacantly! And her eyes were staring almost into a hole. She was staring into it unseeing, a hole going down in the corner, from the lead gutter. It meant nothing to her. Only it frightened her a little more.

Then, suddenly, out of the hole came a sigh and a last

whisper: 'Ah well! Pauline! Get up, it's enough for today.' Good God! Out of the hole of the rain-pipe! The rain-pipe was acting as a speaking-tube! Impossible! No, quite possible. She had read of it even in some book. And Aunt Pauline, like the old and guilty woman she was, talked aloud to herself. That was it!

A sullen exultance sprang in Ciss's breast. *That* was why she would never have anybody, not even Robert, in her bedroom. That was why she never dozed in a chair, never sat absent-minded anywhere, but went to her room, and kept to her room, except when she roused herself to be alert. When she slackened off she talked to herself! She talked in a soft little crazy voice to herself. But she was not crazy. It was only her thoughts murmuring themselves aloud.

So she had qualms about poor Henry! Well she might have! Ciss believed that Aunt Pauline had loved her big, handsome, brilliant first-born much more than she loved Robert, and that his death had been a terrible blow and a chagrin to her. Poor Robert had been only ten years old when Henry died. Since then he had been the substitute.

Ah, how awful!

But Aunt Pauline was a strange woman. She had left her husband when Henry was a small child, some years even before Robert was born. There was no quarrel. Sometimes she saw her husband again, quite amiably, but a little mockingly. And she even gave him money.

For Pauline earned all her own. Her father had been a Consul in the East and in Naples, and a devoted collector of beautiful exotic things. When he died, soon after his grandson Henry was born, he left his collection of treasures to his daughter. And Pauline, who had really a passion and a genius for loveliness, whether in texture or form or colour, had laid the basis of her fortune on her father's collection. She had gone on collecting, buying where she could, and selling to collectors or to museums. She was one of the first to sell old, weird African figures to the museums, and ivory carvings from New Guinea. She bought Renoir as soon as she saw his pictures. But not Rousseau. And all by herself she made a fortune.

After her husband died she had not married again. She was not even *known* to have had lovers. If she did have lovers, it was not among the men who admired her most and paid her devout and open attendance. To these she was a 'friend'.

Cecilia slipped on her clothes and caught up her rug, hastening carefully down the ladder to the loft. As she descended she heard the ringing, musical call: 'All right, Ciss – ' which meant that the lovely lady was finished, and returning to the house. Even her voice was wonderfully young and sonorous, beautifully balanced and self-possessed. So different from the little voice in which she talked to herself. *That* was much more the voice of an old woman.

Ciss hastened round to the yew enclosure, where lay the comfortable chaise longue with the various delicate rugs. Everything Pauline had was choice, to the fine straw mat on the floor. The great yew walls were beginning to cast long shadows. Only in the corner where the rugs tumbled their delicate colours was there hot, still sunshine.

The rugs folded up, the chair lifted away, Cecilia stooped to look at the mouth of the rain-pipe. There it was, in the corner, under a little hood of masonry and just projecting from the thick leaves of the creeper on the wall. If Pauline, lying there, turned her face towards the wall, she would speak into the very mouth of the tube. Cecilia was reassured. She had heard her aunt's thoughts indeed, but by no uncanny agency.

That evening, as if aware of something, Pauline was a little quieter than usual, though she looked her own serene, rather mysterious self. And after coffee she said to Robert and Ciss: 'I'm so sleepy. The sun has made me so sleepy. I feel full of sunshine like a bee. I shall go to bed, if you don't mind. You two sit and have a talk.'

Cecilia looked quickly at her cousin.

'Perhaps you'd rather be alone?' she said to him.

'No – no,' he replied. 'Do keep me company for a while, if it doesn't bore you.'

The windows were open, the scent of honeysuckle wafted in, with the sound of an owl. Robert smoked in silence. There was a sort of despair in his motionless, rather squat body. He looked like a caryatid bearing a weight.

'Do you remember Cousin Henry?' Cecilia asked him suddenly.

He looked up in surprise.

'Yes. Very well,' he said.

'What did he look like?' she said, glancing into her cousin's big, secret-troubled eyes, in which there was so much frustration.

'Oh, he was handsome: tall, and fresh-coloured, with mother's soft brown hair.' As a matter of fact, Pauline's hair was grey. 'The ladies admired him very much; and he was at all the dances.'

'And what kind of character had he?'

'Oh, very good-natured and jolly. He liked to be amused. He was rather quick and clever, like mother, and very good company.'

'And did he love your mother?'

'Very much. She loved him too – better than she does me, as a matter of fact. He was so much more nearly her idea of a man.'

'Why was he more her idea of a man?'

'Tall – handsome – attractive, and very good company – and would, I believe, have been very successful at law. I'm afraid I am merely negative in all those respects.'

Ciss looked at him attentively, with her slow-thinking hazel eyes. Under his impassive mask she knew he suffered.

'Do you think you are so much more negative than he?' she said.

He did not lift his face. But after a few moments he replied: 'My life, certainly, is a negative affair.'

She hesitated before she dared ask him: 'And do you mind?'

He did not answer her at all. Her heart sank.

'You see, I'm afraid my life is as negative as yours is,' she said. 'And I'm beginning to mind bitterly. I'm thirty.'

She saw his creamy, well-bred hand tremble.

'I suppose,' he said, without looking at her, 'one will rebel when it is too late.'

That was queer, from him.

'Robert!' she said. 'Do you like me at all?'

She saw his dusky-creamy face, so changeless in its folds, go pale.

'I am very fond of you,' he murmured.

'Won't you kiss me? Nobody ever kisses me,' she said pathetically.

He looked at her, his eyes strange with fear and a certain haughtiness. Then he rose, and came softly over to her, and kissed her gently on the cheek.

'It's an awful shame, Ciss!' he said softly.

She caught his hand and pressed it to her breast. 'And sit with me sometimes in the garden,' she said, murmuring with difficulty. 'Won't you?'

He looked at her anxiously and searchingly.

'What about mother?'

Ciss smiled a funny little smile, and looked into his eyes. He suddenly flushed crimson, turning aside his face. It was a painful sight.

'I know,' he said. 'I am no lover of women.'

He spoke with sarcastic stoicism, against himself, but even she did not know the shame it was to him.

'You never try to be,' she said.

Again his eyes changed uncannily.

'Does one have to try?' he said.

'Why, yes. One never does anything if one doesn't try.'

He went pale again.

'Perhaps you are right,' he said.

In a few minutes she left him, and went to her rooms. At least she had tried to take off the everlasting lid from things.

The weather continued sunny, Pauline continued her sun-baths, and Ciss lay on the roof eavesdropping, in the literal sense of the word. But Pauline was not to be heard. No sound came up the pipe. She must be lying with her face away into the open. Ciss listened with all her might. She could just detect the faintest, faintest murmur away below, but no audible syllable.

And at night, under the stars, Cecilia sat and waited in silence, on the seat which kept in view the drawing-room windows and the side door into the garden. She saw the light go up in her aunt's room. She saw the lights at last go out in the drawing-room. And she waited. But he did not come. She stayed on in the darkness half the night, while the owl hooted. But she stayed alone.

Two days she heard nothing; her aunt's thoughts were not revealed; and at evening nothing happened. Then, the third night, as she sat with heavy, helpless persistence in the garden, suddenly she started. He had come out. She rose and went softly over the grass to him.

'Don't speak!' he murmured.

And in silence, in the dark, they walked down the garden and over the little bridge to the paddock, where the hay, cut very late, was in cock. There they stood disconsolate under the stars.

'You see,' he said, 'how can I ask for love, if I don't feel any love in myself? You know I have a real regard for you – '

'How *can* you feel any love, when you never feel anything?' she said.

'That is true,' he replied.

And she waited for what would come next.

'And how can I marry?' he said. 'I am a failure even at making money. I can't ask my mother for money.'

She sighed deeply.

'Then don't bother yet about marrying,' she said. 'Only love me a little. Won't you?'

He gave a short laugh.

'It sounds so atrocious, to say it is hard to begin,' he said.

She sighed again. He was so stiff to move.

'Shall we sit down a minute?' she said. And then, as they sat on the hay, she added: 'May I touch you? Do you mind?'

'Yes, I mind. But do as you wish,' he replied, with that mixture of shyness and queer candour which made him a little ridiculous, as he knew quite well. But in his heart there was almost murder.

She touched his black, always tidy, hair, with her fingers.

'I suppose I shall rebel one day,' he said again suddenly.

They sat some time, till it grew chilly. And he held her hand fast, but he never put his arms round her. At last she rose, and went indoors, saying good-night.

The next day, as Cecilia lay stunned and angry on the roof, taking her sun-bath, and becoming hot and fierce with sunshine, suddenly she started. A terror seized her in spite of herself. It was the voice.

'Caro, caro, tu non l'hai visto!' it was murmuring away, in a language Cecilia did not understand. She lay and writhed her limbs in the sun, listening intently to words she could not follow. Softly, whisperingly, with infinite caressiveness and yet with that subtle, insidious arrogance under its velvet, came the voice, murmuring in Italian: 'Bravo, si, molto bravo, poverino, ma uomo come te non sarà mai, mai, mai!' Oh, especially in Italian Cecilia heard the poisonous charm of the voice, so caressive, so soft and flexible, yet so utterly egoistic. She hated it with intensity as it sighed and whispered out of nowhere. Why, why should it be so delicate, so subtle and flexible and beautifully controlled, when she herself was so clumsy? Oh, poor Cecilia, she writhed in the afternoon sun, knowing her own clownish clumsiness and lack of suavity, in comparison.

'No, Robert dear, you will never be the man your father was, though you have some of his looks. He was a marvellous lover, soft as a flower yet piercing as a humming-bird. Cara, cara mia bellissima, ti ho aspettato come l'agonissante aspetta la morte, morte deliziosa, quasi quasi troppo deliziosa per una mera anima humana. He gave himself to a woman as he gave himself to God. Mauro! Mauro! How you loved me! How you loved me!'

The voice ceased in reverie, and Cecilia knew what she had guessed before – that Robert was not the son of her Uncle Ronald, but of some Italian.

'I am disappointed in you, Robert. There is no poignancy in you. Your father was a Jesuit, but he was the most perfect and poignant lover in the world. You are a Jesuit like a fish in a tank. And that Ciss of yours is the cat fishing for you. It is less edifying even than poor Henry.'

Cecilia suddenly bent her mouth down to the tube, and said in a deep voice: 'Leave Robert alone! Don't kill him as well.'

There was dead silence in the hot July afternoon that was lowering for thunder. Cecilia lay prostrate, her heart beating in great thumps. She was listening as if her whole soul were an ear. At last she caught the whisper: 'Did someone speak?'

She leaned again to the mouth of the tube: 'Don't kill Robert as you killed me,' she said, with slow enunciation, and a deep but small voice.

'Ah!' came the sharp little cry. 'Who is that speaking?'

'Henry,' said the deep voice.

There was dead silence. Poor Cecilia lay with all the use gone out of her. And there was dead silence. Till at last came the whisper: 'I didn't kill Henry. No, no! No, no! Henry, surely you can't blame me! I loved you, dearest; I only wanted to help you.'

'You killed me!' came the deep, artificial, accusing voice. 'Now let Robert live. Let him go! Let him marry!'

There was a pause.

'How very, very awful!' mused the whispering voice. 'Is it possible, Henry, you are a spirit, and you condemn me?'

'Yes, I condemn you!'

Cecilia felt all the pent-up rage going down that rain-pipe. At the same time, she almost laughed. It was awful.

She lay and listened and listened. No sound! As if time had ceased, she lay inert in the weakening sun, till she heard a far-off rumble of thunder. She sat up. The sky was yellowing. Quickly she dressed herself, went down, and out to the corner of the stables.

'Aunt Pauline!' she called discreetly. 'Did you hear thunder?'

'Yes. I am going in. Don't wait,' came a feeble voice.

Cecilia retired, and from the loft watched, spying, as the figure of the lovely lady, wrapped in a lovely wrap of old blue silk, went rather totteringly to the house.

The sky gradually darkened. Cecilia hastened in with the rugs. Then the storm broke. Aunt Pauline did not appear to tea. She found the thunder trying. Robert also did not arrive till after tea, in the pouring rain. Cecilia went down the covered passage to her own house, and dressed carefully for dinner, putting some white columbines at her breast.

The drawing-room was lit with a softly shaded lamp. Robert, dressed, was waiting, listening to the rain. He too seemed strangely crackling and on edge. Cecilia came in, with the white flowers nodding at her dusky breast. Robert was watching her curiously, a new look on his face. Cecilia went to the book-shelves near the door, and was peering for something, listening acutely. She heard a rustle, then the door softly opening. And as it opened, Ciss suddenly switched on the strong electric light by the door.

Her aunt, in a dress of black lace over ivory colour, stood in the doorway. Her face was made up, but haggard with a look of unspeakable irritability, as if years of suppressed exasperation and dislike of her fellow men had suddenly crumpled her into an old witch.

'Oh, aunt!' cried Cecilia.

'Why, mother, you're a little old lady!' came the astounded voice of Robert – like an astonished boy, as if it were a joke.

'Have you only just found it out?' snapped the old woman venomously.

'Yes! Why, I thought – ' his voice tailed out in misgiving.

The haggard, old Pauline, in a frenzy of exasperation, said: 'Aren't we going down?'

She had not even noticed the excess of light, a thing she shunned. And she went downstairs almost tottering.

At table she sat with her face like a crumpled mask of unspeakable irritability. She looked old, very old, and like a witch. Robert and Cecilia fetched furtive glances at her. And Ciss, watching Robert, saw that he was so astonished and repelled by his mother's looks that he was another man.

'What kind of a drive home did you have?' snapped Pauline, with an almost gibbering irritability.

'It rained, of course,' he said.

'How clever of you to have found that out!' said his mother, with the grisly grin of malice that had succeeded her arch smile.

'I don't understand,' he said, with quiet suavity.

'It's apparent,' said his mother, rapidly and sloppily eating her food.

She rushed through the meal like a crazy dog, to the utter consternation of the servant. And the moment it was over she darted in a queer, crab-like way upstairs. Robert and Cecilia followed her, thunderstruck, like two conspirators.

'You pour the coffee. I loathe it! I'm going. Good-night!' said the old woman, in a succession of sharp shots. And she scrambled out of the room.

There was a dead silence. At last he said: 'I'm afraid mother isn't well. I must persuade her to see a doctor.'

'Yes,' said Cecilia.

The evening passed in silence. Robert and Ciss stayed on in the drawing-room, having lit a fire. Outside was cold rain. Each pretended to read. They did not want to separate. The evening passed with ominous mysteriousness, yet quickly.

At about ten o'clock the door suddenly opened, and Pauline appeared, in a blue wrap. She shut the door behind her, and came to the fire. Then she looked at the two young people in hate, real hate.

'You two had better get married quickly,' she said, in an ugly voice. 'It would look more decent; such a passionate pair of lovers!'

Robert looked up at her quietly.

'I thought you believed that cousins should not marry, mother,' he said.

'I do. But you're not cousins. Your father was an Italian priest.' Pauline held her daintily-slippered foot to the fire, in an old coquettish gesture. Her body tried to repeat all the old graceful gestures. But the nerve had snapped, so it was a rather dreadful caricature.

'Is that really true, mother?' he asked.

'True! What do you think? He was a distinguished man, or he wouldn't have been my lover. He was far too distinguished a man to have had you for a son. But that joy fell to me.'

'How unfortunate all round,' he said slowly.

'Unfortunate for you? *You* were lucky. It was *my* misfortune,' she said acidly to him.

She was really a dreadful sight, like a piece of lovely Venetian glass that has been dropped and gathered up again in horrible, sharp-edged fragments.

Suddenly she left the room again.

For a week it went on. She did not recover. It was as if every nerve in her body had suddenly started screaming in an insanity of discordance. The doctor came, and gave her sedatives, for she never slept. Without drugs she never slept at all, only paced back and forth in her room, looking hideous and evil, reeking with malevolence. She could not bear to see either her son or her niece. Only when either of them came she asked, in pure malice: 'Well! When's the wedding? Have you celebrated the nuptials yet?'

At first Cecilia was stunned by what she had done. She realised vaguely that her aunt, once a definite thrust of condemnation had penetrated her beautiful armour, had just collapsed, squirming, inside her shell. It was too terrible. Ciss was almost terrified into repentance. Then she thought; 'This is what she always was. Now let her live the rest of her days in her true colours.'

But Pauline would not live long. She was literally shrivelling away. She kept her room, and saw no one. She had her mirrors taken away.

Robert and Cecilia sat a good deal together. The jeering of the mad Pauline had not driven them apart, as she had hoped. But Cecilia dared not confess to him what she had done.

'Do you think your mother ever loved anybody?' Ciss asked him tentatively, rather wistfully, one evening.

He looked at her fixedly.

'Herself!' he said at last.

'She didn't even *love* herself,' said Ciss. 'It was something else. What was it?' She lifted a troubled, utterly puzzled face to him.

'Power,' he said curtly.

'But what power?' she asked. 'I don't understand.'

'Power to feed on other lives,' he said bitterly. 'She was beautiful, and she fed on life. She has fed on me as she fed on Henry. She put a sucker into one's soul, and sucked up one's essential life.'

'And don't you forgive her?'

'No.'

'Poor Aunt Pauline!'

But even Ciss did not mean it. She was only aghast.

'I *know* I've got a heart,' he said, passionately striking his breast. 'But it's almost sucked dry. I *know* I've got a soul, somewhere. But it's gnawed bare. I *hate* people who want power over others.'

Ciss was silent. What was there to say?

And two days later Pauline was found dead in her bed, having taken too much veronal, for her heart was weakened.

From the grave even she hit back at her son and her niece. She left Robert the noble sum of one thousand pounds, and Ciss one hundred. All the rest, with the nucleus of her valuable antiques, went to form the 'Pauline Attenborough Museum'.